Pokémon™ Journeys

4

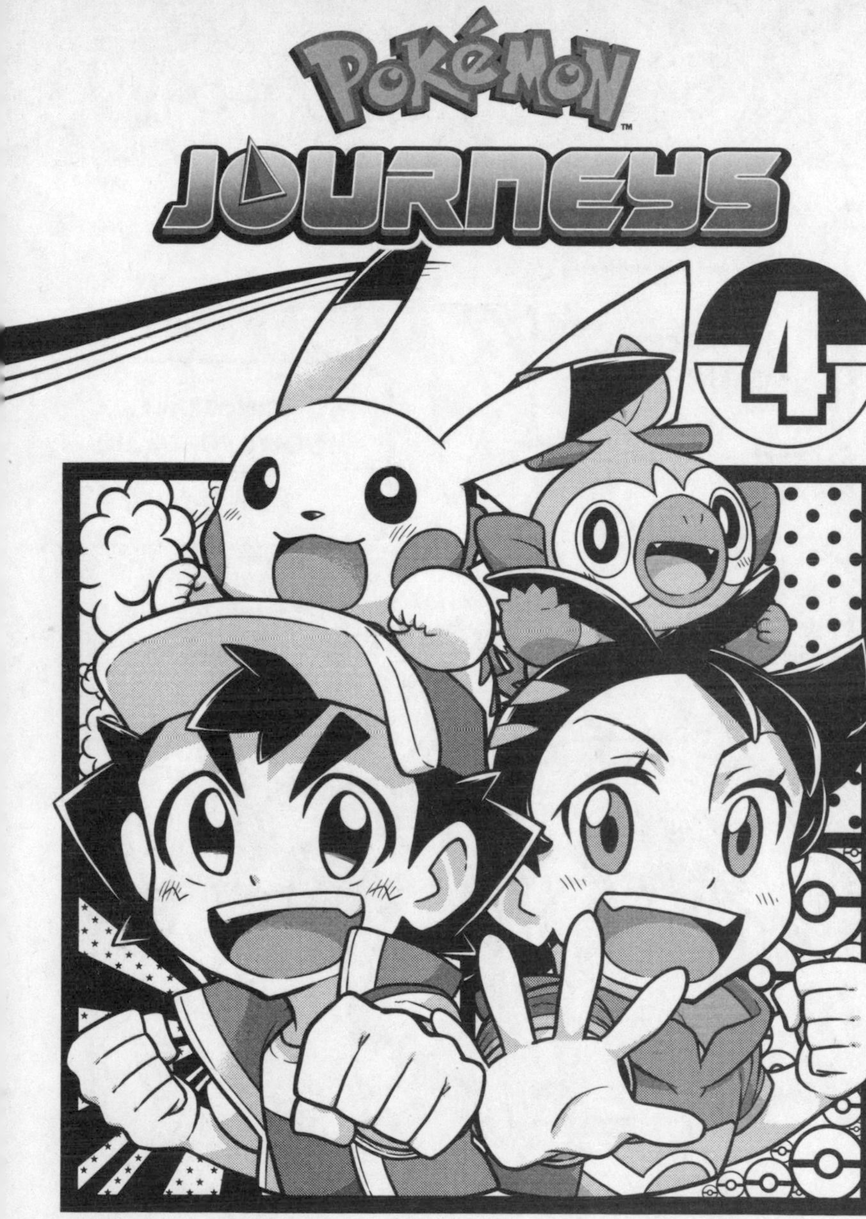

STORY AND ART BY

MACHITO GOMI

Original Concept by Satoshi Tajiri, Junichi Masuda & Ken Sugimori
Supervised by Tsunekazu Ishihara

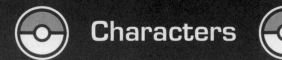

Characters

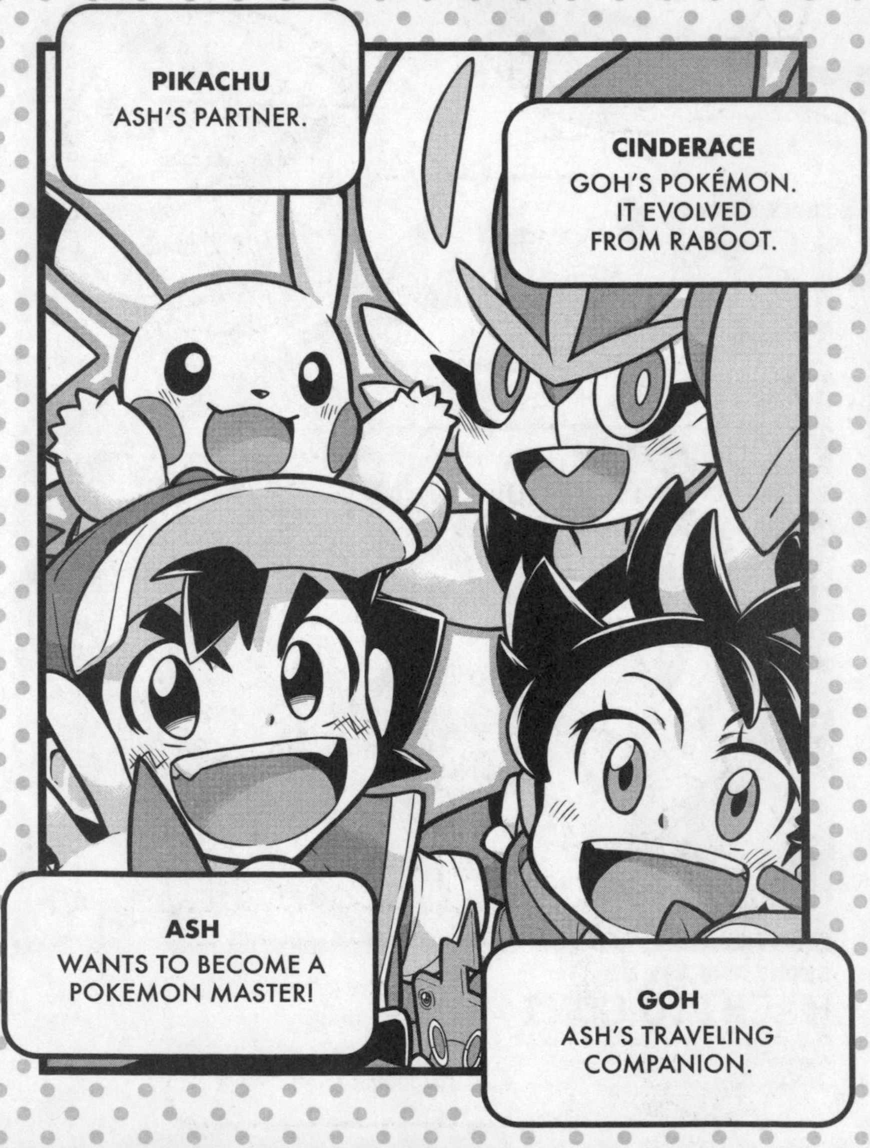

CINDERACE
GOH'S POKÉMON. IT EVOLVED FROM RABOOT.
PIKACHU
ASH'S PARTNER.
GOH
ASH'S TRAVELING COMPANION.
ASH
WANTS TO BECOME A POKEMON MASTER!

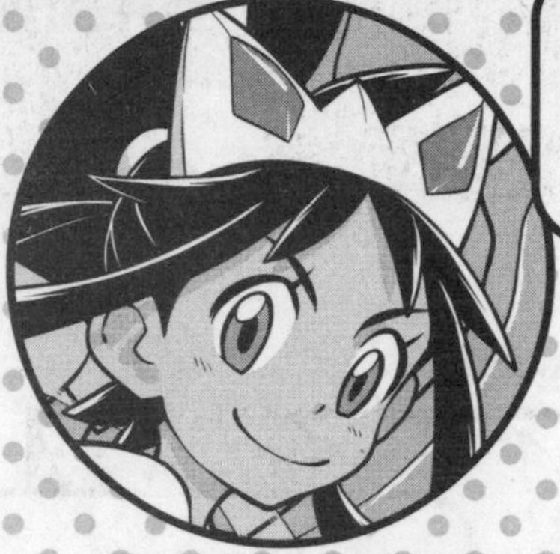

IRIS
CHAMPION OF THE
UNOVA REGION.
A DRAGON-TYPE USER.

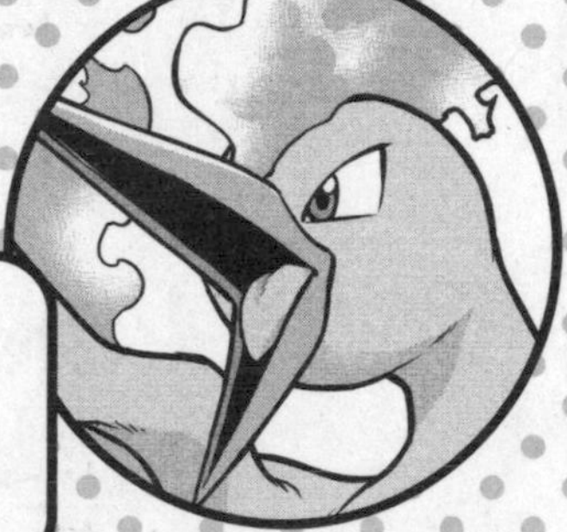

MOLTRES
FIRE/FLYING
LEGENDARY POKÉMON.

DANIKA **QUILLON**
MEMBERS OF PROJECT MEW.

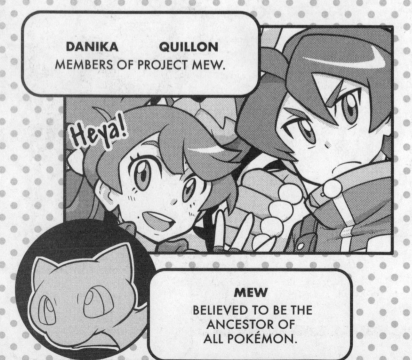

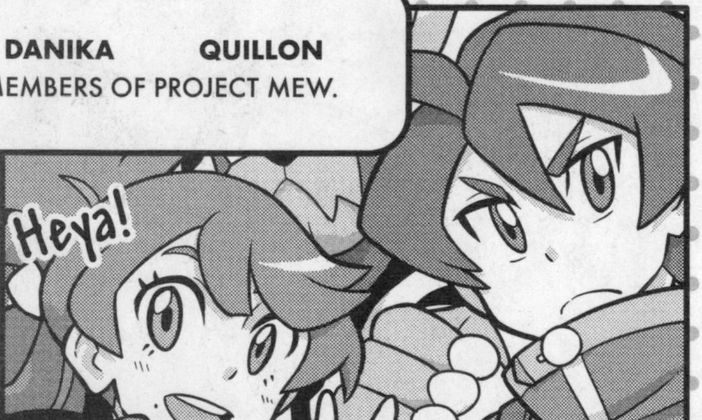
Heya!

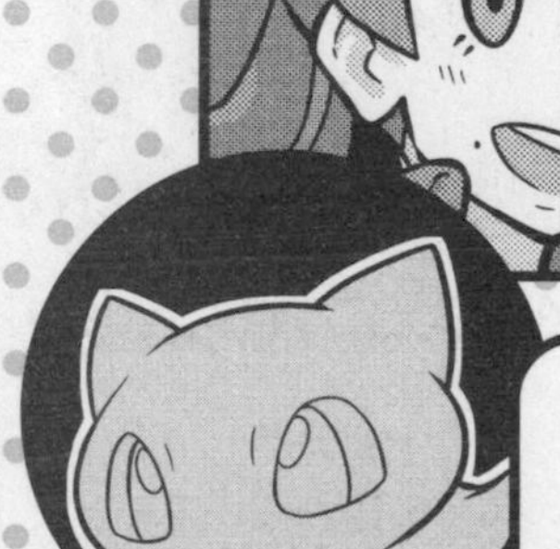

MEW
BELIEVED TO BE THE
ANCESTOR OF
ALL POKÉMON.

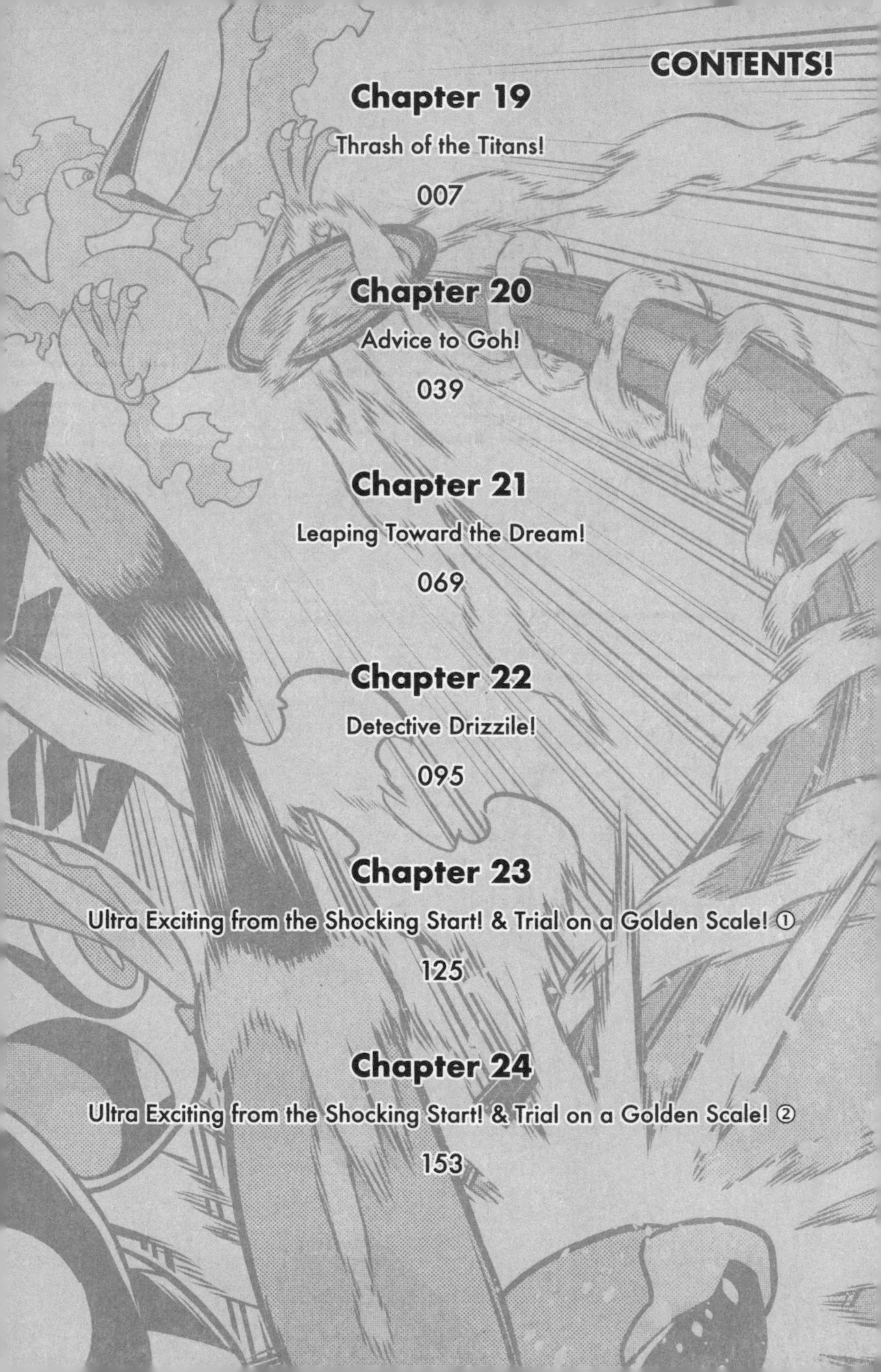

CONTENTS!

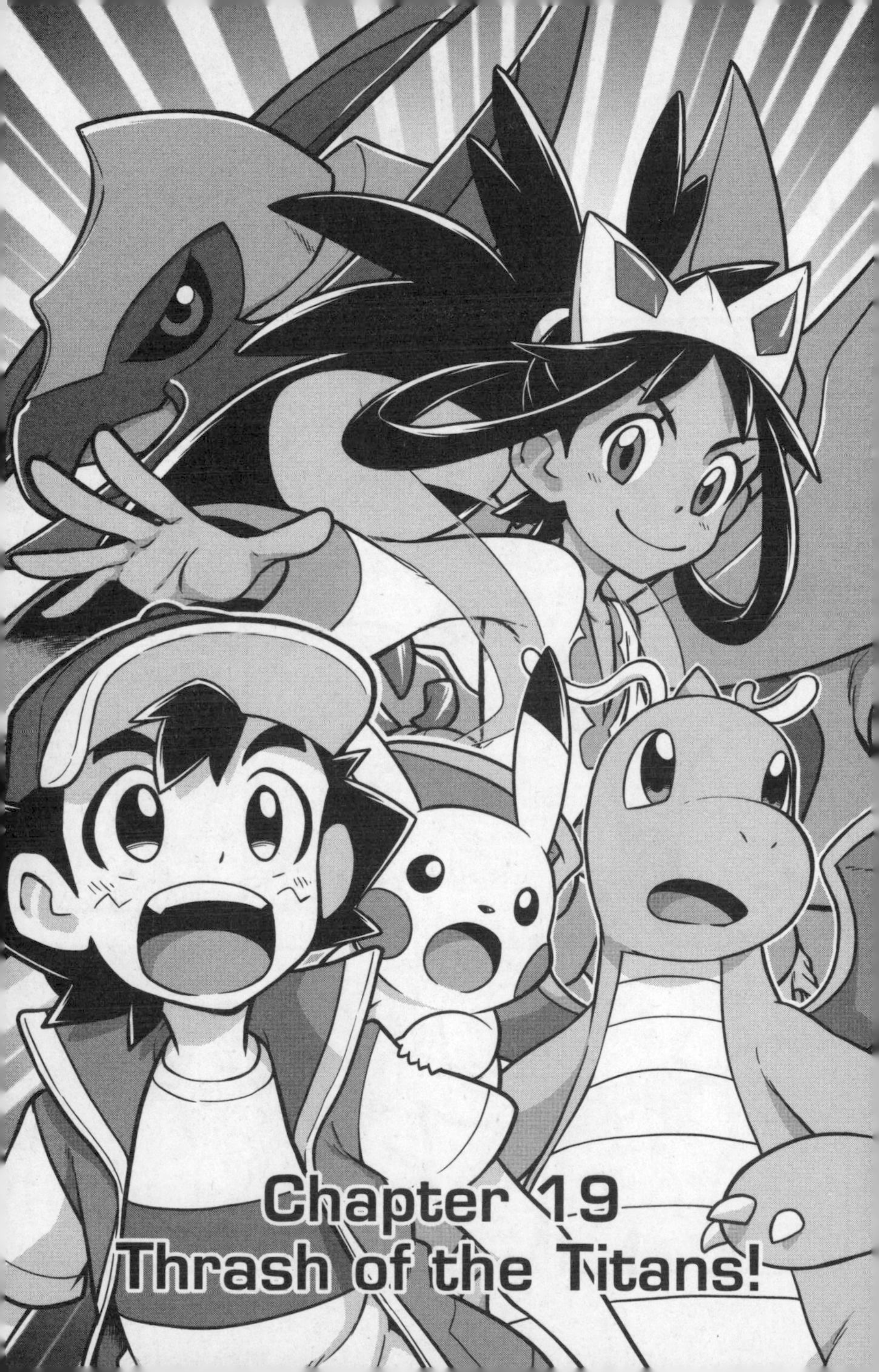
Chapter 19
Thrash of the Titans!

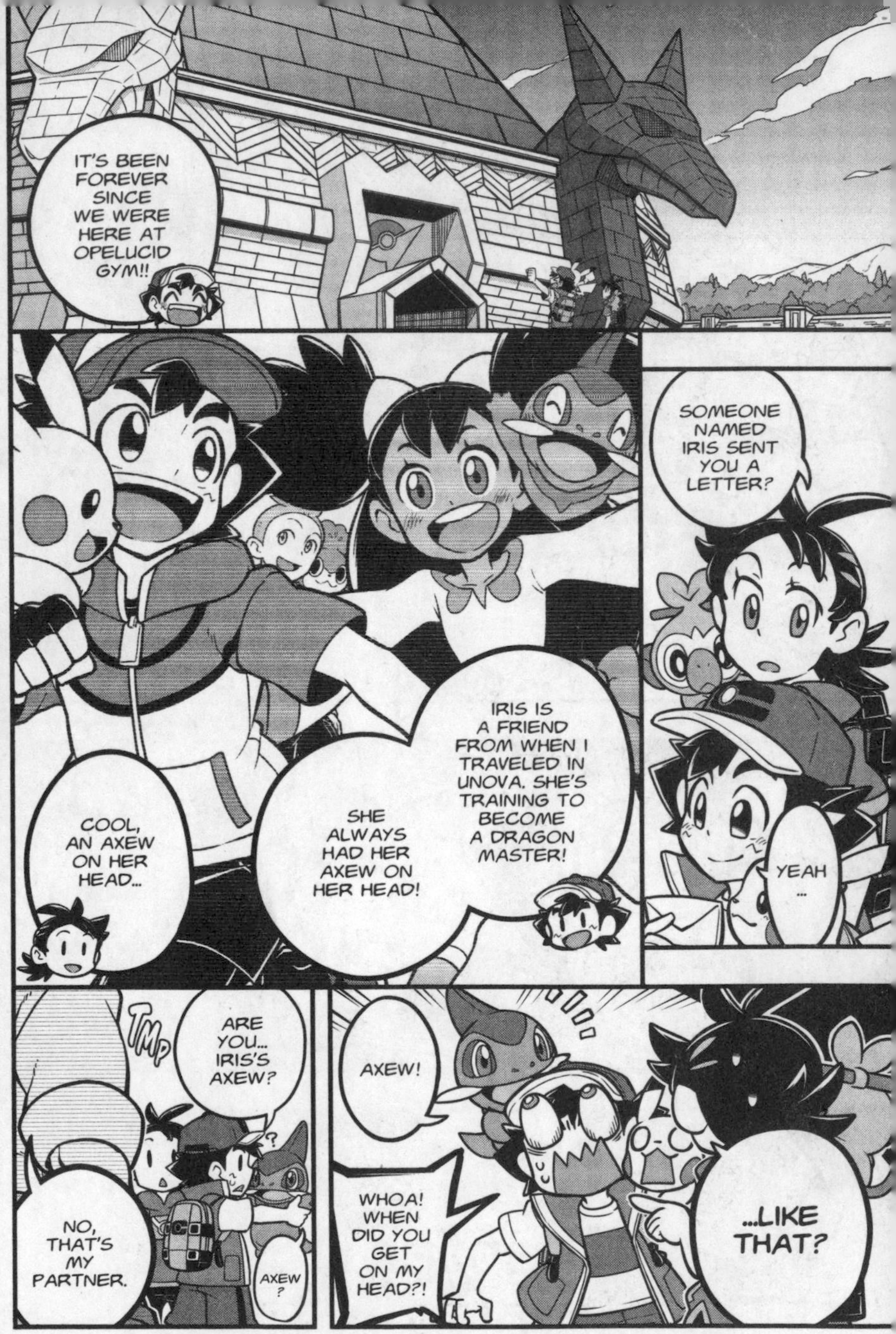
IT'S BEEN FOREVER SINCE WE WERE HERE AT OPELUCID GYM!!
SOMEONE NAMED IRIS SENT YOU A LETTER?
YEAH ...
IRIS IS A FRIEND FROM WHEN I TRAVELED IN UNOVA. SHE'S TRAINING TO BECOME A DRAGON MASTER!
SHE ALWAYS HAD HER AXEW ON HER HEAD!
COOL, AN AXEW ON HER HEAD...
...LIKE THAT?
AXEW!
WHOA! WHEN DID YOU GET ON MY HEAD?!
TMP
ARE YOU... IRIS'S AXEW?
AXEW ?
NO, THAT'S MY PARTNER.

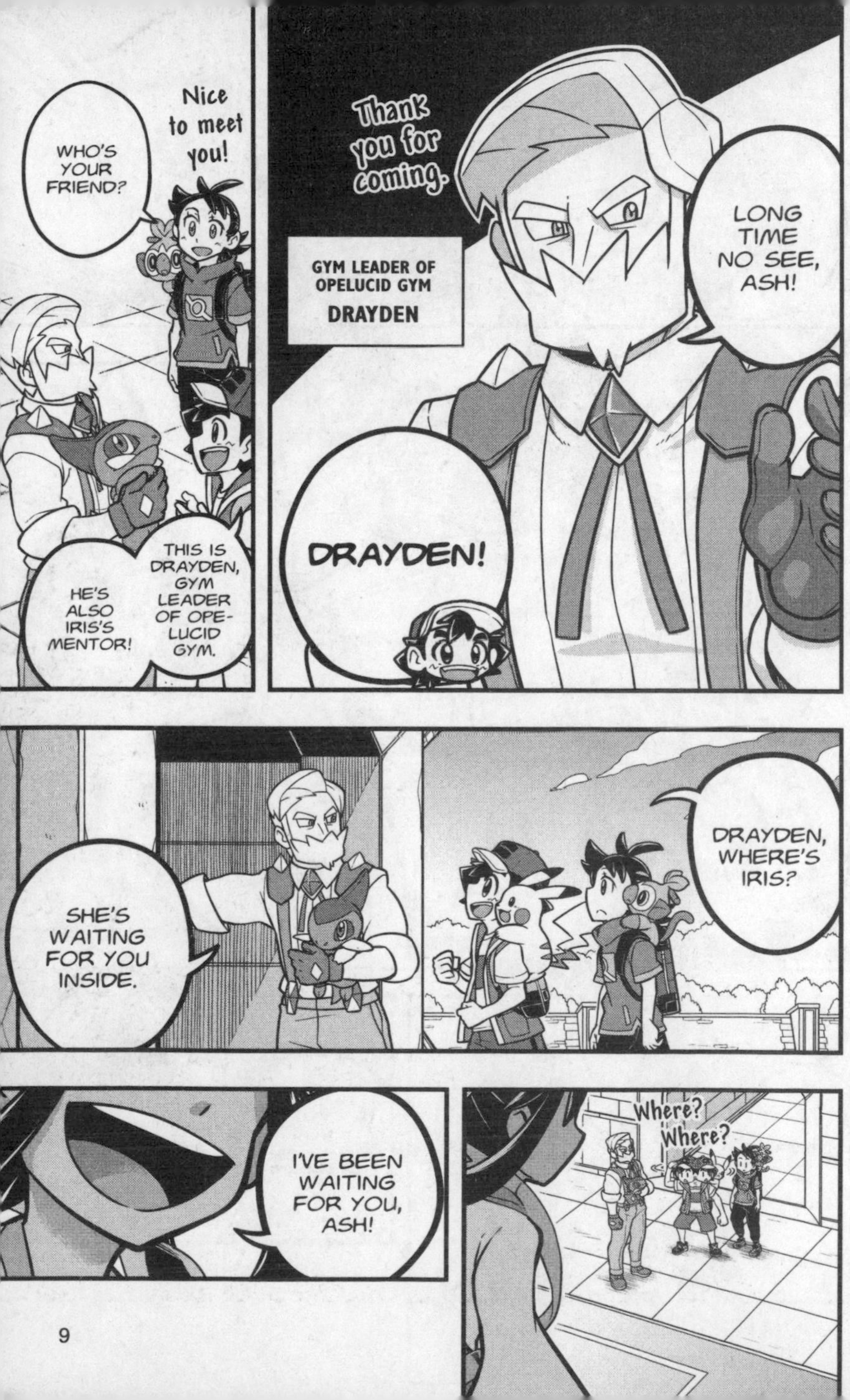
LONG TIME NO SEE, ASH!
Thank you for coming.
GYM LEADER OF OPELUCID GYM DRAYDEN
DRAYDEN!
Nice to meet you!
WHO'S YOUR FRIEND?
THIS IS DRAYDEN, GYM LEADER OF OPE-LUCID GYM.
HE'S ALSO IRIS'S MENTOR!
DRAYDEN, WHERE'S IRIS?
SHE'S WAITING FOR YOU INSIDE.
Where? Where?
I'VE BEEN WAITING FOR YOU, ASH!

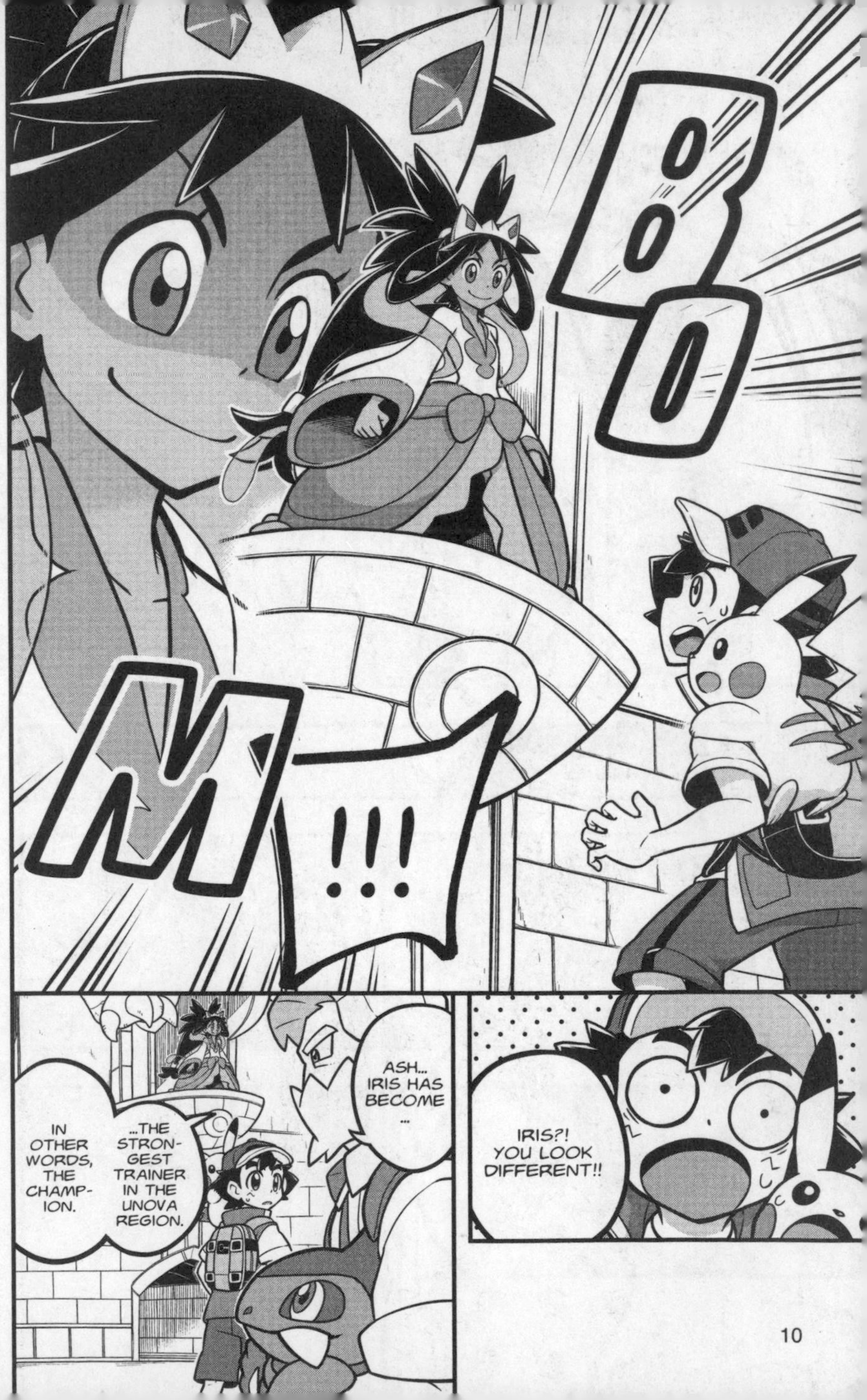
BOO
M—!!!
IRIS?! YOU LOOK DIFFERENT!!
ASH... IRIS HAS BECOME ...
...THE STRONG-EST TRAINER IN THE UNOVA REGION.
IN OTHER WORDS, THE CHAMP-ION.

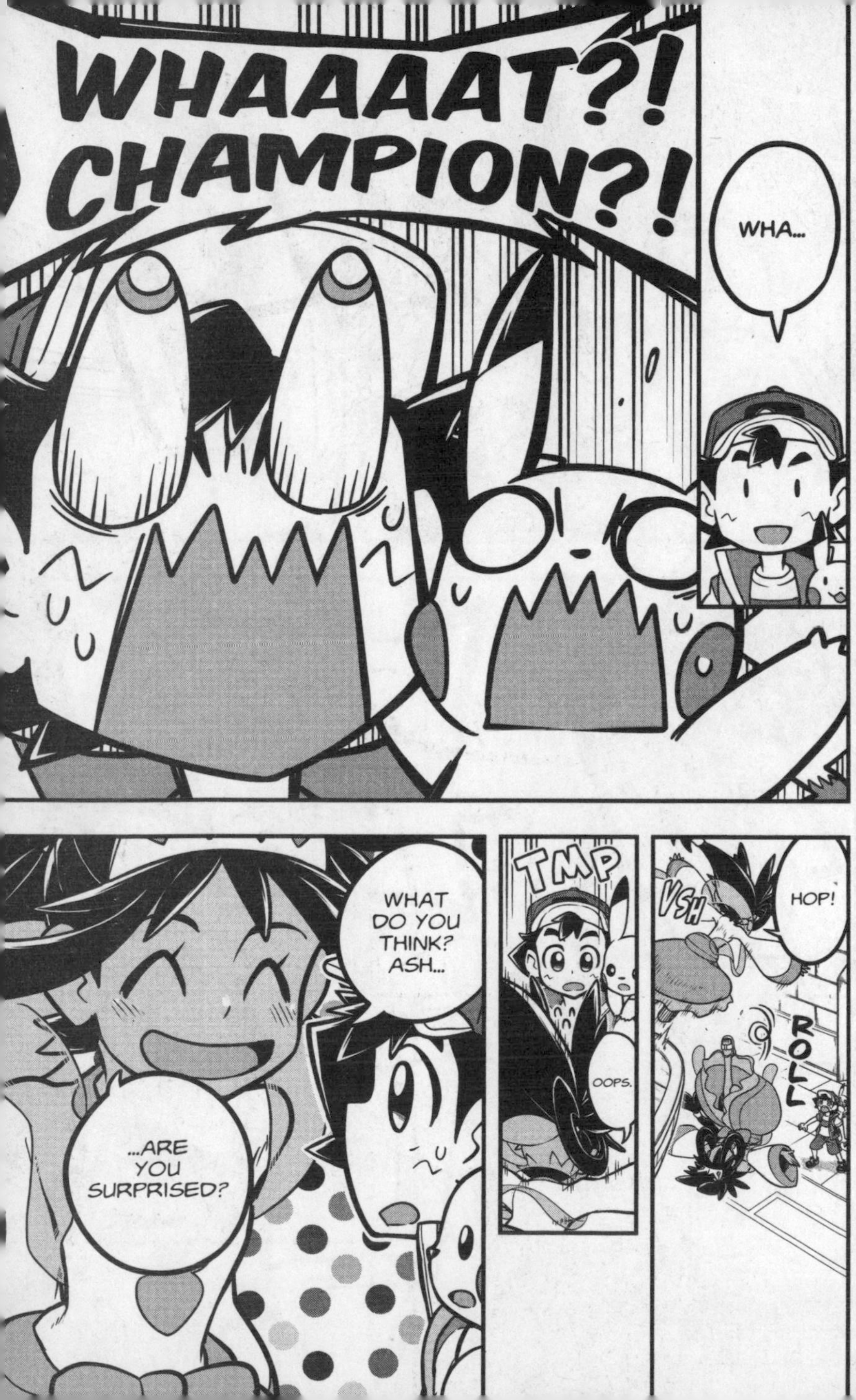
WHA...
WHAAAAT?! CHAMPION?!
HOP!
VSH
ROLL
TMP
OOPS.
WHAT DO YOU THINK? ASH...
...ARE YOU SURPRISED?

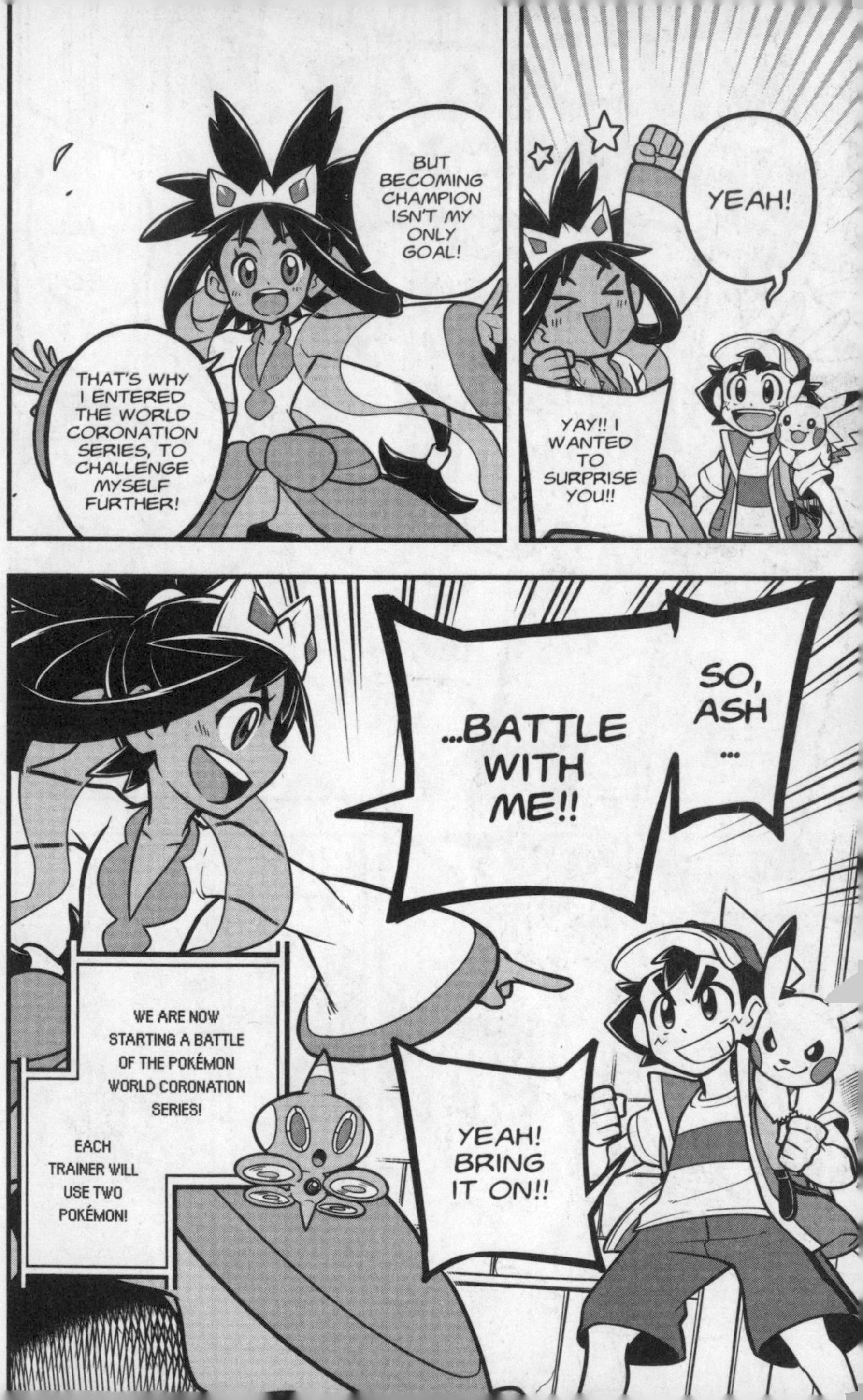
YEAH!
YAY!! I WANTED TO SURPRISE YOU!!
BUT BECOMING CHAMPION ISN'T MY ONLY GOAL!
THAT'S WHY I ENTERED THE WORLD CORONATION SERIES, TO CHALLENGE MYSELF FURTHER!
SO, ASH ...
...BATTLE WITH ME!!
YEAH! BRING IT ON!!
WE ARE NOW STARTING A BATTLE OF THE POKÉMON WORLD CORONATION SERIES!
EACH TRAINER WILL USE TWO POKÉMON!

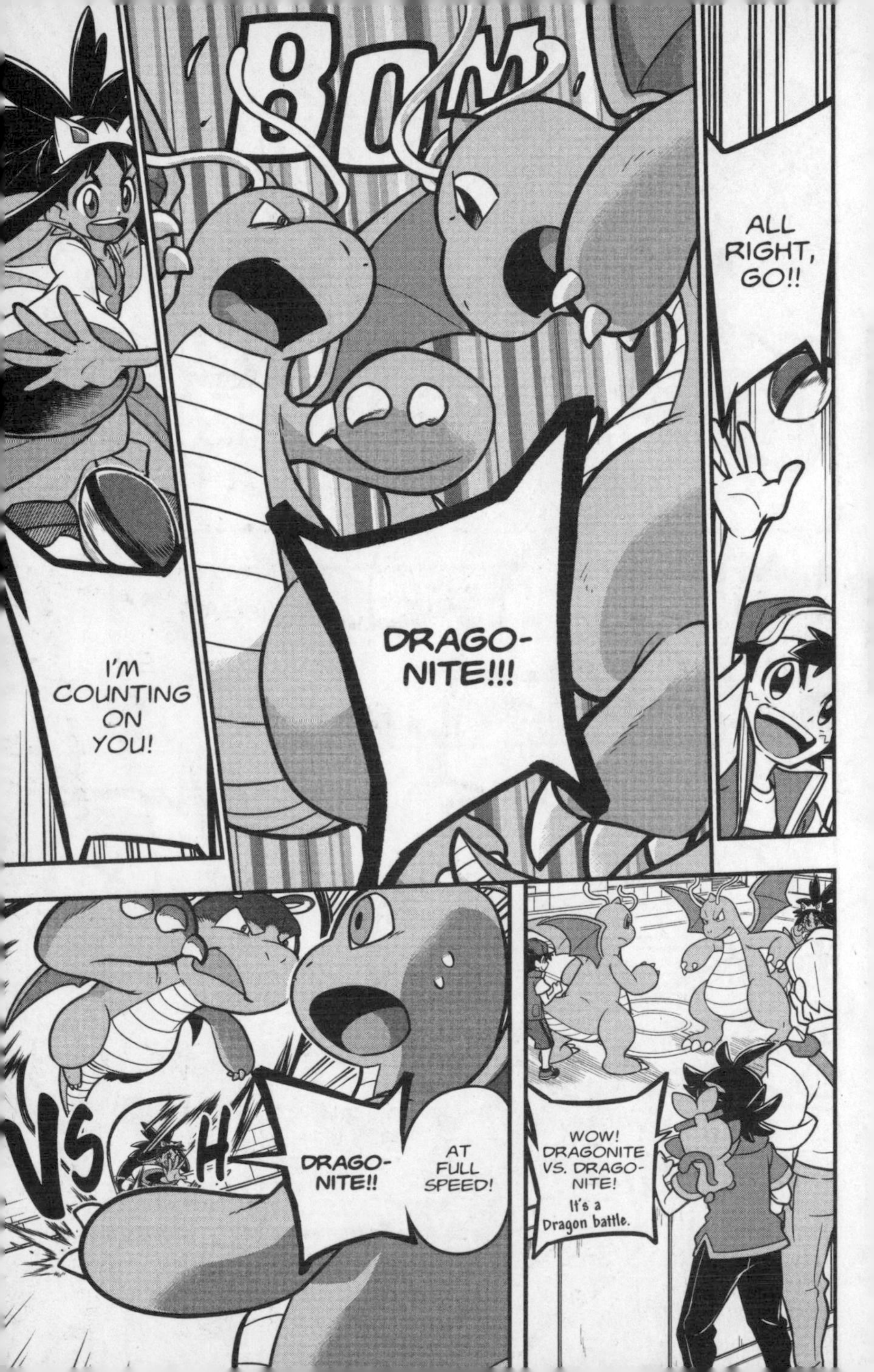
ALL RIGHT, GO!!
BOOM
DRAGO-NITE!!!
I'M COUNTING ON YOU!
WOW! DRAGONITE VS. DRAGO-NITE!
It's a Dragon battle.
AT FULL SPEED!
DRAGO-NITE!!

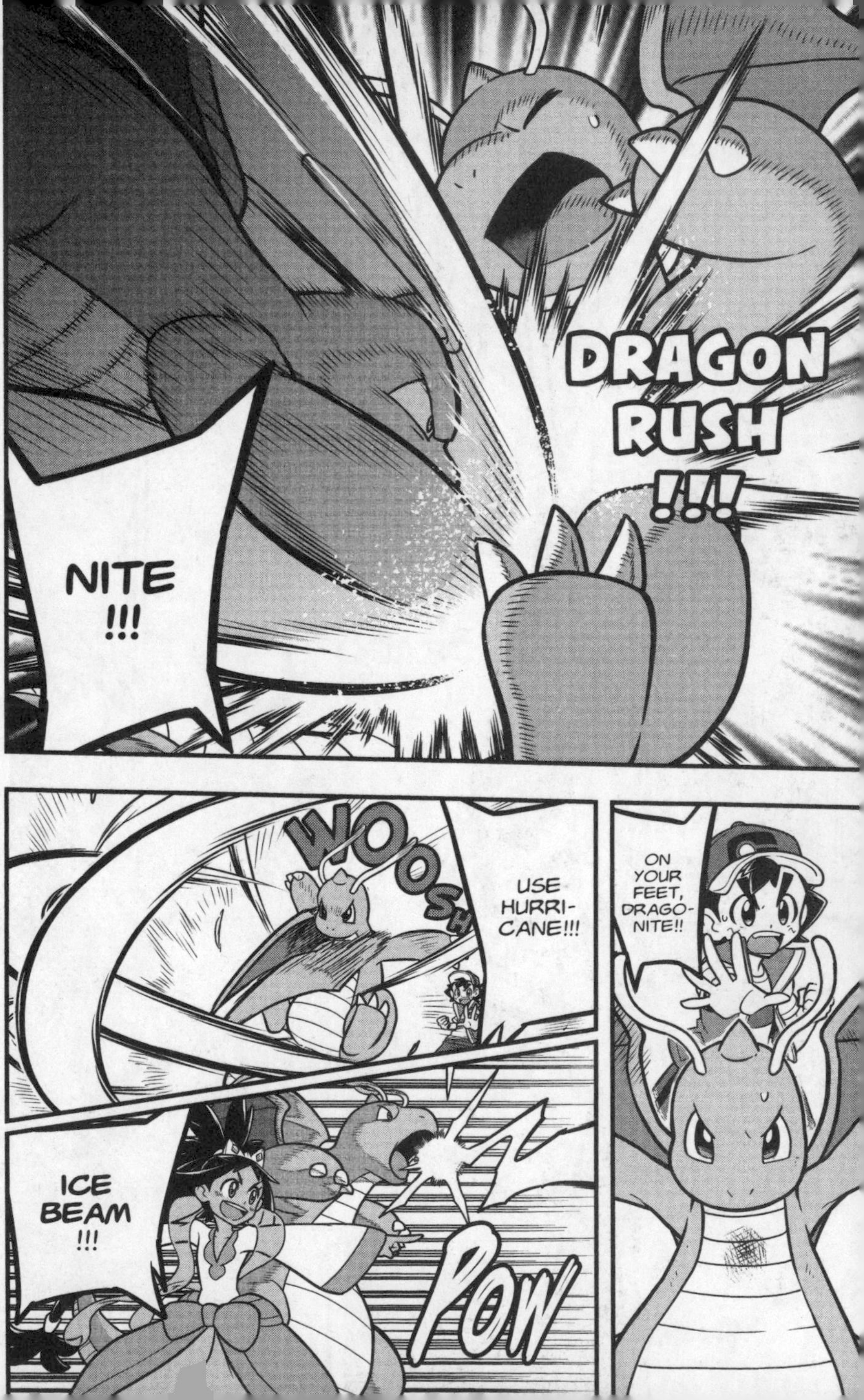
DRAGON RUSH !!!
NITE !!!
ON YOUR FEET, DRAGO-NITE!!
USE HURRI-CANE!!!
WOOSH
ICE BEAM !!!
POW

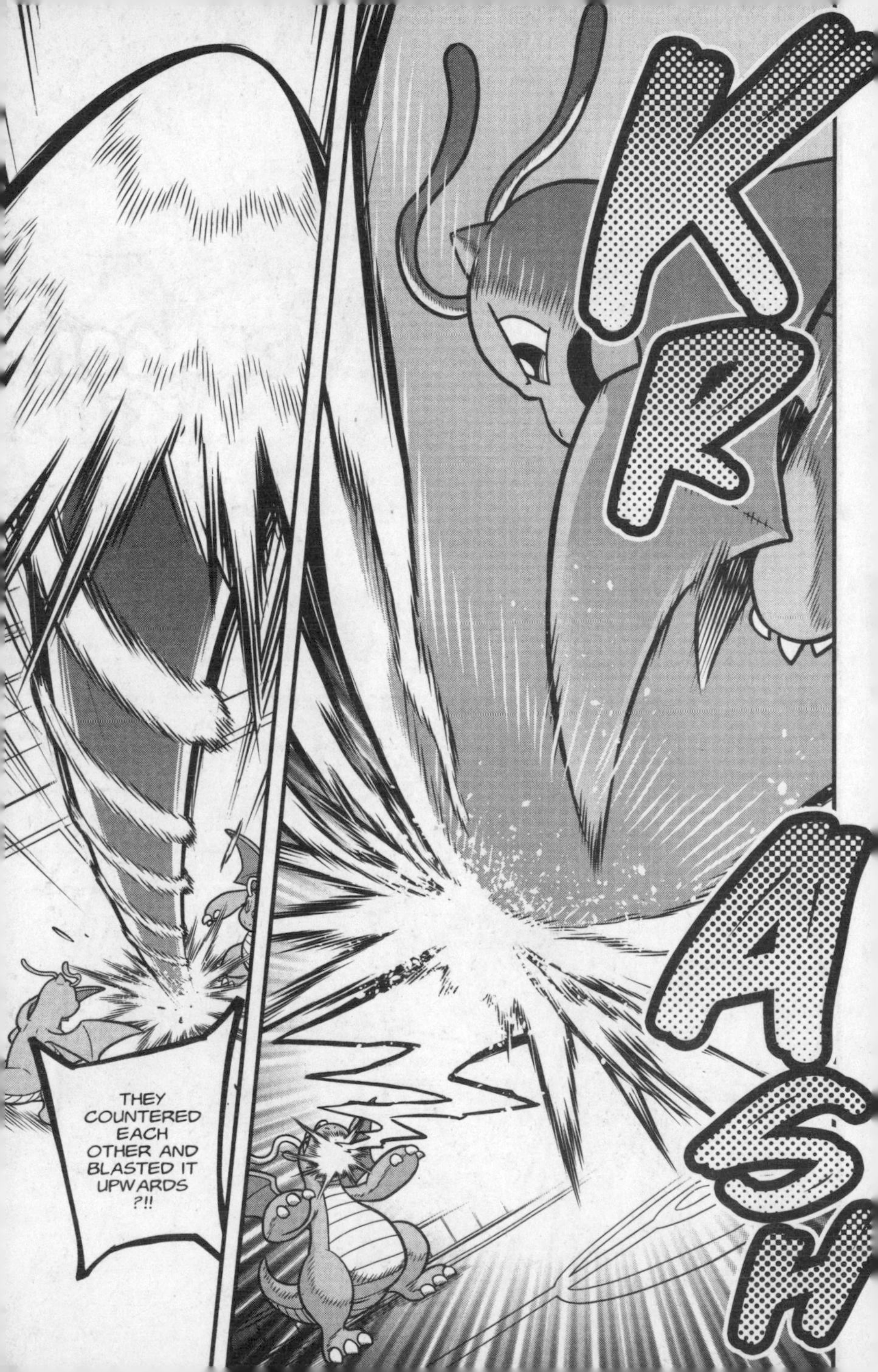
KRASH
THEY COUNTERED EACH OTHER AND BLASTED IT UPWARDS ?!!

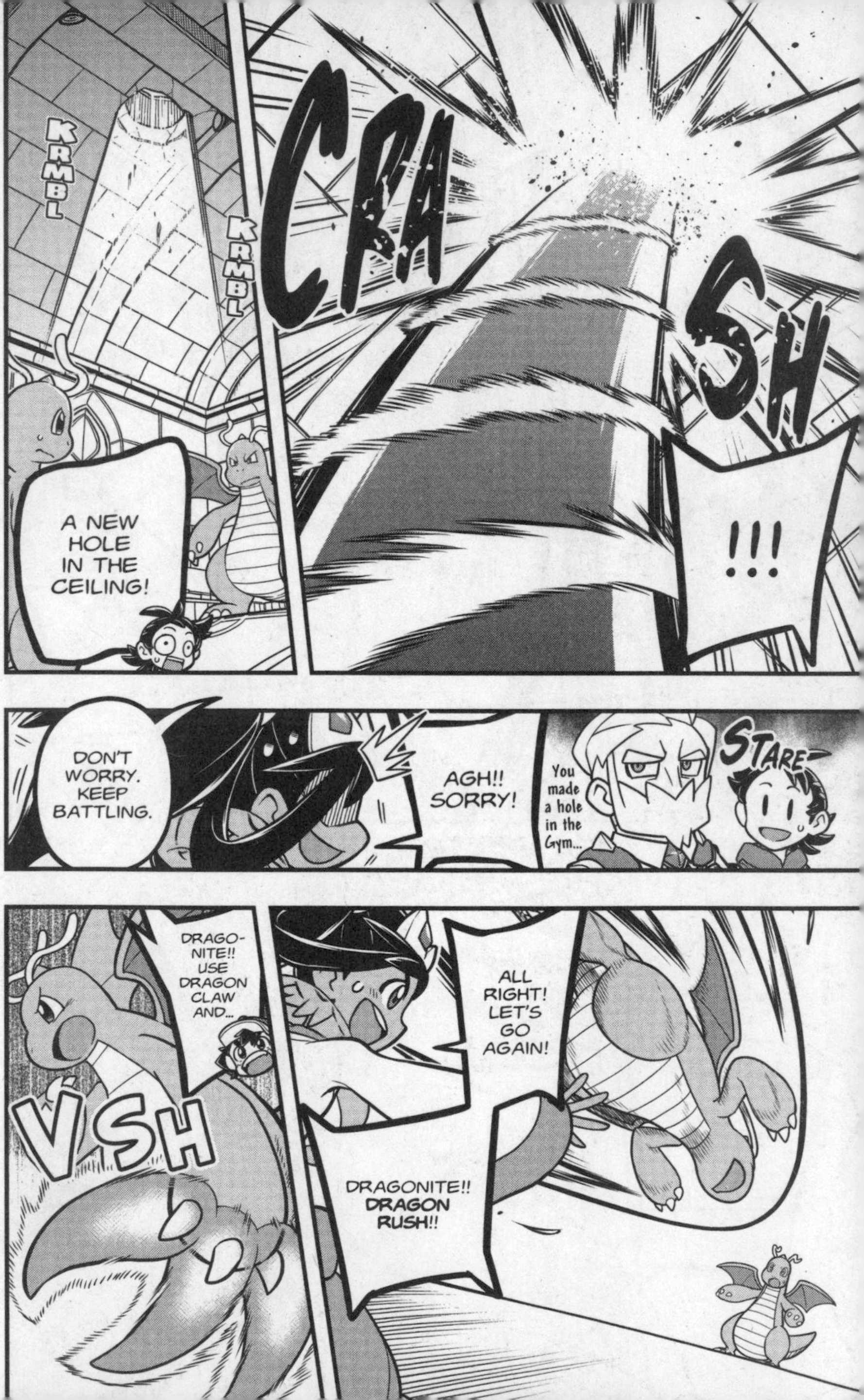

CRA
SH
!!!
KRMBL
KRMBL
A NEW HOLE IN THE CEILING!
STARE
You made a hole in the Gym...
AGH!! SORRY!
DON'T WORRY. KEEP BATTLING.
ALL RIGHT! LET'S GO AGAIN!
DRAGONITE!! USE DRAGON CLAW AND...
VSH
DRAGONITE!! DRAGON RUSH!!

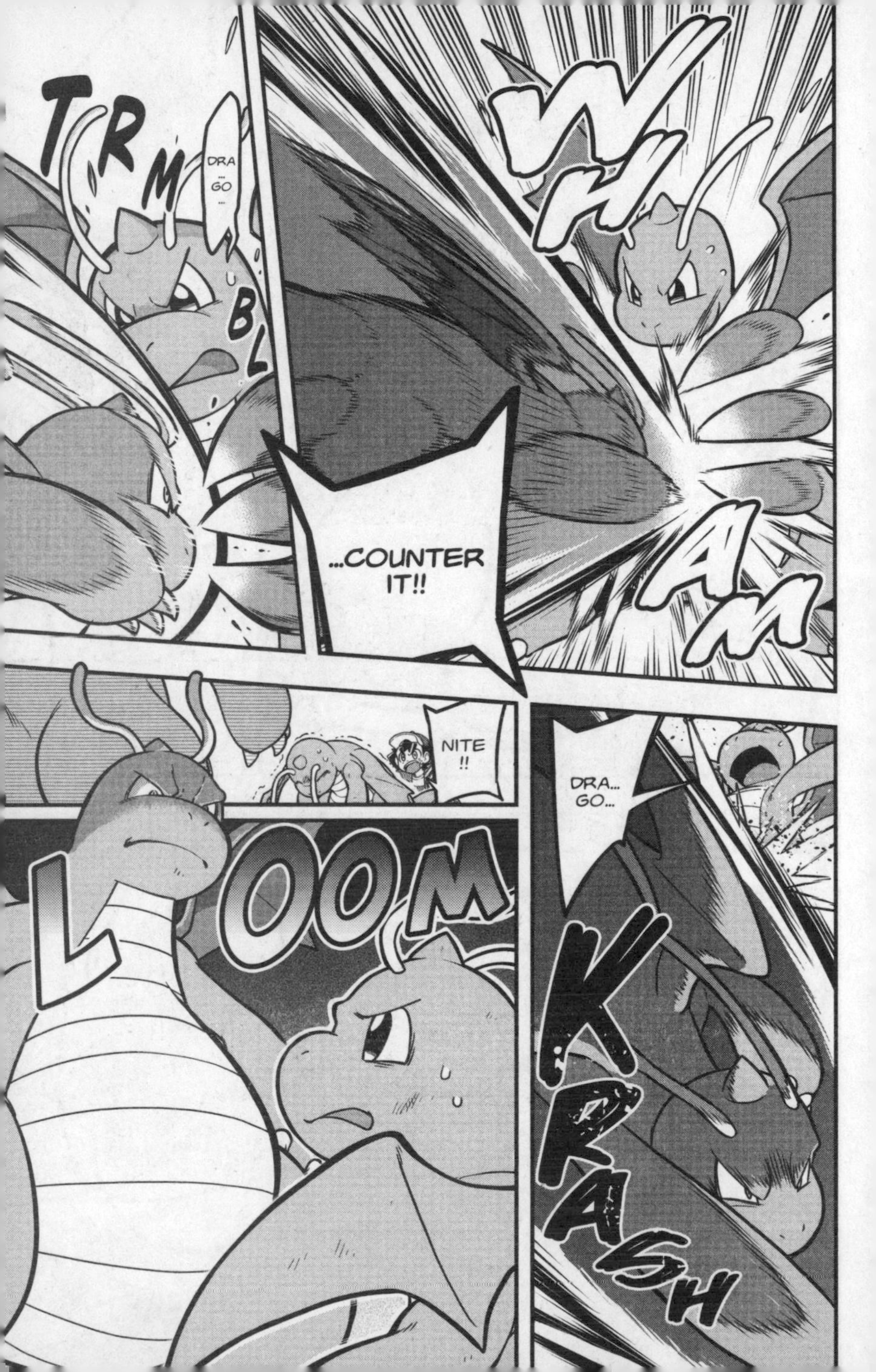
WHAM
...COUNTER IT!!
TRMBL
DRA ... GO ...
DRA... GO...
KRASH
NITE !!
LOOM

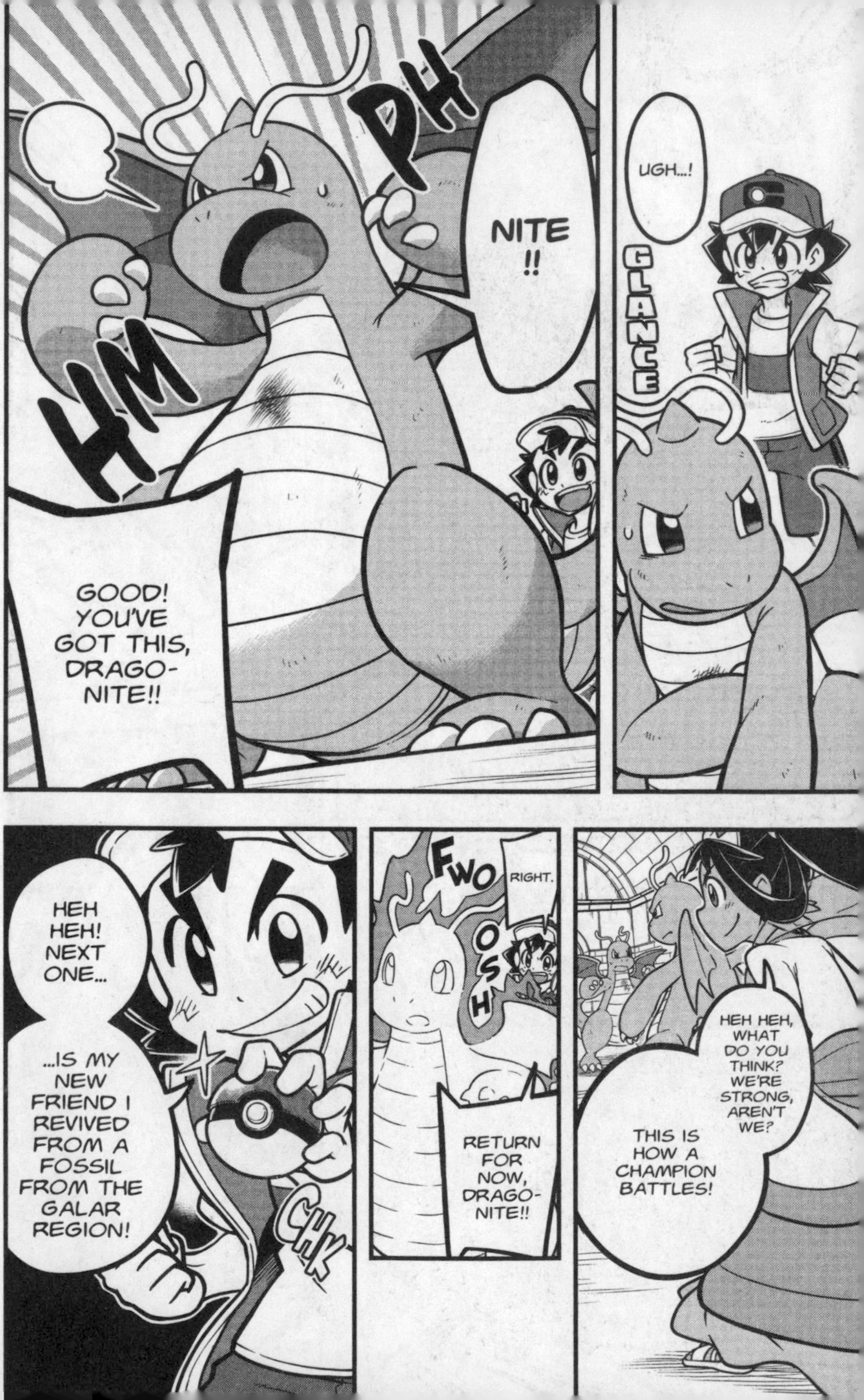
UGH...!
GLANCE
HMPH
NITE !!
GOOD! YOU'VE GOT THIS, DRAGO-NITE!!
HEH HEH, WHAT DO YOU THINK? WE'RE STRONG, AREN'T WE?
THIS IS HOW A CHAMPION BATTLES!
RIGHT.
FWOOSH
RETURN FOR NOW, DRAGO-NITE!!
HEH HEH! NEXT ONE...
...IS MY NEW FRIEND I REVIVED FROM A FOSSIL FROM THE GALAR REGION!
CHK

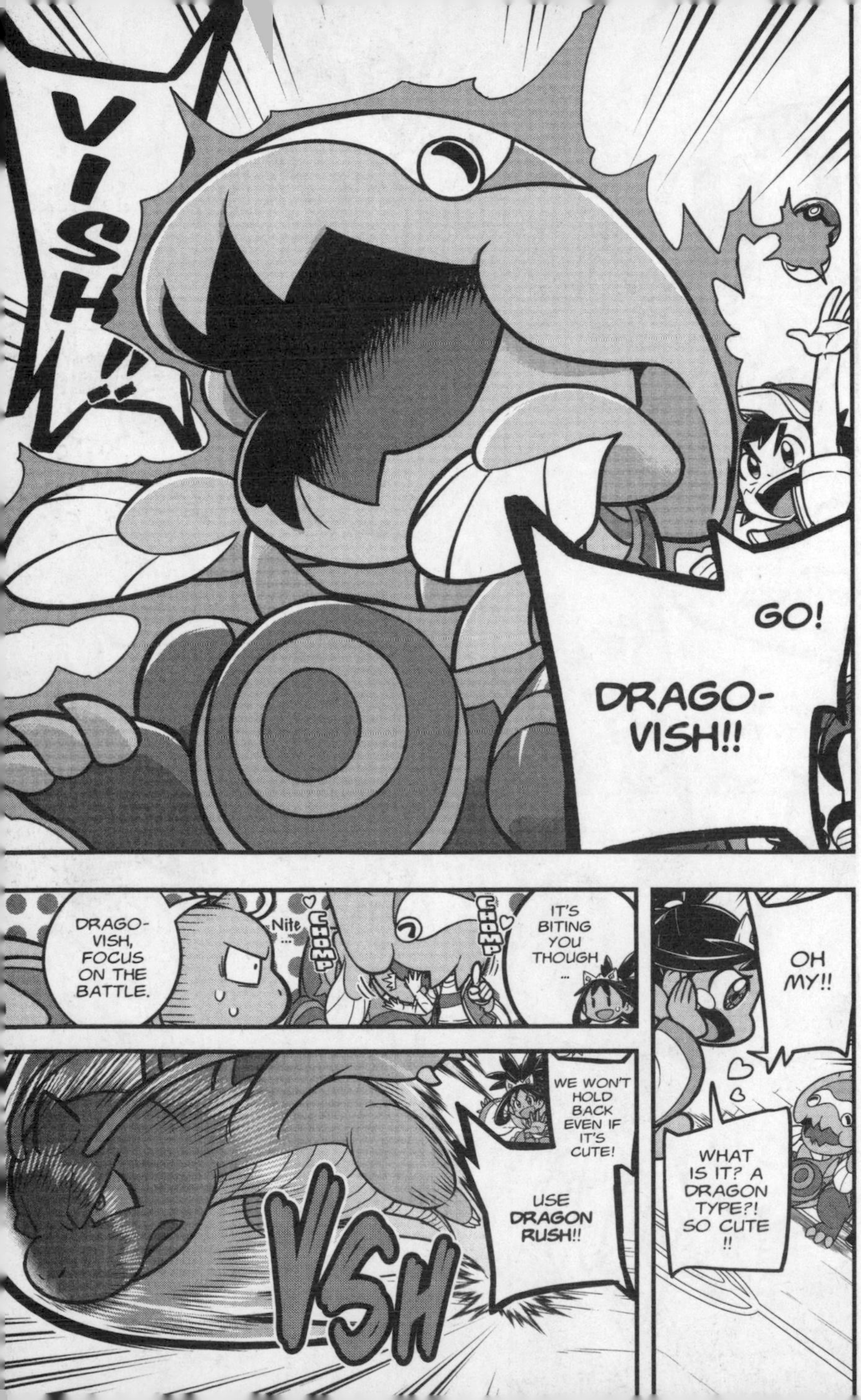
GO!
DRAGO-VISH!!
VISH!!
OH MY!!
WHAT IS IT? A DRAGON TYPE?! SO CUTE!!
IT'S BITING YOU THOUGH...
CHOMP
Nite...
CHOMP
DRAGO-VISH, FOCUS ON THE BATTLE.
WE WON'T HOLD BACK EVEN IF IT'S CUTE!
USE DRAGON RUSH!!
VSH

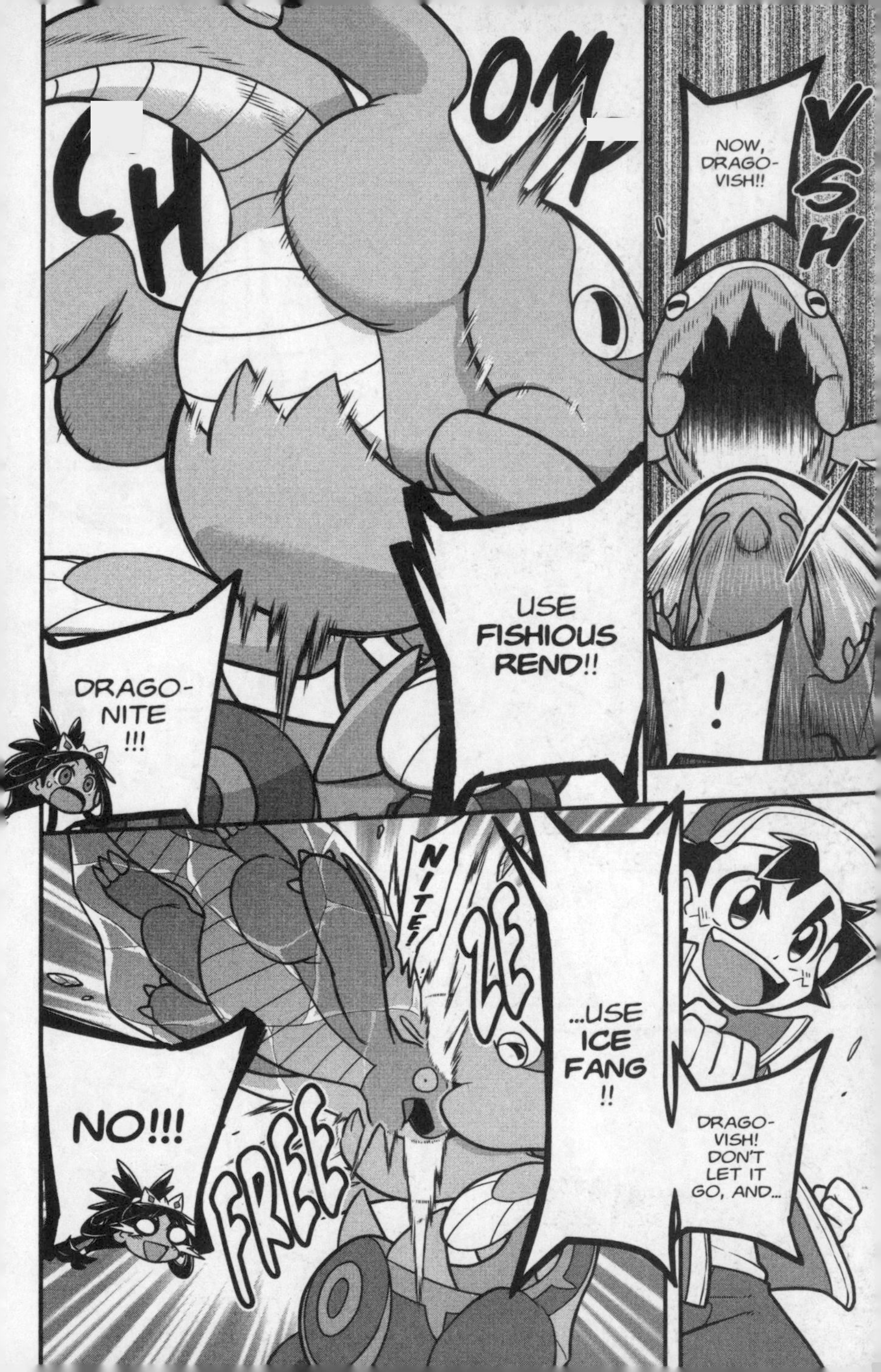
VSH
NOW, DRAGO-VISH!!
!
CHOMP
USE FISHIOUS REND!!
DRAGO-NITE!!!
DRAGO-VISH! DON'T LET IT GO, AND...
...USE ICE FANG!!
NITE!
FREEZE
NO!!!

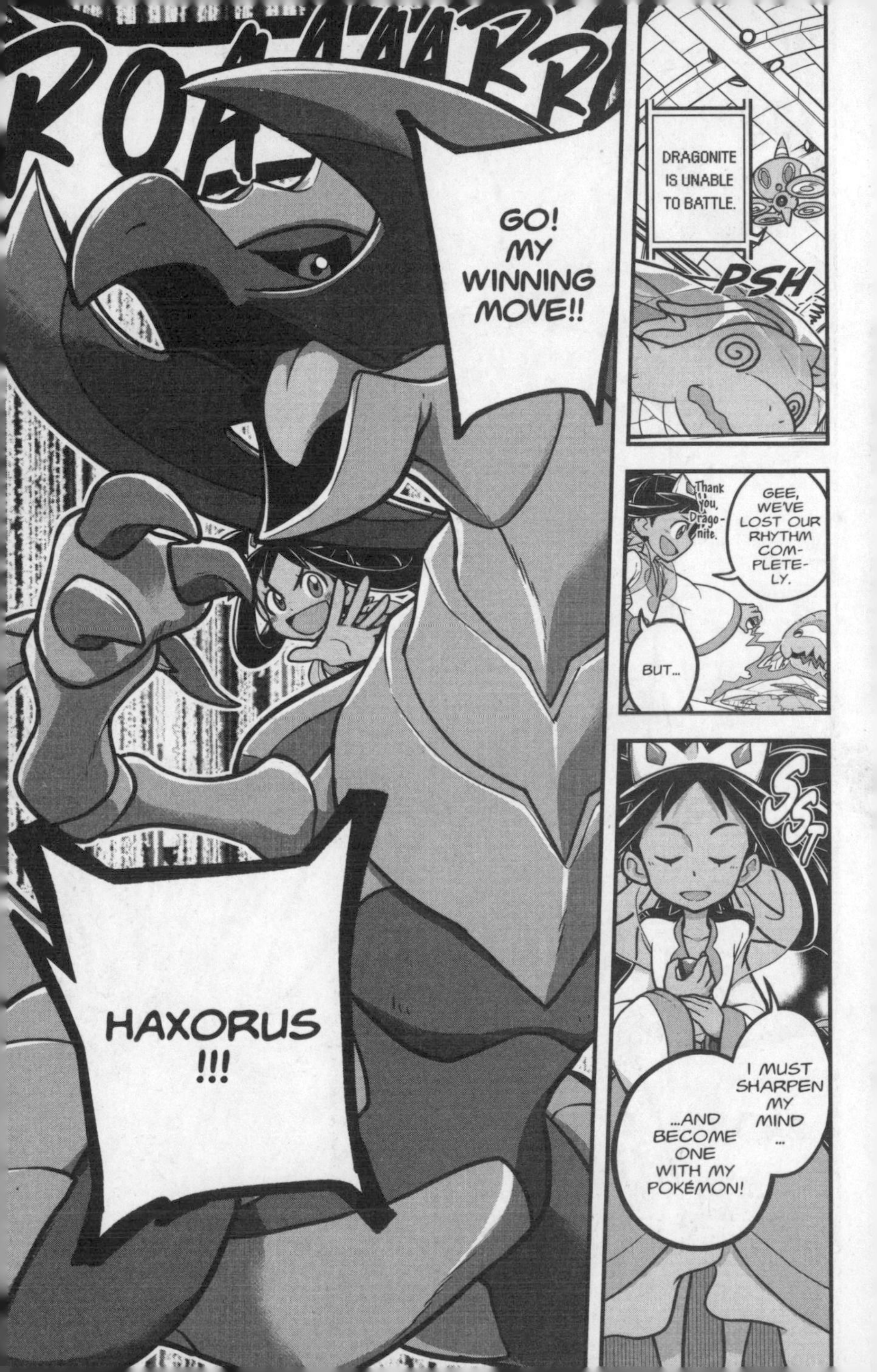
DRAGONITE IS UNABLE TO BATTLE.
PSH
GEE, WE'VE LOST OUR RHYTHM COM-PLETE-LY.
Thank you, Drago-nite.
BUT...
SST
I MUST SHARPEN MY MIND ...
...AND BECOME ONE WITH MY POKÉMON!
ROAAAARR
GO! MY WINNING MOVE!!
HAXORUS !!!

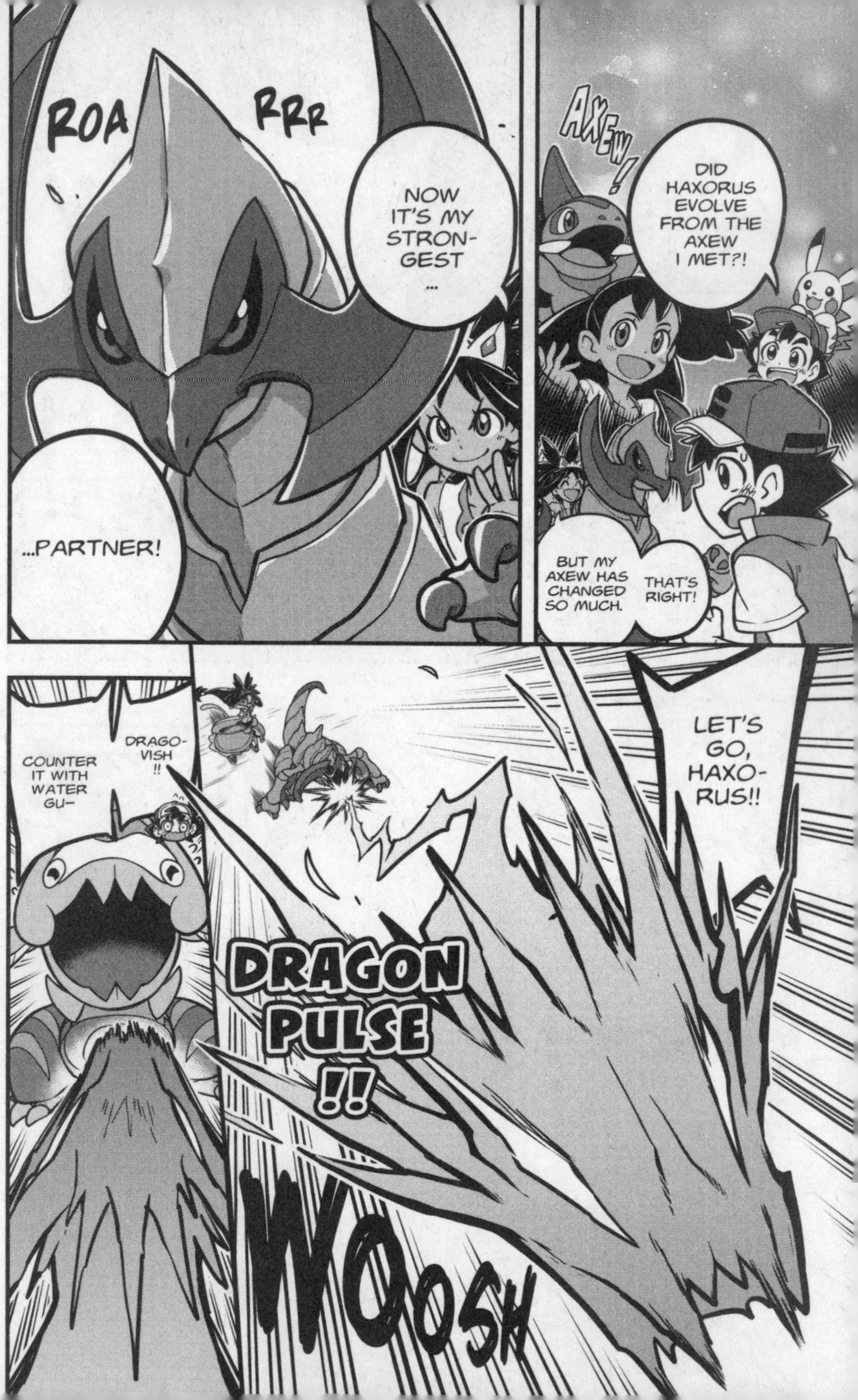
AXEW!
DID HAXORUS EVOLVE FROM THE AXEW I MET?!
THAT'S RIGHT!
BUT MY AXEW HAS CHANGED SO MUCH.
ROA RRR
NOW IT'S MY STRONGEST ...
...PARTNER!
LET'S GO, HAXORUS!!
DRAGON PULSE!!
WOOSH
DRAGOVISH!!
COUNTER IT WITH WATER GU-

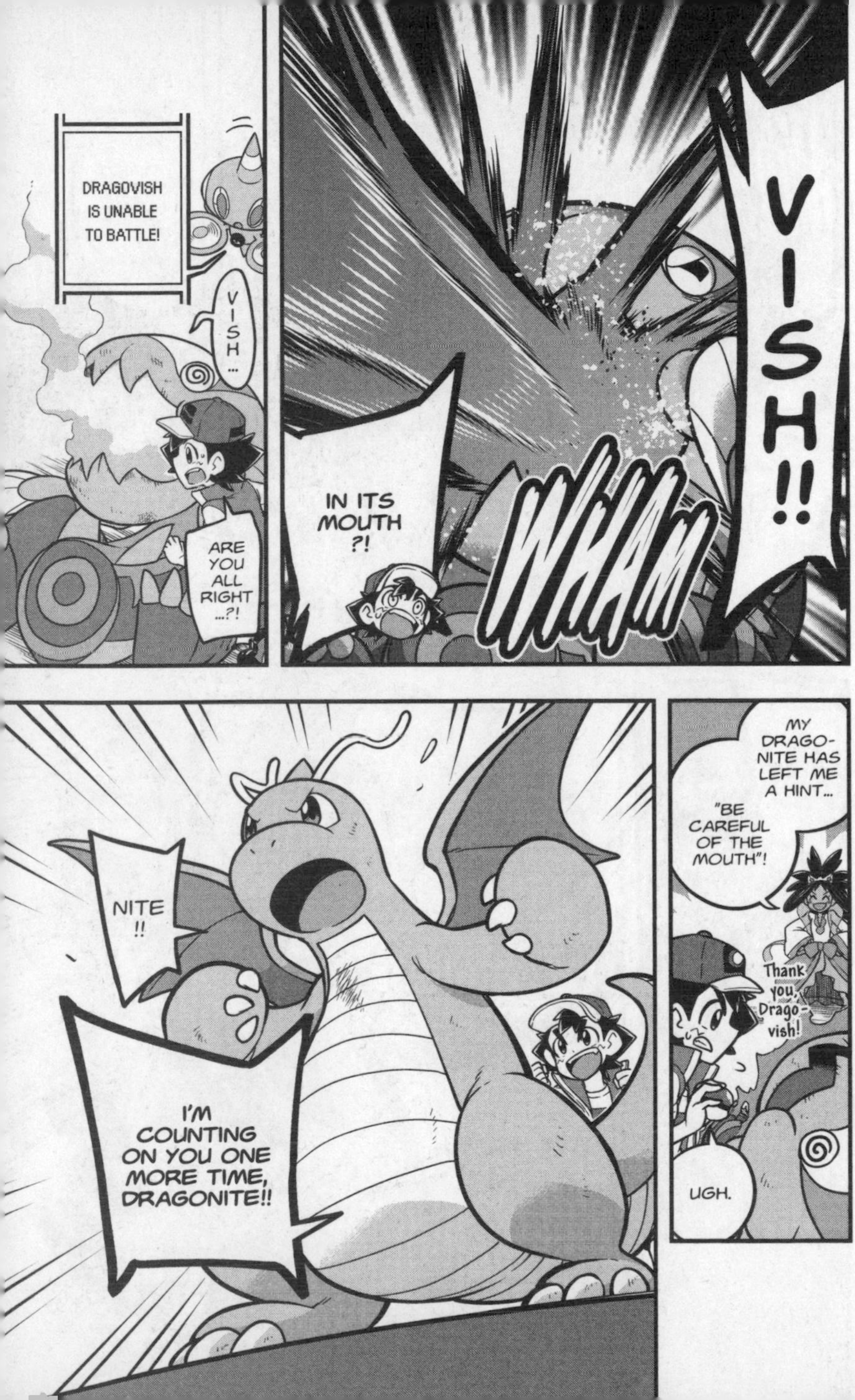
VISH!!
WHAM
IN ITS MOUTH ?!
DRAGOVISH IS UNABLE TO BATTLE!
VISH...
ARE YOU ALL RIGHT ...?!
MY DRAGO-NITE HAS LEFT ME A HINT...
"BE CAREFUL OF THE MOUTH"!
Thank you, Drago-vish!
UGH.
NITE !!
I'M COUNTING ON YOU ONE MORE TIME, DRAGONITE!!

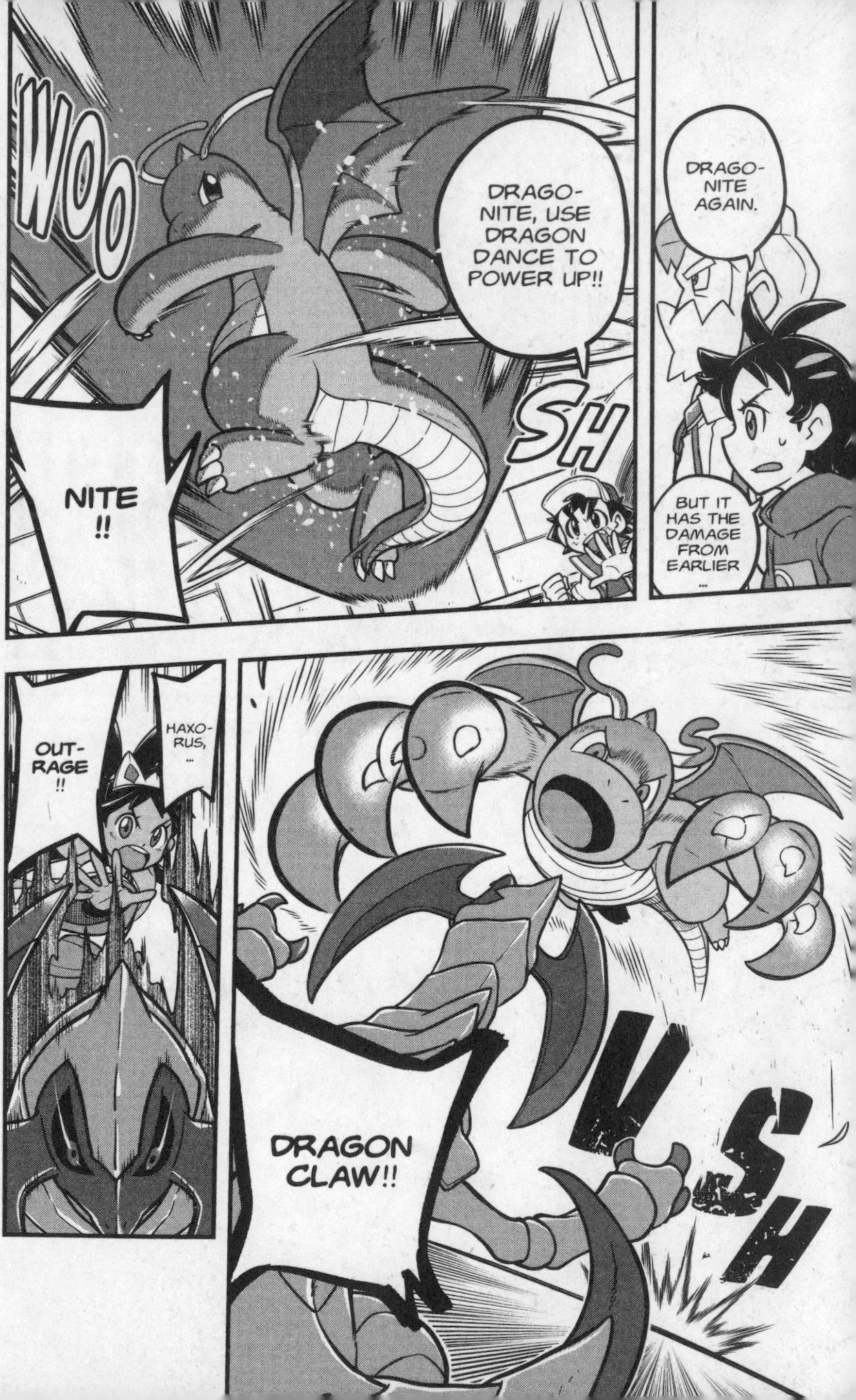
DRAGO-NITE AGAIN.
BUT IT HAS THE DAMAGE FROM EARLIER ...
DRAGO-NITE, USE DRAGON DANCE TO POWER UP!!
WOO
SH
NITE !!
VSH
DRAGON CLAW!!
HAXO-RUS, ...
OUT-RAGE !!

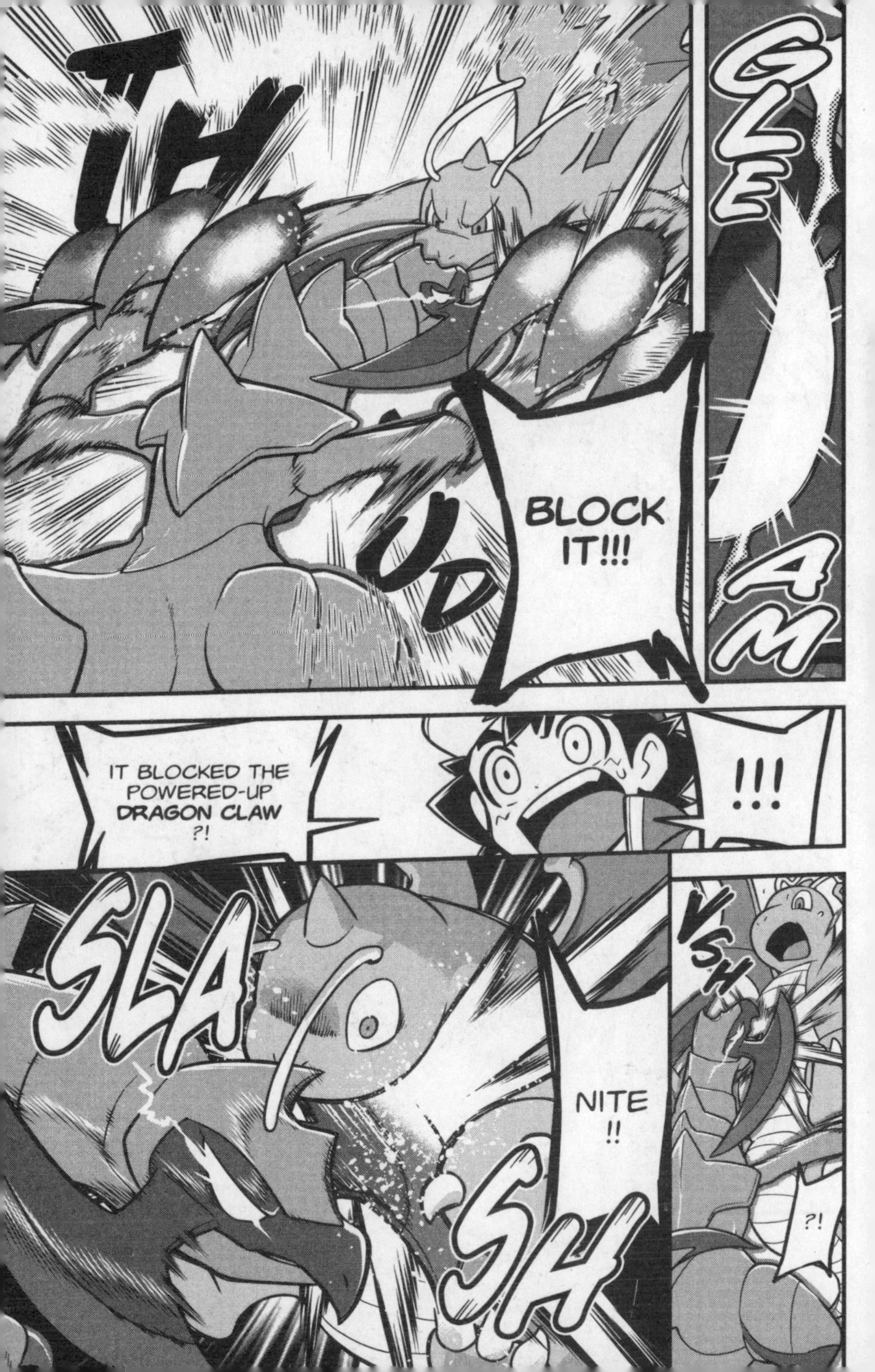
GLEAM
BLOCK IT!!!
THUD
!!!
IT BLOCKED THE POWERED-UP DRAGON CLAW ?!
VSH
?!
NITE !!
SLASH

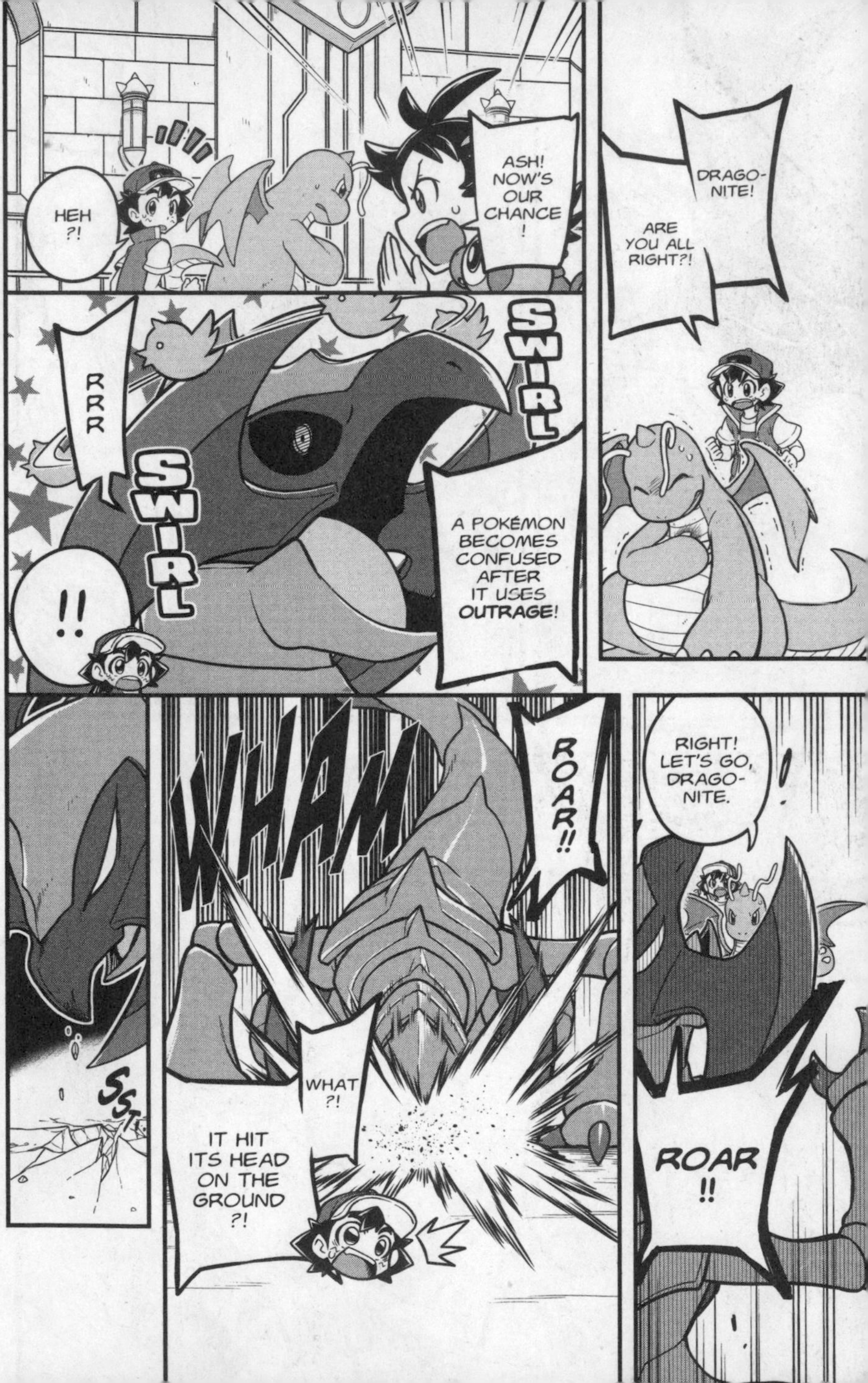
DRAGO-NITE!
ARE YOU ALL RIGHT?!
ASH! NOW'S OUR CHANCE!
HEH?!
SWIRL
SWIRL
A POKÉMON BECOMES CONFUSED AFTER IT USES OUTRAGE!
RRR
!!
RIGHT! LET'S GO, DRAGO-NITE.
ROAR!!
ROAR!!
WHAM
WHAT?!
IT HIT ITS HEAD ON THE GROUND?!
SST

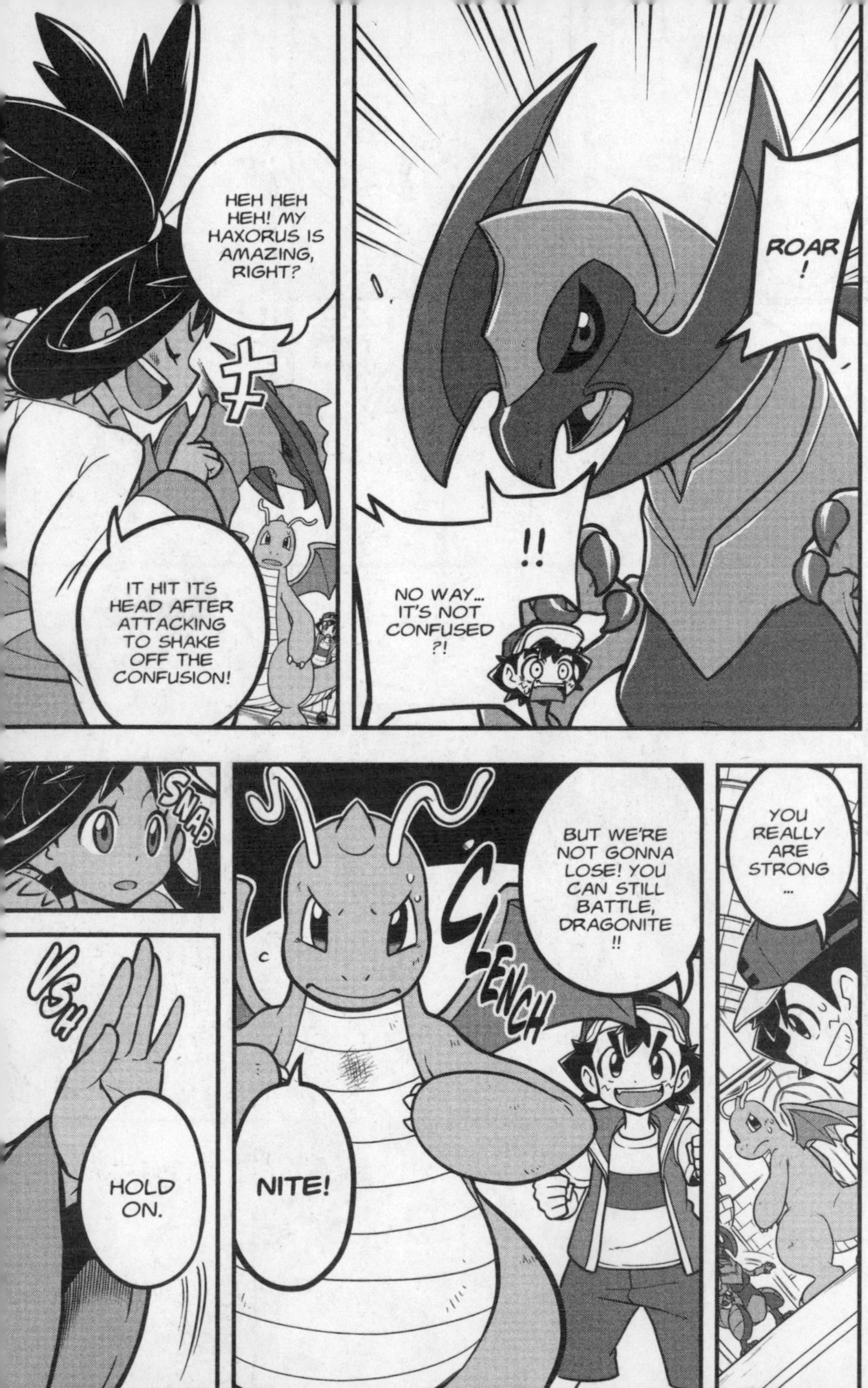

ROAR!
!!
NO WAY... IT'S NOT CONFUSED?!
HEH HEH HEH! MY HAXORUS IS AMAZING, RIGHT?
IT HIT ITS HEAD AFTER ATTACKING TO SHAKE OFF THE CONFUSION!
YOU REALLY ARE STRONG...
BUT WE'RE NOT GONNA LOSE! YOU CAN STILL BATTLE, DRAGONITE!!
CLENCH
NITE!
SNAP
VSH
HOLD ON.

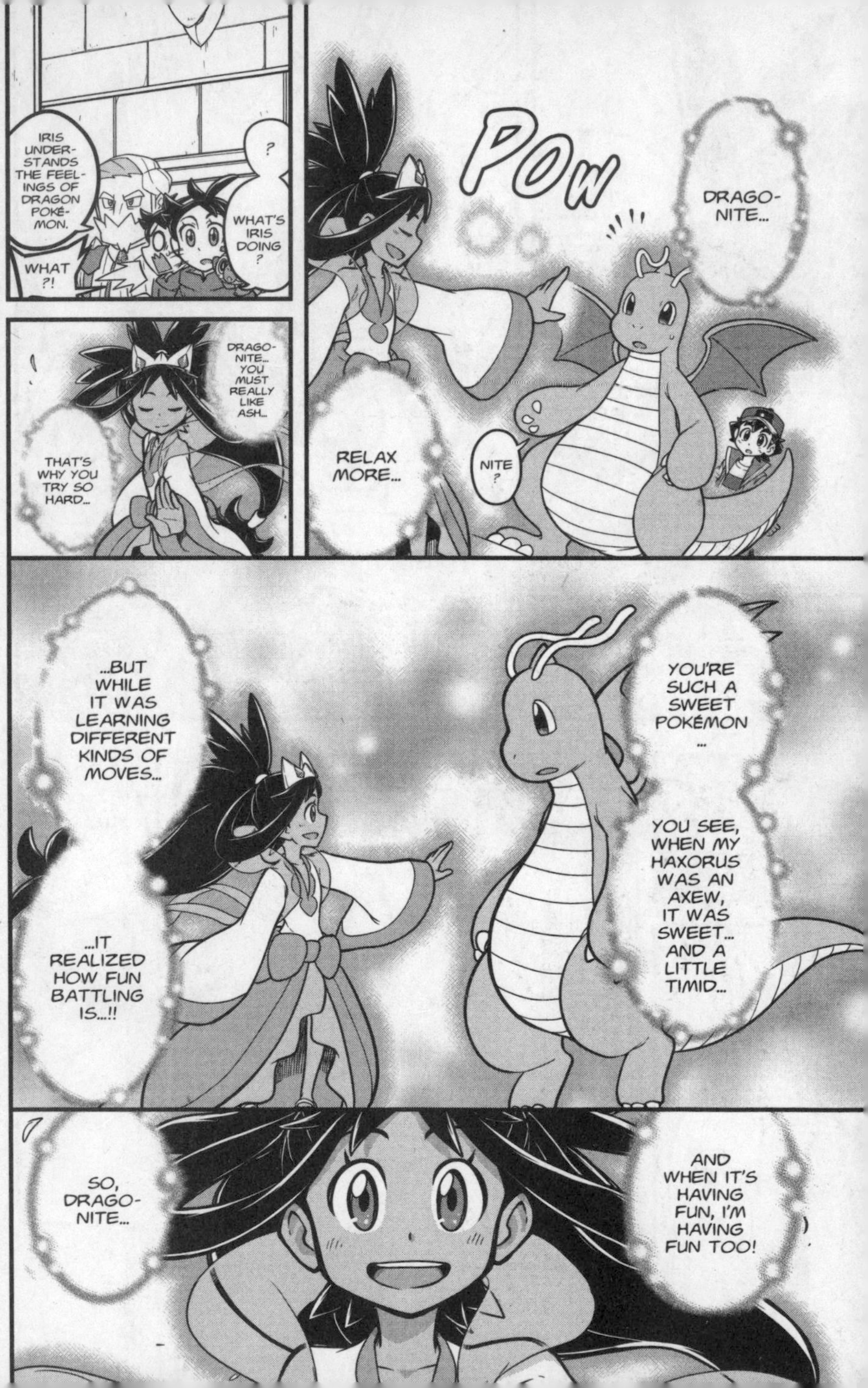
POW
DRAGONITE...
NITE?
RELAX MORE...
?
WHAT'S IRIS DOING?
IRIS UNDERSTANDS THE FEELINGS OF DRAGON POKÉMON.
WHAT?!
DRAGONITE... YOU MUST REALLY LIKE ASH...
THAT'S WHY YOU TRY SO HARD...
YOU'RE SUCH A SWEET POKÉMON...
YOU SEE, WHEN MY HAXORUS WAS AN AXEW, IT WAS SWEET... AND A LITTLE TIMID...
...BUT WHILE IT WAS LEARNING DIFFERENT KINDS OF MOVES...
...IT REALIZED HOW FUN BATTLING IS...!!
AND WHEN IT'S HAVING FUN, I'M HAVING FUN TOO!
SO, DRAGONITE...

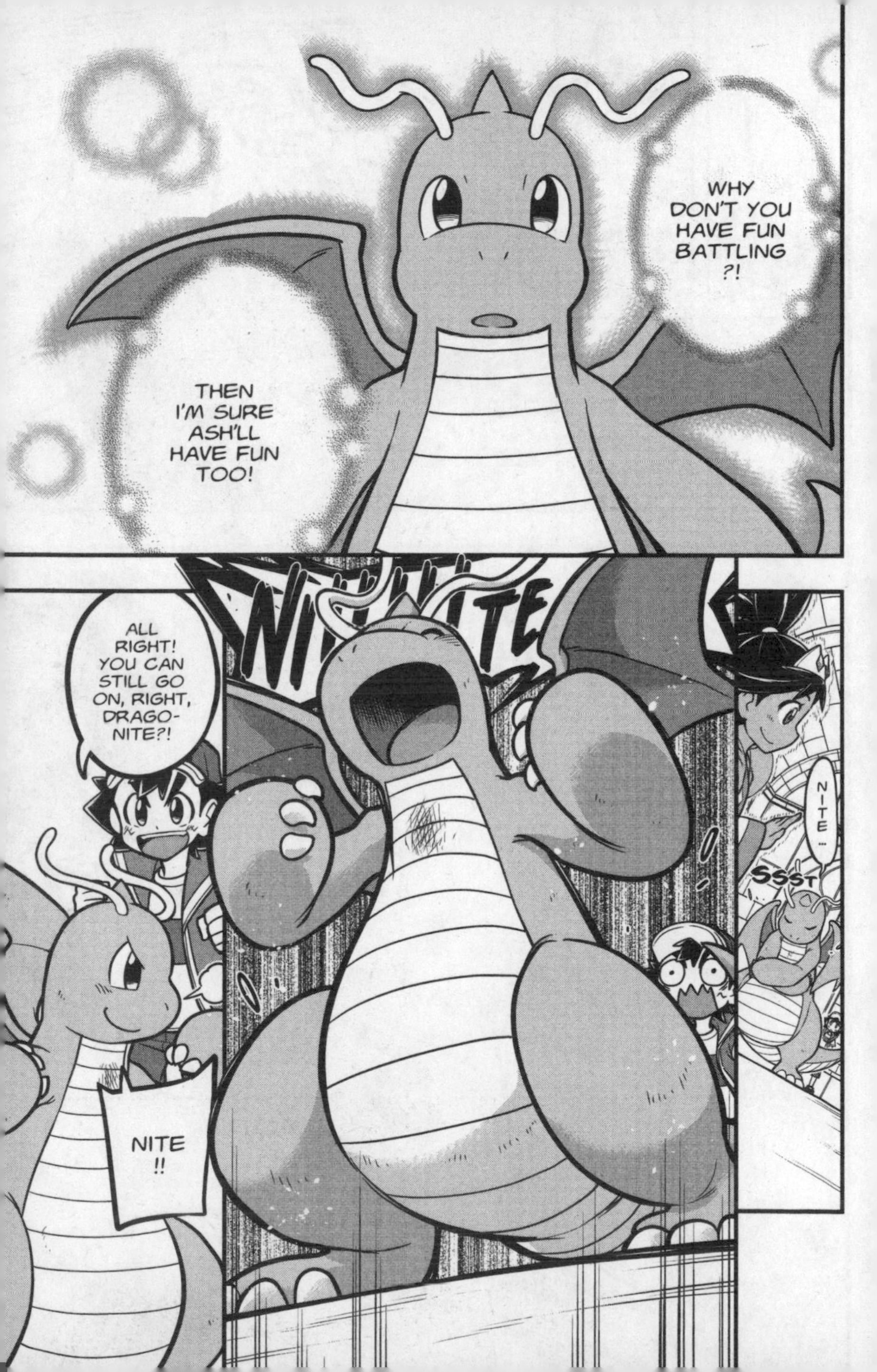
WHY DON'T YOU HAVE FUN BATTLING?!
THEN I'M SURE ASH'LL HAVE FUN TOO!
NITE...
SSST
ALL RIGHT! YOU CAN STILL GO ON, RIGHT, DRAGONITE?!
NITE!!

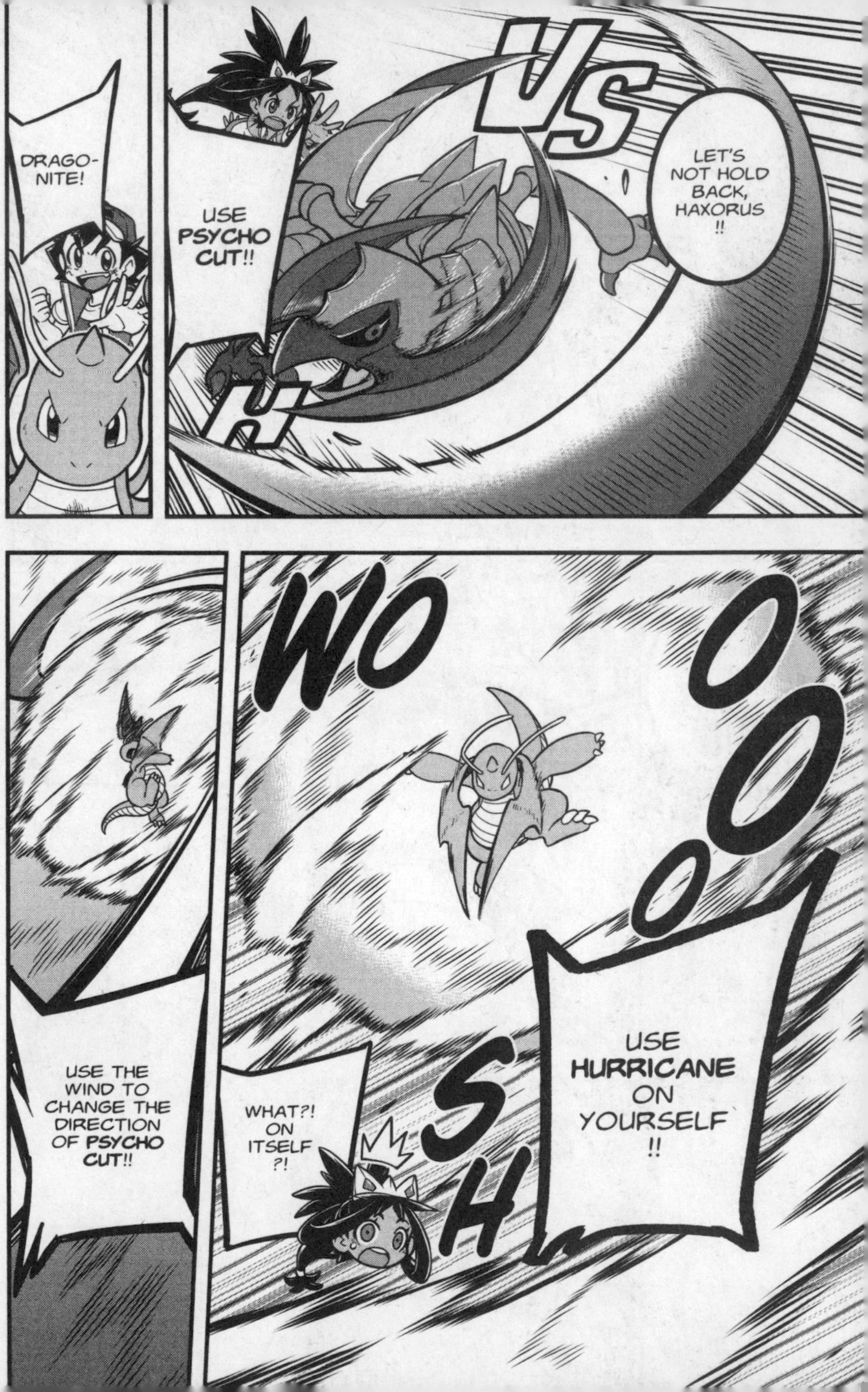
VS
LET'S NOT HOLD BACK, HAXORUS!!
USE PSYCHO CUT!!
H
DRAGO-NITE!
WOOOOO
USE HURRICANE ON YOURSELF!!
SH
WHAT?! ON ITSELF?!
USE THE WIND TO CHANGE THE DIRECTION OF PSYCHO CUT!!

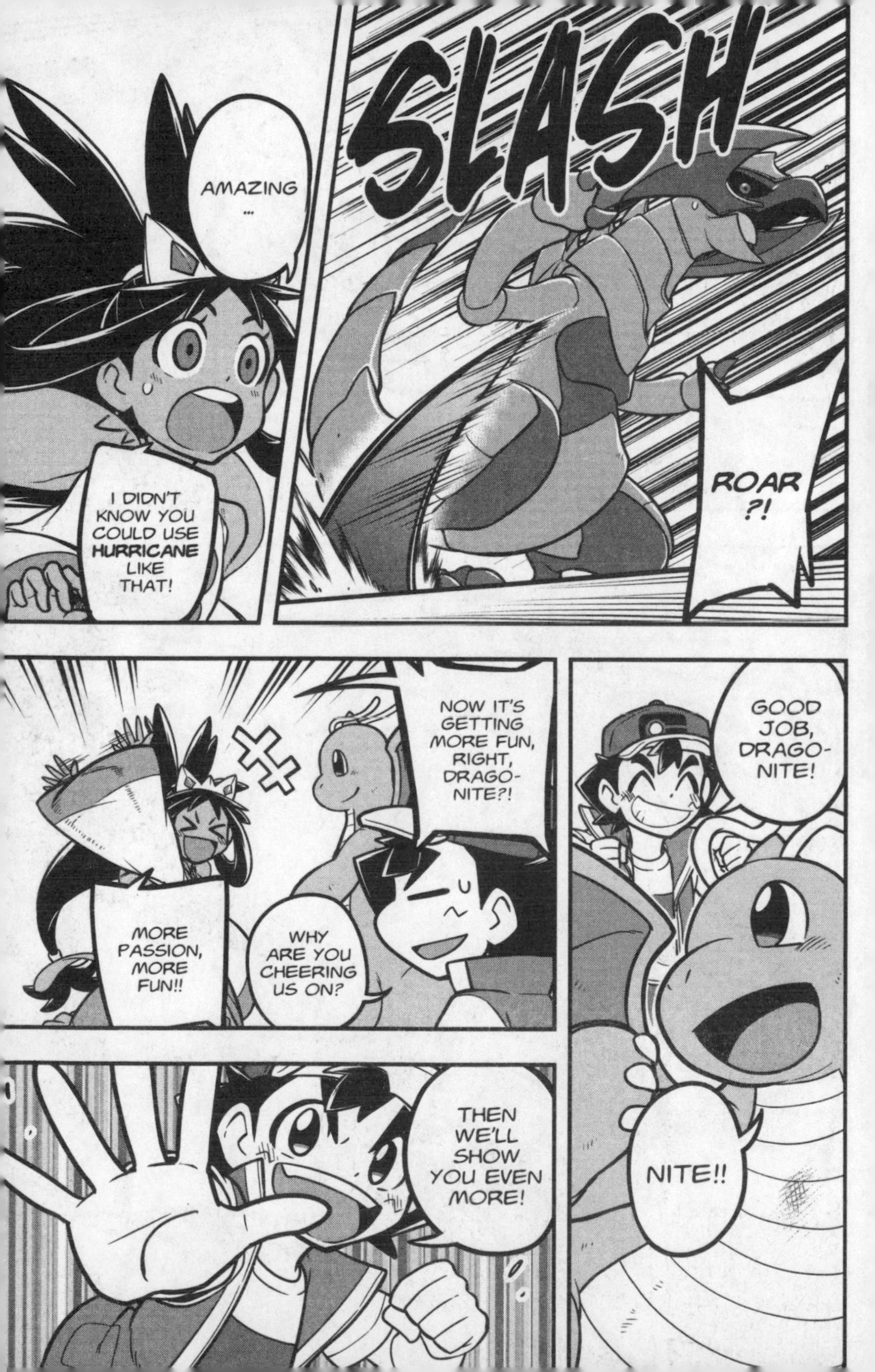
SLASH
ROAR?!
AMAZING...
I DIDN'T KNOW YOU COULD USE **HURRICANE** LIKE THAT!
GOOD JOB, DRAGONITE!
NITE!!
NOW IT'S GETTING MORE FUN, RIGHT, DRAGONITE?!
WHY ARE YOU CHEERING US ON?
MORE PASSION, MORE FUN!!
THEN WE'LL SHOW YOU EVEN MORE!

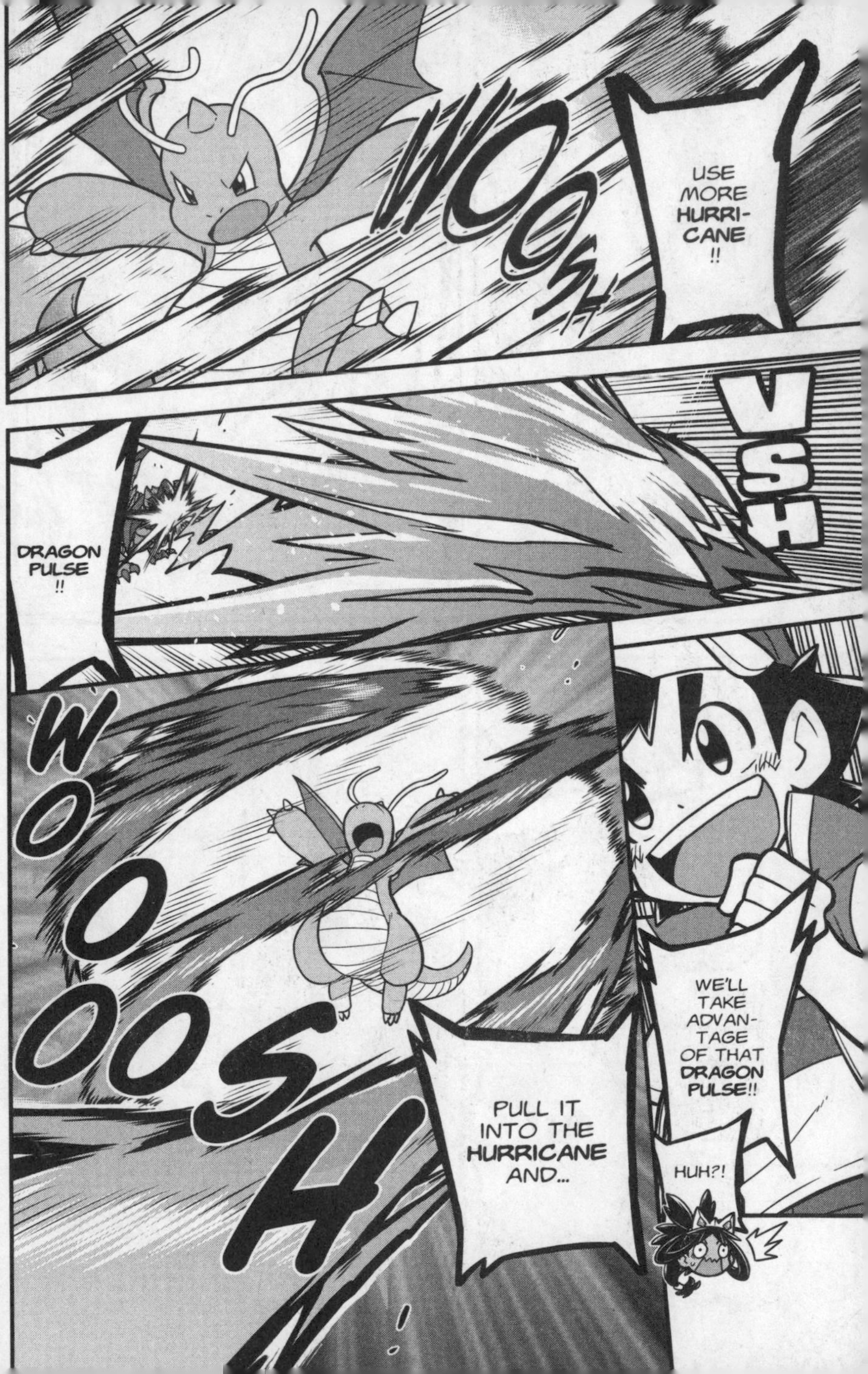
USE MORE HURRICANE!!
WOOSH
VSH
DRAGON PULSE!!
WE'LL TAKE ADVANTAGE OF THAT DRAGON PULSE!!
HUH?!
PULL IT INTO THE HURRICANE AND...
WOOOOSH

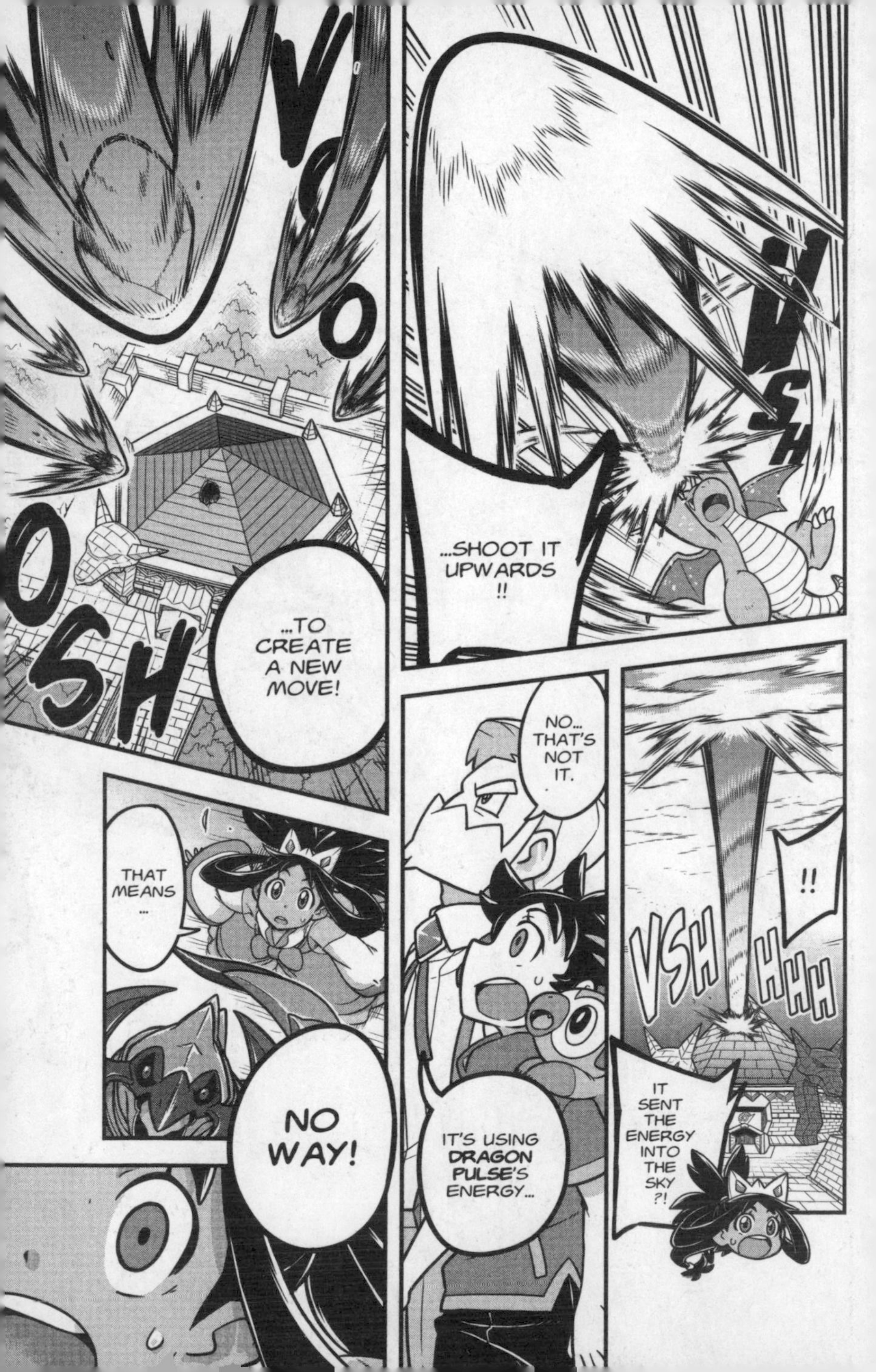
...SHOOT IT UPWARDS !!
...TO CREATE A NEW MOVE!
!!
VSHHHHH
IT SENT THE ENERGY INTO THE SKY ?!
NO... THAT'S NOT IT.
IT'S USING **DRAGON PULSE**'S ENERGY...
THAT MEANS ...
NO WAY!

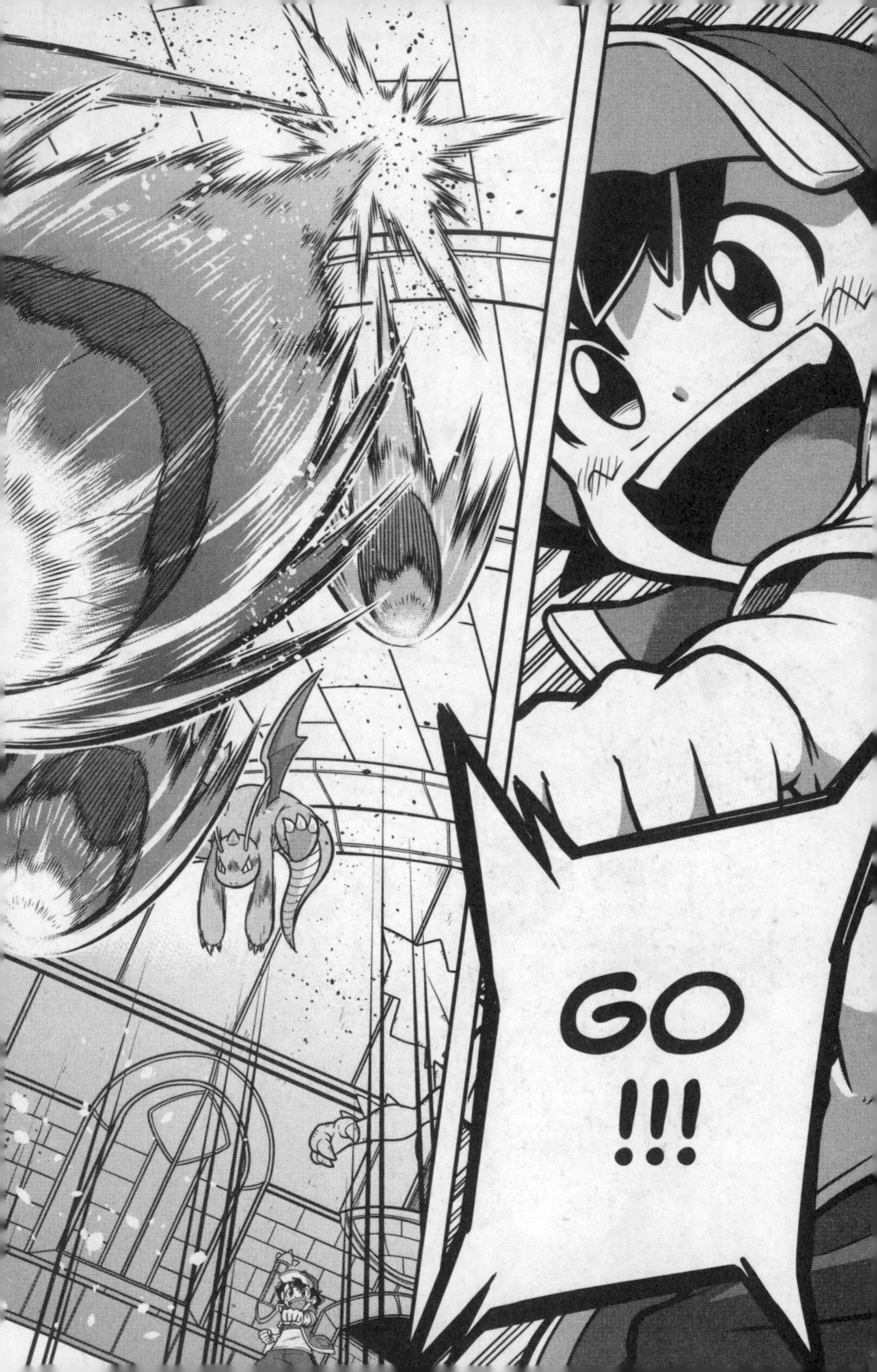
GO !!!

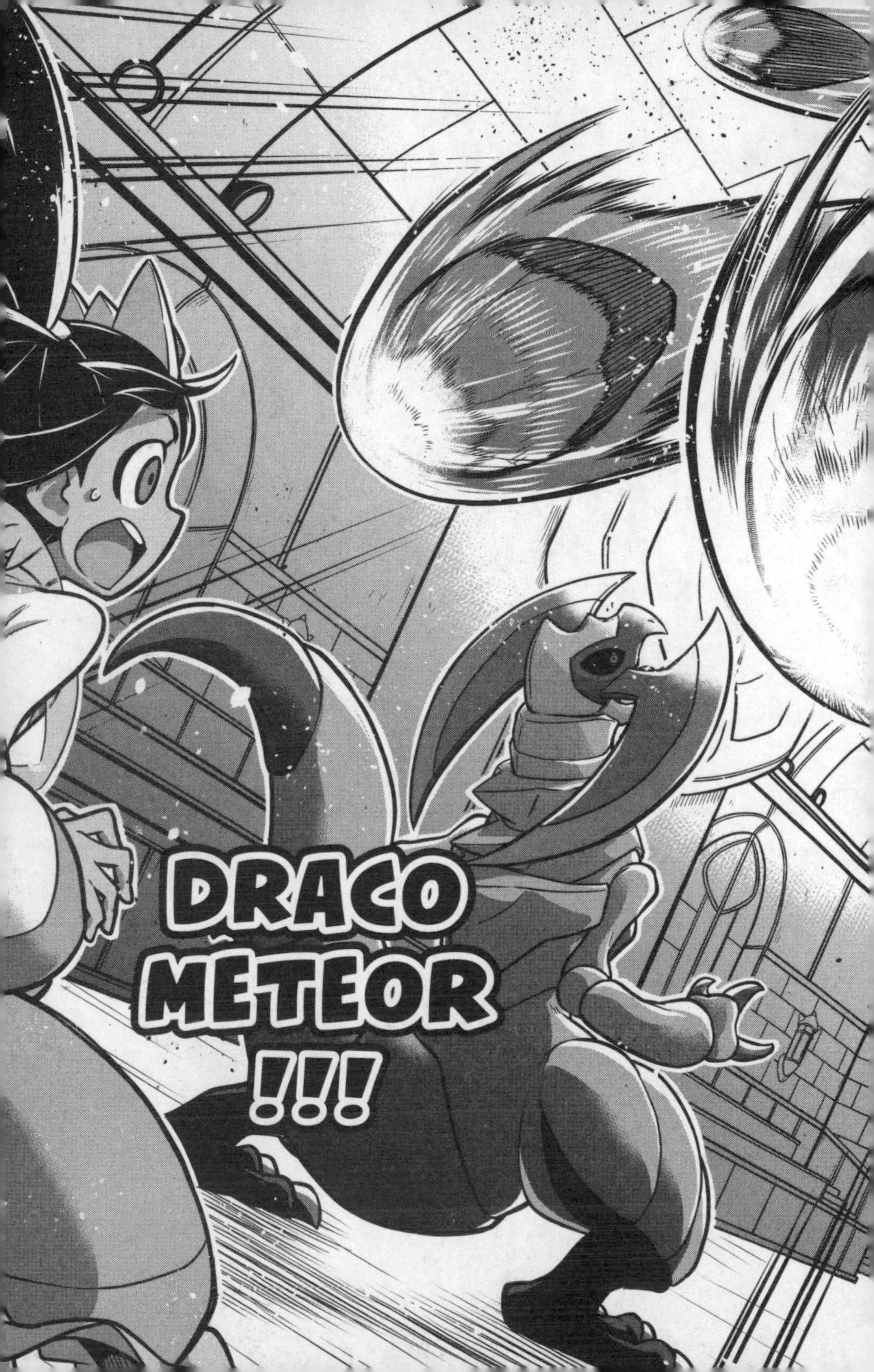
DRACO METEOR !!!

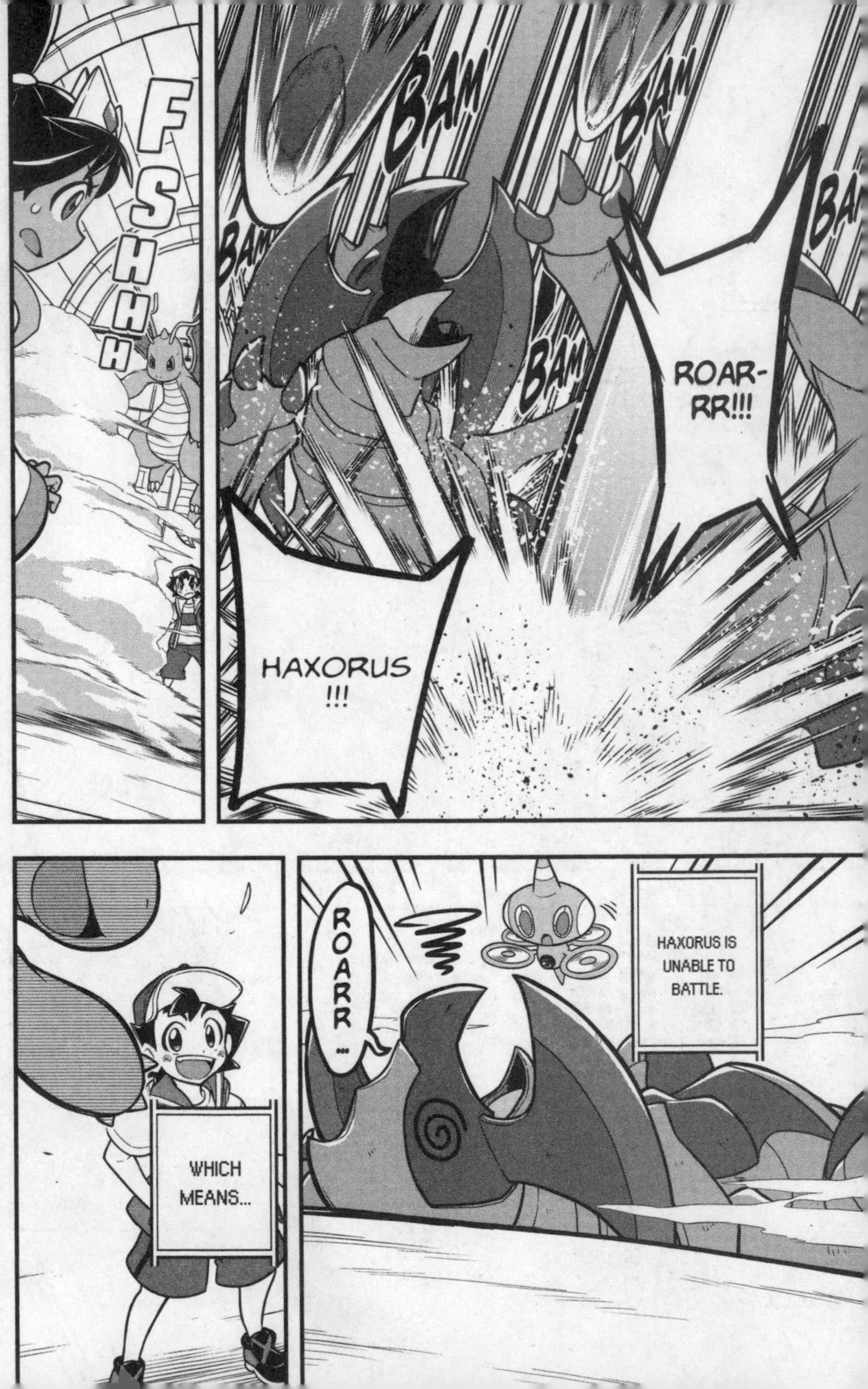
BAM
BAM
BAM
ROAR-RR!!!
BAM
BAM
HAXORUS!!!
FSHHHH
HAXORUS IS UNABLE TO BATTLE.
ROARR...
WHICH MEANS...

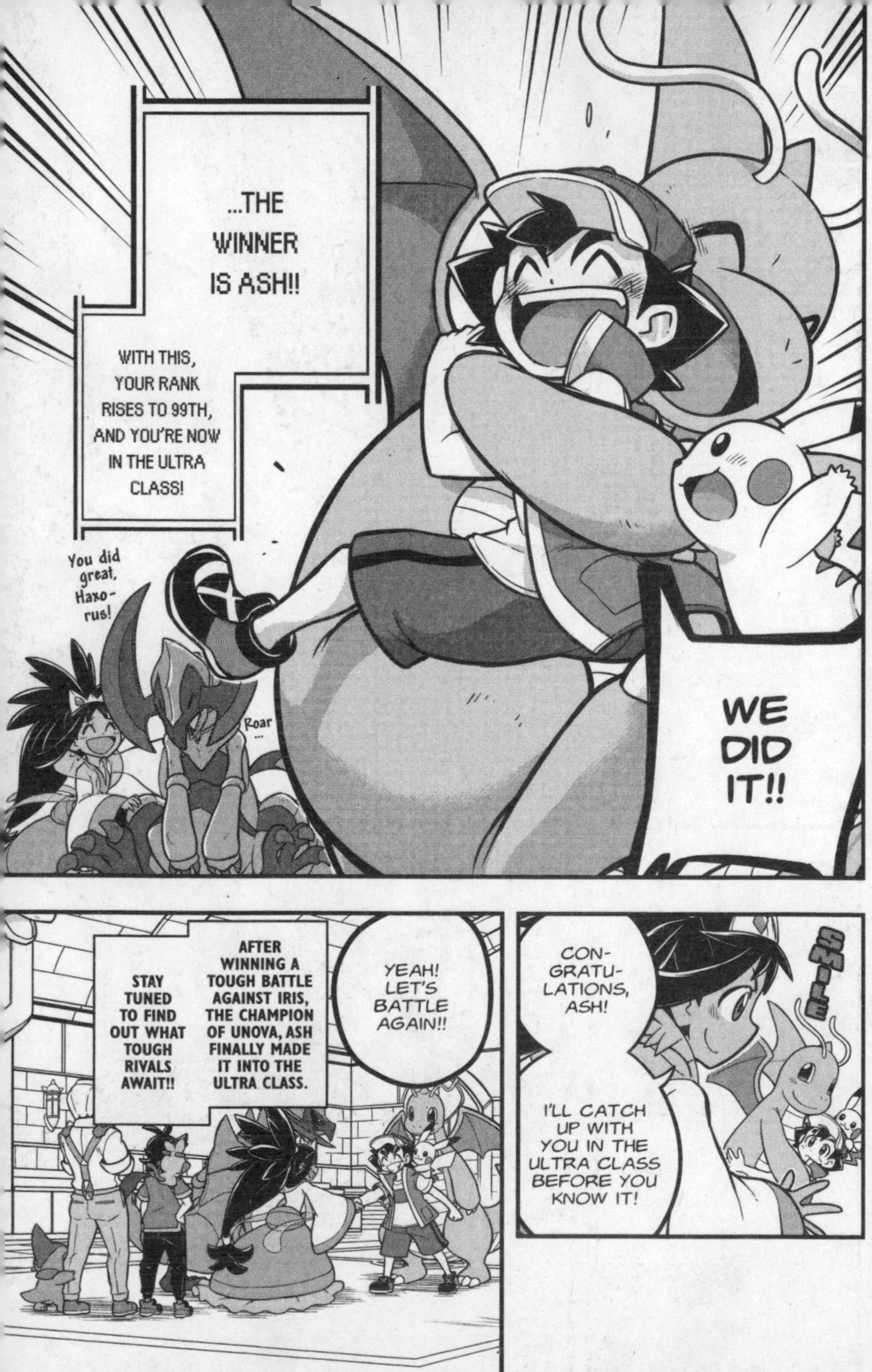
...THE WINNER IS ASH!!
WE DID IT!!
WITH THIS, YOUR RANK RISES TO 99TH, AND YOU'RE NOW IN THE ULTRA CLASS!
You did great, Haxo-rus!
Roar ...
SMILE
CON-GRATU-LATIONS, ASH!
I'LL CATCH UP WITH YOU IN THE ULTRA CLASS BEFORE YOU KNOW IT!
YEAH! LET'S BATTLE AGAIN!!
AFTER WINNING A TOUGH BATTLE AGAINST IRIS, THE CHAMPION OF UNOVA, ASH FINALLY MADE IT INTO THE ULTRA CLASS.
STAY TUNED TO FIND OUT WHAT TOUGH RIVALS AWAIT!!

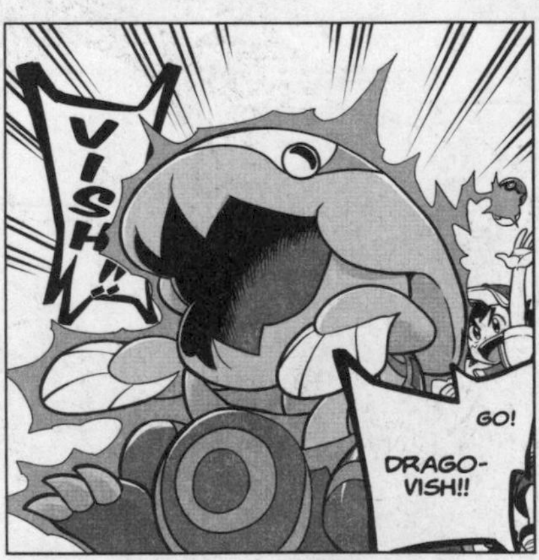
GO!
DRAGO-
VISH!!
VISH!!

Chapter 20
Advice to Goh!

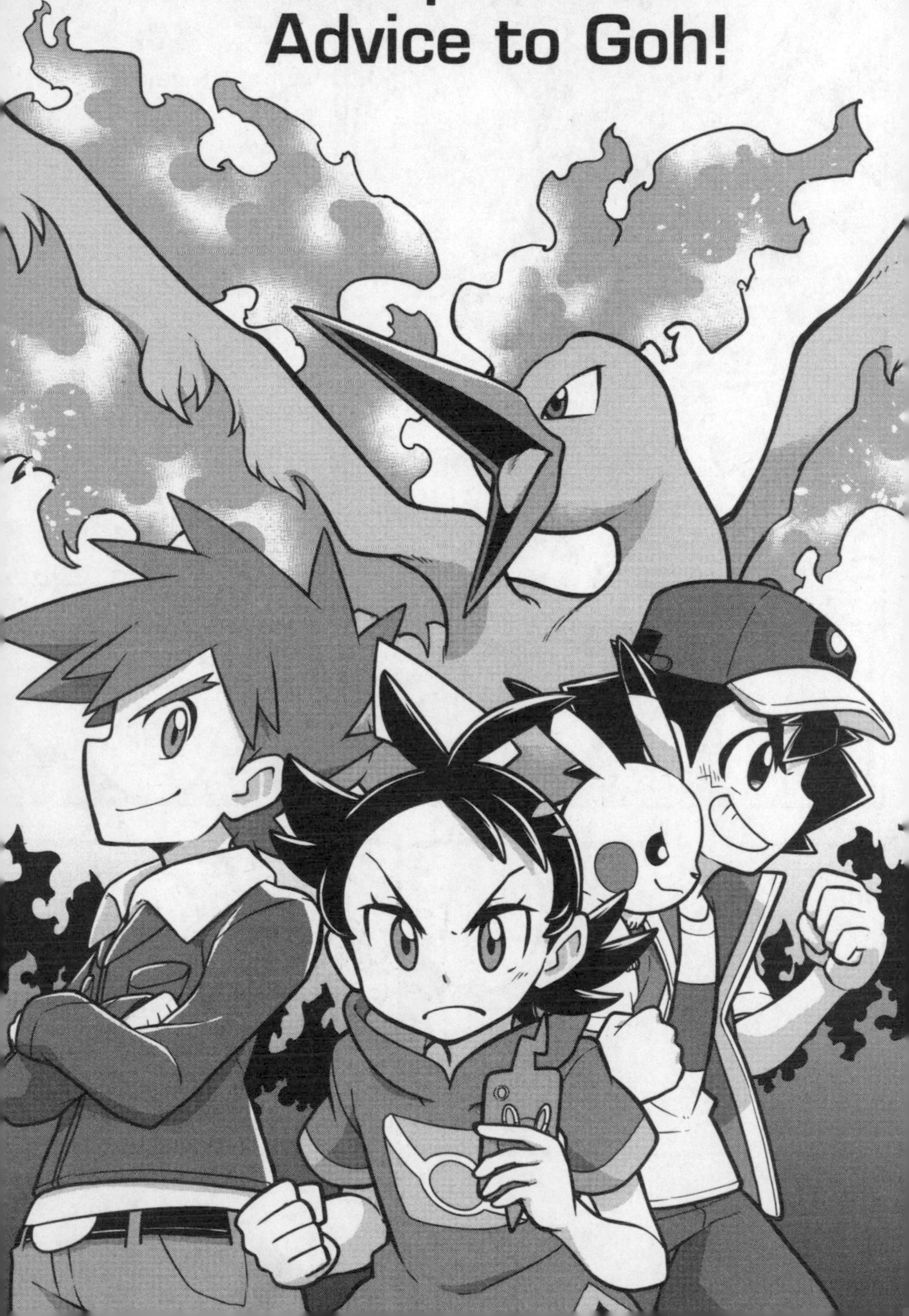

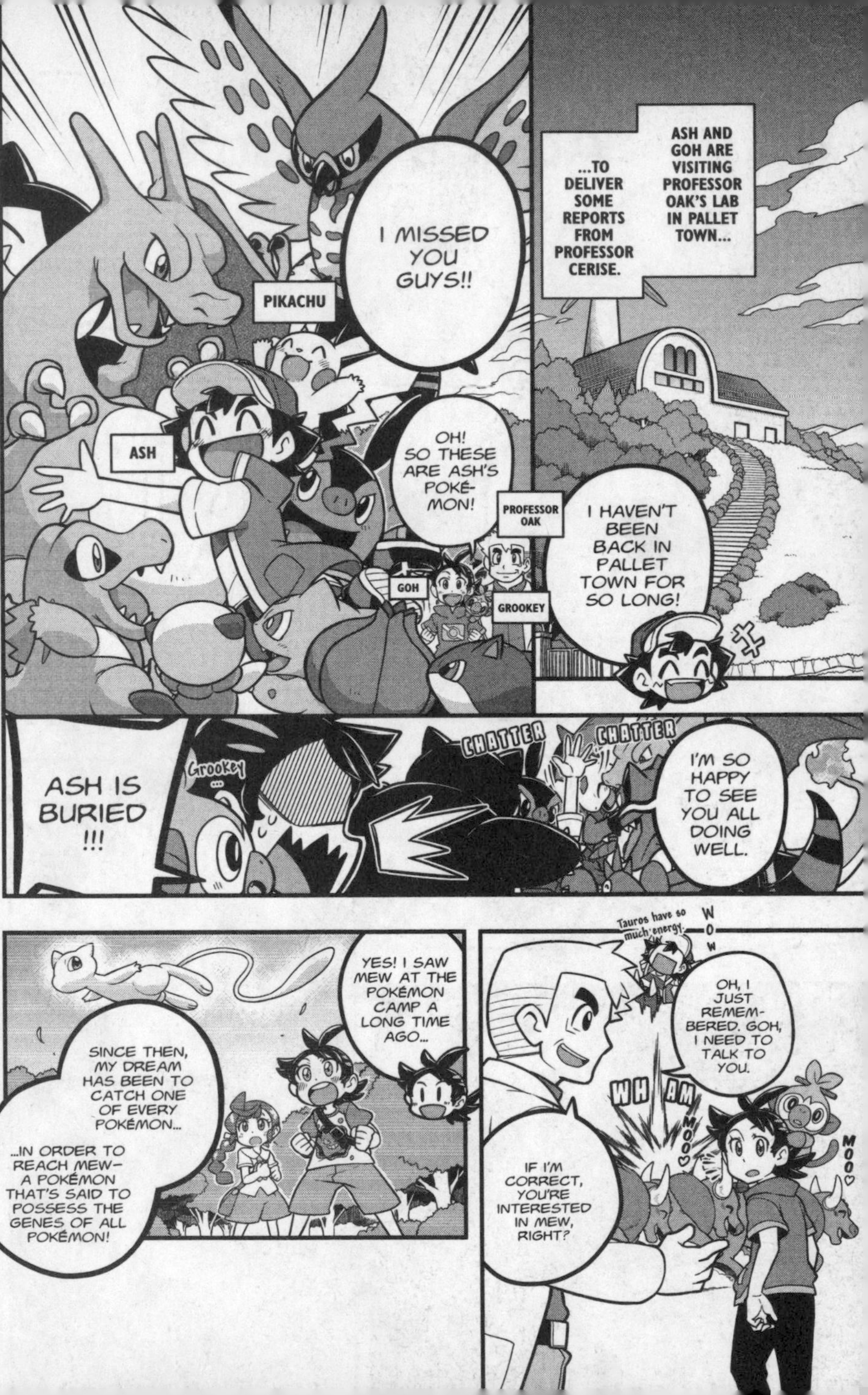
ASH AND GOH ARE VISITING PROFESSOR OAK'S LAB IN PALLET TOWN...
...TO DELIVER SOME REPORTS FROM PROFESSOR CERISE.
I HAVEN'T BEEN BACK IN PALLET TOWN FOR SO LONG!
I MISSED YOU GUYS!!
PIKACHU
ASH
OH! SO THESE ARE ASH'S POKÉMON!
PROFESSOR OAK
GOH
GROOKEY
I'M SO HAPPY TO SEE YOU ALL DOING WELL.
CHATTER
CHATTER
Grookey ...
ASH IS BURIED !!!
Tauros have so much energy...
WOW
OH, I JUST REMEMBERED. GOH, I NEED TO TALK TO YOU.
WHAM
MOO♡
MOO♡
IF I'M CORRECT, YOU'RE INTERESTED IN MEW, RIGHT?
YES! I SAW MEW AT THE POKÉMON CAMP A LONG TIME AGO...
SINCE THEN, MY DREAM HAS BEEN TO CATCH ONE OF EVERY POKÉMON...
...IN ORDER TO REACH MEW—A POKÉMON THAT'S SAID TO POSSESS THE GENES OF ALL POKÉMON!

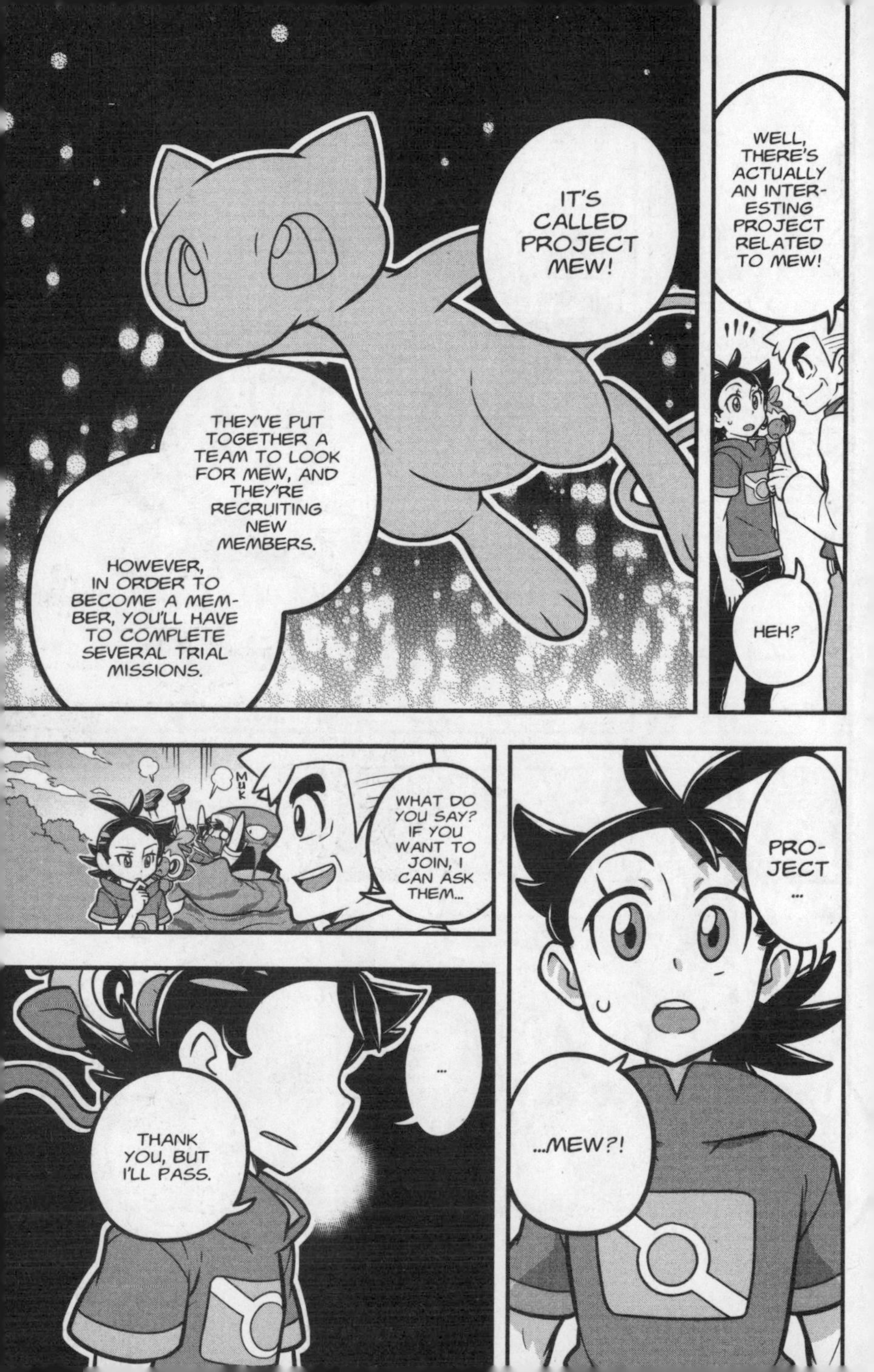
WELL, THERE'S ACTUALLY AN INTERESTING PROJECT RELATED TO MEW!
HEH?
IT'S CALLED PROJECT MEW!
THEY'VE PUT TOGETHER A TEAM TO LOOK FOR MEW, AND THEY'RE RECRUITING NEW MEMBERS.
HOWEVER, IN ORDER TO BECOME A MEMBER, YOU'LL HAVE TO COMPLETE SEVERAL TRIAL MISSIONS.
PROJECT...
...MEW?!
MUK
WHAT DO YOU SAY? IF YOU WANT TO JOIN, I CAN ASK THEM...
...
THANK YOU, BUT I'LL PASS.

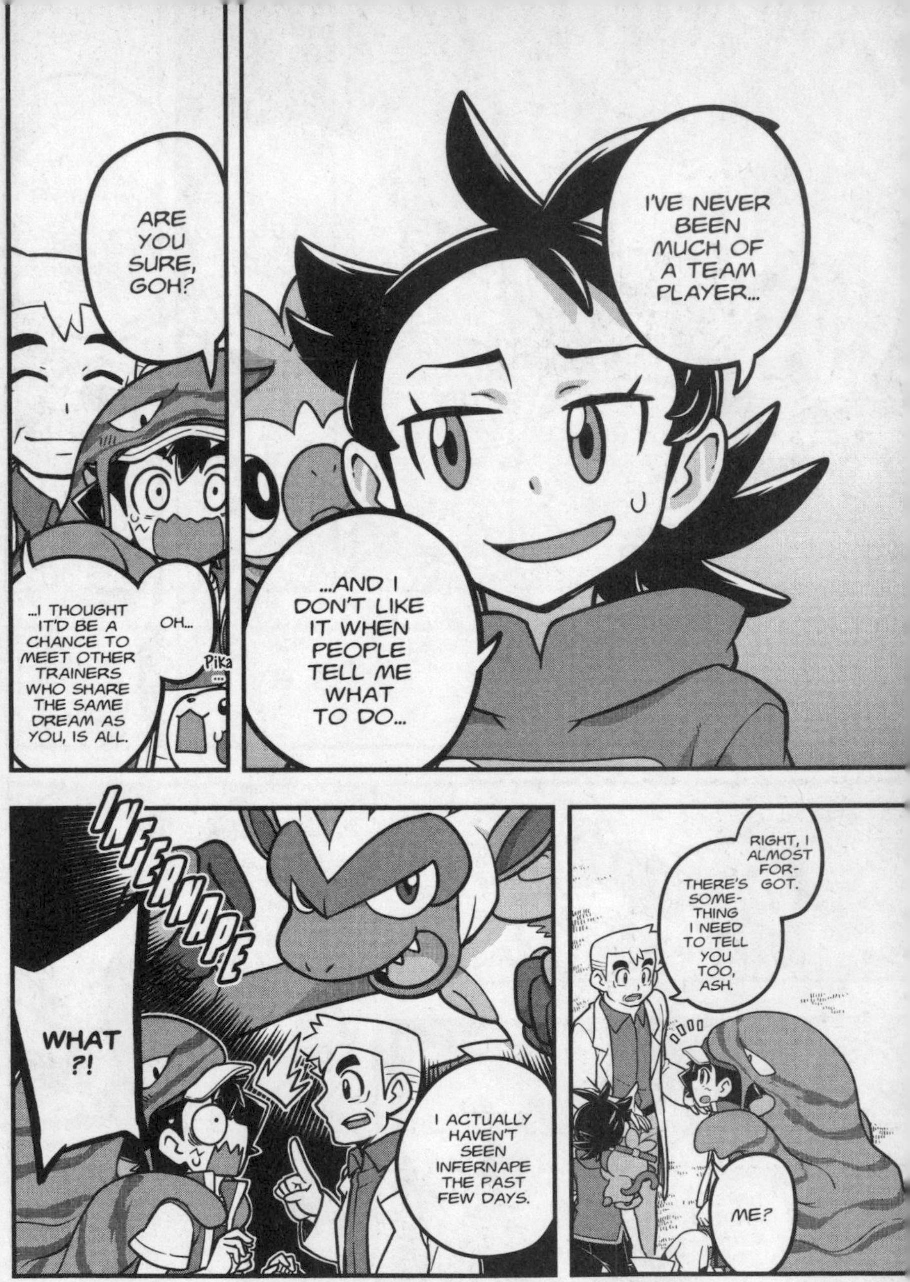
I'VE NEVER BEEN MUCH OF A TEAM PLAYER...
...AND I DON'T LIKE IT WHEN PEOPLE TELL ME WHAT TO DO...
ARE YOU SURE, GOH?
OH...
Pika ...
...I THOUGHT IT'D BE A CHANCE TO MEET OTHER TRAINERS WHO SHARE THE SAME DREAM AS YOU, IS ALL.
RIGHT, I ALMOST FOR-GOT.
THERE'S SOME-THING I NEED TO TELL YOU TOO, ASH.
ME?
I ACTUALLY HAVEN'T SEEN INFERNAPE THE PAST FEW DAYS.
INFERNAPE
WHAT ?!

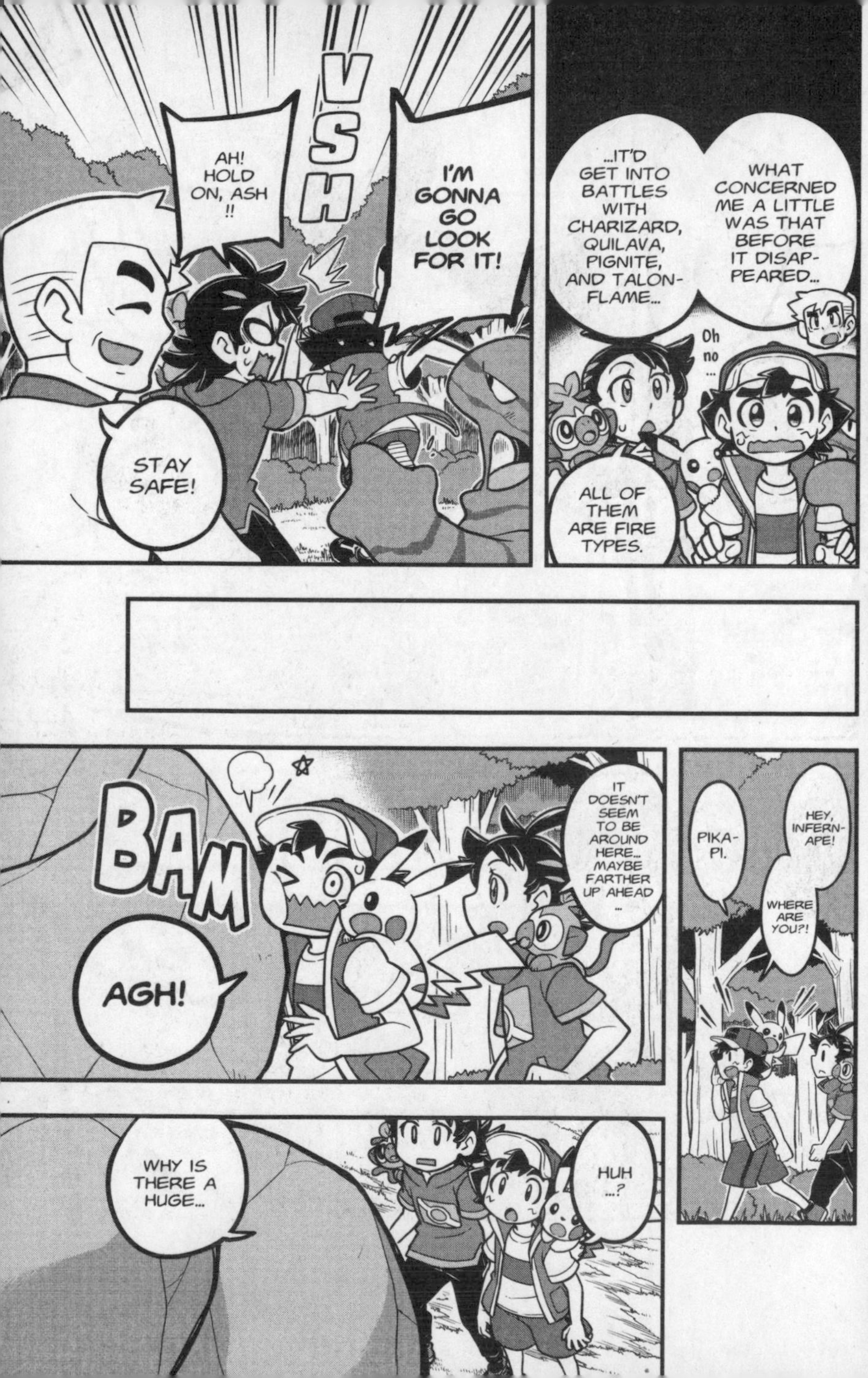
WHAT CONCERNED ME A LITTLE WAS THAT BEFORE IT DISAPPEARED...
...IT'D GET INTO BATTLES WITH CHARIZARD, QUILAVA, PIGNITE, AND TALONFLAME...
Oh no ...
ALL OF THEM ARE FIRE TYPES.
I'M GONNA GO LOOK FOR IT!
VSH
AH! HOLD ON, ASH!!
STAY SAFE!
HEY, INFERNAPE!
WHERE ARE YOU?!
PIKA-PI.
IT DOESN'T SEEM TO BE AROUND HERE... MAYBE FARTHER UP AHEAD ...
BAM
AGH!
HUH ...?
WHY IS THERE A HUGE...

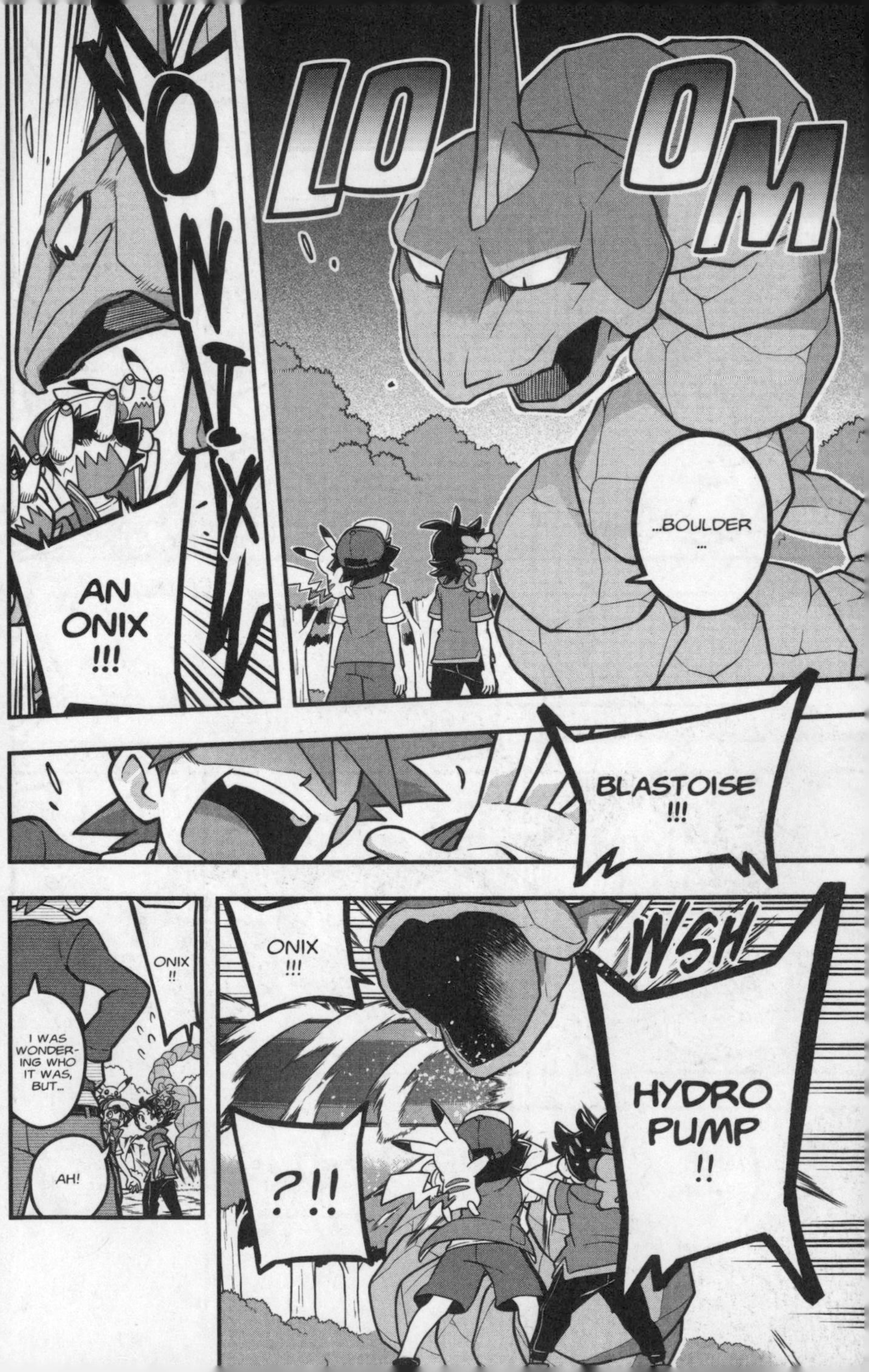
LOOM
...BOULDER
...
AN ONIX !!!
BLASTOISE !!!
WSH
HYDRO PUMP !!
ONIX !!!
?!!
ONIX !!
I WAS WONDERING WHO IT WAS, BUT...
AH!

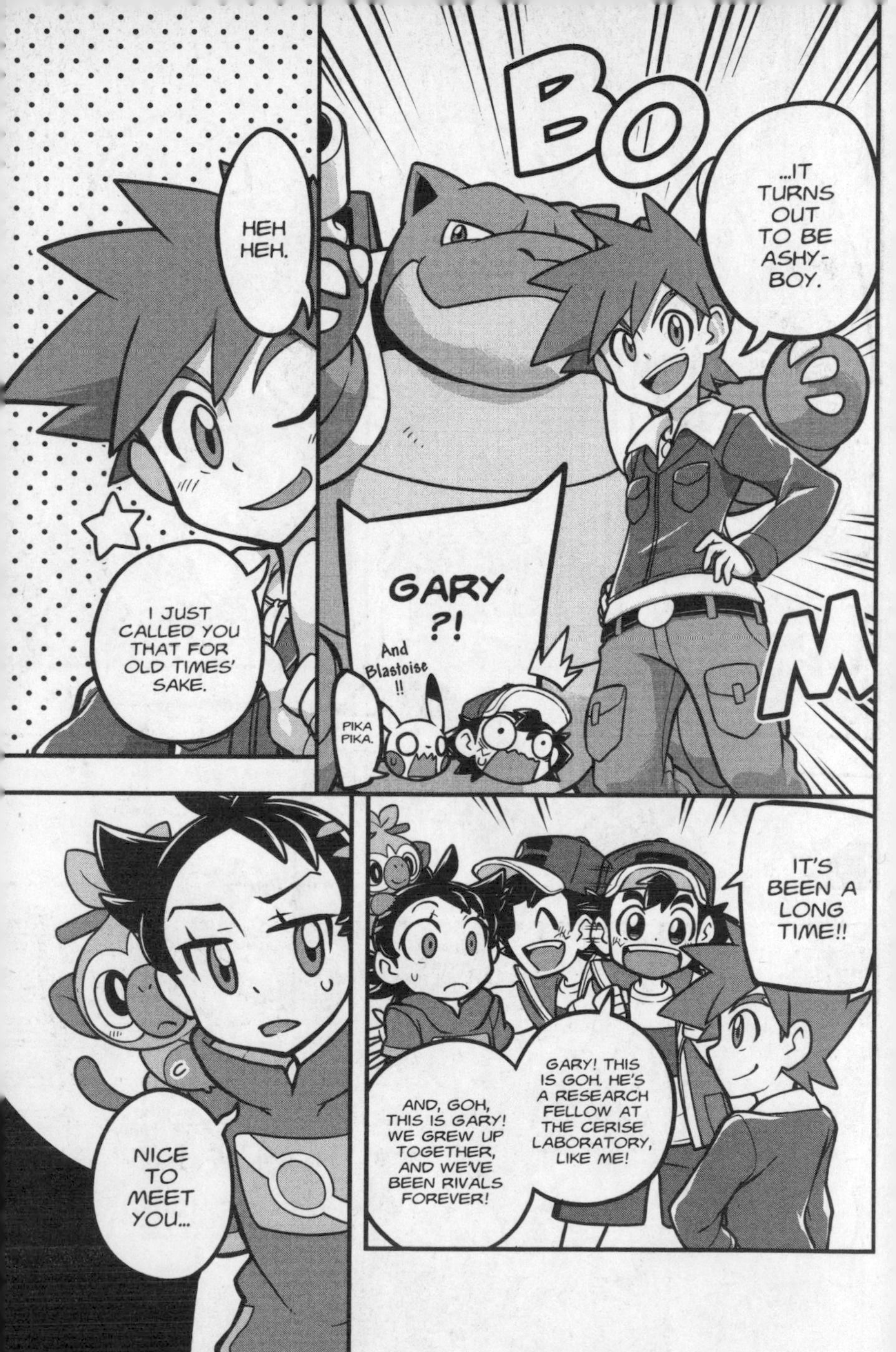
BO
...IT TURNS OUT TO BE ASHY-BOY.
M
GARY ?!
And Blastoise !!
PIKA PIKA.
HEH HEH.
I JUST CALLED YOU THAT FOR OLD TIMES' SAKE.
IT'S BEEN A LONG TIME!!
GARY! THIS IS GOH. HE'S A RESEARCH FELLOW AT THE CERISE LABORATORY, LIKE ME!
AND, GOH, THIS IS GARY! WE GREW UP TOGETHER, AND WE'VE BEEN RIVALS FOREVER!
NICE TO MEET YOU...

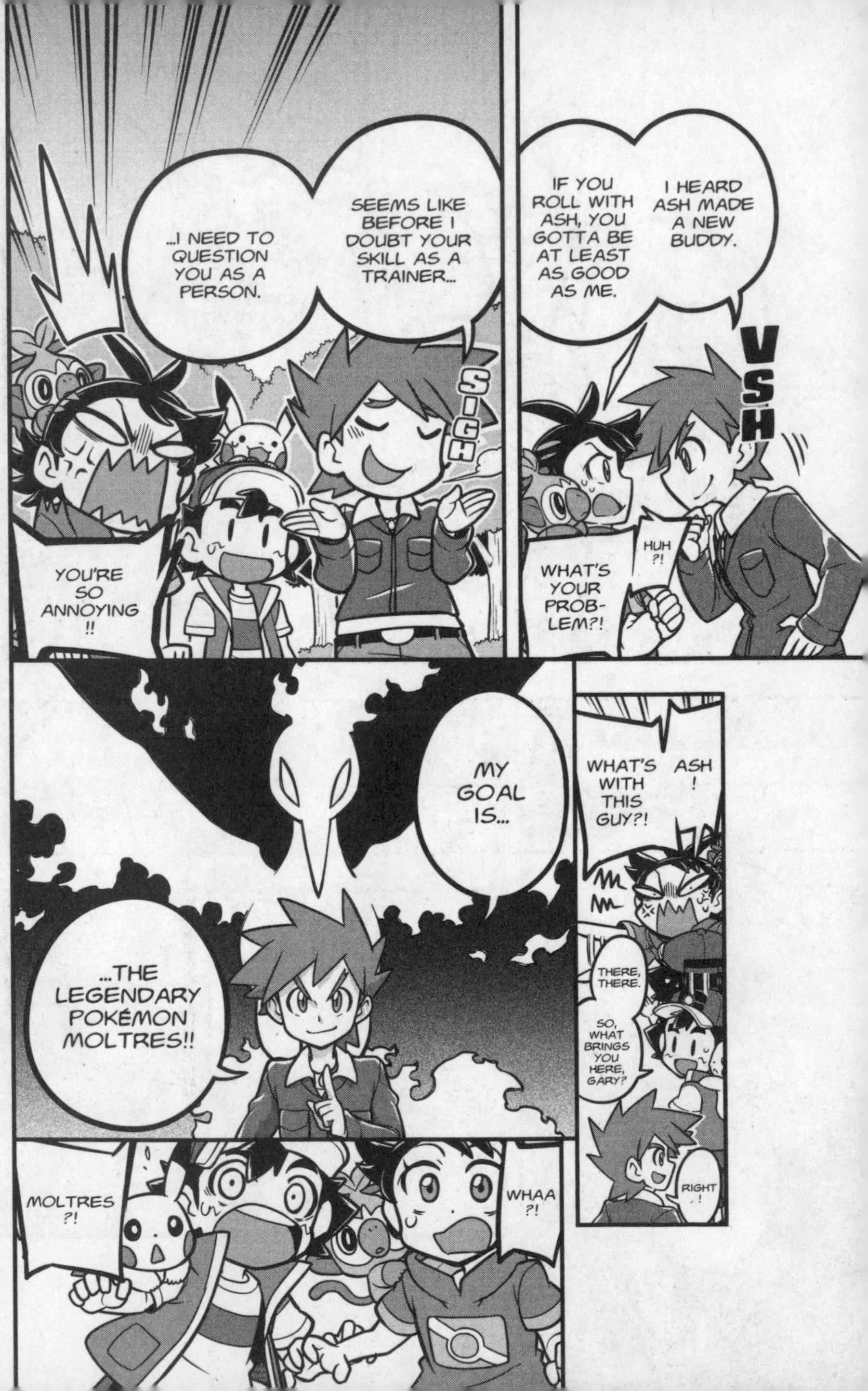
I HEARD ASH MADE A NEW BUDDY.
IF YOU ROLL WITH ASH, YOU GOTTA BE AT LEAST AS GOOD AS ME.
VSH
HUH ?!
WHAT'S YOUR PROB-LEM?!
SEEMS LIKE BEFORE I DOUBT YOUR SKILL AS A TRAINER...
...I NEED TO QUESTION YOU AS A PERSON.
SIGH
YOU'RE SO ANNOYING !!
ASH !
WHAT'S WITH THIS GUY?!
THERE, THERE.
SO, WHAT BRINGS YOU HERE, GARY?
RIGHT !
MY GOAL IS...
...THE LEGENDARY POKÉMON MOLTRES!!
WHAA ?!
MOLTRES ?!

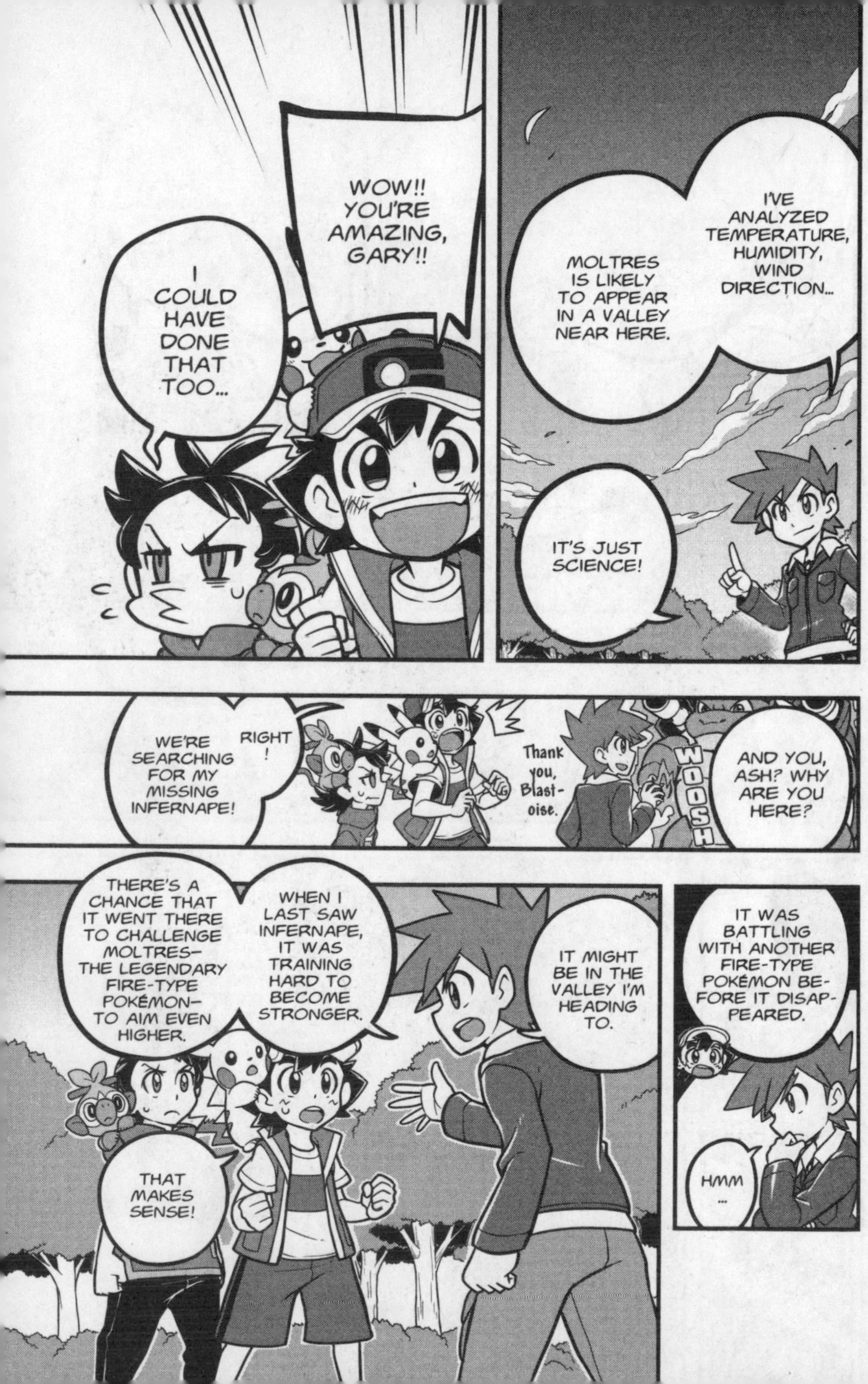
I'VE ANALYZED TEMPERATURE, HUMIDITY, WIND DIRECTION...
MOLTRES IS LIKELY TO APPEAR IN A VALLEY NEAR HERE.
IT'S JUST SCIENCE!
WOW!! YOU'RE AMAZING, GARY!!
I COULD HAVE DONE THAT TOO...
AND YOU, ASH? WHY ARE YOU HERE?
WOOSH
Thank you, Blastoise.
RIGHT!
WE'RE SEARCHING FOR MY MISSING INFERNAPE!
IT WAS BATTLING WITH ANOTHER FIRE-TYPE POKÉMON BEFORE IT DISAPPEARED.
HMM...
IT MIGHT BE IN THE VALLEY I'M HEADING TO.
WHEN I LAST SAW INFERNAPE, IT WAS TRAINING HARD TO BECOME STRONGER.
THERE'S A CHANCE THAT IT WENT THERE TO CHALLENGE MOLTRES—THE LEGENDARY FIRE-TYPE POKÉMON—TO AIM EVEN HIGHER.
THAT MAKES SENSE!

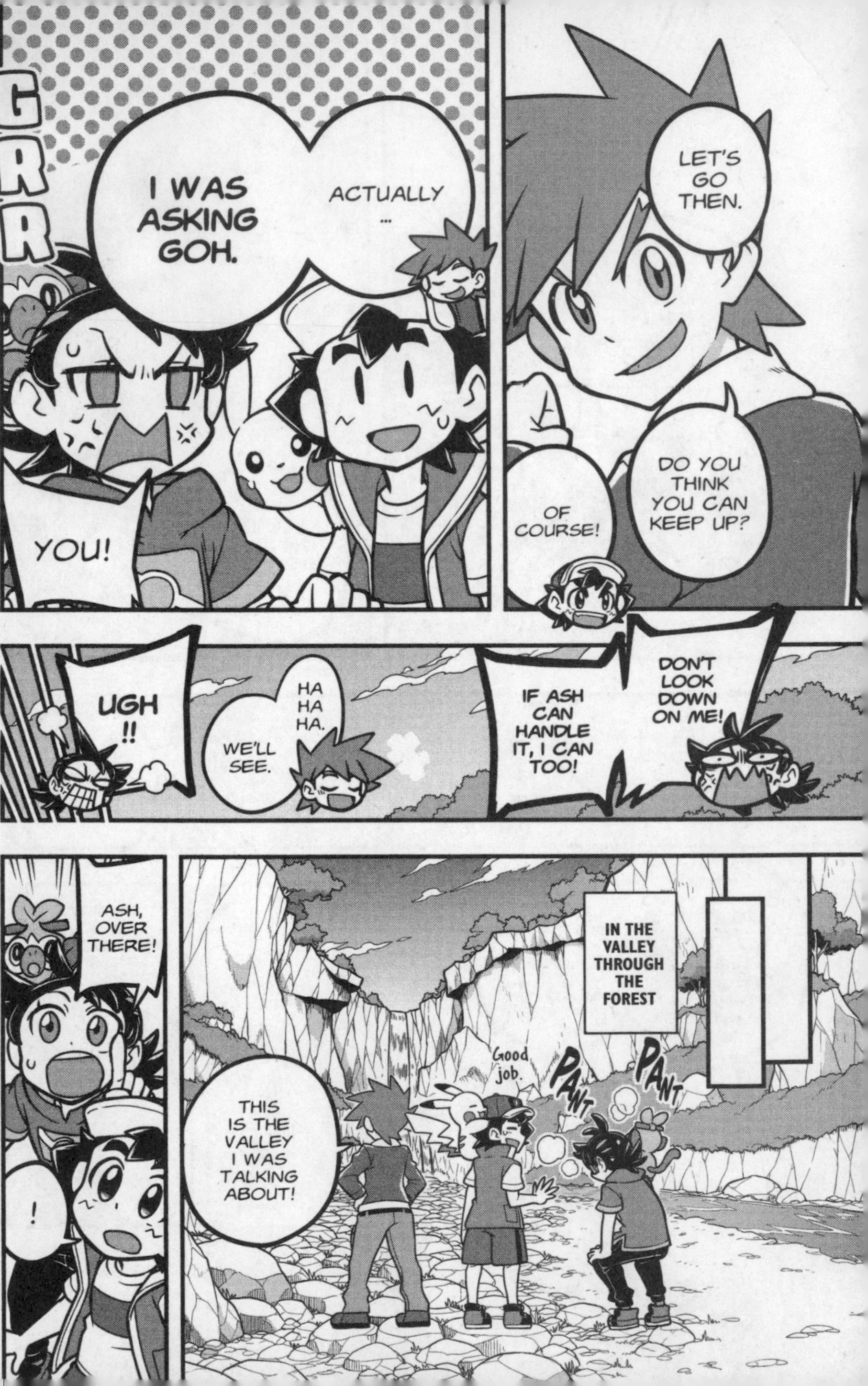
LET'S GO THEN.
DO YOU THINK YOU CAN KEEP UP?
OF COURSE!
ACTUALLY ...
I WAS ASKING GOH.
GRR
YOU!
DON'T LOOK DOWN ON ME!
IF ASH CAN HANDLE IT, I CAN TOO!
HA HA HA.
WE'LL SEE.
UGH !!
IN THE VALLEY THROUGH THE FOREST
PANT PANT
Good job.
THIS IS THE VALLEY I WAS TALKING ABOUT!
ASH, OVER THERE!
!

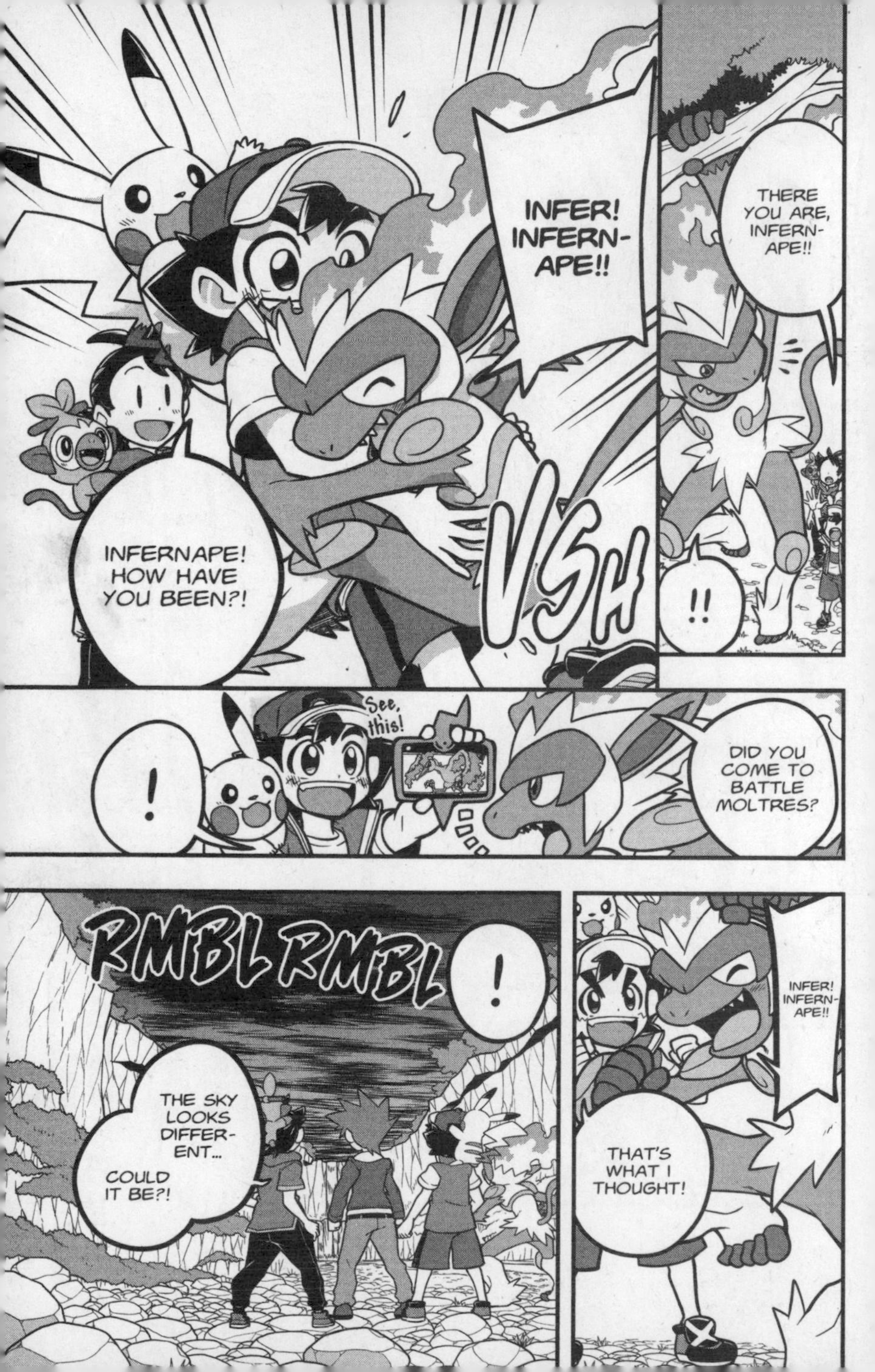
THERE YOU ARE, INFERN-APE!!
!!
INFER! INFERN-APE!!
VSH
INFERNAPE! HOW HAVE YOU BEEN?!
DID YOU COME TO BATTLE MOLTRES?
See, this!
!
INFER! INFERN-APE!!
THAT'S WHAT I THOUGHT!
!
RMBL RMBL
THE SKY LOOKS DIFFER-ENT...
COULD IT BE?!

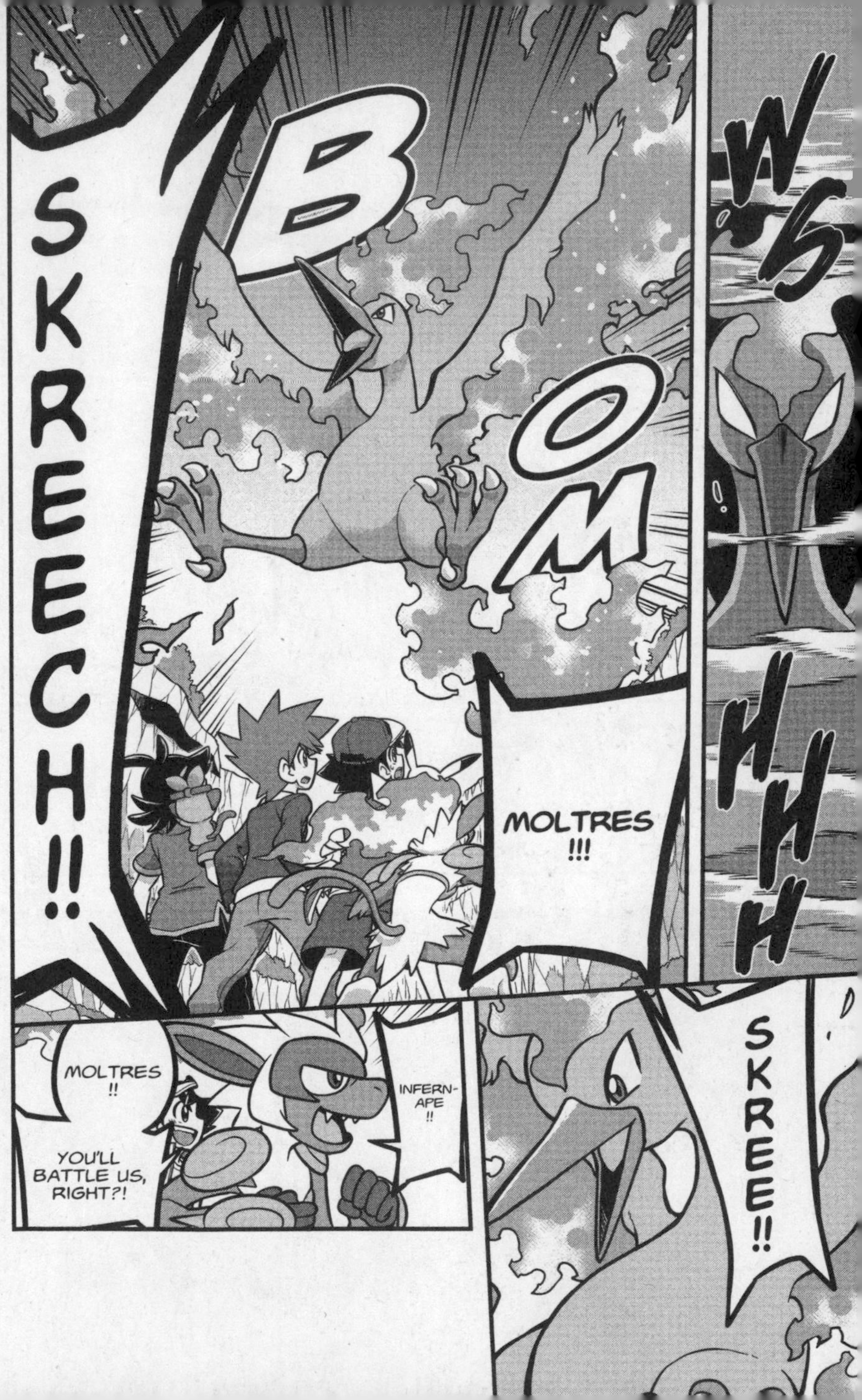
WSHHHH
SKREECH!!
BOOM
MOLTRES!!!
SKREE!!
INFERN-APE!!
MOLTRES!!
YOU'LL BATTLE US, RIGHT?!

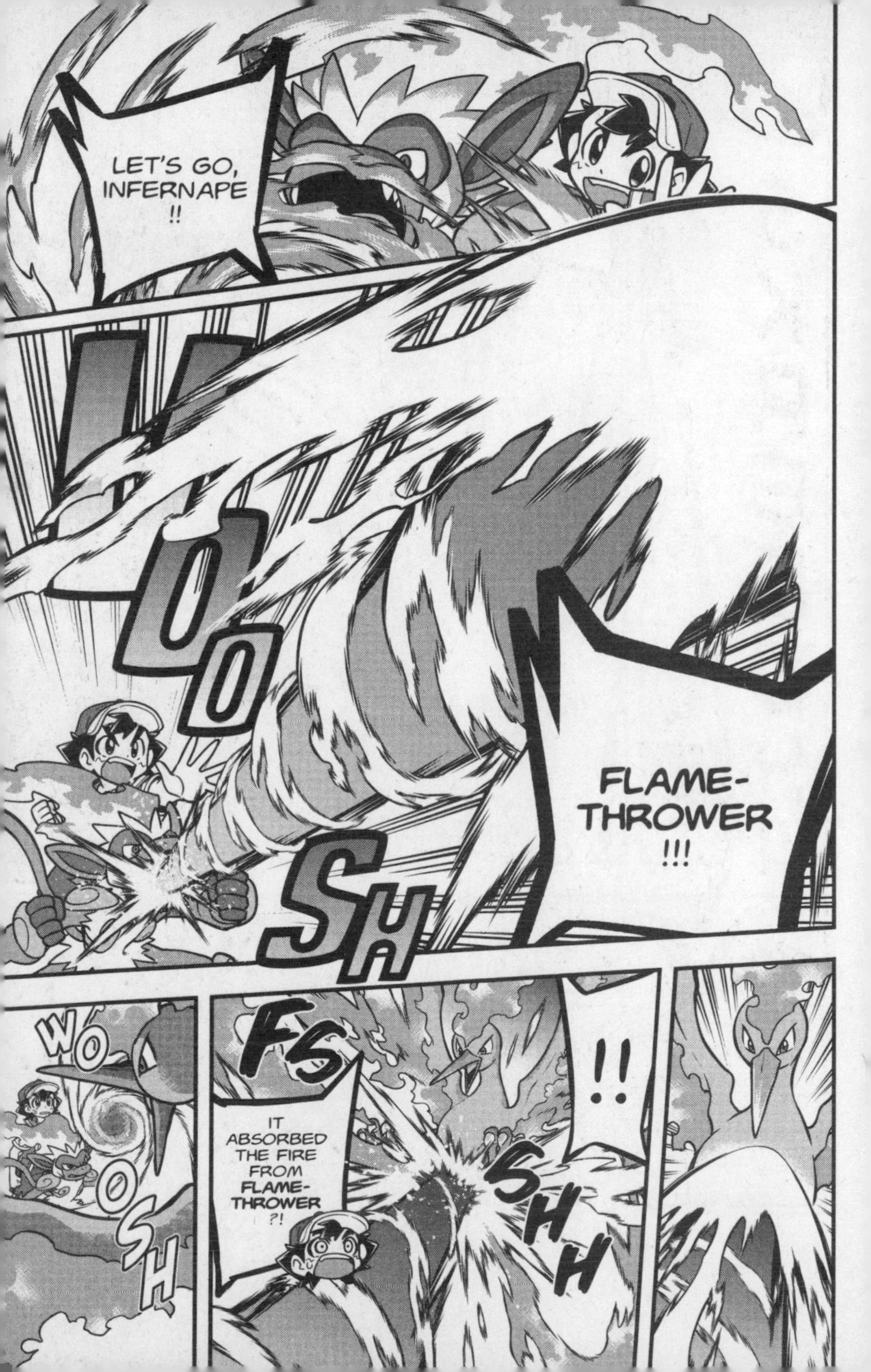
LET'S GO, INFERNAPE !!
WOOSH
FLAME-THROWER !!!
!!
FS
IT ABSORBED THE FIRE FROM FLAME-THROWER ?!
SHH
WOOSH

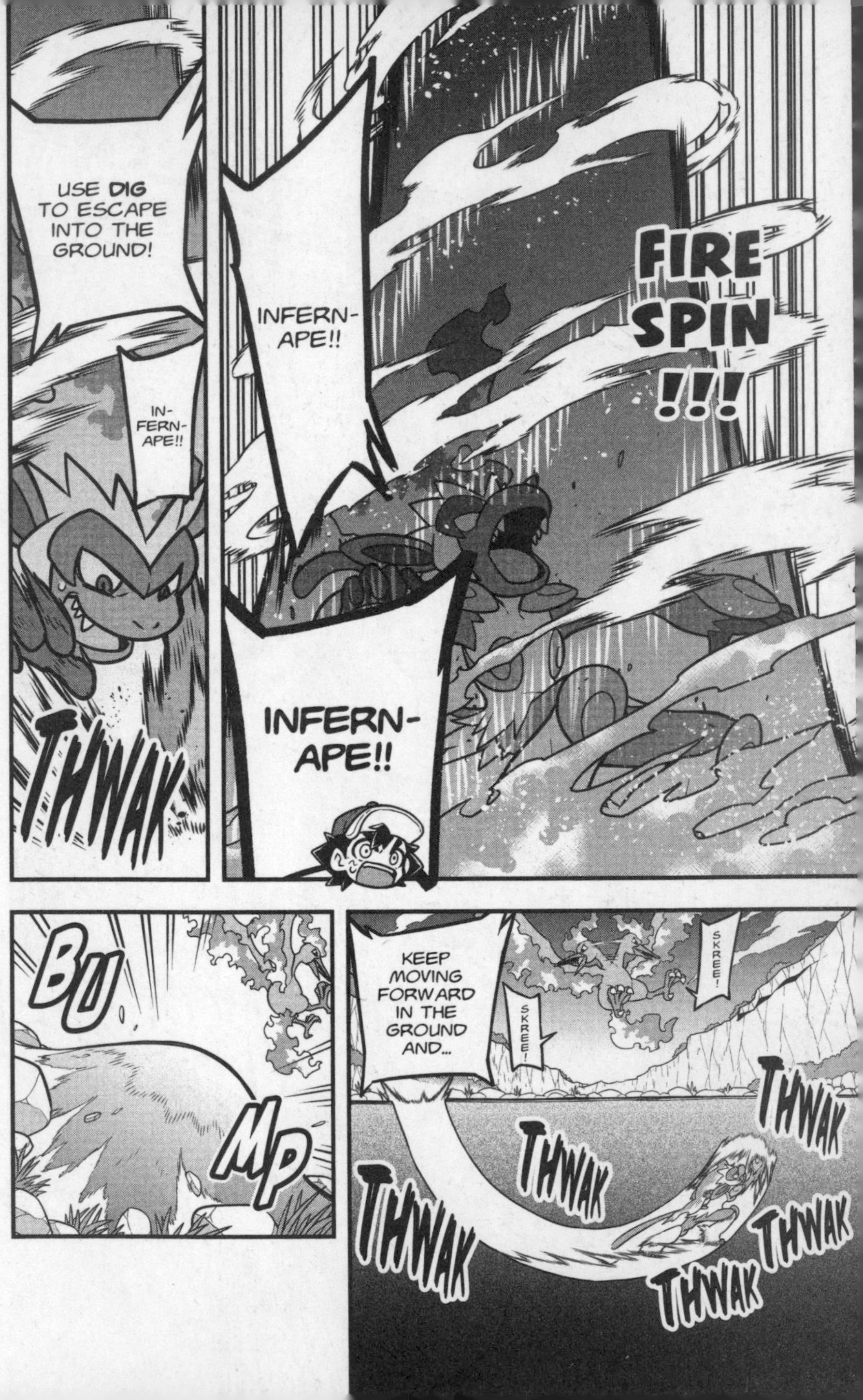
FIRE SPIN!!!
INFERN-APE!!
INFERN-APE!!
USE DIG TO ESCAPE INTO THE GROUND!
IN-FERN-APE!!
THWAK
SKREE!
SKREE!
KEEP MOVING FORWARD IN THE GROUND AND...
THWAK
THWAK
THWAK
THWAK
THWAK
BU
MP

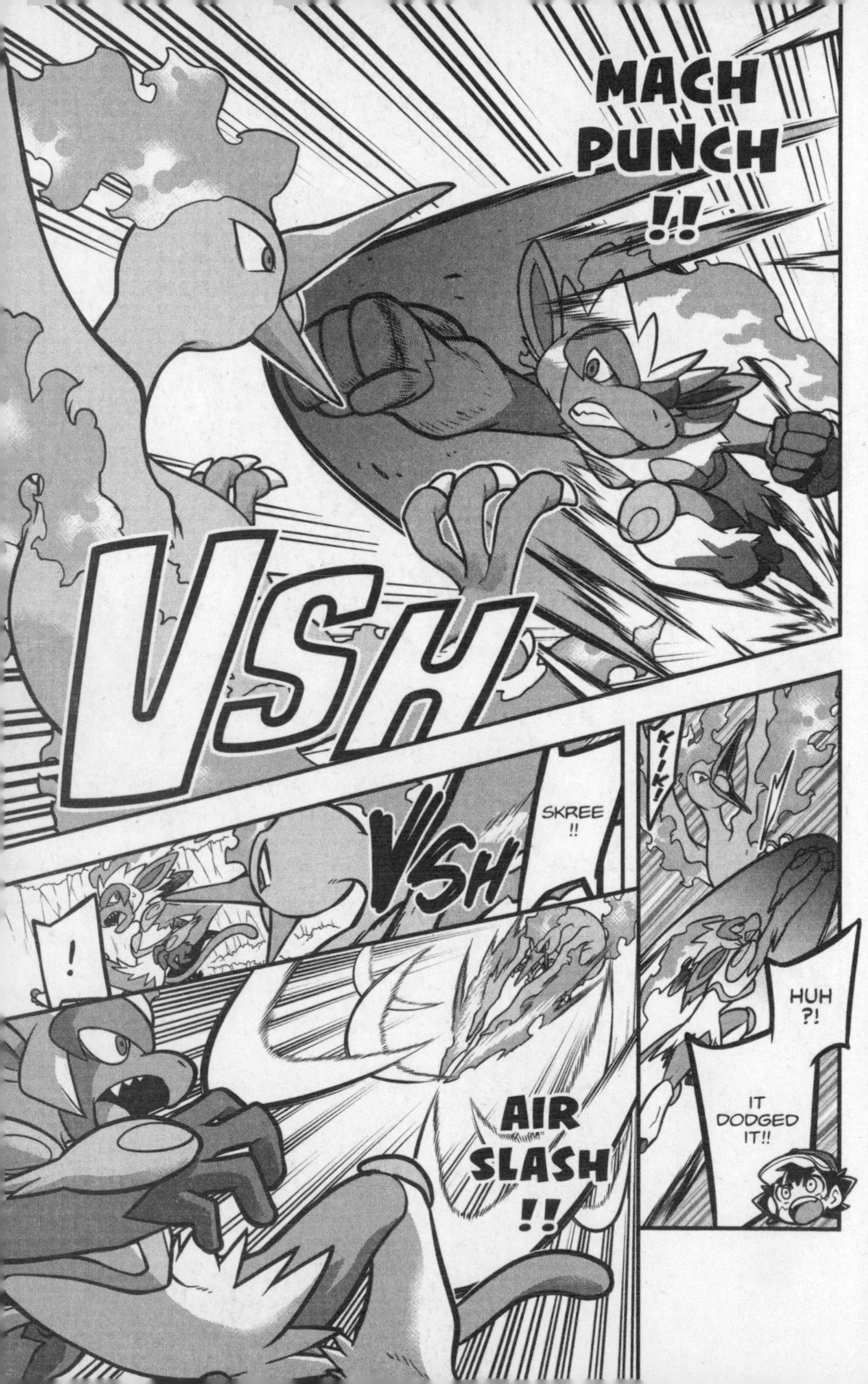
MACH PUNCH!!
VSH
KIIK!!
HUH?!
IT DODGED IT!!
SKREE!!
VSH
!
AIR SLASH!!

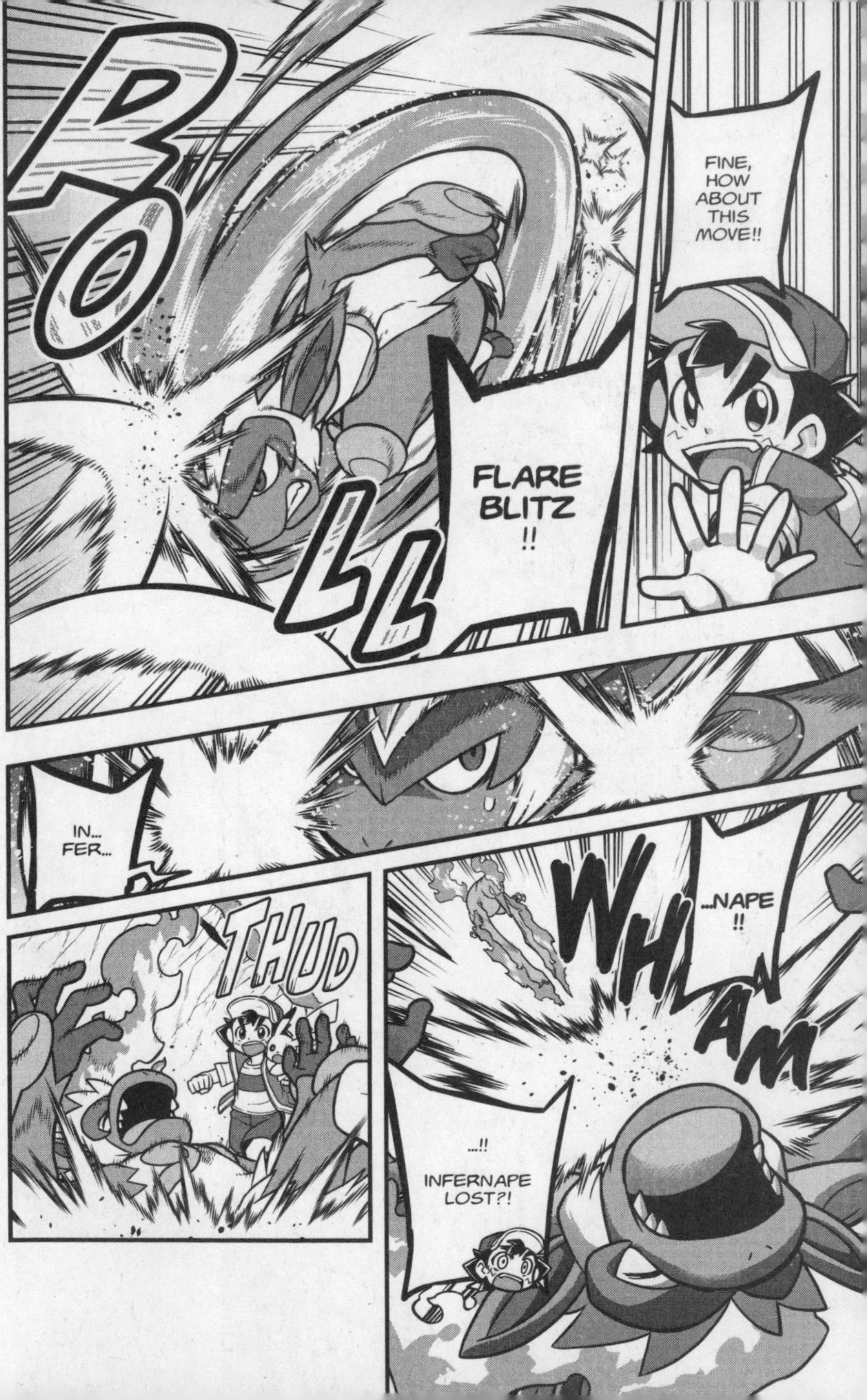
FINE, HOW ABOUT THIS MOVE!!
FLARE BLITZ !!
BOLL
IN... FER...
...NAPE !!
WHAM
...!!
INFERNAPE LOST?!
THUD

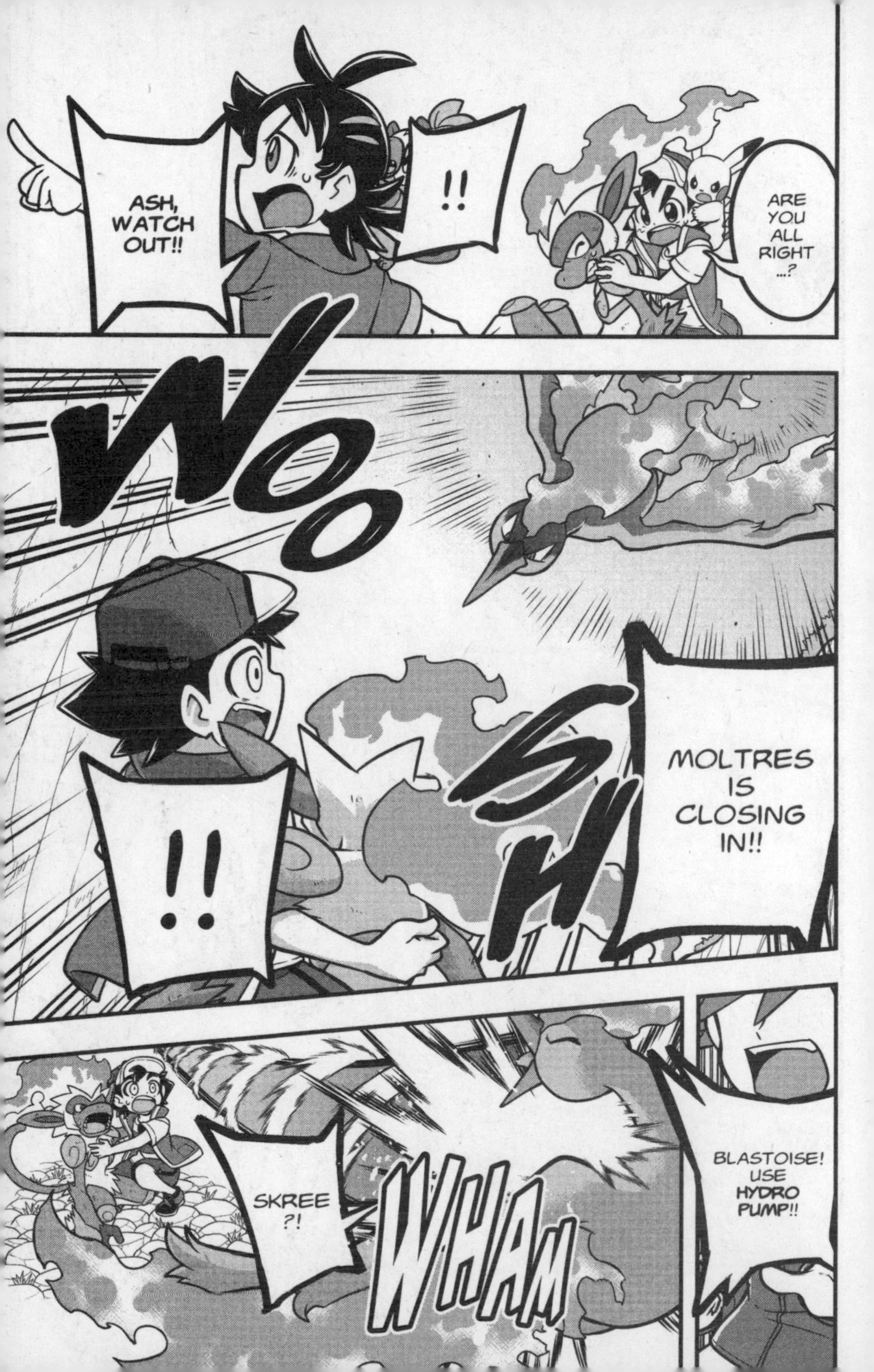
ARE YOU ALL RIGHT ...?
!!
ASH, WATCH OUT!!
WOOO
MOLTRES IS CLOSING IN!!
SHH
!!
BLASTOISE! USE HYDRO PUMP!!
WHAM
SKREE ?!

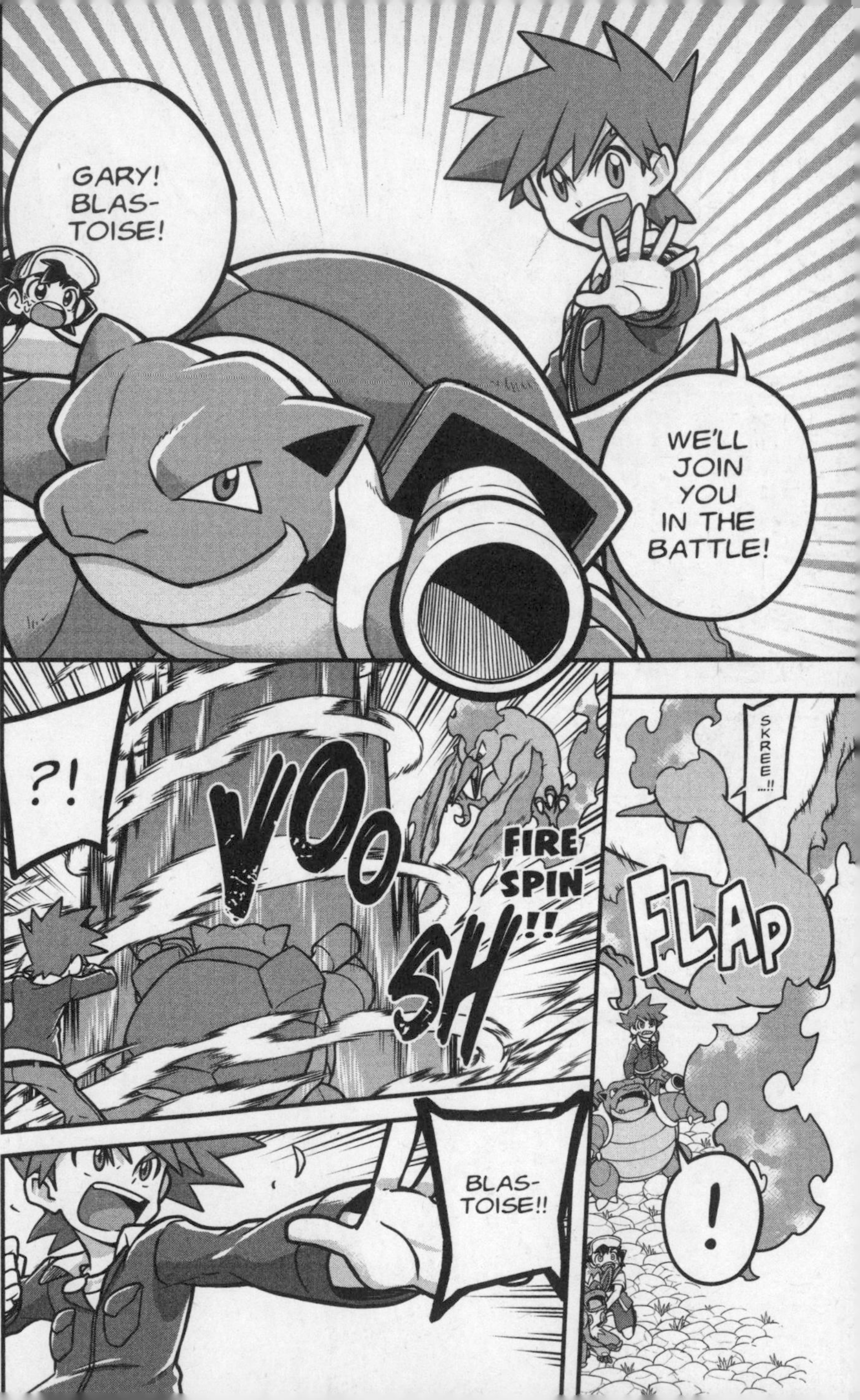
GARY! BLAS-TOISE!
WE'LL JOIN YOU IN THE BATTLE!
SKREE...!!
FLAP
!
?!
VOOSH
FIRE SPIN!!
BLAS-TOISE!!

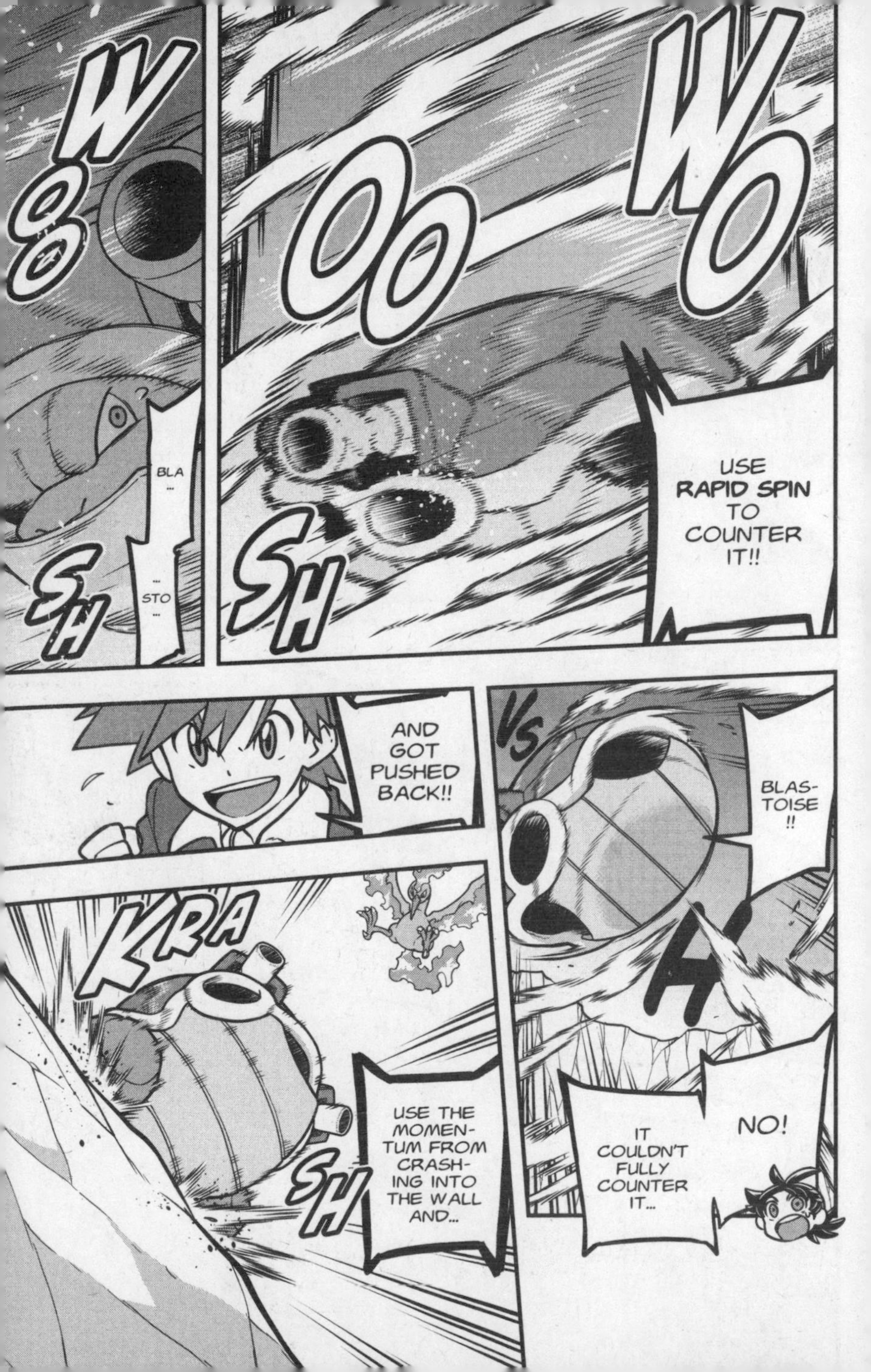
WOOO
USE RAPID SPIN TO COUNTER IT!!
SH
WOO
BLA…
…STO…
SH
BLASTOISE!!
VS
AND GOT PUSHED BACK!!
NO!
IT COULDN'T FULLY COUNTER IT…
KRA
USE THE MOMENTUM FROM CRASHING INTO THE WALL AND…
SH

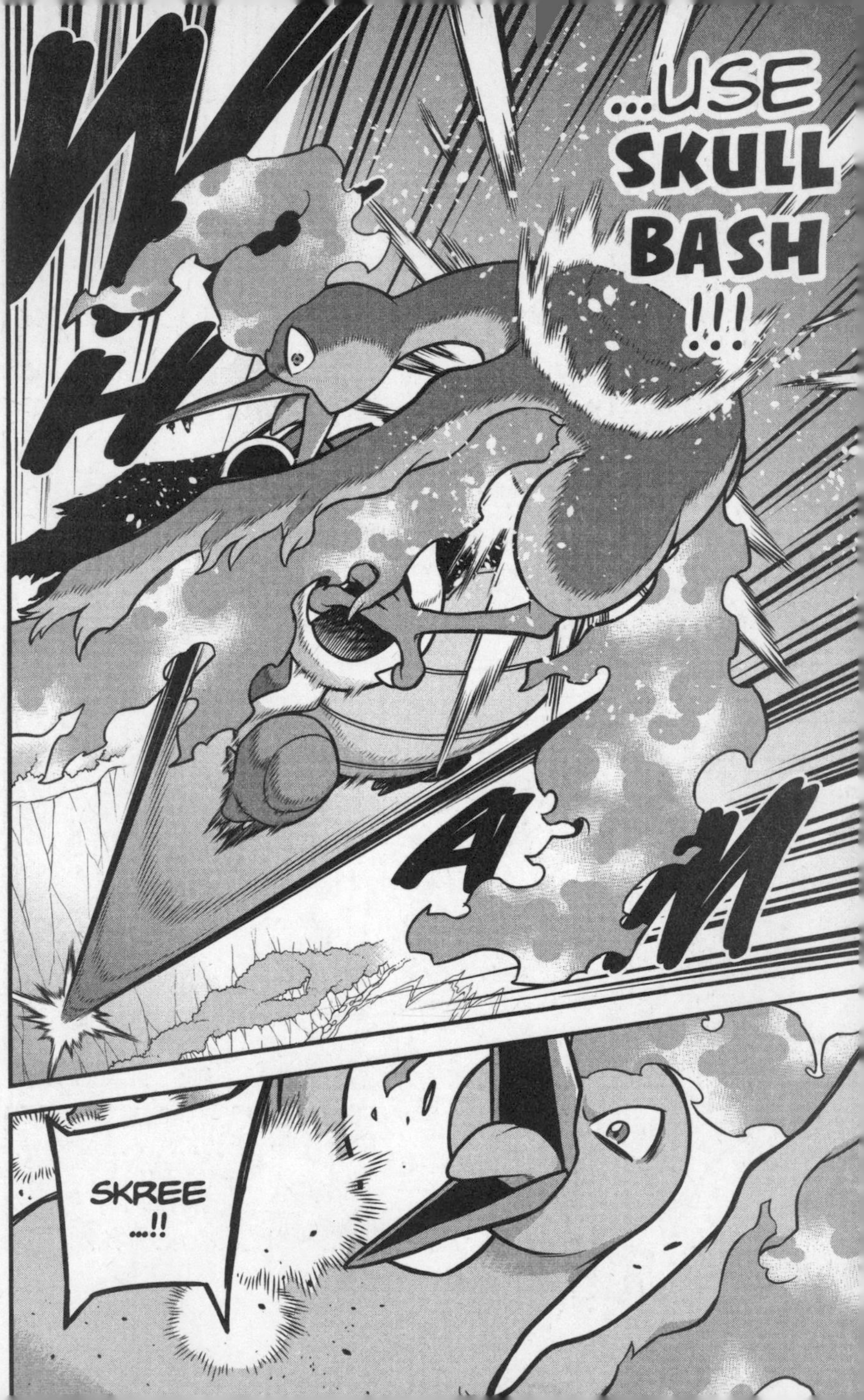
...USE SKULL BASH !!!
WHAM
SKREE ...!!

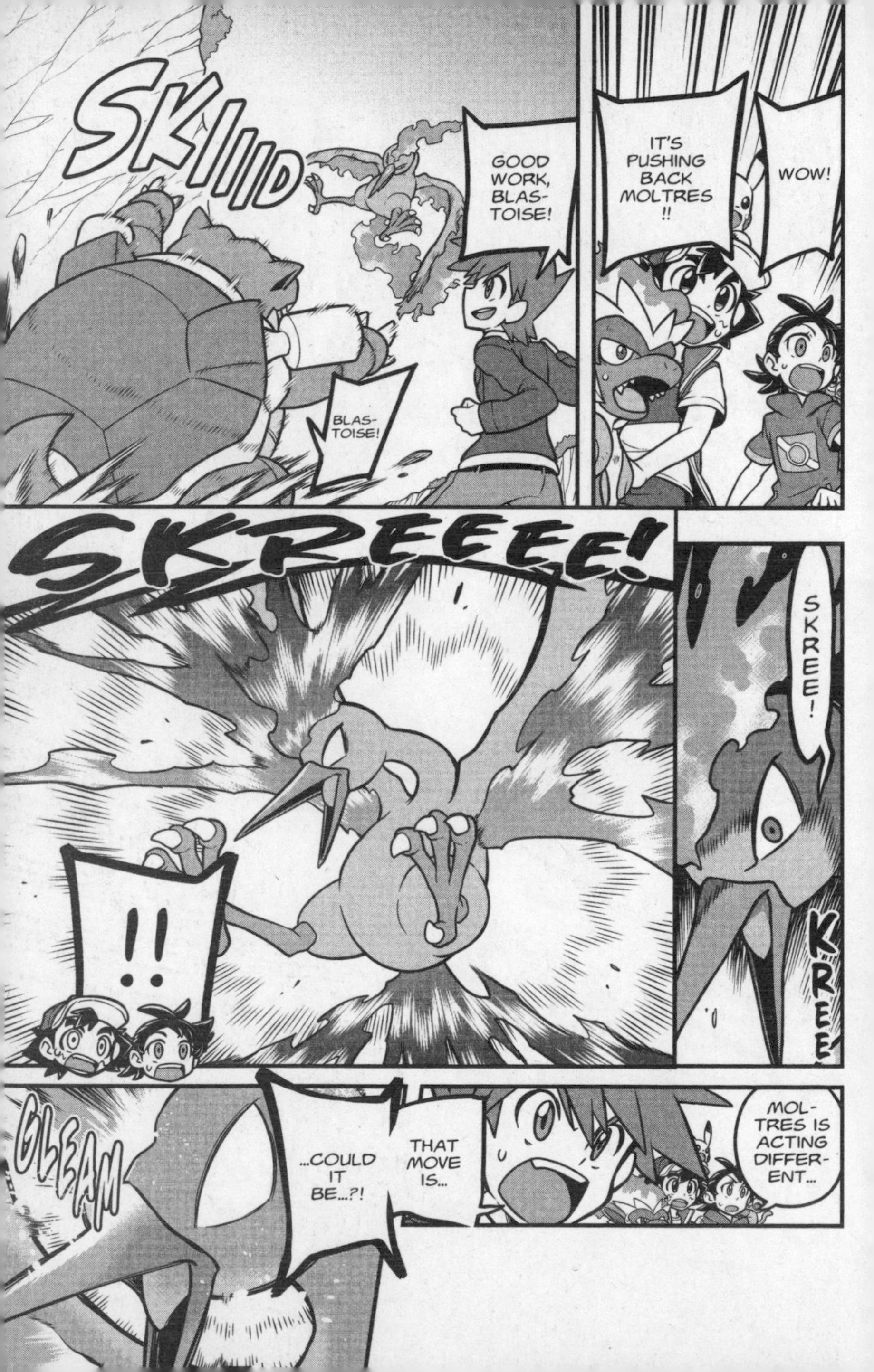
WOW!
IT'S PUSHING BACK MOLTRES !!
GOOD WORK, BLAS-TOISE!
SKIIID
BLAS-TOISE!
SKREE!
KREE
SKREEEEE!
!!
MOL-TRES IS ACTING DIFFER-ENT...
THAT MOVE IS...
...COULD IT BE...?!
GLEAM

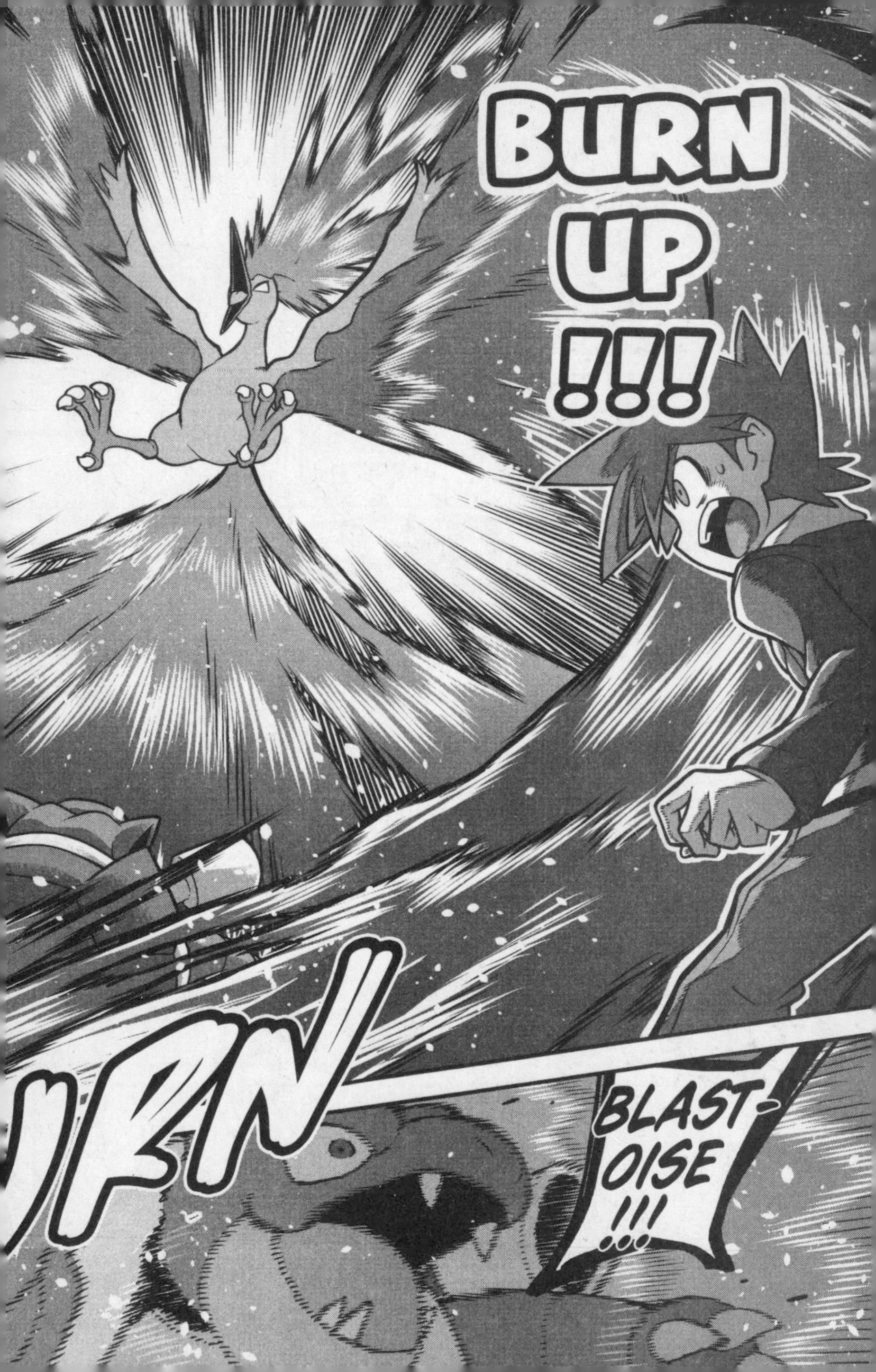
BURN UP !!!
BLAST-OISE !!!

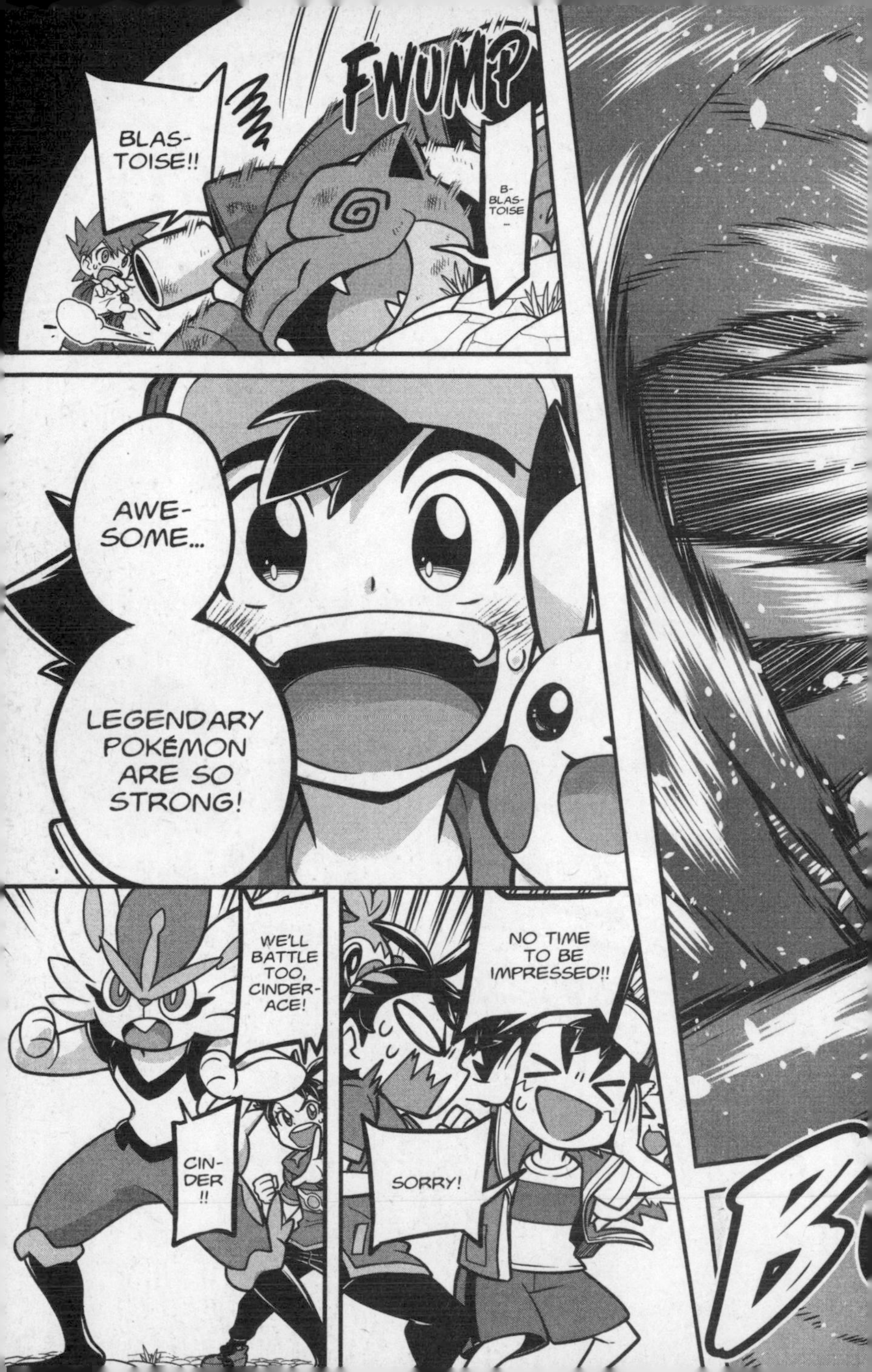
FWUMP
B-BLAS-TOISE...
BLAS-TOISE!!
AWE-SOME...
LEGENDARY POKÉMON ARE SO STRONG!
NO TIME TO BE IMPRESSED!!
SORRY!
WE'LL BATTLE TOO, CINDER-ACE!
CIN-DER!!

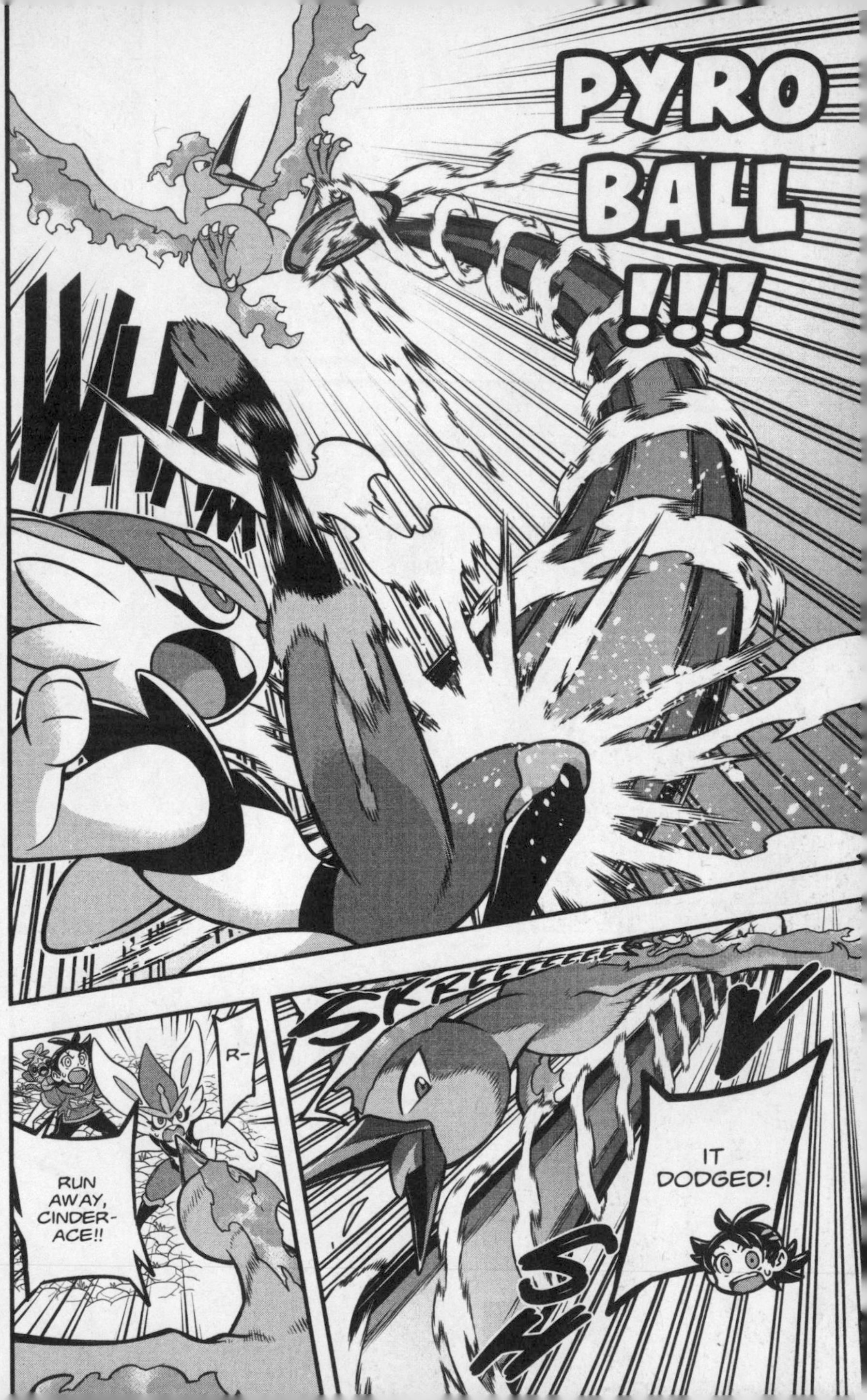
PYRO BALL!!!
WHAM
IT DODGED!
R-
RUN AWAY, CINDER-ACE!!

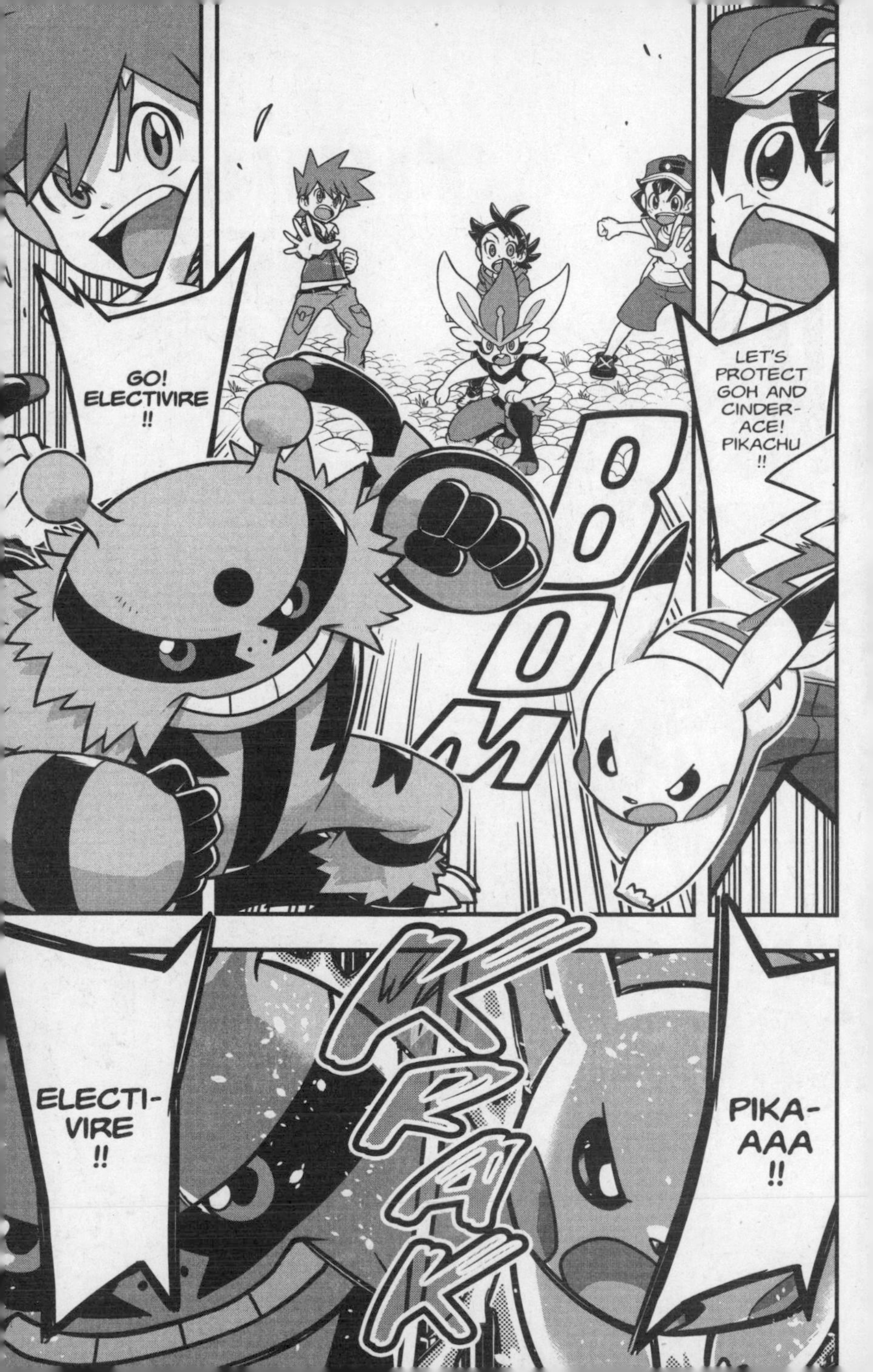
LET'S PROTECT GOH AND CINDER-ACE! PIKACHU !!
GO! ELECTIVIRE !!
BOOM
PIKA-AAA !!
ELECTI-VIRE !!

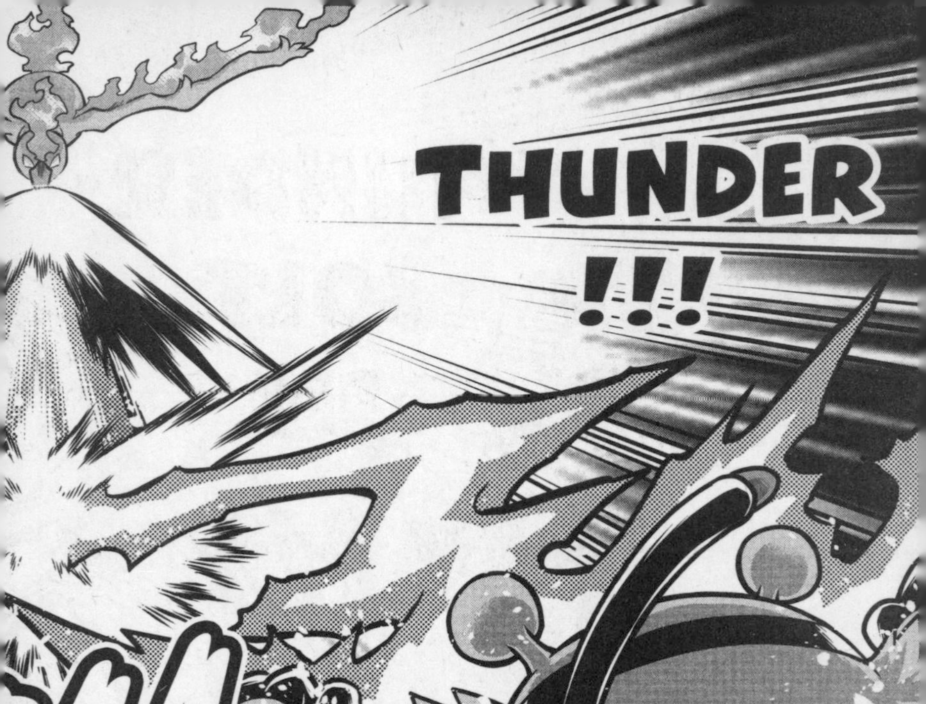
THUNDER !!!
AAK
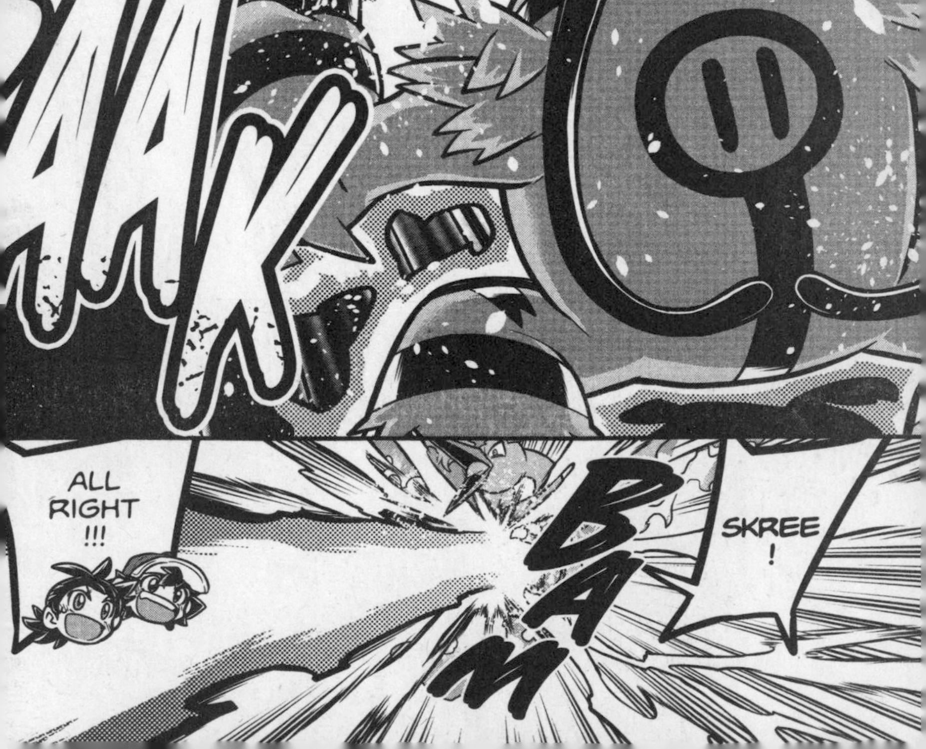
SKREE !
BAM
ALL RIGHT !!!

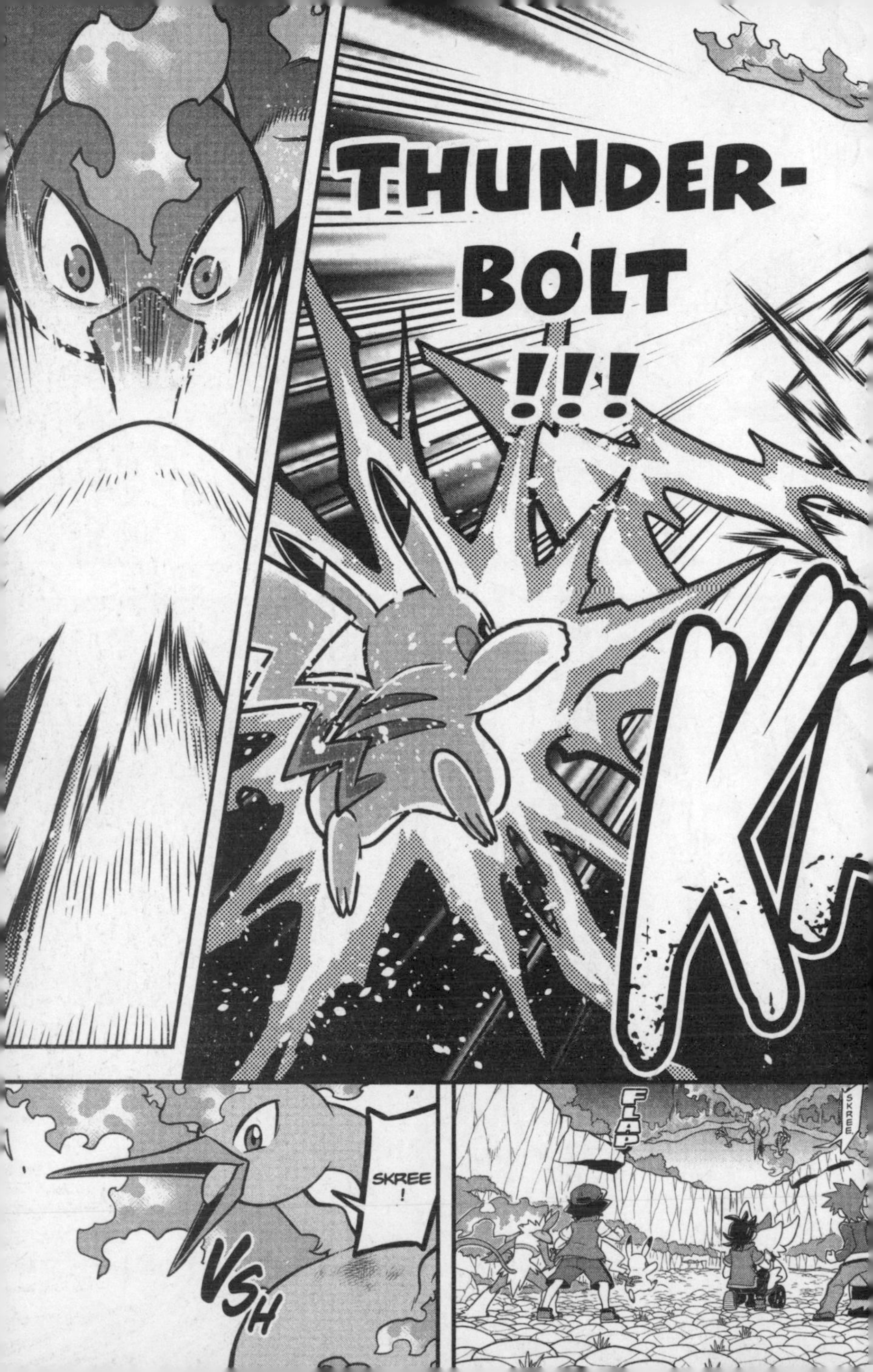
THUNDER-
BOLT
!!!
K
FLAP
SKREE
SKREE
!
VSH

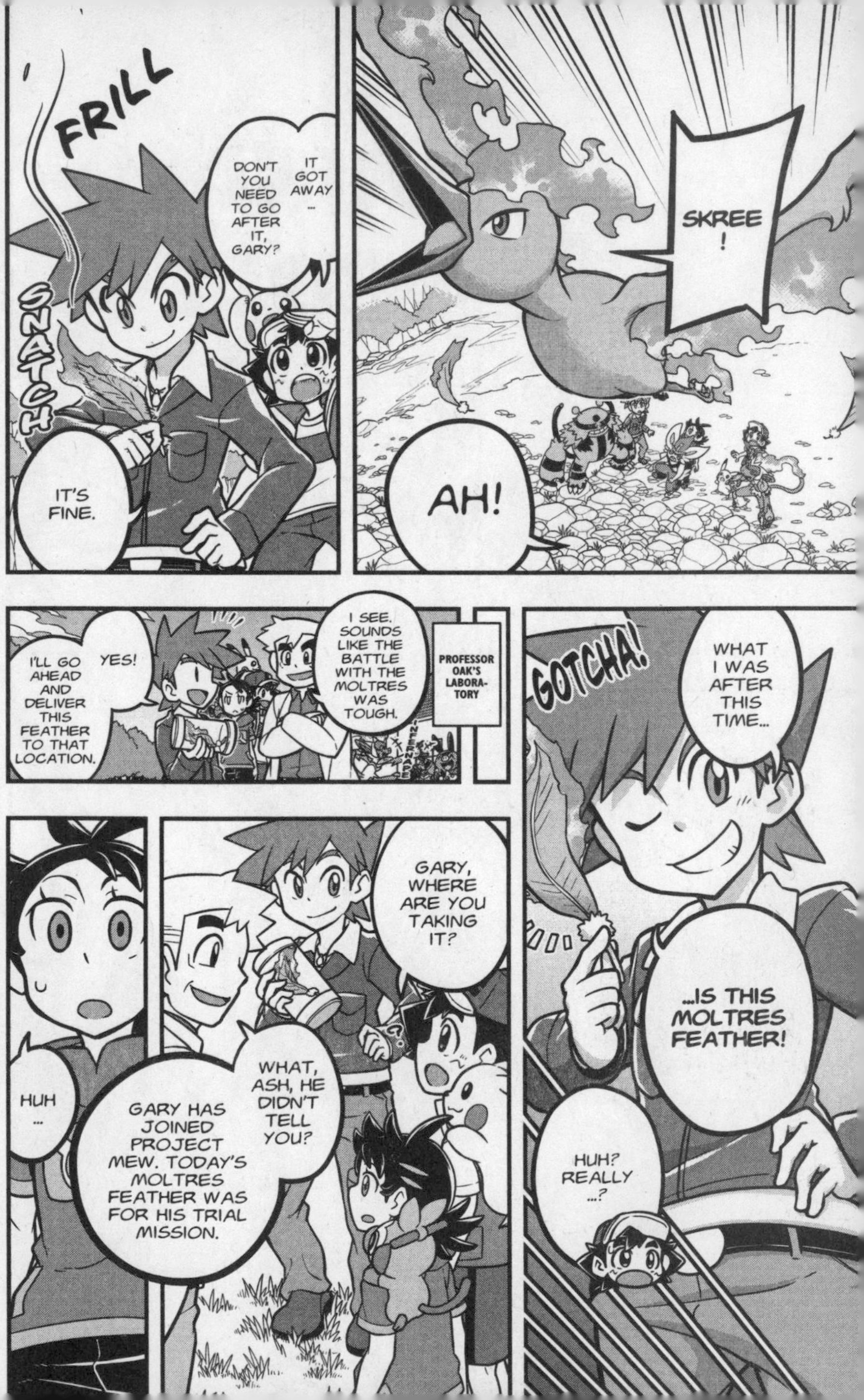
SKREE!
AH!
IT GOT AWAY...
DON'T YOU NEED TO GO AFTER IT, GARY?
FRILL
SNATCH
IT'S FINE.
GOTCHA!
WHAT I WAS AFTER THIS TIME...
...IS THIS MOLTRES FEATHER!
HUH? REALLY...?
PROFESSOR OAK'S LABORATORY
I SEE. SOUNDS LIKE THE BATTLE WITH THE MOLTRES WAS TOUGH.
INFERNAPE
YES!
I'LL GO AHEAD AND DELIVER THIS FEATHER TO THAT LOCATION.
GARY, WHERE ARE YOU TAKING IT?
WHAT, ASH, HE DIDN'T TELL YOU?
GARY HAS JOINED PROJECT MEW. TODAY'S MOLTRES FEATHER WAS FOR HIS TRIAL MISSION.
HUH...

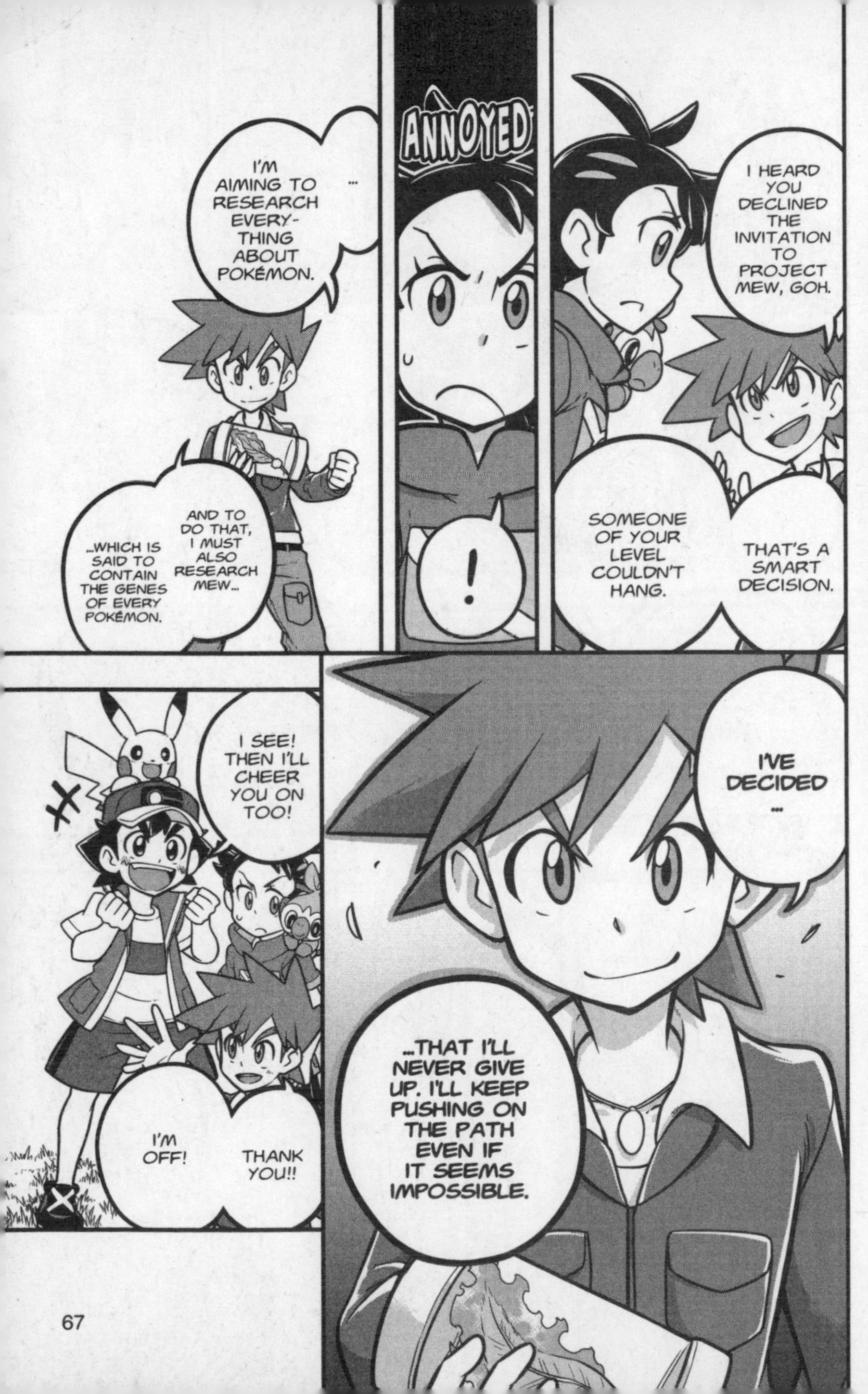
I HEARD YOU DECLINED THE INVITATION TO PROJECT MEW, GOH.
THAT'S A SMART DECISION.
SOMEONE OF YOUR LEVEL COULDN'T HANG.
ANNOYED
!
...
I'M AIMING TO RESEARCH EVERY-THING ABOUT POKÉMON.
AND TO DO THAT, I MUST ALSO RESEARCH MEW...
...WHICH IS SAID TO CONTAIN THE GENES OF EVERY POKÉMON.
I'VE DECIDED ...
...THAT I'LL NEVER GIVE UP. I'LL KEEP PUSHING ON THE PATH EVEN IF IT SEEMS IMPOSSIBLE.
I SEE! THEN I'LL CHEER YOU ON TOO!
THANK YOU!!
I'M OFF!

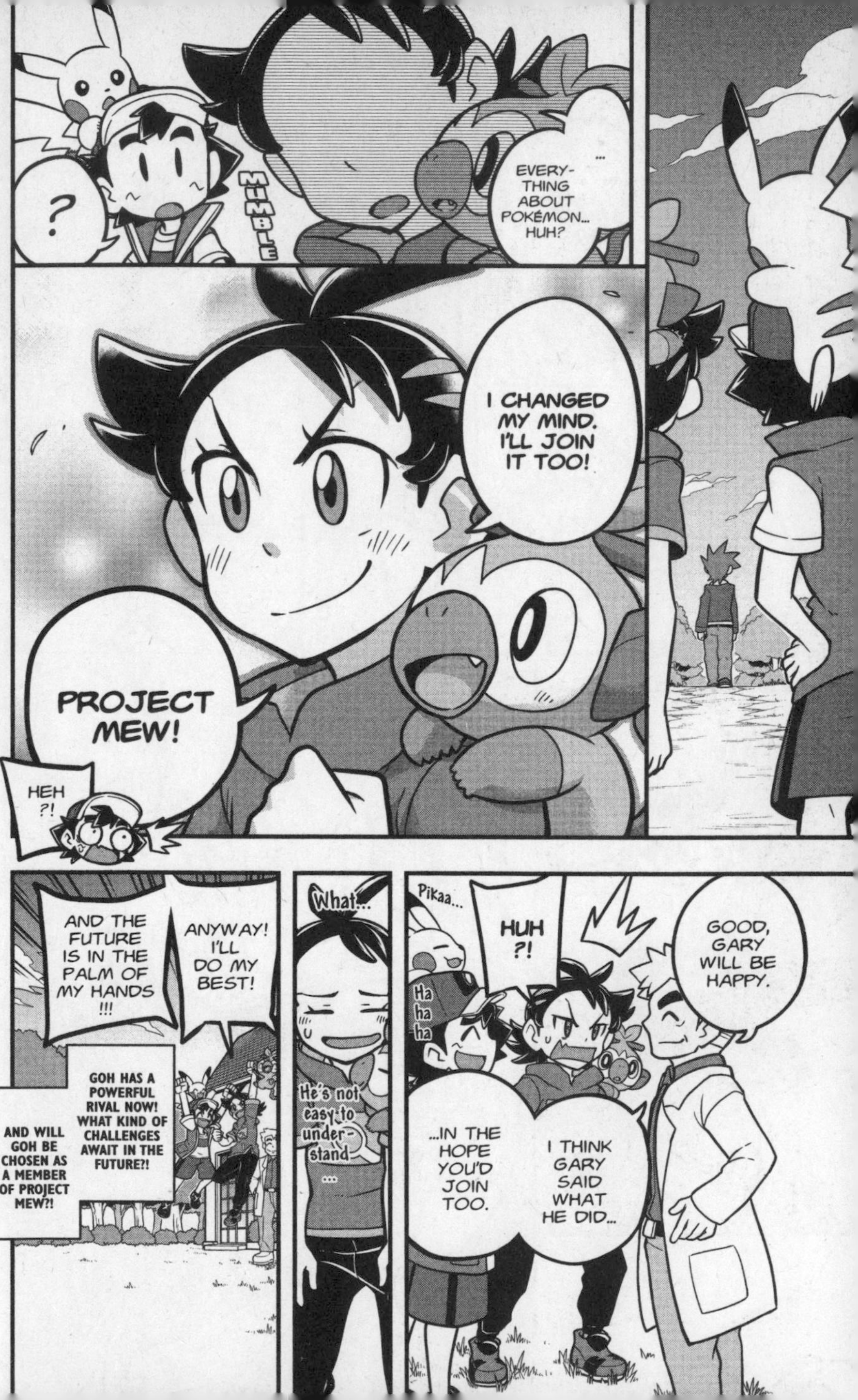

...EVERYTHING ABOUT POKÉMON... HUH?
MUMBLE
?
I CHANGED MY MIND. I'LL JOIN IT TOO!
PROJECT MEW!
HEH ?!
GOOD, GARY WILL BE HAPPY.
HUH ?!
Pikaa...
Ha ha ha
I THINK GARY SAID WHAT HE DID...
...IN THE HOPE YOU'D JOIN TOO.
What...
He's not easy to under-stand
...
ANYWAY! I'LL DO MY BEST!
AND THE FUTURE IS IN THE PALM OF MY HANDS!!!
GOH HAS A POWERFUL RIVAL NOW! WHAT KIND OF CHALLENGES AWAIT IN THE FUTURE?!
AND WILL GOH BE CHOSEN AS A MEMBER OF PROJECT MEW?!

Chapter 21
Leaping Toward the Dream!

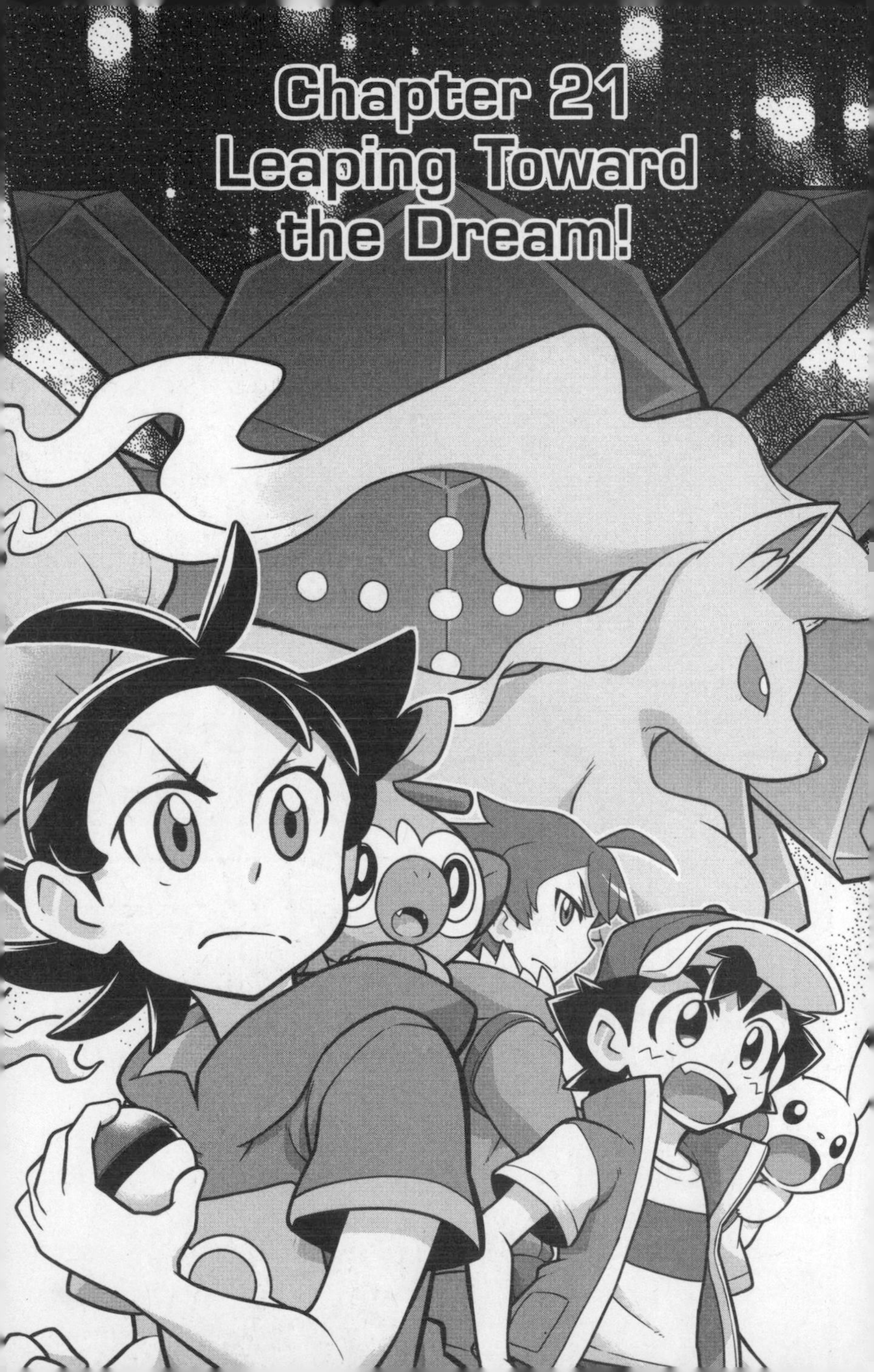

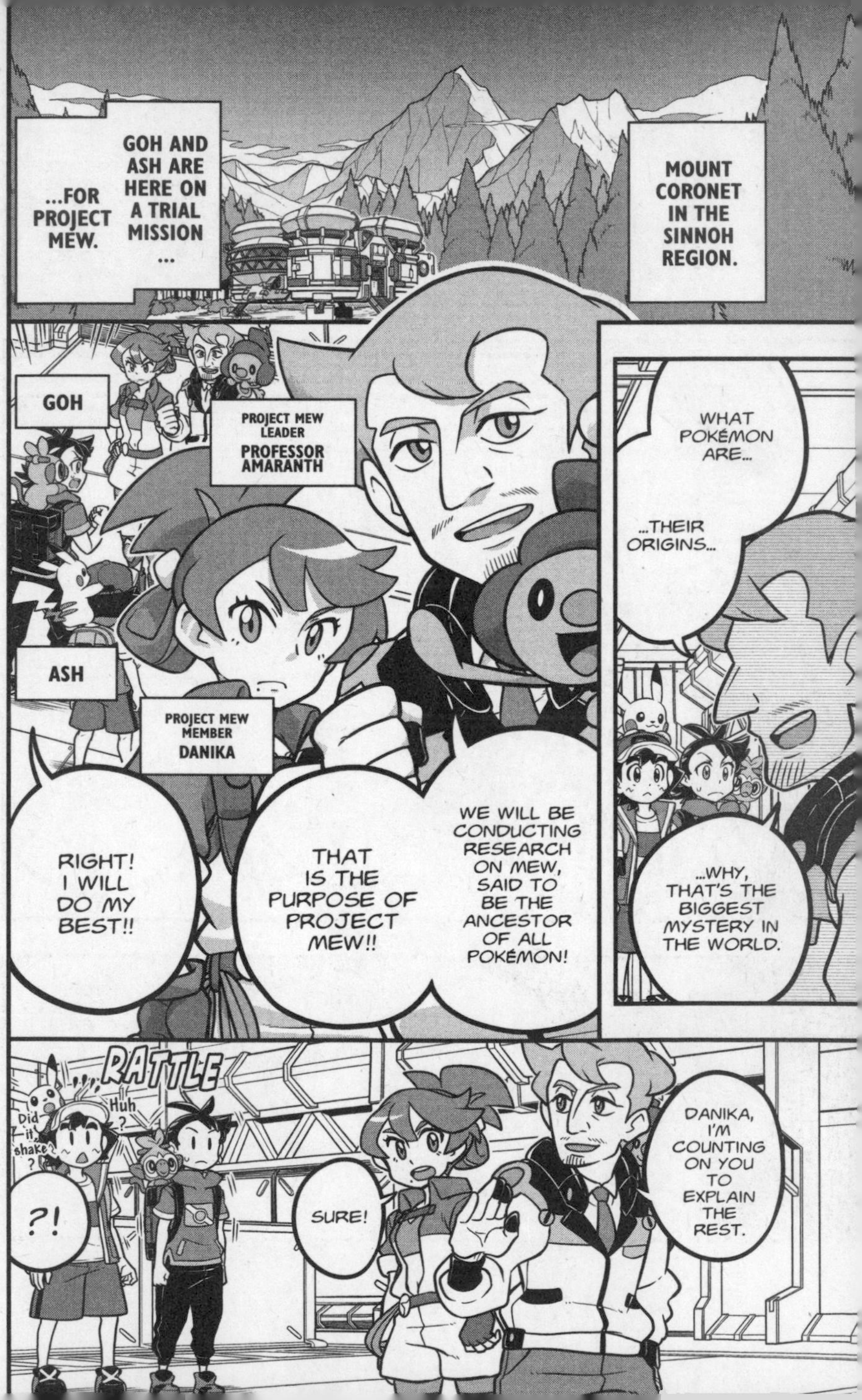
MOUNT CORONET IN THE SINNOH REGION.
GOH AND ASH ARE HERE ON A TRIAL MISSION ...
...FOR PROJECT MEW.
WHAT POKÉMON ARE...
...THEIR ORIGINS...
...WHY, THAT'S THE BIGGEST MYSTERY IN THE WORLD.
PROJECT MEW LEADER PROFESSOR AMARANTH
GOH
PROJECT MEW MEMBER DANIKA
ASH
WE WILL BE CONDUCTING RESEARCH ON MEW, SAID TO BE THE ANCESTOR OF ALL POKÉMON!
THAT IS THE PURPOSE OF PROJECT MEW!!
RIGHT! I WILL DO MY BEST!!
DANIKA, I'M COUNTING ON YOU TO EXPLAIN THE REST.
SURE!
RATTLE
Huh?
Did it shake?
?!

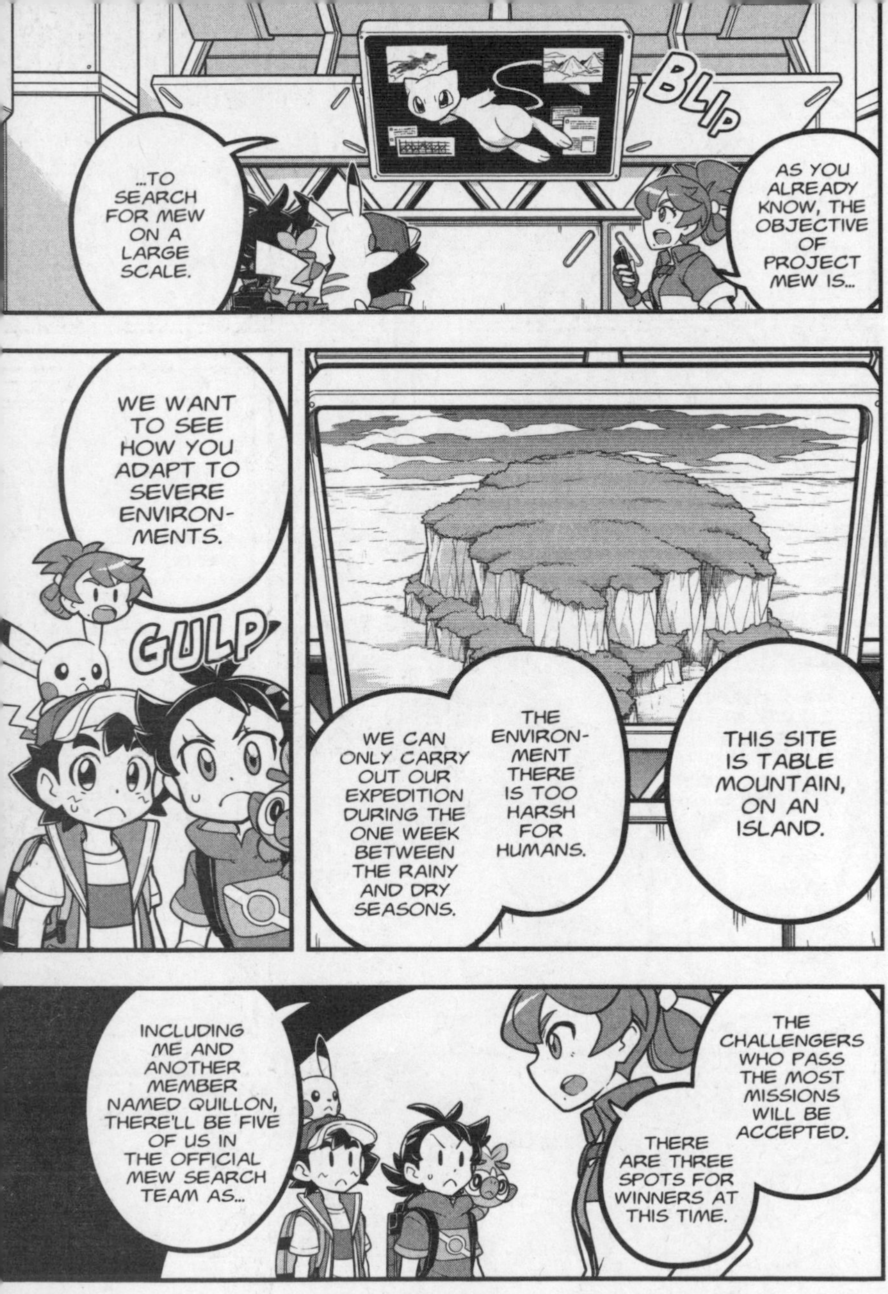
BLIP
AS YOU ALREADY KNOW, THE OBJECTIVE OF PROJECT MEW IS...
...TO SEARCH FOR MEW ON A LARGE SCALE.
THIS SITE IS TABLE MOUNTAIN, ON AN ISLAND.
THE ENVIRONMENT THERE IS TOO HARSH FOR HUMANS.
WE CAN ONLY CARRY OUT OUR EXPEDITION DURING THE ONE WEEK BETWEEN THE RAINY AND DRY SEASONS.
WE WANT TO SEE HOW YOU ADAPT TO SEVERE ENVIRONMENTS.
GULP
THE CHALLENGERS WHO PASS THE MOST MISSIONS WILL BE ACCEPTED.
THERE ARE THREE SPOTS FOR WINNERS AT THIS TIME.
INCLUDING ME AND ANOTHER MEMBER NAMED QUILLON, THERE'LL BE FIVE OF US IN THE OFFICIAL MEW SEARCH TEAM AS...

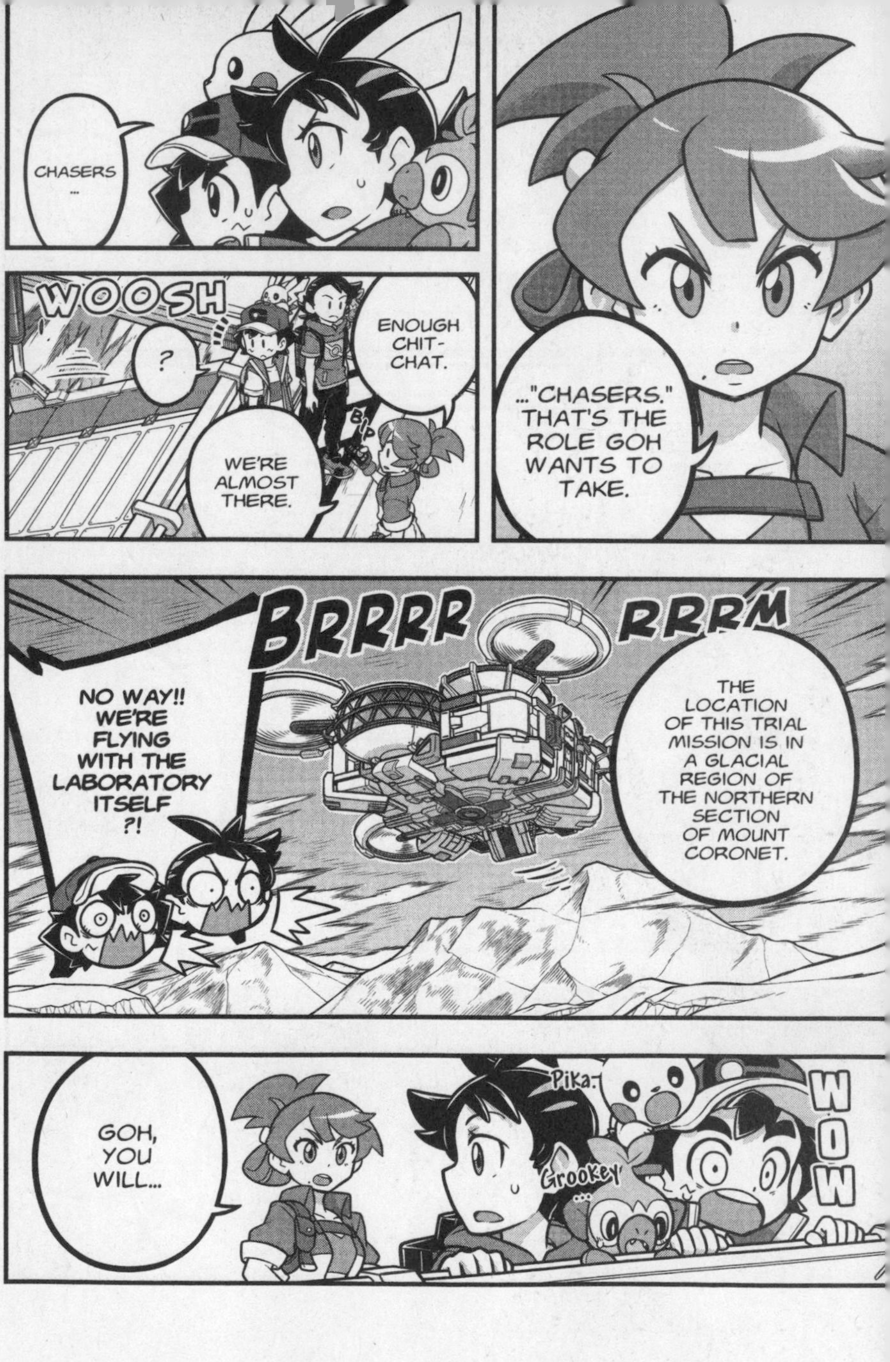
..."CHASERS." THAT'S THE ROLE GOH WANTS TO TAKE.
CHASERS ...
WOOSH
ENOUGH CHIT-CHAT.
?
BIP
WE'RE ALMOST THERE.
BRRRR RRRM
THE LOCATION OF THIS TRIAL MISSION IS IN A GLACIAL REGION OF THE NORTHERN SECTION OF MOUNT CORONET.
NO WAY!! WE'RE FLYING WITH THE LABORATORY ITSELF ?!
WOW
Pika.
Grookey ...
GOH, YOU WILL...

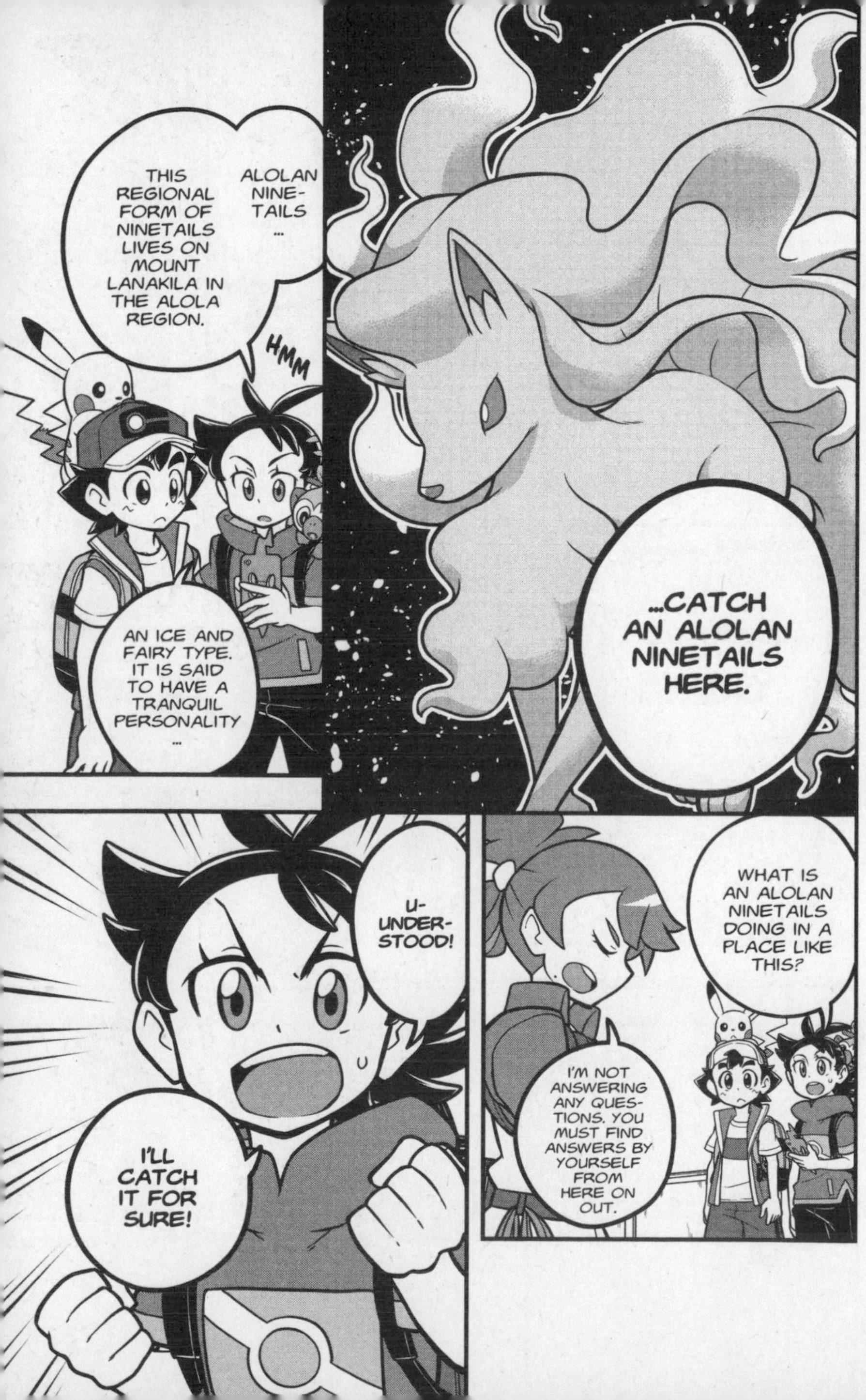
...CATCH AN ALOLAN NINETAILS HERE.
ALOLAN NINE-TAILS ...
THIS REGIONAL FORM OF NINETAILS LIVES ON MOUNT LANAKILA IN THE ALOLA REGION.
HMM
AN ICE AND FAIRY TYPE. IT IS SAID TO HAVE A TRANQUIL PERSONALITY ...
WHAT IS AN ALOLAN NINETAILS DOING IN A PLACE LIKE THIS?
I'M NOT ANSWERING ANY QUES-TIONS. YOU MUST FIND ANSWERS BY YOURSELF FROM HERE ON OUT.
U-UNDER-STOOD!
I'LL CATCH IT FOR SURE!

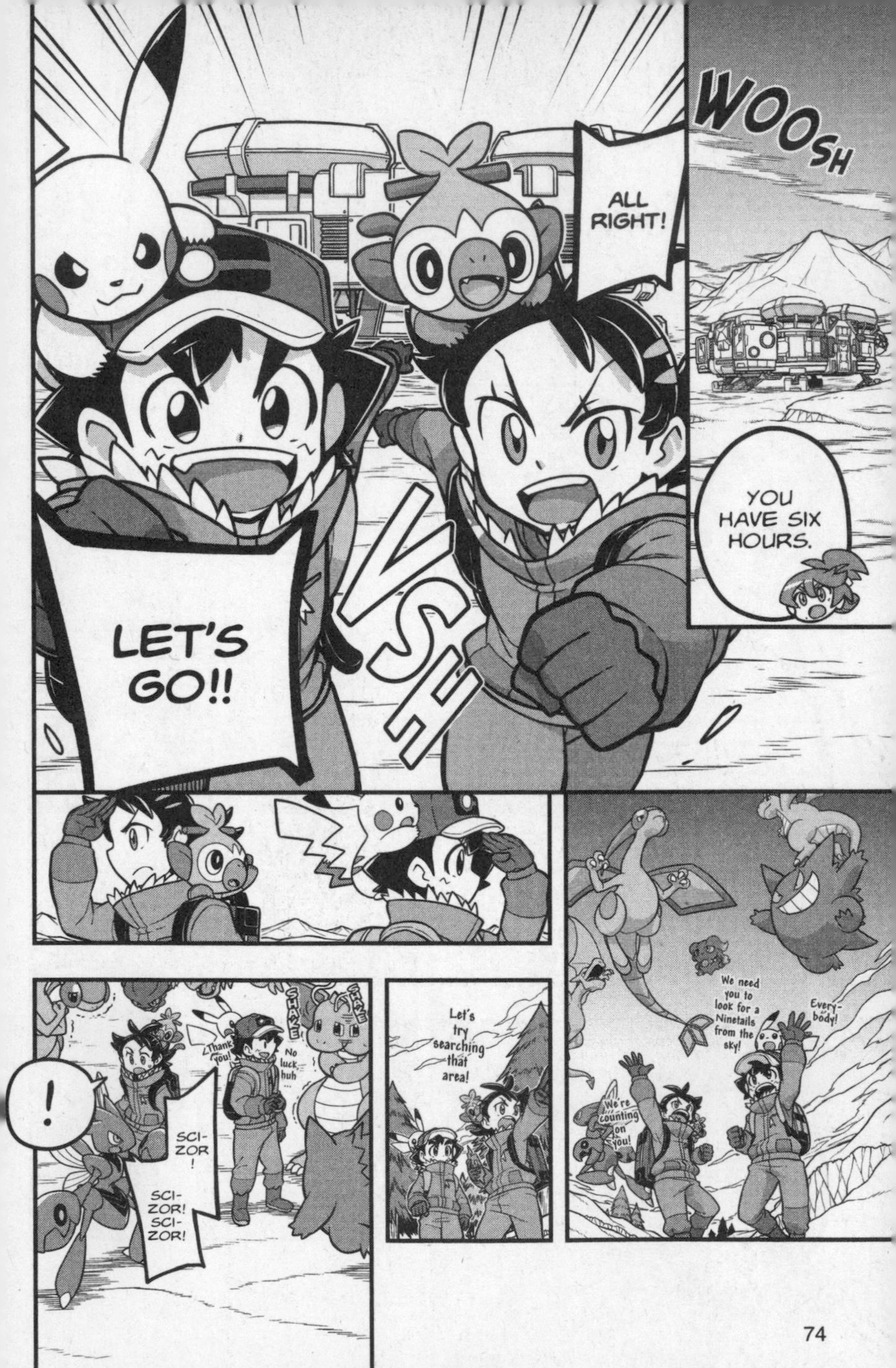
WOOSH
YOU HAVE SIX HOURS.
ALL RIGHT!
LET'S GO!!
VSH
Every-body!
We need you to look for a Ninetails from the sky!
We're counting on you!
Let's try searching that area!
SHAKE SHAKE
No luck, huh...
Thank you!
SCI-ZOR!
SCI-ZOR! SCI-ZOR!
!

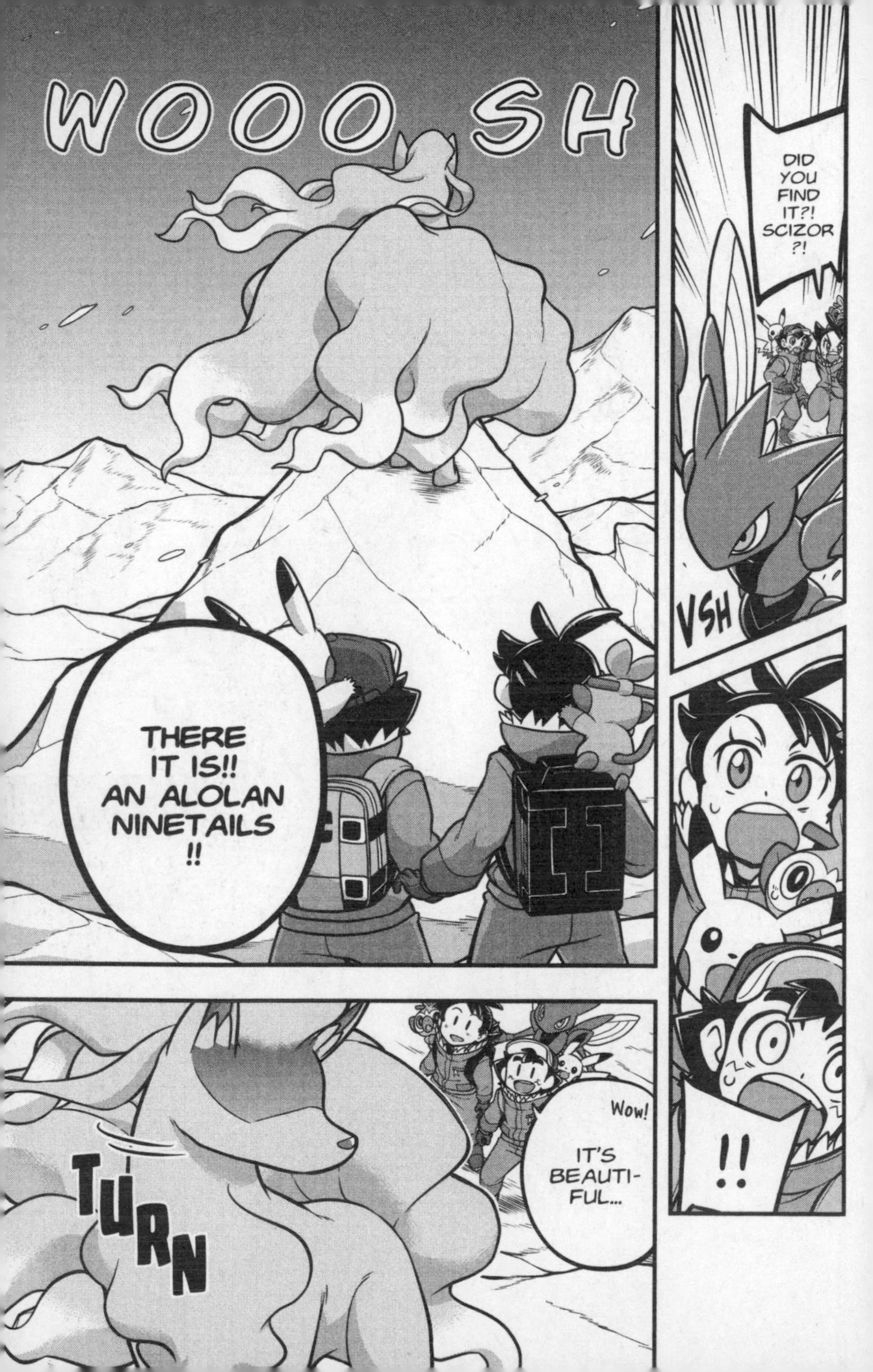
DID YOU FIND IT?! SCIZOR ?!
VSH
!!
WOOOSH
THERE IT IS!! AN ALOLAN NINETAILS !!
Wow!
IT'S BEAUTIFUL...
TURN

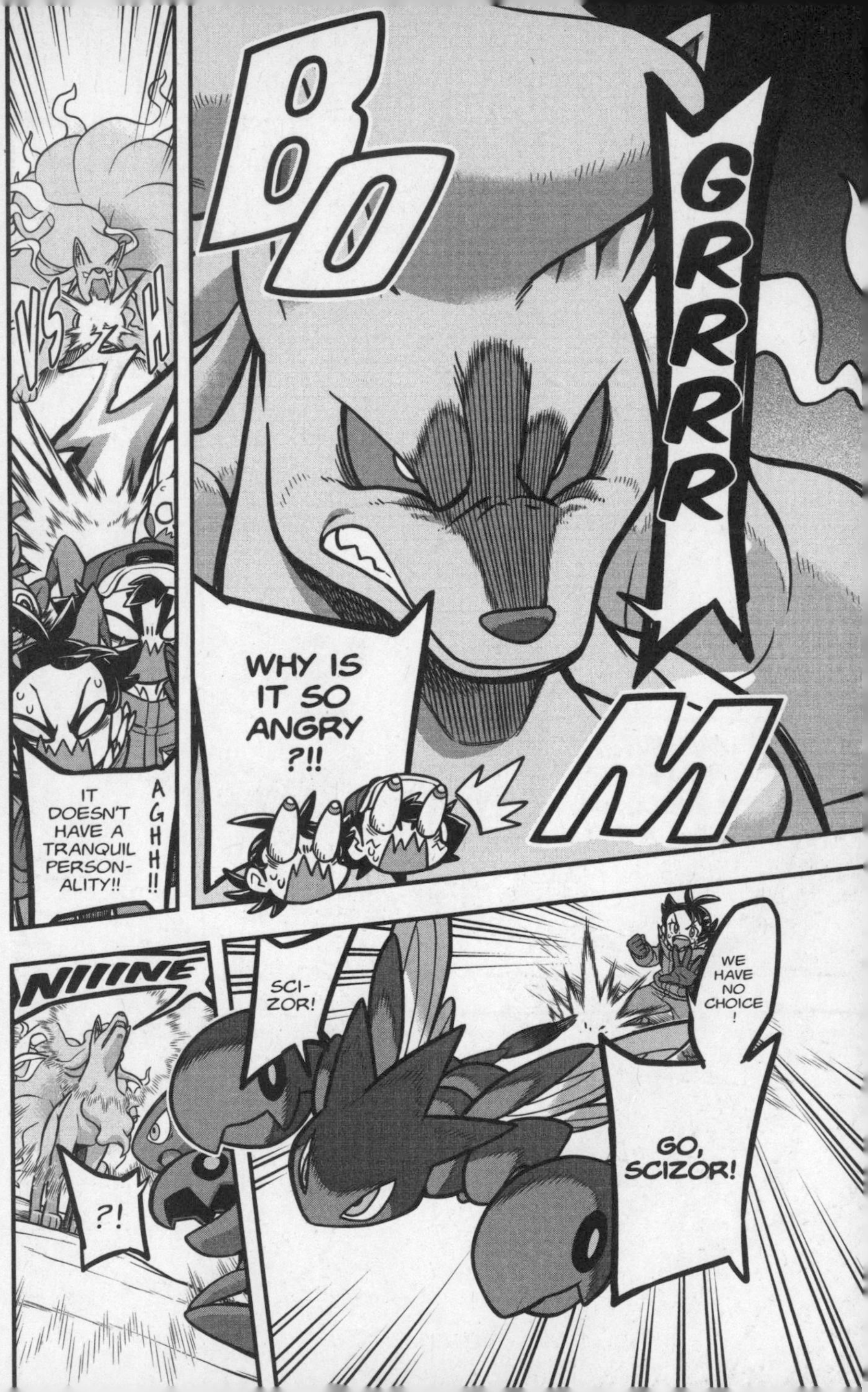
BOO
GRRRR
M
WHY IS IT SO ANGRY?!!
IT DOESN'T HAVE A TRANQUIL PERSONALITY!!
AGHHH!!
WE HAVE NO CHOICE!
GO, SCIZOR!
SCI-ZOR!
NIIIINE
?!

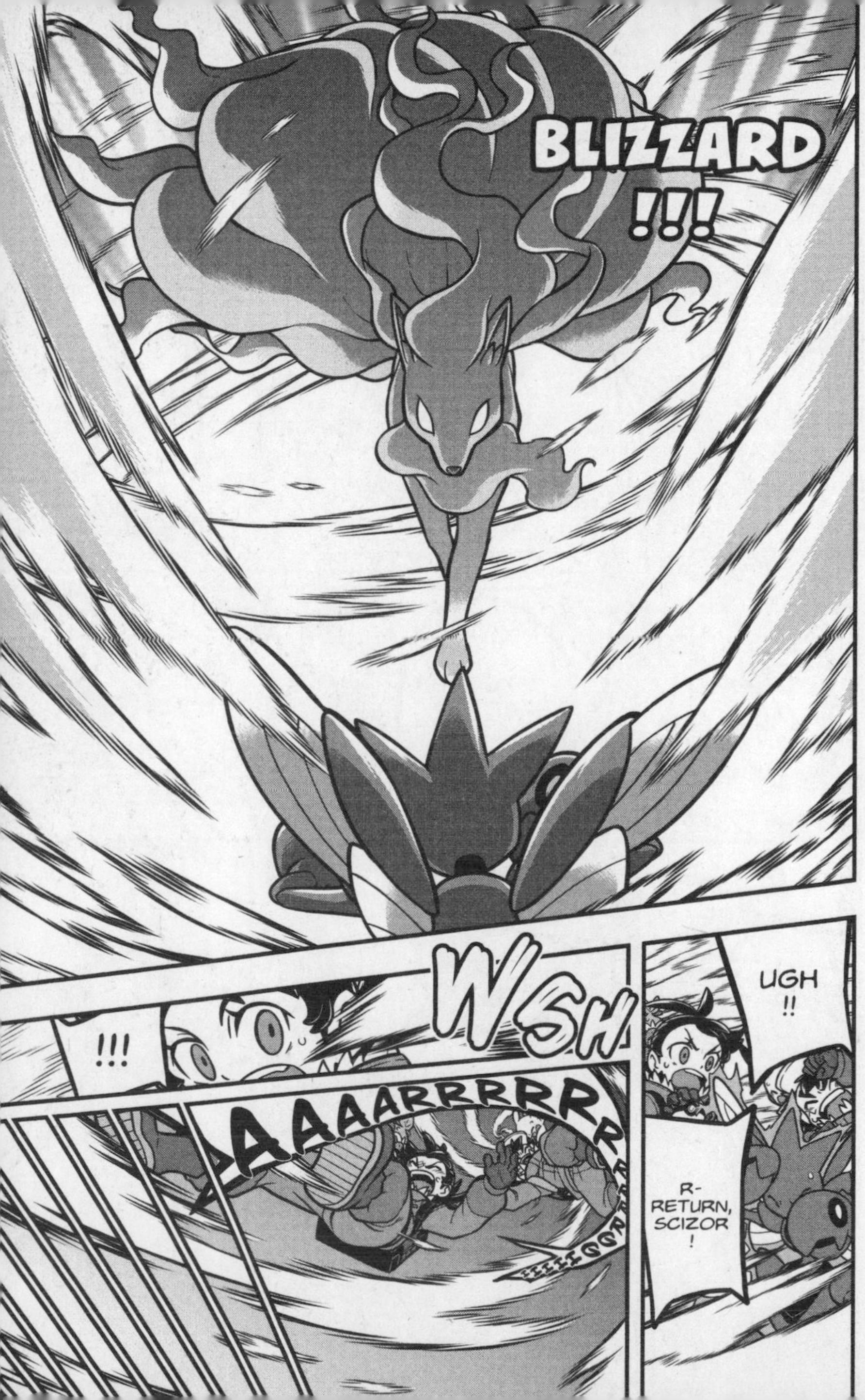
BLIZZARD!!!
UGH!!
R-RETURN, SCIZOR!
WSH
!!!
AAAARRRRRR

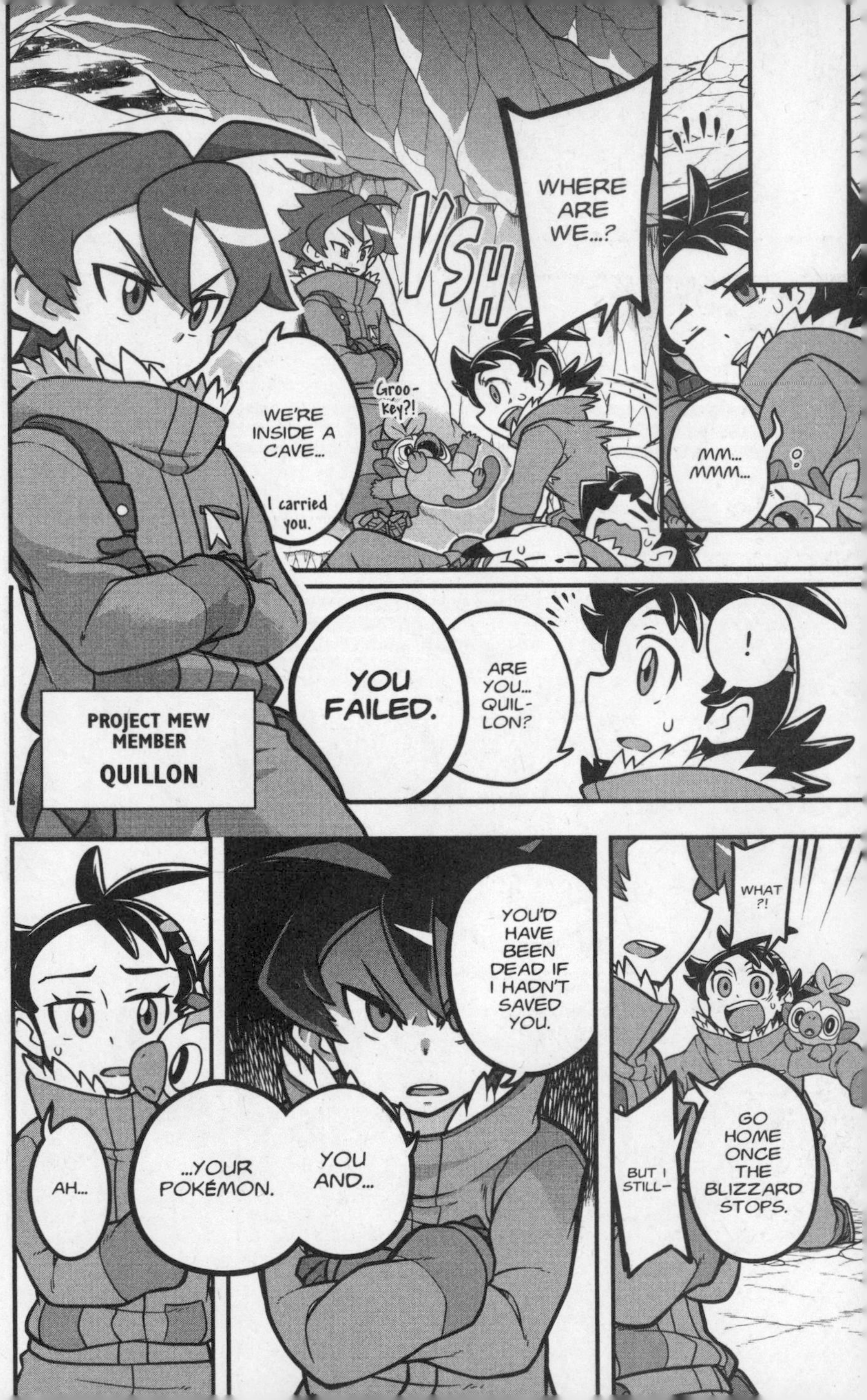
MM... MMM...
WHERE ARE WE...?
VSH
Groo-key?!
WE'RE INSIDE A CAVE...
I carried you.
!
ARE YOU... QUIL-LON?
YOU FAILED.
PROJECT MEW MEMBER
QUILLON
WHAT?!
GO HOME ONCE THE BLIZZARD STOPS.
BUT I STILL—
YOU'D HAVE BEEN DEAD IF I HADN'T SAVED YOU.
YOU AND...
...YOUR POKÉMON.
AH...

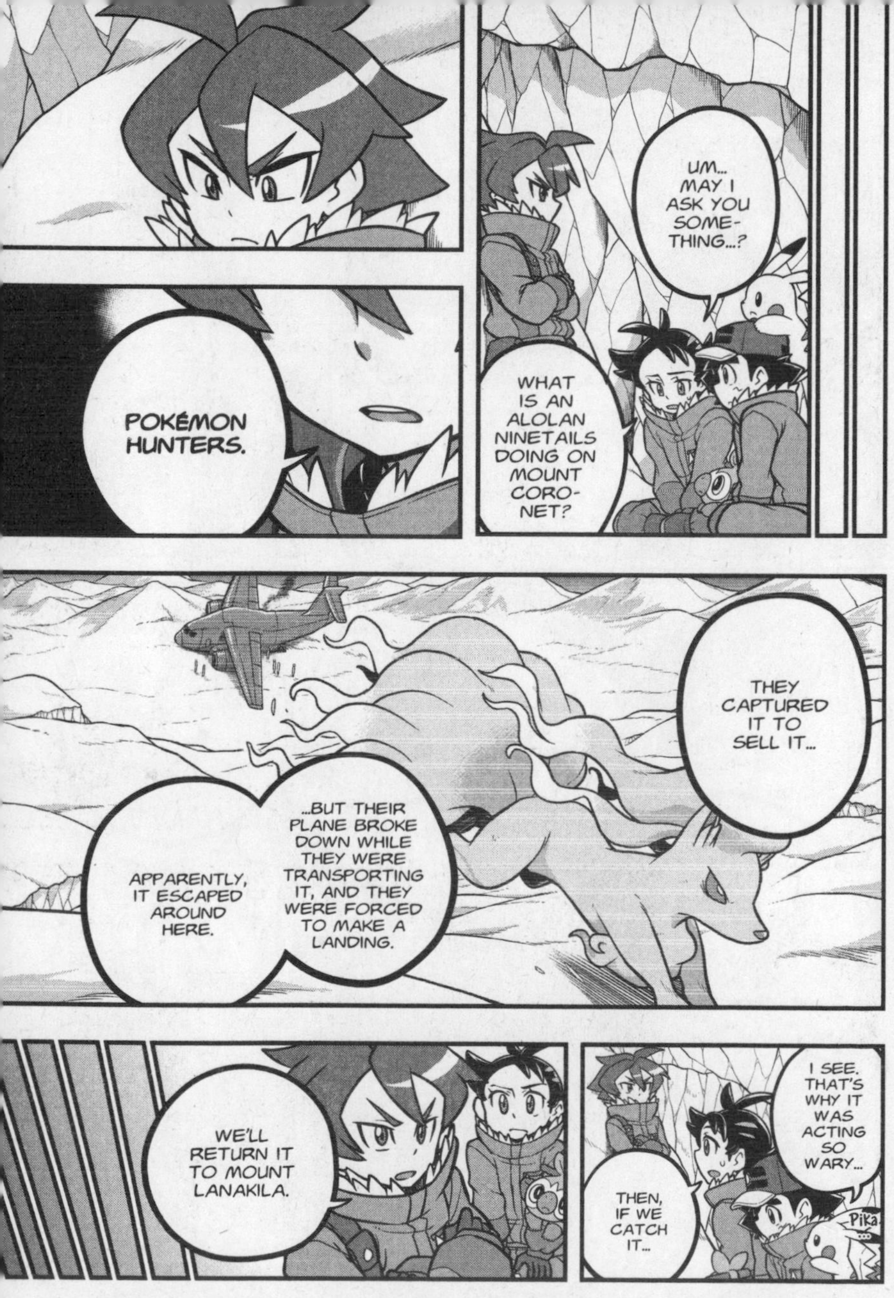
UM... MAY I ASK YOU SOME-THING...?
WHAT IS AN ALOLAN NINETAILS DOING ON MOUNT CORO-NET?
POKÉMON HUNTERS.
THEY CAPTURED IT TO SELL IT...
...BUT THEIR PLANE BROKE DOWN WHILE THEY WERE TRANSPORTING IT, AND THEY WERE FORCED TO MAKE A LANDING.
APPARENTLY, IT ESCAPED AROUND HERE.
I SEE. THAT'S WHY IT WAS ACTING SO WARY...
Pika...
THEN, IF WE CATCH IT...
WE'LL RETURN IT TO MOUNT LANAKILA.

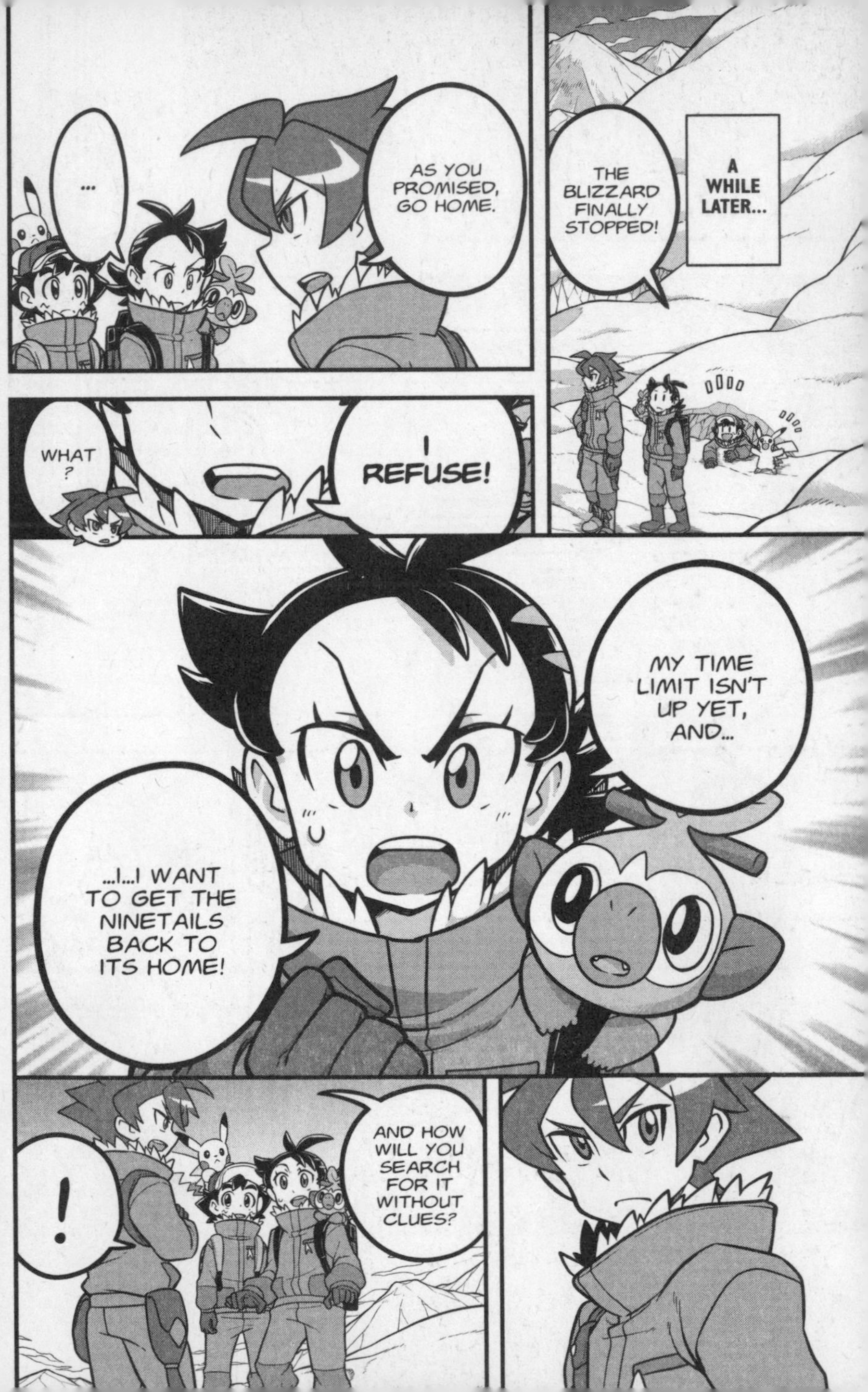
A WHILE LATER...
THE BLIZZARD FINALLY STOPPED!
AS YOU PROMISED, GO HOME.
...
I REFUSE!
WHAT?
MY TIME LIMIT ISN'T UP YET, AND...
...I...I WANT TO GET THE NINETAILS BACK TO ITS HOME!
AND HOW WILL YOU SEARCH FOR IT WITHOUT CLUES?
!

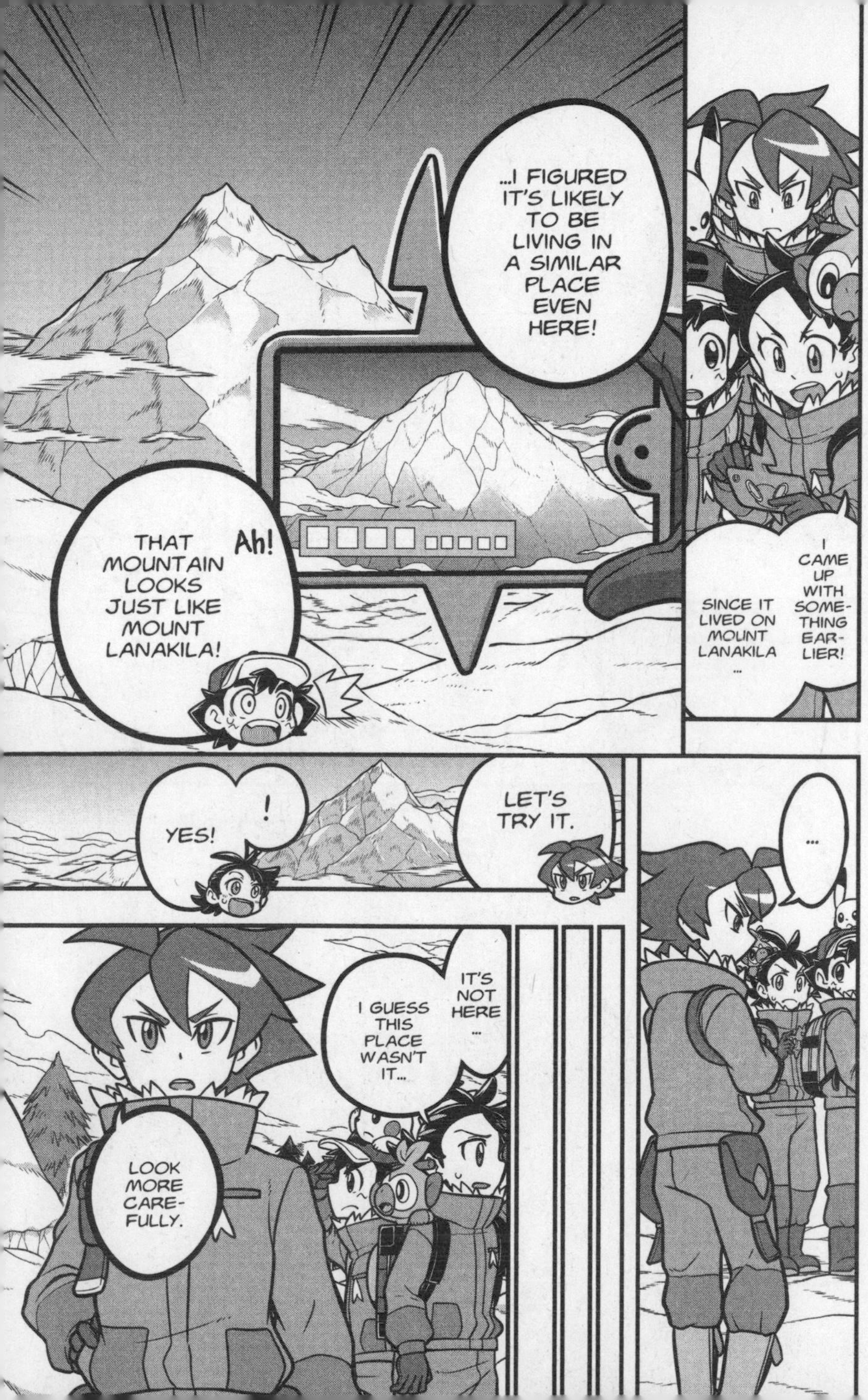
I CAME UP WITH SOMETHING EARLIER!
SINCE IT LIVED ON MOUNT LANAKILA...
...I FIGURED IT'S LIKELY TO BE LIVING IN A SIMILAR PLACE EVEN HERE!
Ah!
THAT MOUNTAIN LOOKS JUST LIKE MOUNT LANAKILA!
...
LET'S TRY IT.
!
YES!
IT'S NOT HERE...
I GUESS THIS PLACE WASN'T IT...
LOOK MORE CAREFULLY.

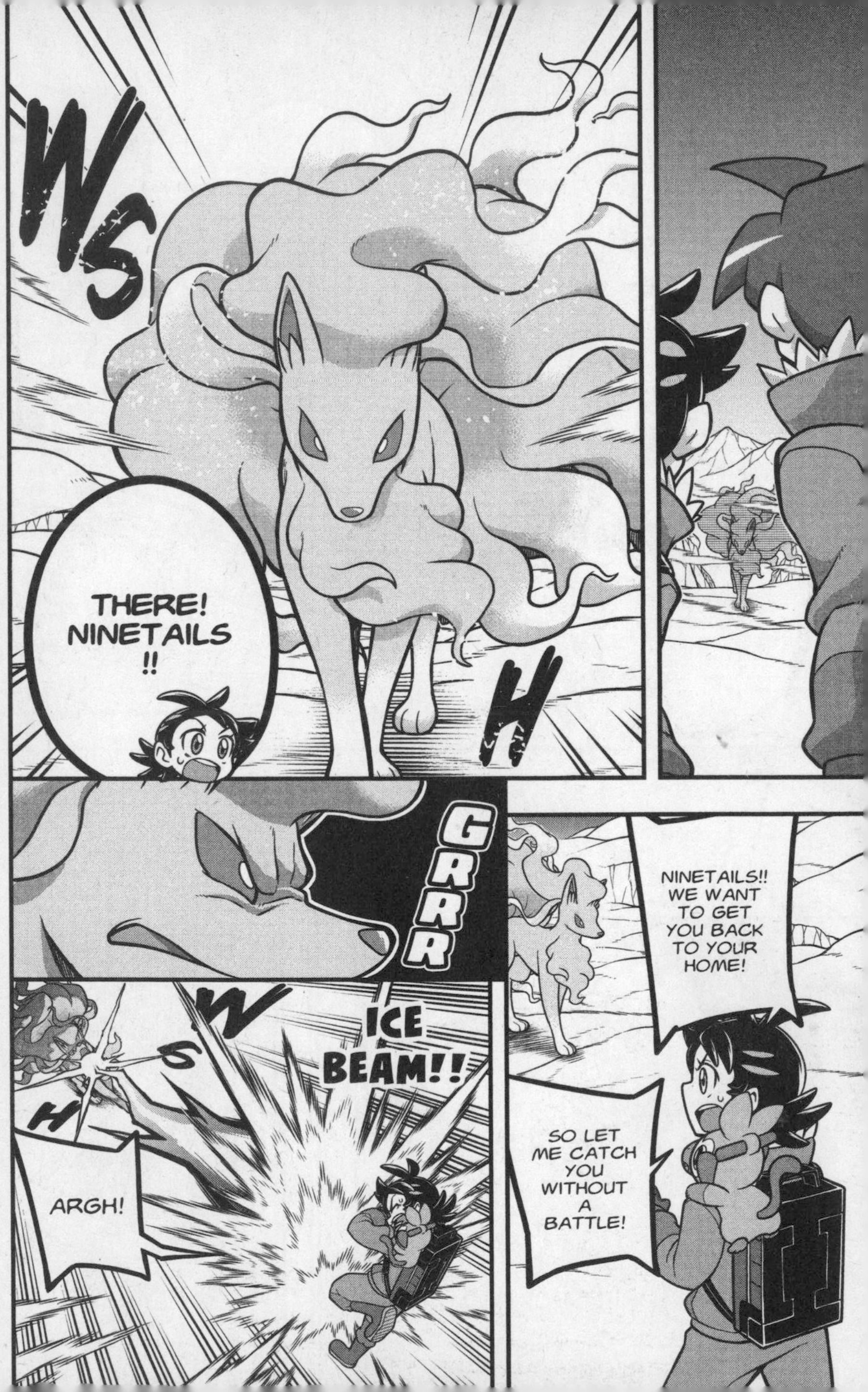
WS
THERE! NINETAILS !!
H
NINETAILS!! WE WANT TO GET YOU BACK TO YOUR HOME!
SO LET ME CATCH YOU WITHOUT A BATTLE!
GRRR
W
S
H
ICE BEAM!!
ARGH!

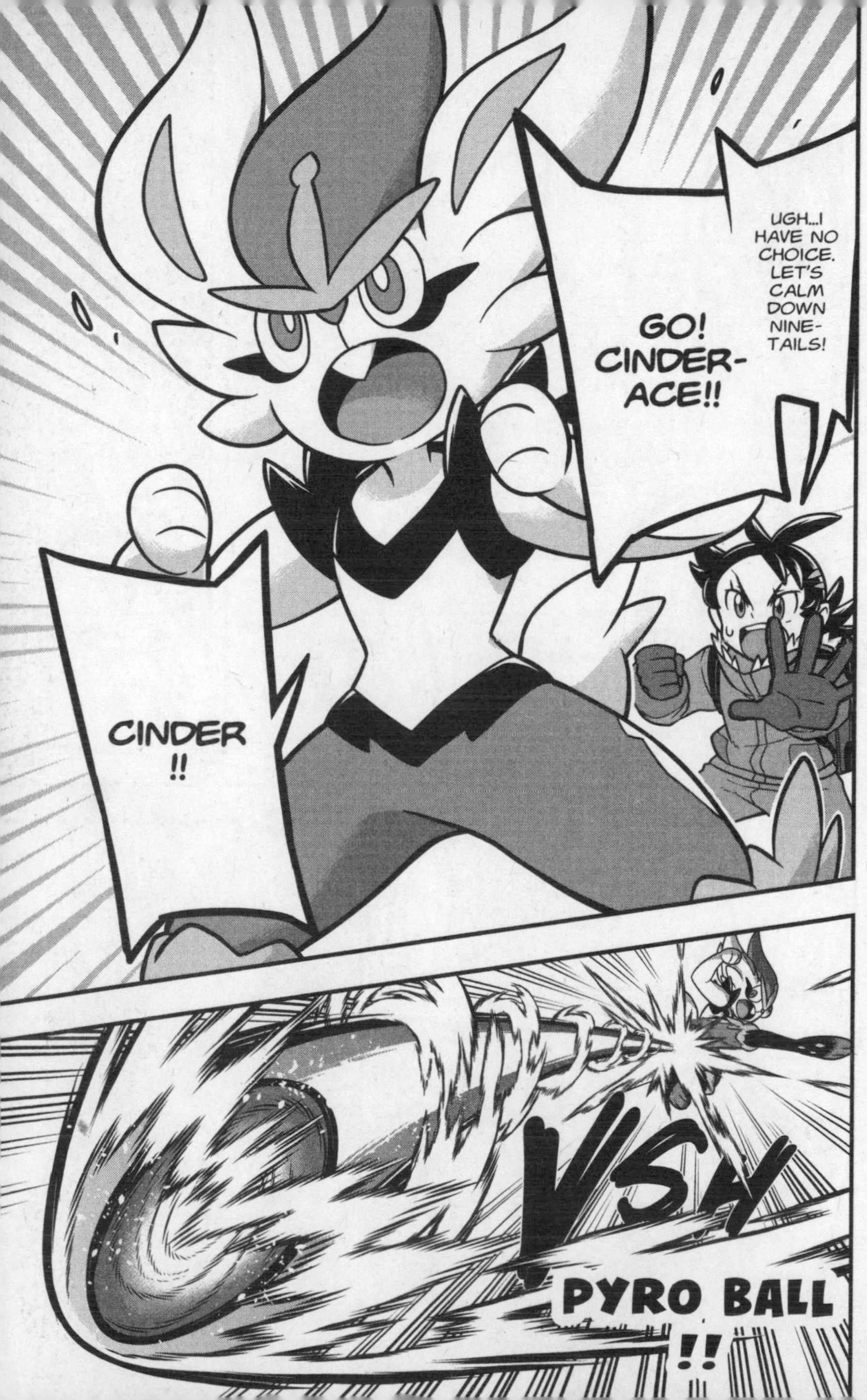
UGH...I HAVE NO CHOICE. LET'S CALM DOWN NINE-TAILS!
GO! CINDER-ACE!!
CINDER !!
VSH
PYRO BALL !!

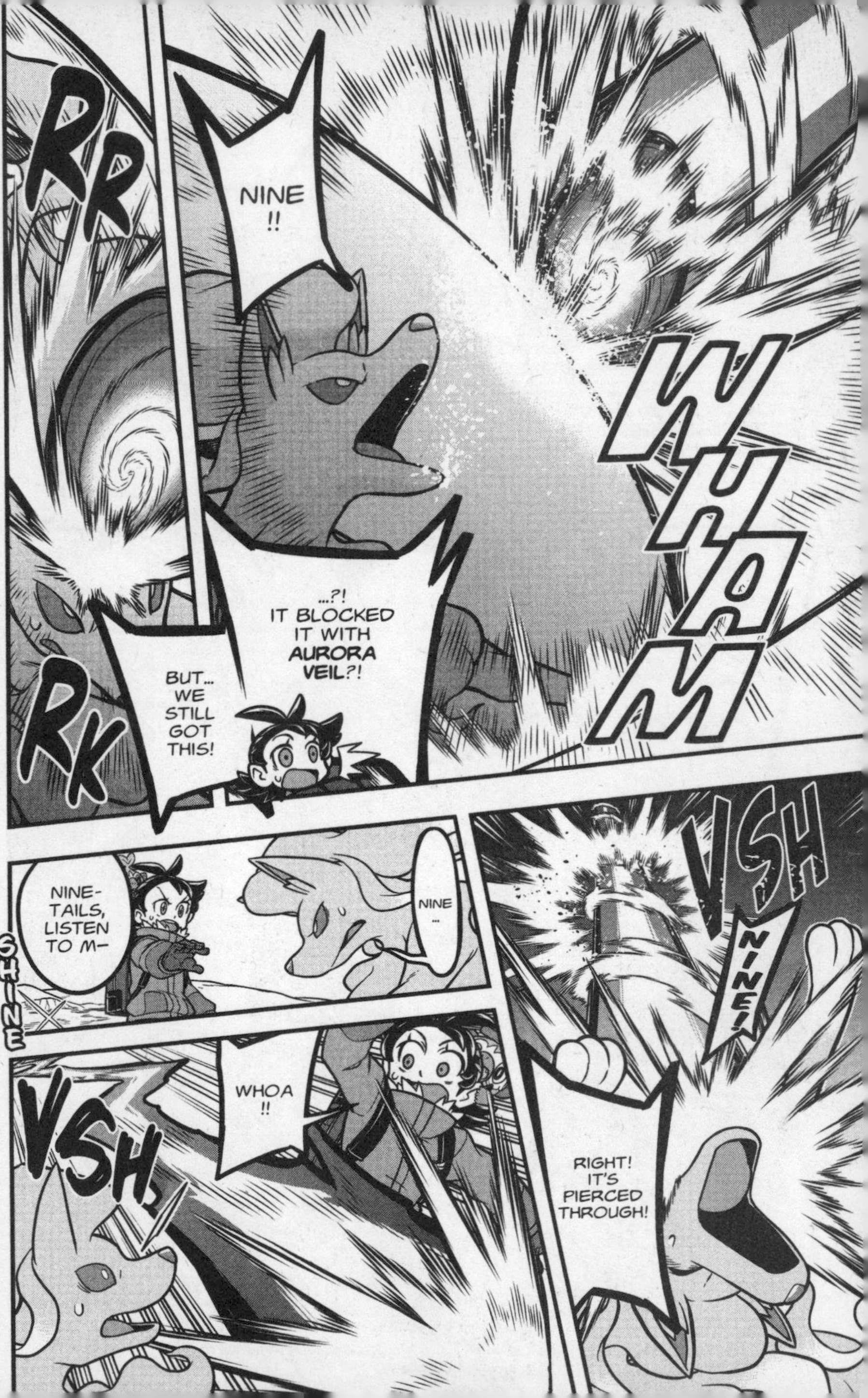
WHAM
NINE!!
...?! IT BLOCKED IT WITH AURORA VEIL?!
BUT... WE STILL GOT THIS!
RR
RK
VSH
NINE!
RIGHT! IT'S PIERCED THROUGH!
NINE...
NINE-TAILS, LISTEN TO M—
SHINE
WHOA!!
VSH

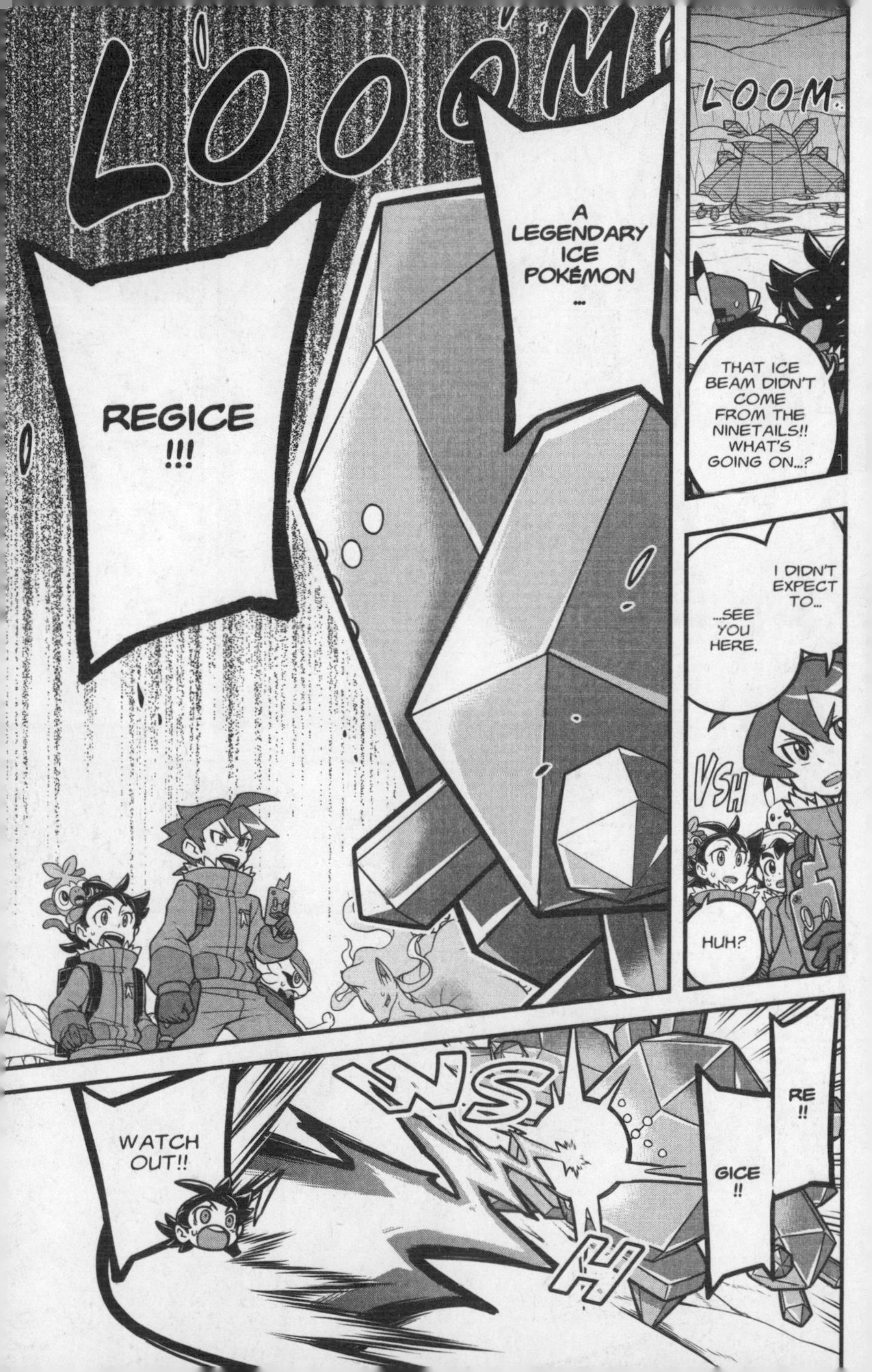
LOOM
THAT ICE BEAM DIDN'T COME FROM THE NINETAILS!! WHAT'S GOING ON...?
I DIDN'T EXPECT TO...
...SEE YOU HERE.
VSH
HUH?
LOOOM
A LEGENDARY ICE POKÉMON ...
REGICE !!!
RE !!
GICE !!
WSH
WATCH OUT!!

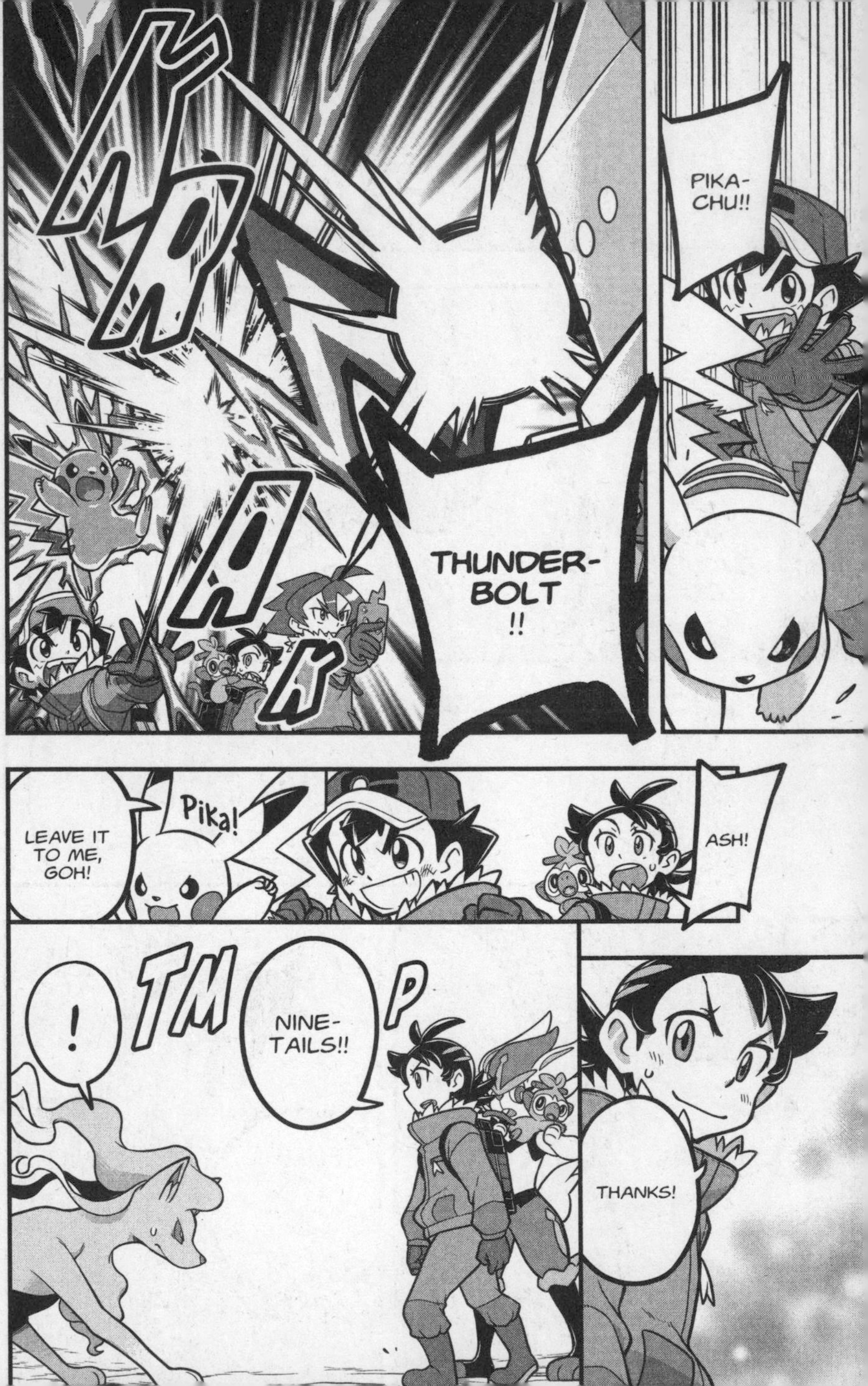
PIKA-CHU!!
THUNDER-BOLT !!
ASH!
Pika!
LEAVE IT TO ME, GOH!
THANKS!
TMP
NINE-TAILS!!
!

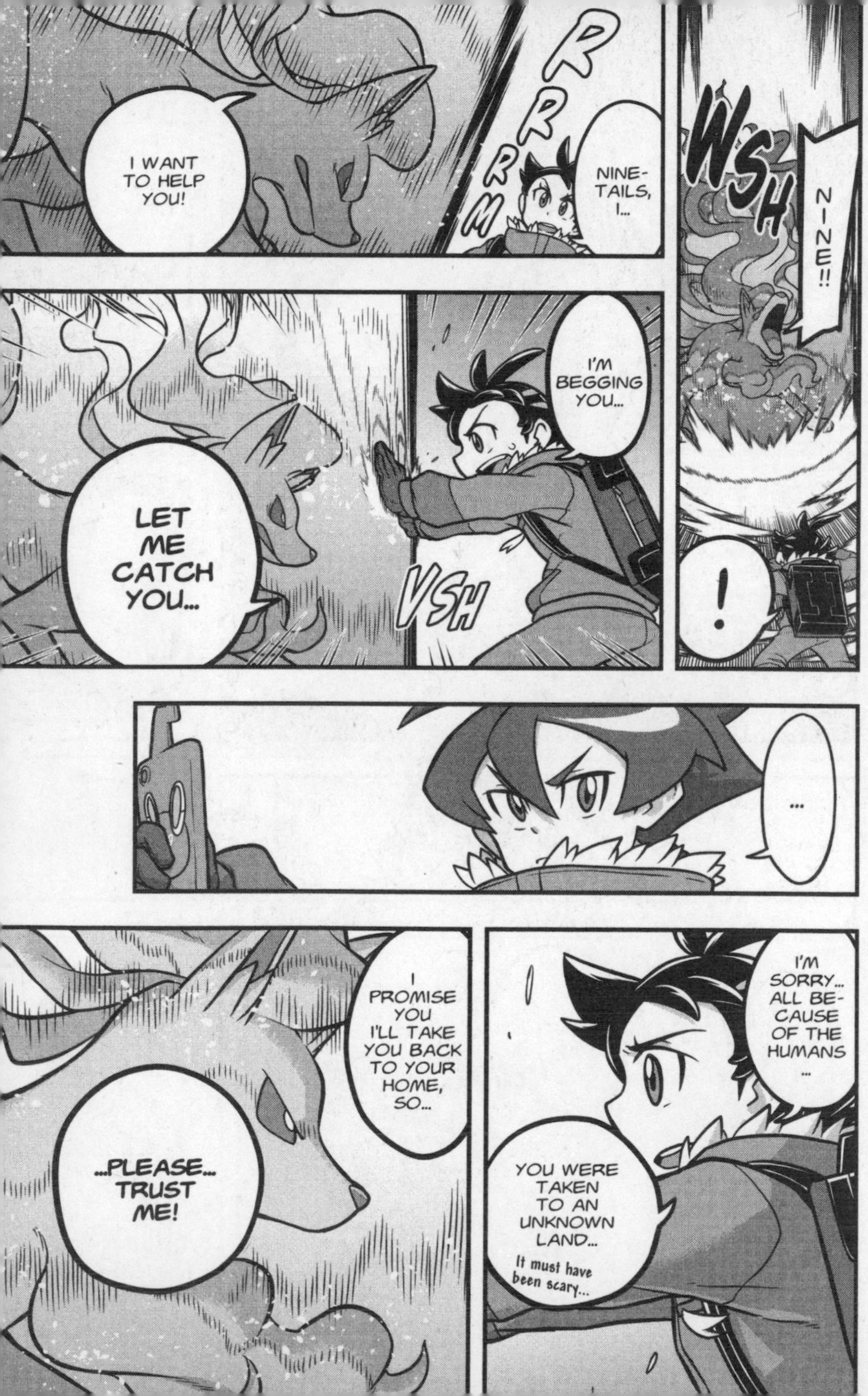
WSH
NINE!!
!
RRRM
NINE-TAILS, I...
I WANT TO HELP YOU!
I'M BEGGING YOU...
VSH
LET ME CATCH YOU...
...
I'M SORRY... ALL BECAUSE OF THE HUMANS...
YOU WERE TAKEN TO AN UNKNOWN LAND...
It must have been scary...
I PROMISE YOU I'LL TAKE YOU BACK TO YOUR HOME, SO...
...PLEASE... TRUST ME!

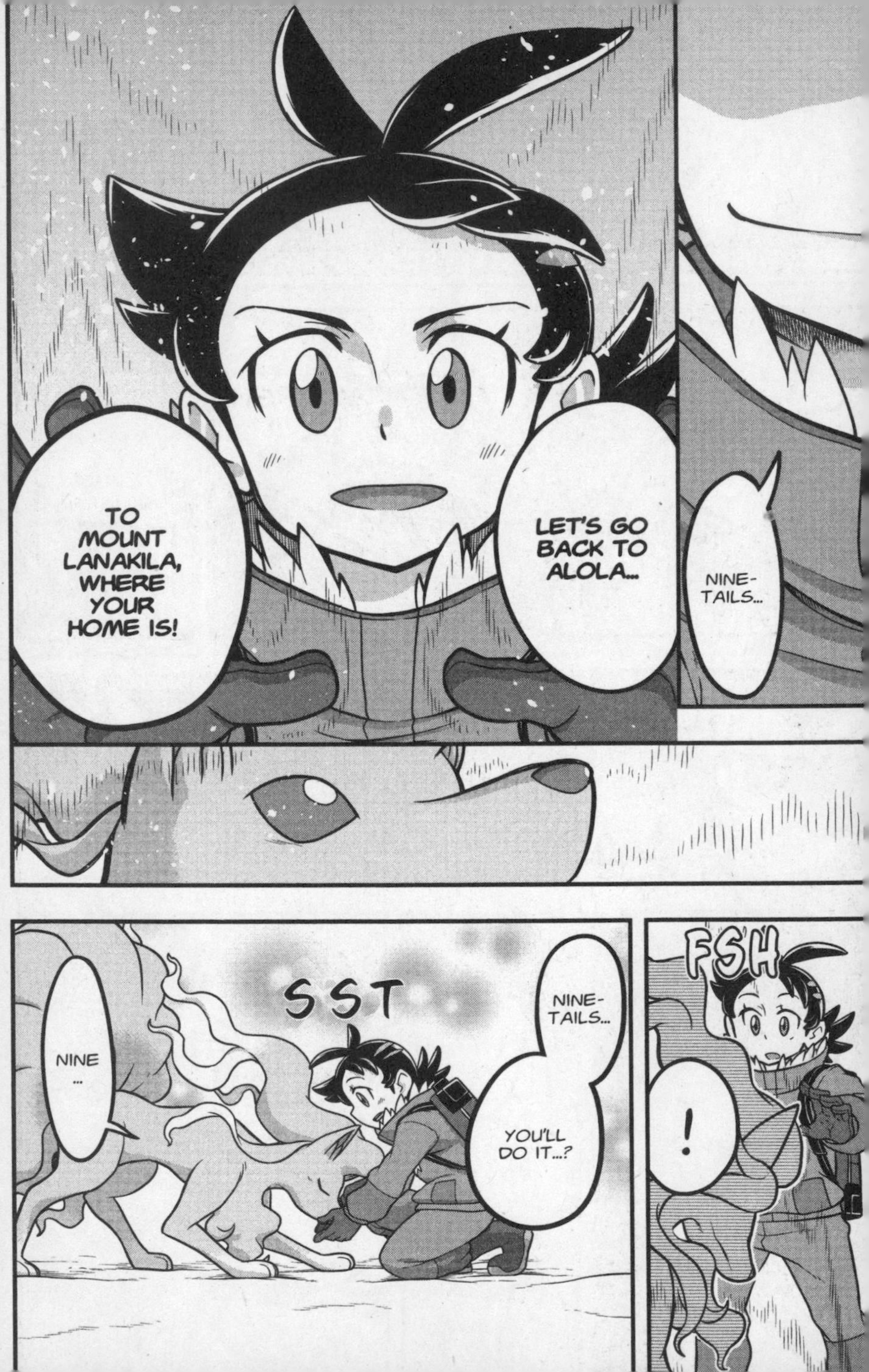
NINE-TAILS...
LET'S GO BACK TO ALOLA...
TO MOUNT LANAKILA, WHERE YOUR HOME IS!
FSH
!
NINE-TAILS...
YOU'LL DO IT...?
SST
NINE ...

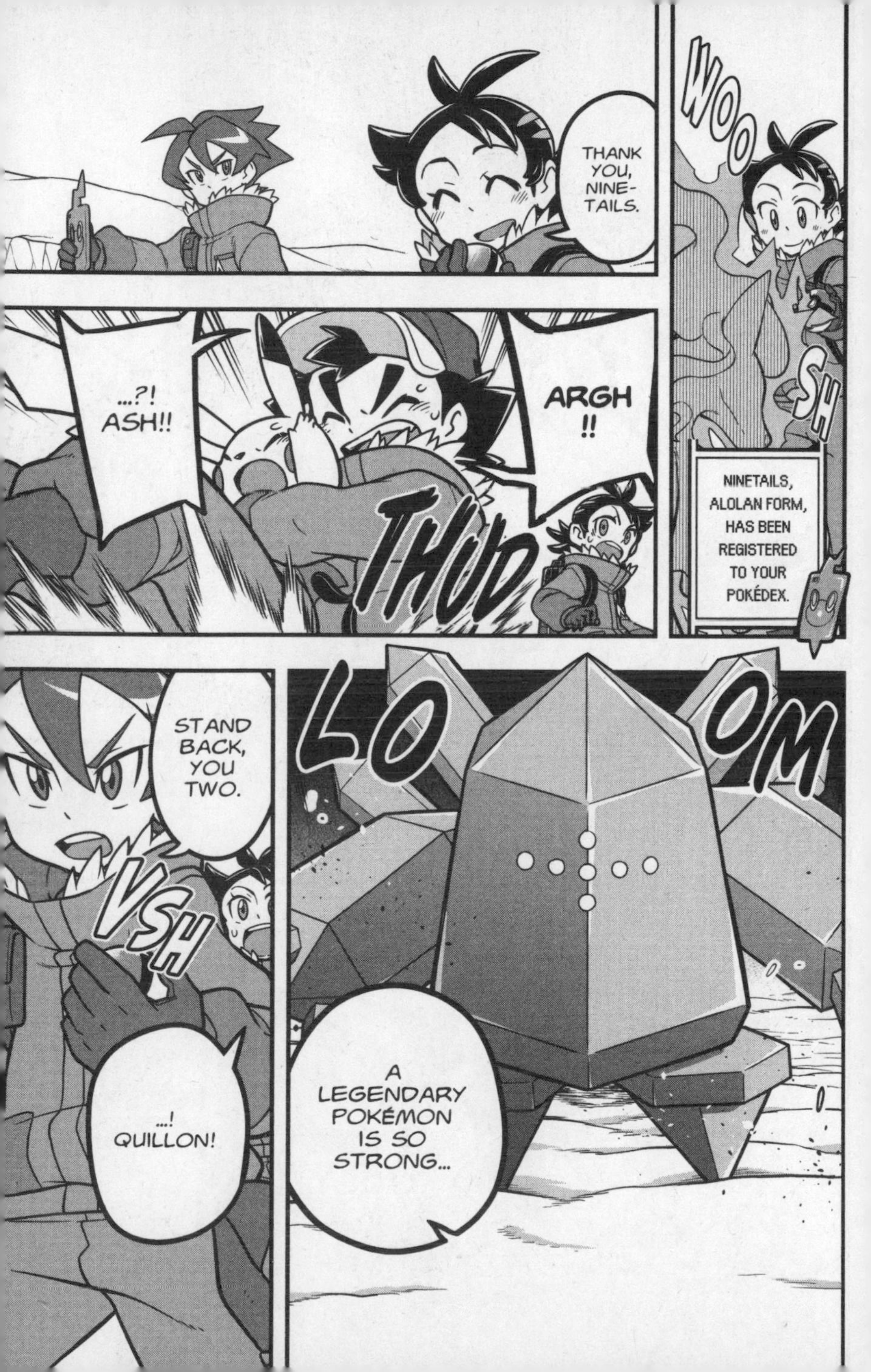
WOO
SH
NINETAILS, ALOLAN FORM, HAS BEEN REGISTERED TO YOUR POKÉDEX.
THANK YOU, NINE-TAILS.
ARGH !!
...?! ASH!!
THUD
LO
OM
A LEGENDARY POKÉMON IS SO STRONG...
STAND BACK, YOU TWO.
VSH
...! QUILLON!

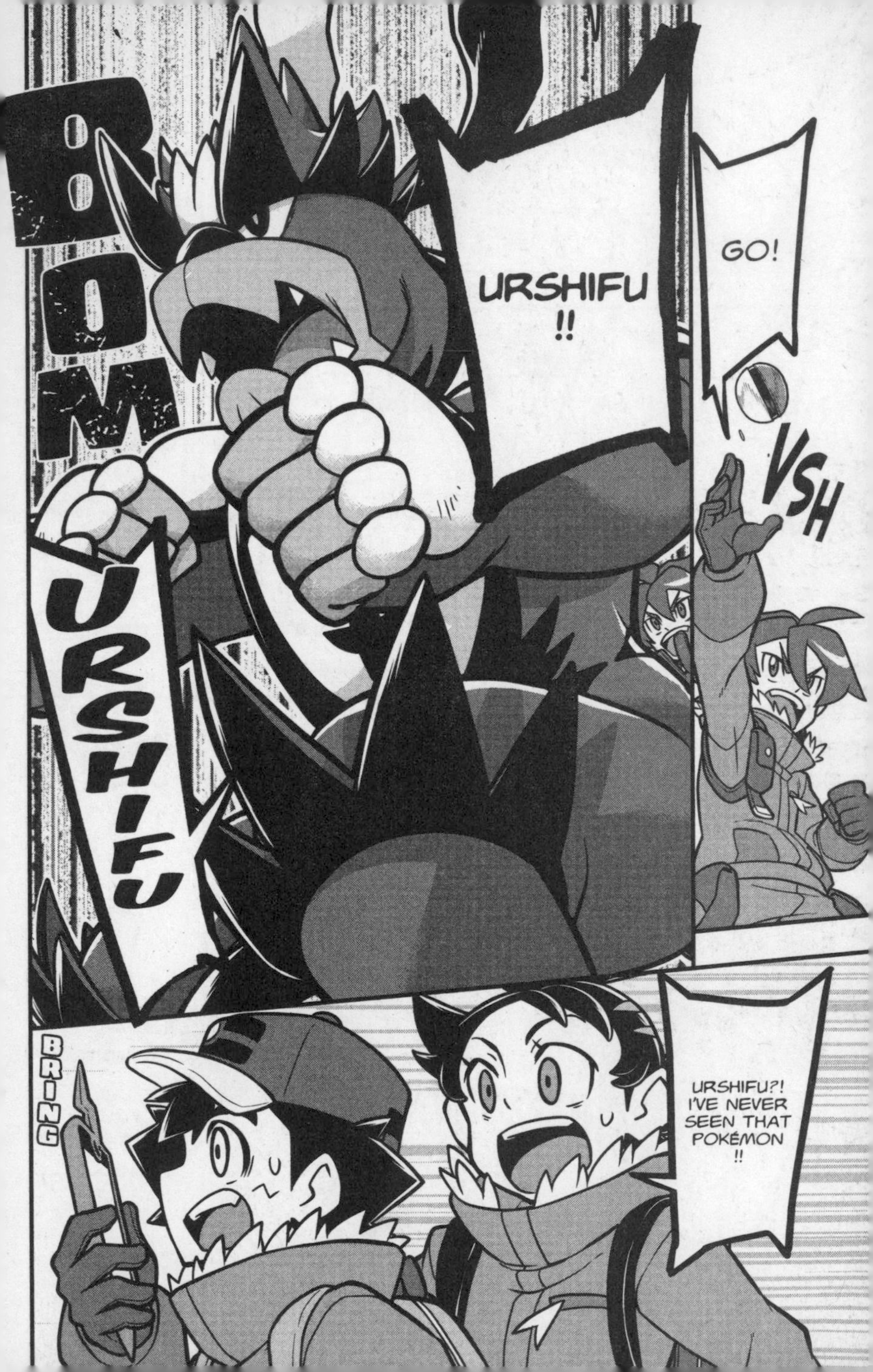
GO!
VSH
URSHIFU!!
BOOM
URSHIFU
URSHIFU?! I'VE NEVER SEEN THAT POKÉMON!!
BRING

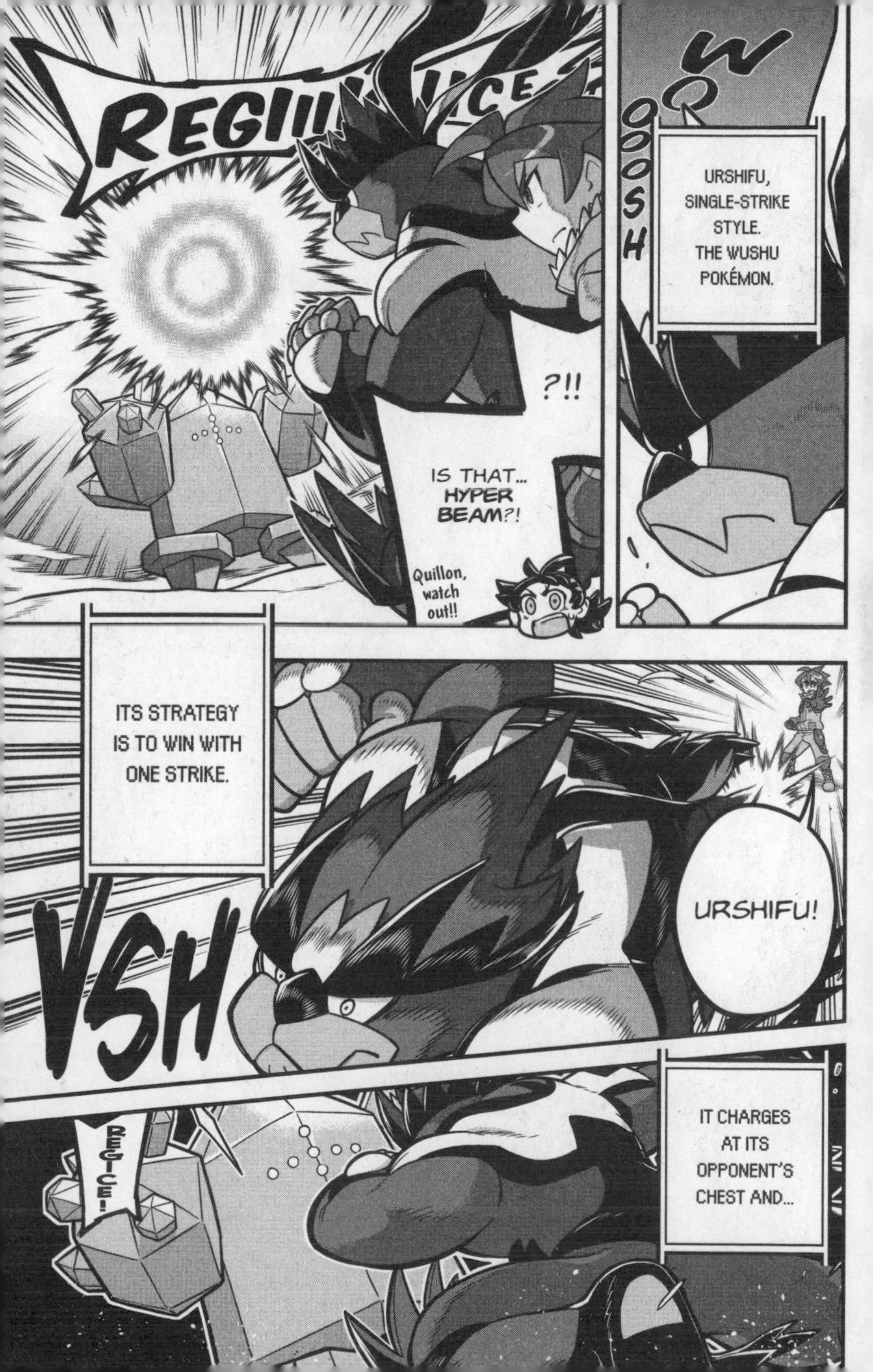
WOOOOOSH
URSHIFU, SINGLE-STRIKE STYLE. THE WUSHU POKÉMON.
REGIII ICE
?!!
IS THAT... HYPER BEAM?!
Quillon, watch out!!
URSHIFU!
ITS STRATEGY IS TO WIN WITH ONE STRIKE.
VSH
IT CHARGES AT ITS OPPONENT'S CHEST AND...
REGICE!

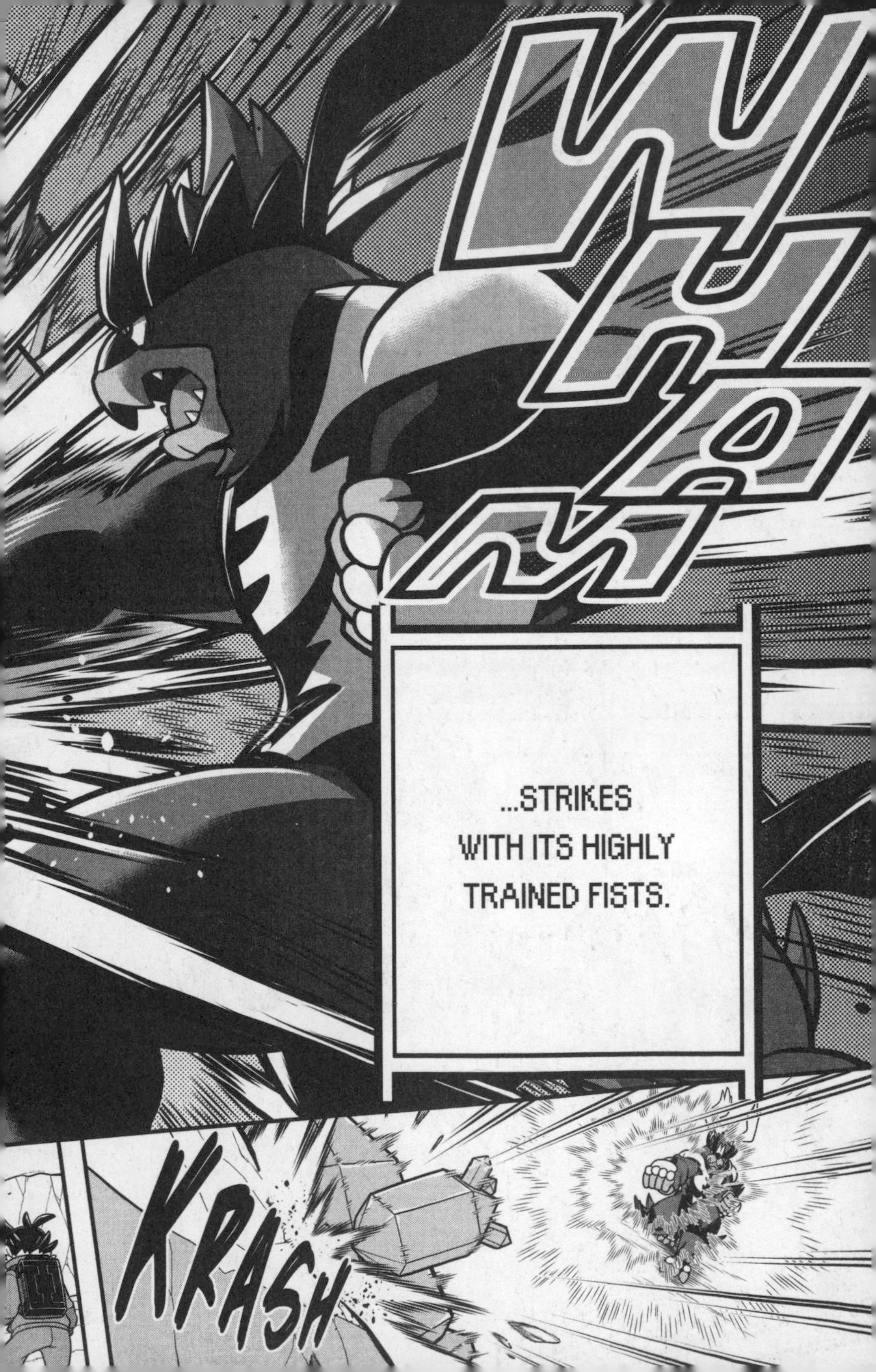
...STRIKES
WITH ITS HIGHLY
TRAINED FISTS.
KRASH

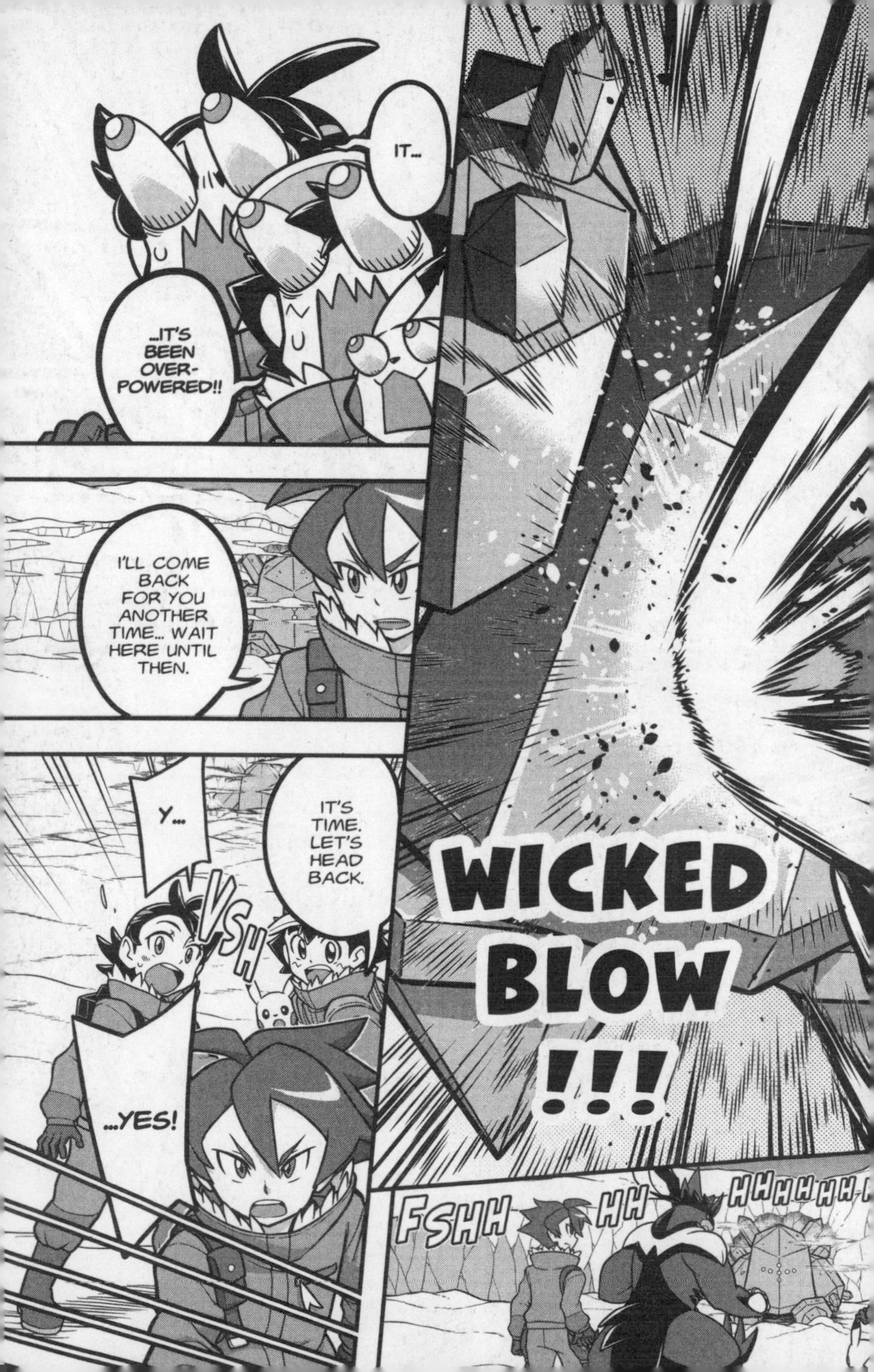
WICKED BLOW!!!
FSHH
HH
HHHHHHH
IT...
...IT'S BEEN OVER-POWERED!!
I'LL COME BACK FOR YOU ANOTHER TIME... WAIT HERE UNTIL THEN.
IT'S TIME. LET'S HEAD BACK.
Y...
VSH
...YES!

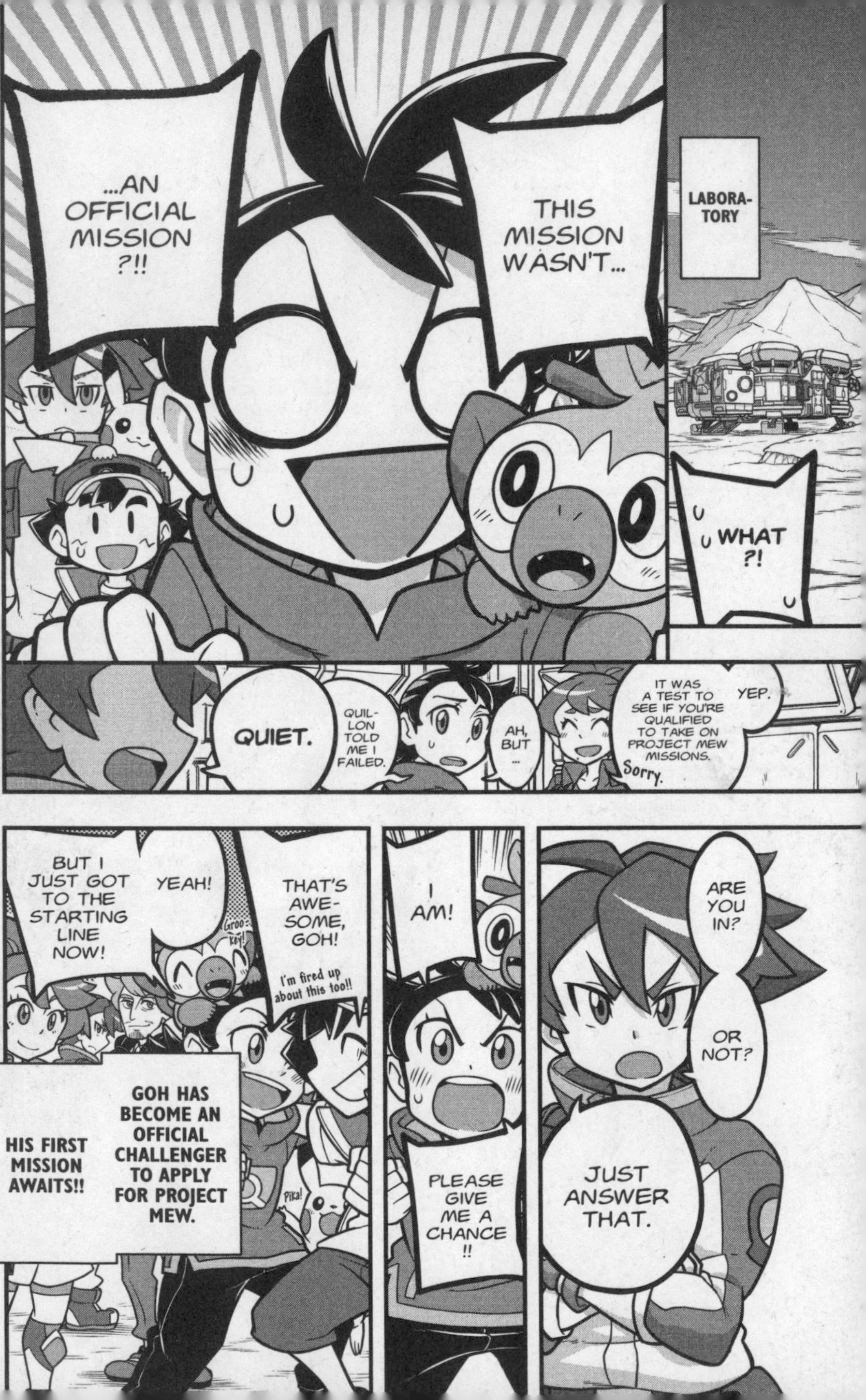
LABORA-TORY
WHAT?!
THIS MISSION WASN'T...
...AN OFFICIAL MISSION?!!
YEP.
IT WAS A TEST TO SEE IF YOU'RE QUALIFIED TO TAKE ON PROJECT MEW MISSIONS.
Sorry.
AH, BUT ...
QUIL-LON TOLD ME I FAILED.
QUIET.
ARE YOU IN?
OR NOT?
JUST ANSWER THAT.
I AM!
PLEASE GIVE ME A CHANCE!!
THAT'S AWE-SOME, GOH!
I'm fired up about this too!!
YEAH!
Groo-key!
BUT I JUST GOT TO THE STARTING LINE NOW!
Pika!
GOH HAS BECOME AN OFFICIAL CHALLENGER TO APPLY FOR PROJECT MEW.
HIS FIRST MISSION AWAITS!!

Chapter 22
Detective Drizzile!

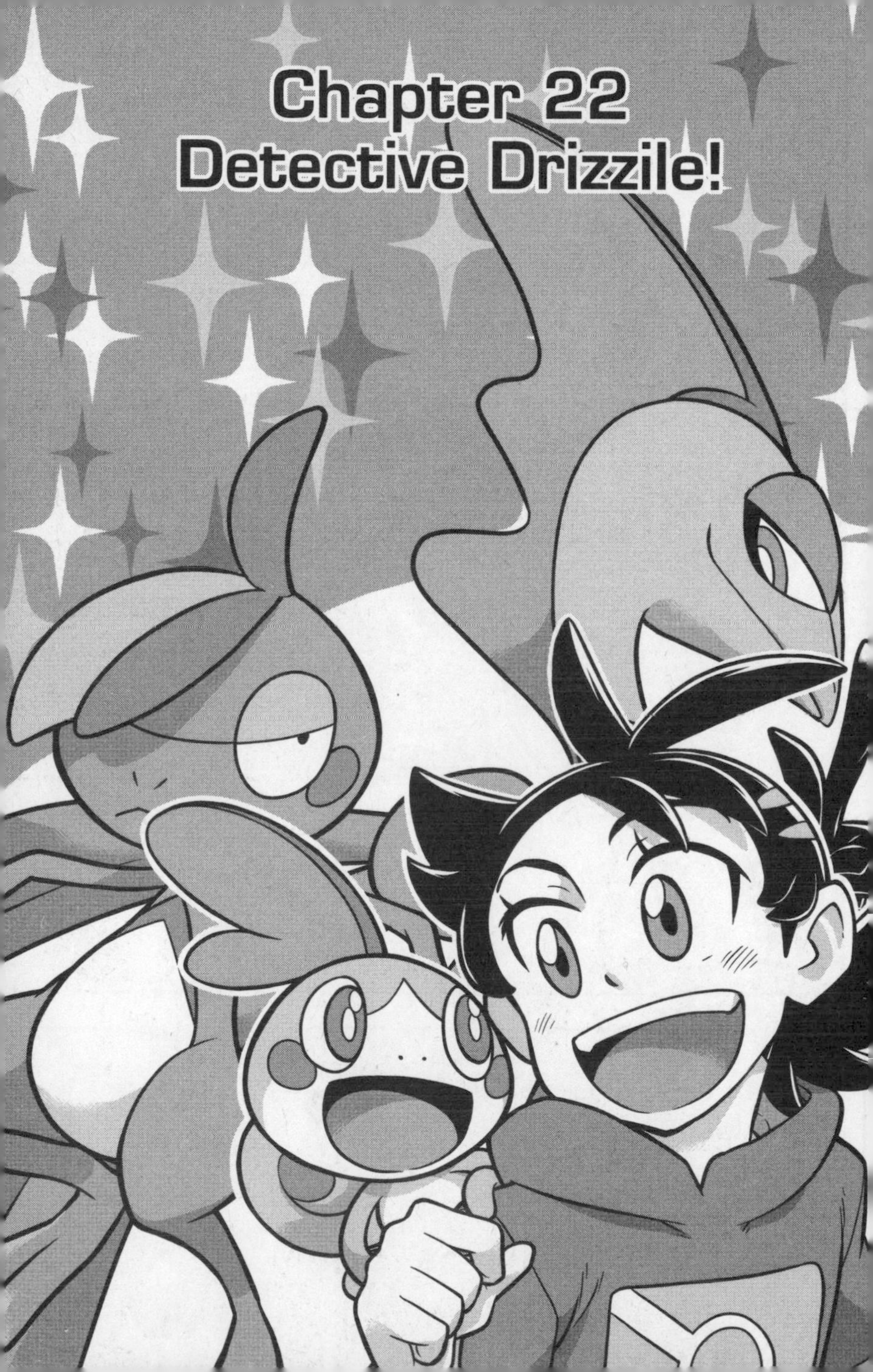

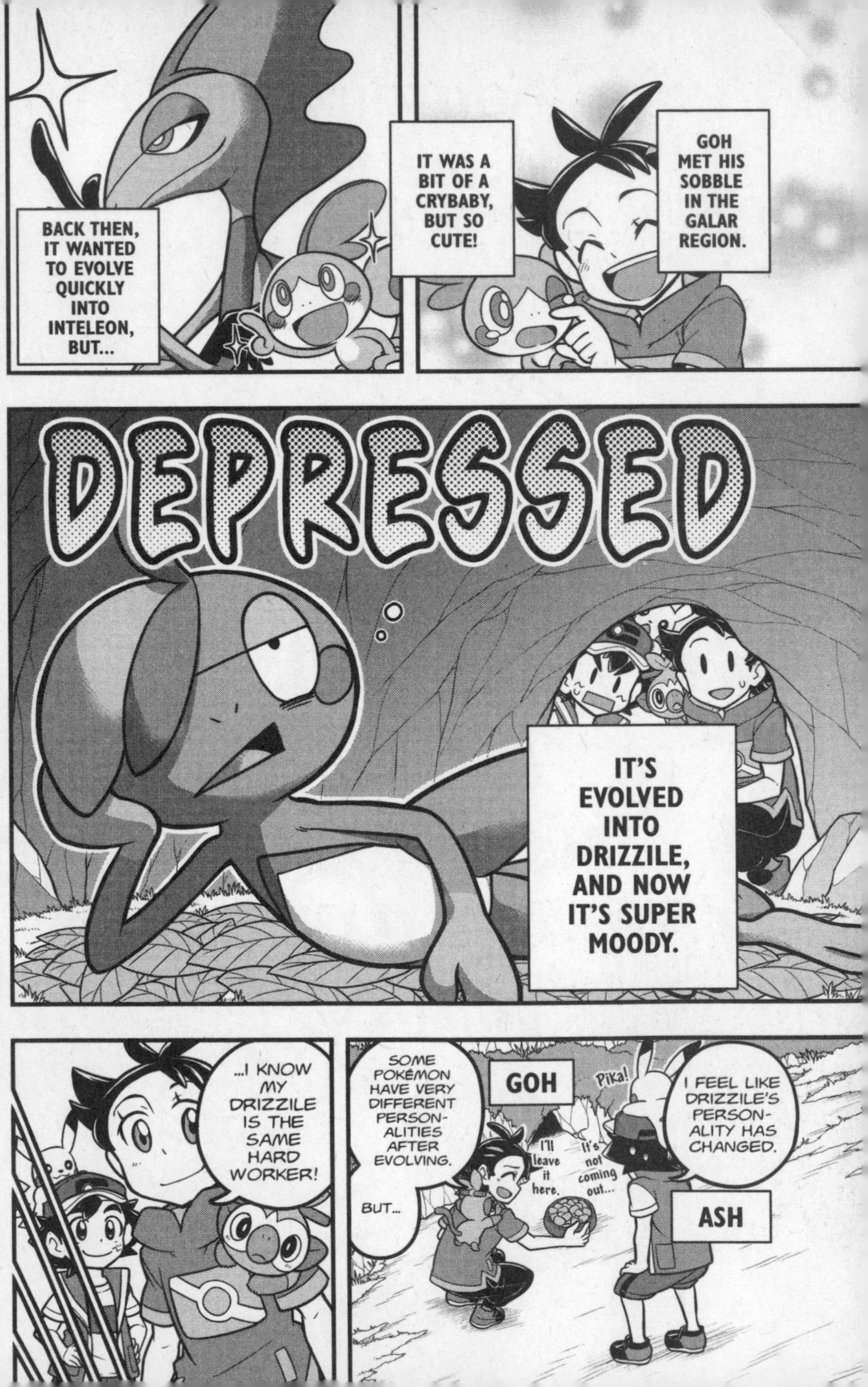
GOH MET HIS SOBBLE IN THE GALAR REGION.
IT WAS A BIT OF A CRYBABY, BUT SO CUTE!
BACK THEN, IT WANTED TO EVOLVE QUICKLY INTO INTELEON, BUT...
DEPRESSED
IT'S EVOLVED INTO DRIZZILE, AND NOW IT'S SUPER MOODY.
I FEEL LIKE DRIZZILE'S PERSON-ALITY HAS CHANGED.
Pika!
ASH
GOH
It's not coming out...
I'll leave it here.
SOME POKÉMON HAVE VERY DIFFERENT PERSON-ALITIES AFTER EVOLVING.
BUT...
...I KNOW MY DRIZZILE IS THE SAME HARD WORKER!

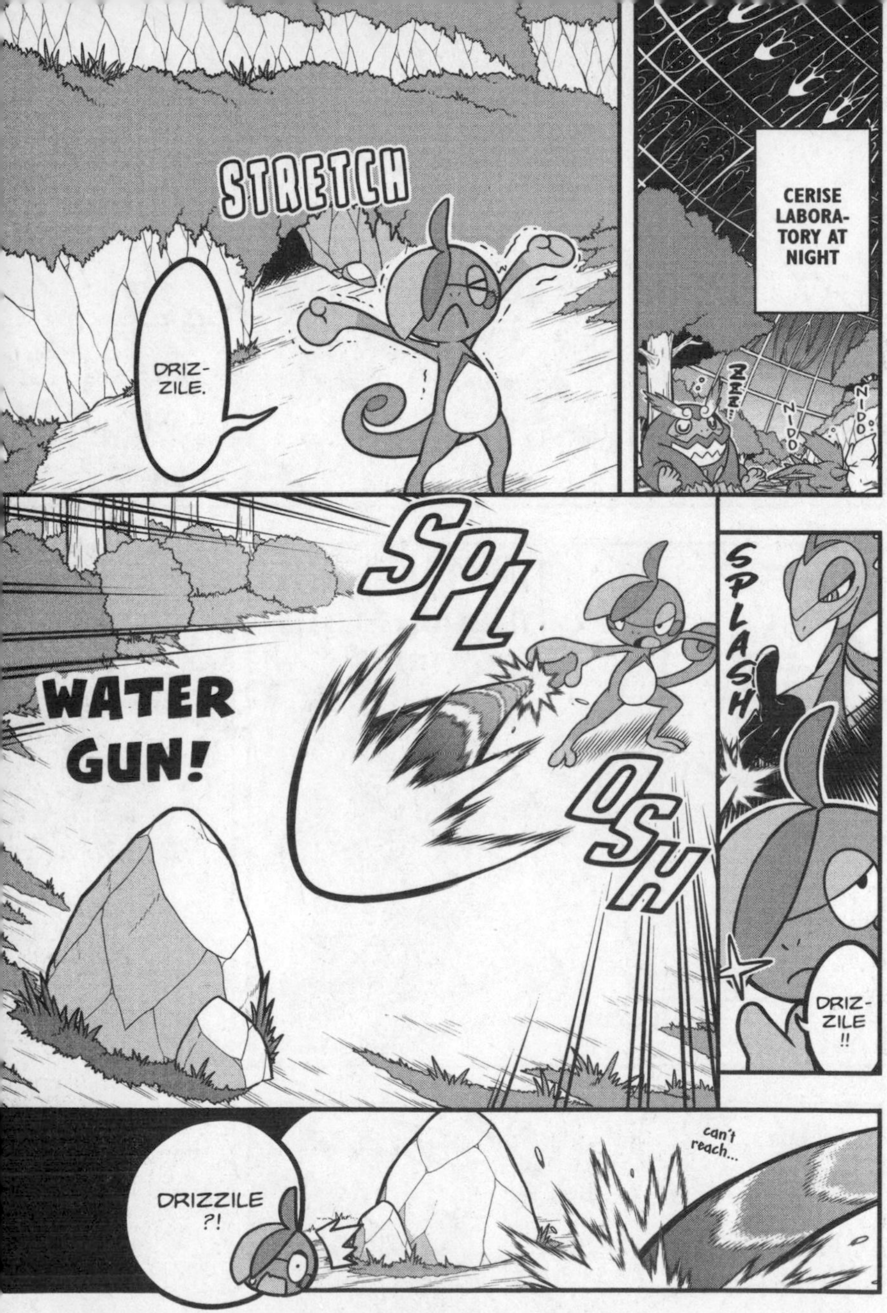
CERISE LABORA-TORY AT NIGHT
ZZZ...
NIDO
NIDO
STRETCH
DRIZ-ZILE.
SPLASH
DRIZ-ZILE!!
SPLOSH
WATER GUN!
can't reach...
DRIZZILE?!

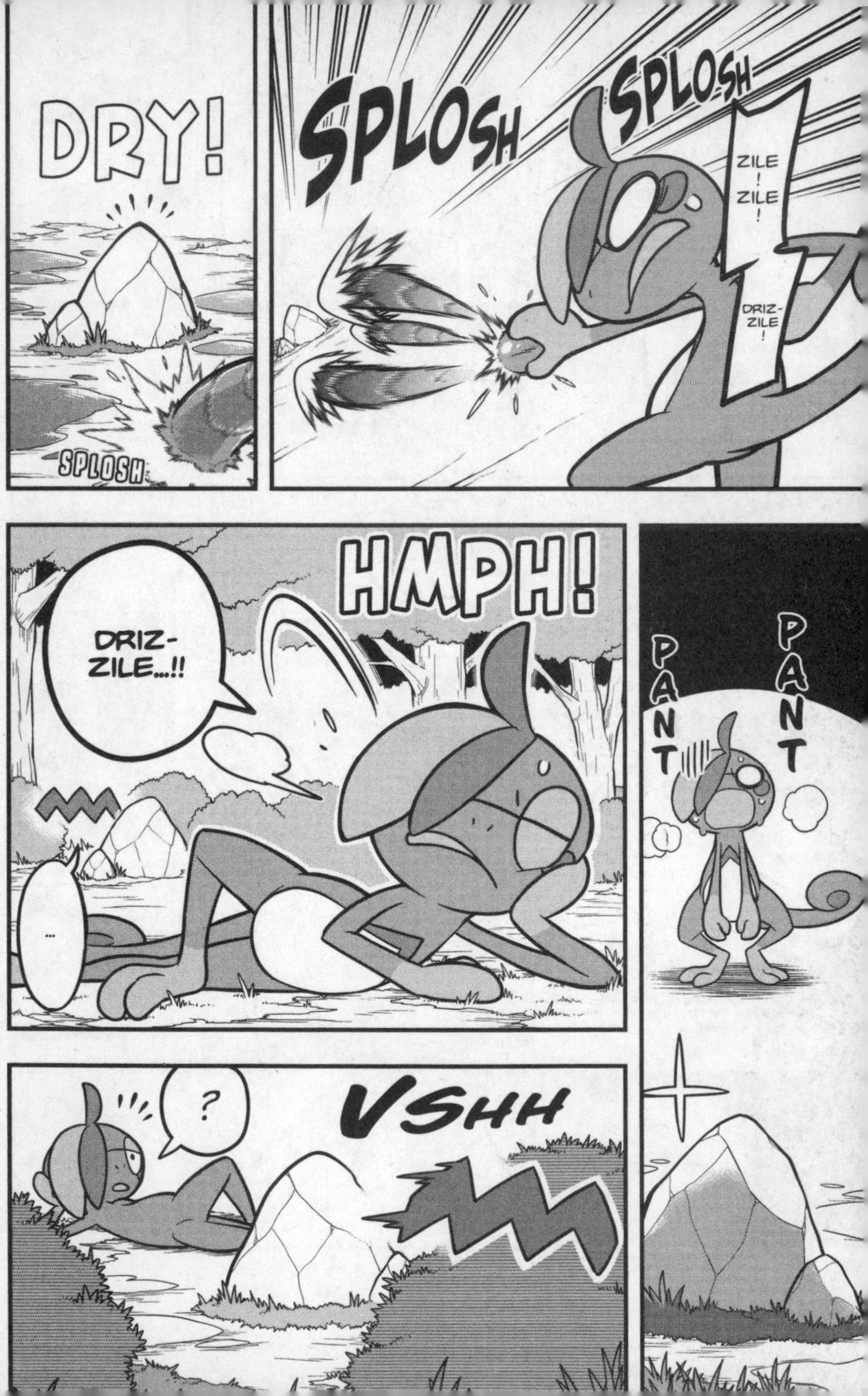
SPLOSH
SPLOSH
ZILE! ZILE!
DRIZ-ZILE!
DRY!
SPLOSH
PANT
PANT
HMPH!
DRIZ-ZILE...!!
...
?
VSHH

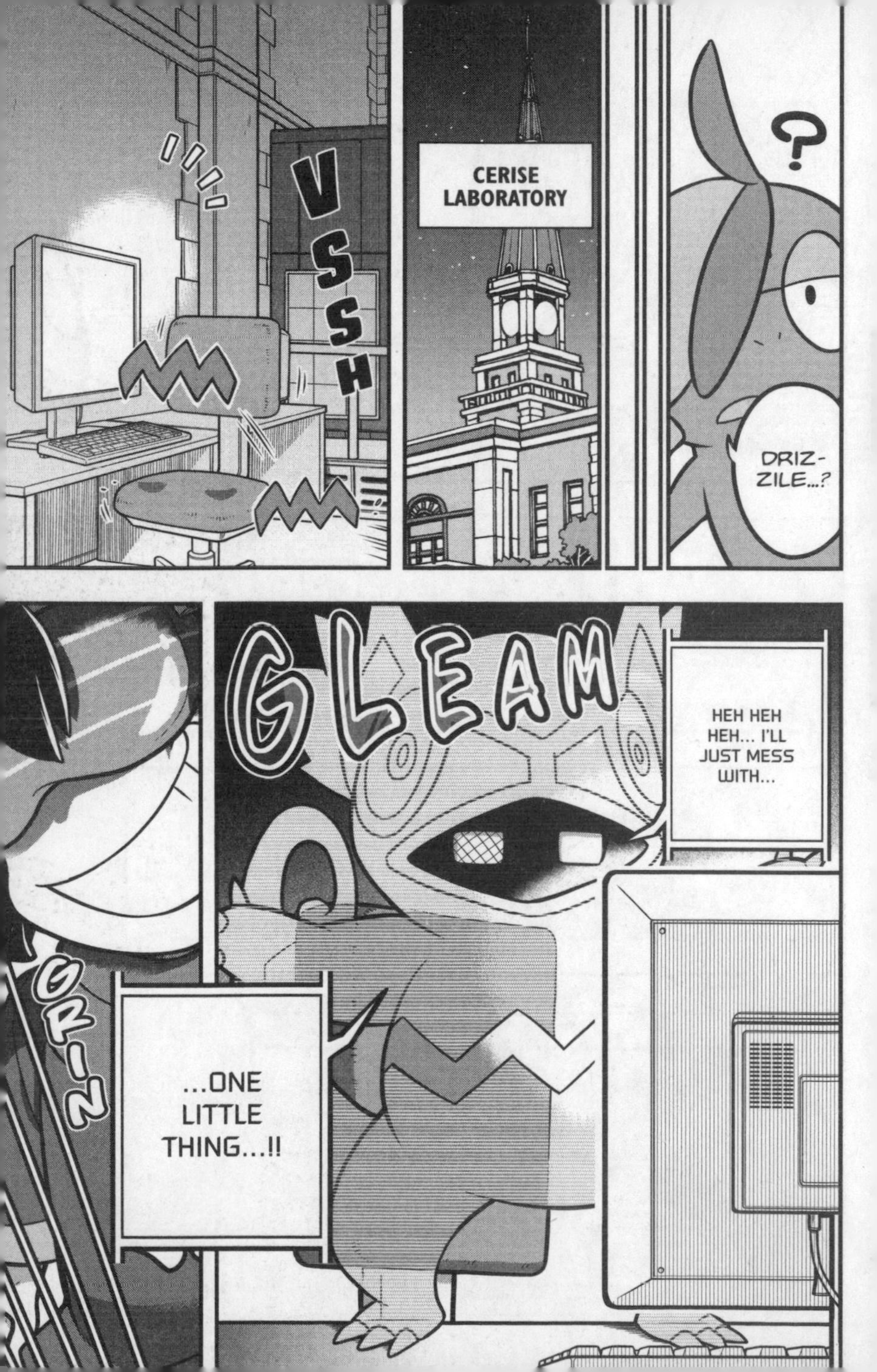
?
DRIZ-ZILE...?
CERISE LABORATORY
VSSH
GLEAM
HEH HEH HEH... I'LL JUST MESS WITH...
GRIN
...ONE LITTLE THING...!!

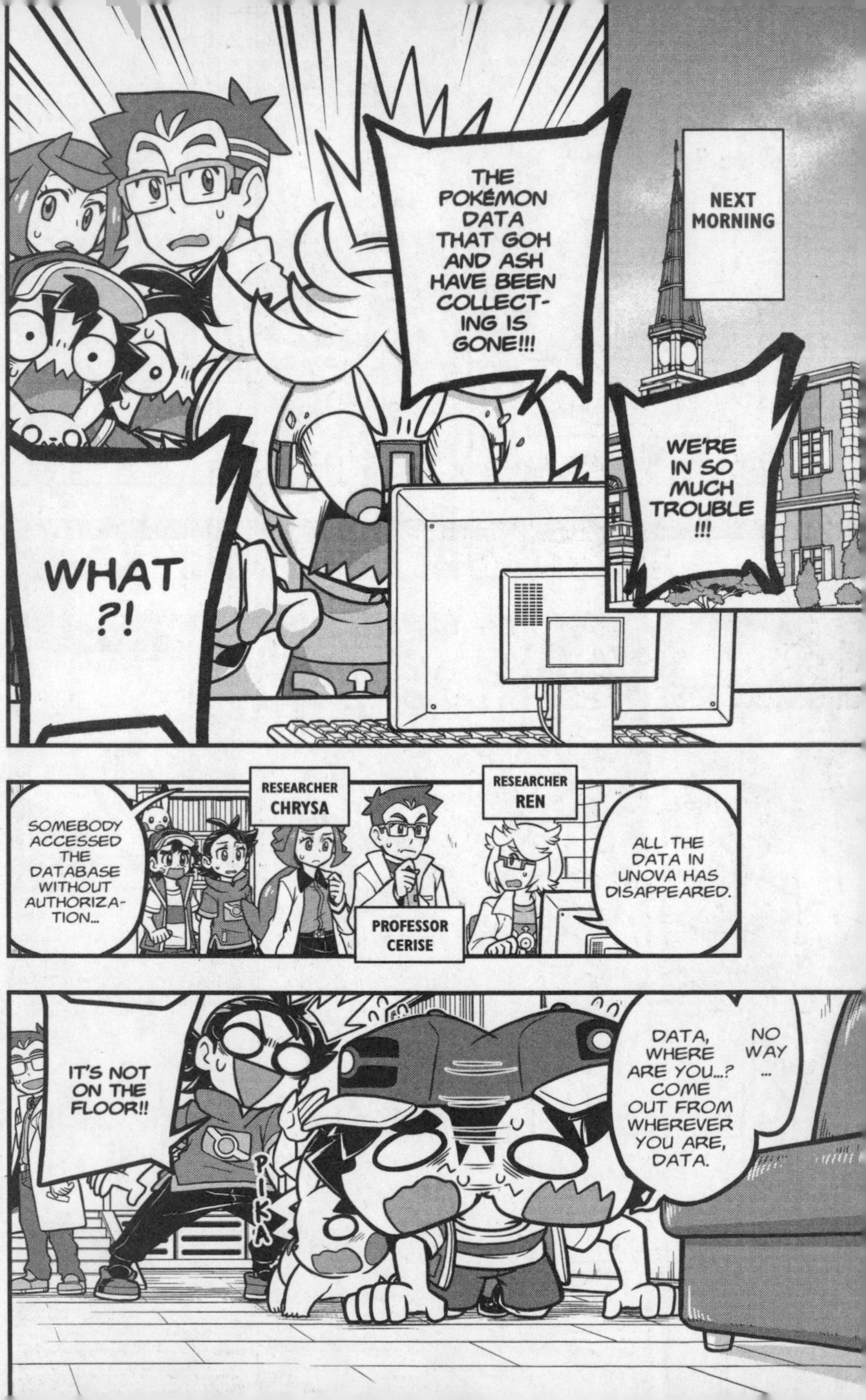
NEXT MORNING
WE'RE IN SO MUCH TROUBLE!!!
THE POKÉMON DATA THAT GOH AND ASH HAVE BEEN COLLECTING IS GONE!!!
WHAT?!
ALL THE DATA IN UNOVA HAS DISAPPEARED.
RESEARCHER REN
PROFESSOR CERISE
RESEARCHER CHRYSA
SOMEBODY ACCESSED THE DATABASE WITHOUT AUTHORIZATION...
NO WAY...
DATA, WHERE ARE YOU...? COME OUT FROM WHEREVER YOU ARE, DATA.
PIKA
IT'S NOT ON THE FLOOR!!

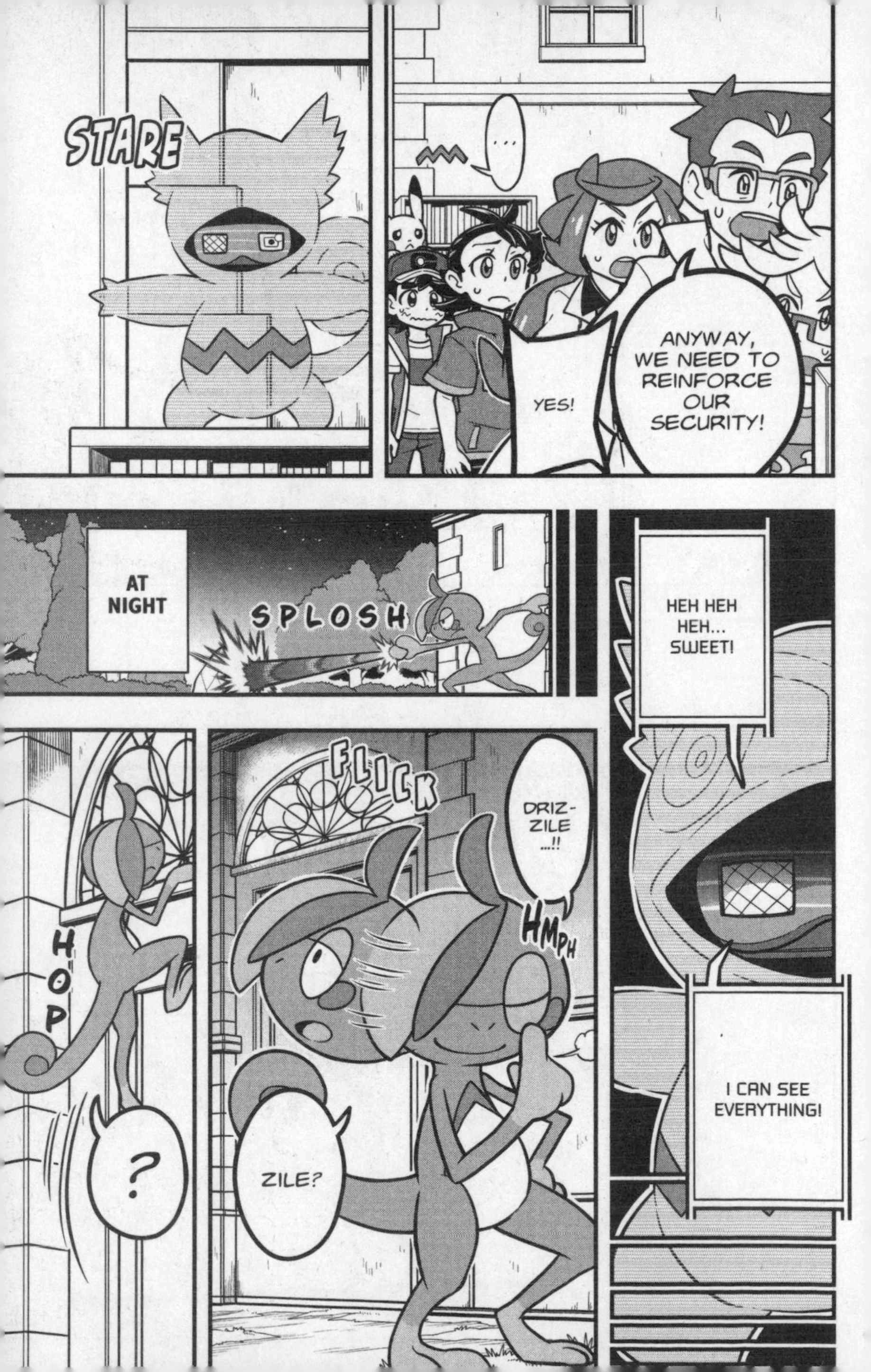
...
ANYWAY, WE NEED TO REINFORCE OUR SECURITY!
YES!
STARE
HEH HEH HEH... SWEET!
I CAN SEE EVERYTHING!
AT NIGHT
SPLOSH
FLICK
DRIZ-ZILE ...!!
HMPH
ZILE?
HOP
?

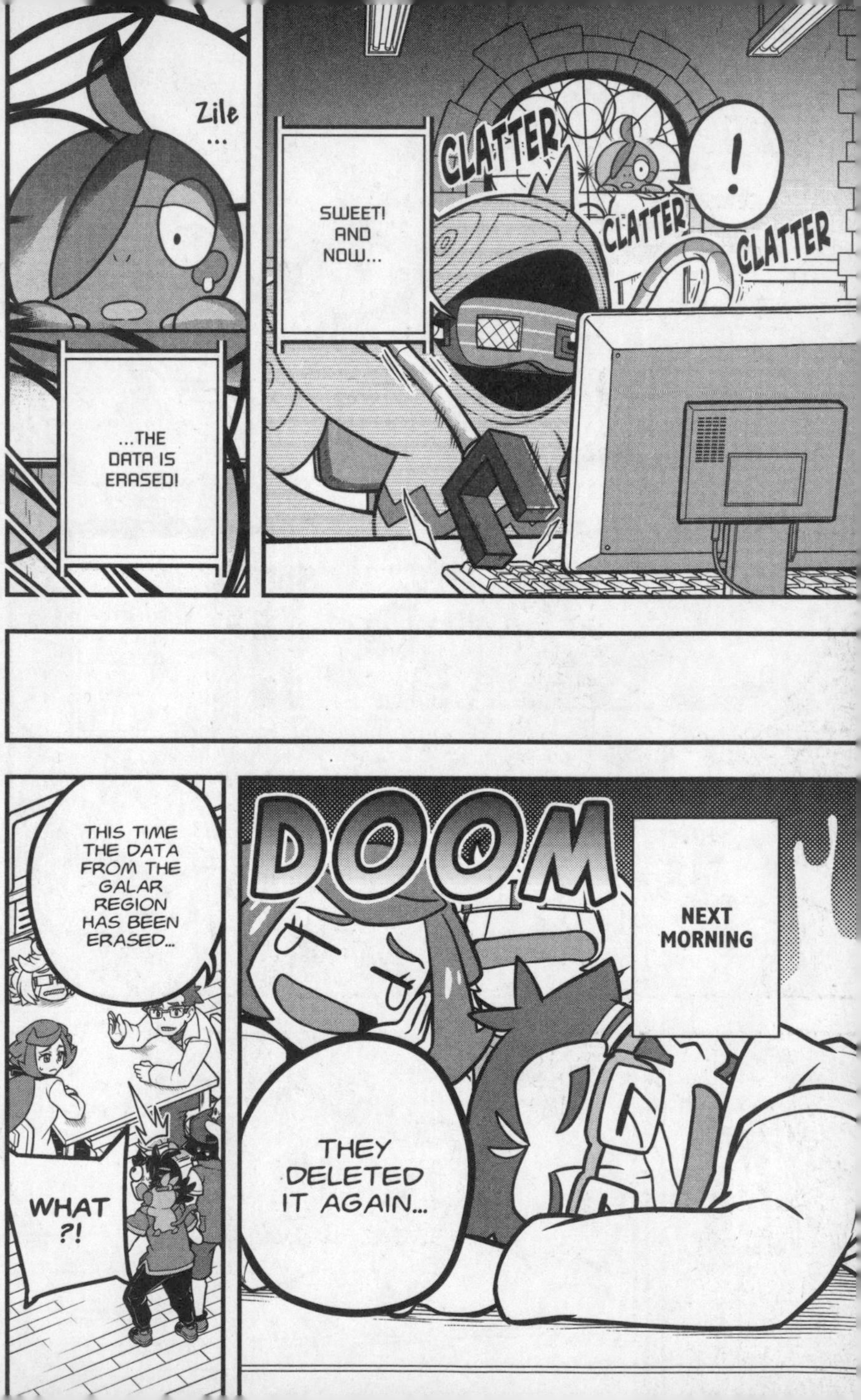
!
CLATTER
CLATTER
CLATTER
SWEET! AND NOW...
Zile ...
...THE DATA IS ERASED!
NEXT MORNING
DOOM
THEY DELETED IT AGAIN...
THIS TIME THE DATA FROM THE GALAR REGION HAS BEEN ERASED...
WHAT ?!

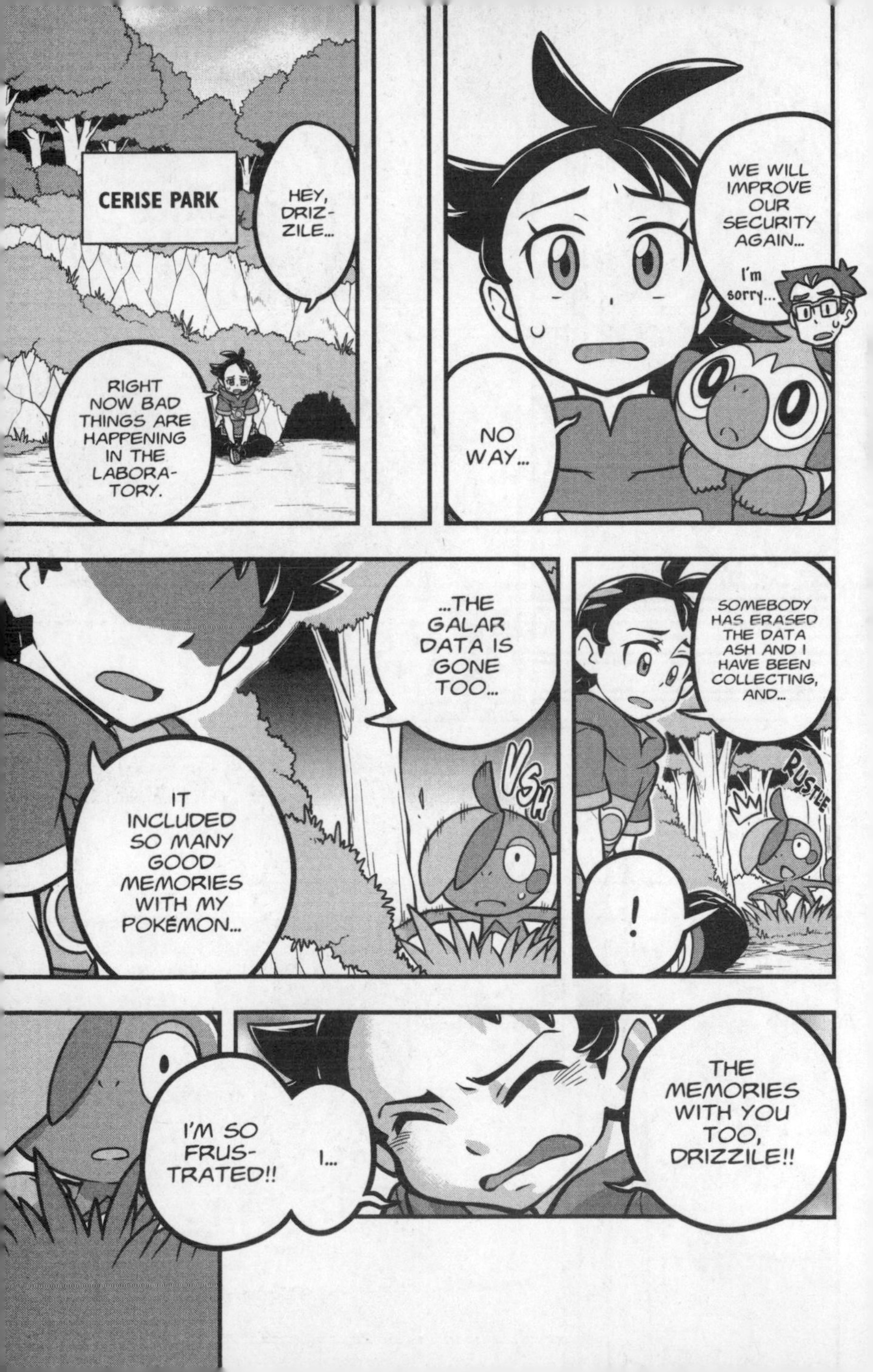
WE WILL IMPROVE OUR SECURITY AGAIN...
I'm sorry...
NO WAY...
CERISE PARK
HEY, DRIZ-ZILE...
RIGHT NOW BAD THINGS ARE HAPPENING IN THE LABORA-TORY.
SOMEBODY HAS ERASED THE DATA ASH AND I HAVE BEEN COLLECTING, AND...
RUSTLE
!
...THE GALAR DATA IS GONE TOO...
VSH
IT INCLUDED SO MANY GOOD MEMORIES WITH MY POKÉMON...
THE MEMORIES WITH YOU TOO, DRIZZILE!!
I...
I'M SO FRUS-TRATED!!

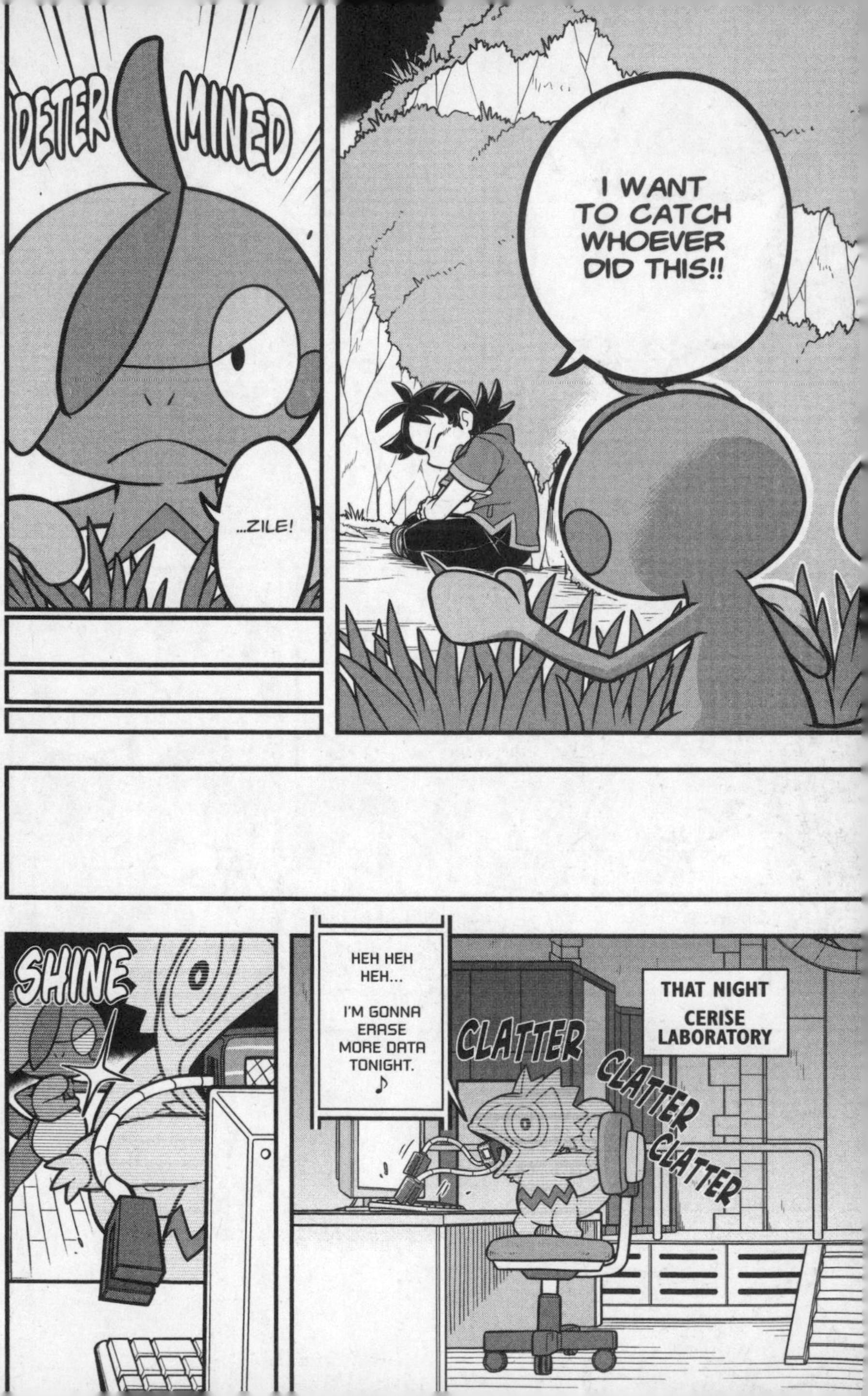
I WANT TO CATCH WHOEVER DID THIS!!
DETER MINED
...ZILE!
THAT NIGHT
CERISE LABORATORY
HEH HEH HEH...
I'M GONNA ERASE MORE DATA TONIGHT. ♪
CLATTER
CLATTER
CLATTER
SHINE

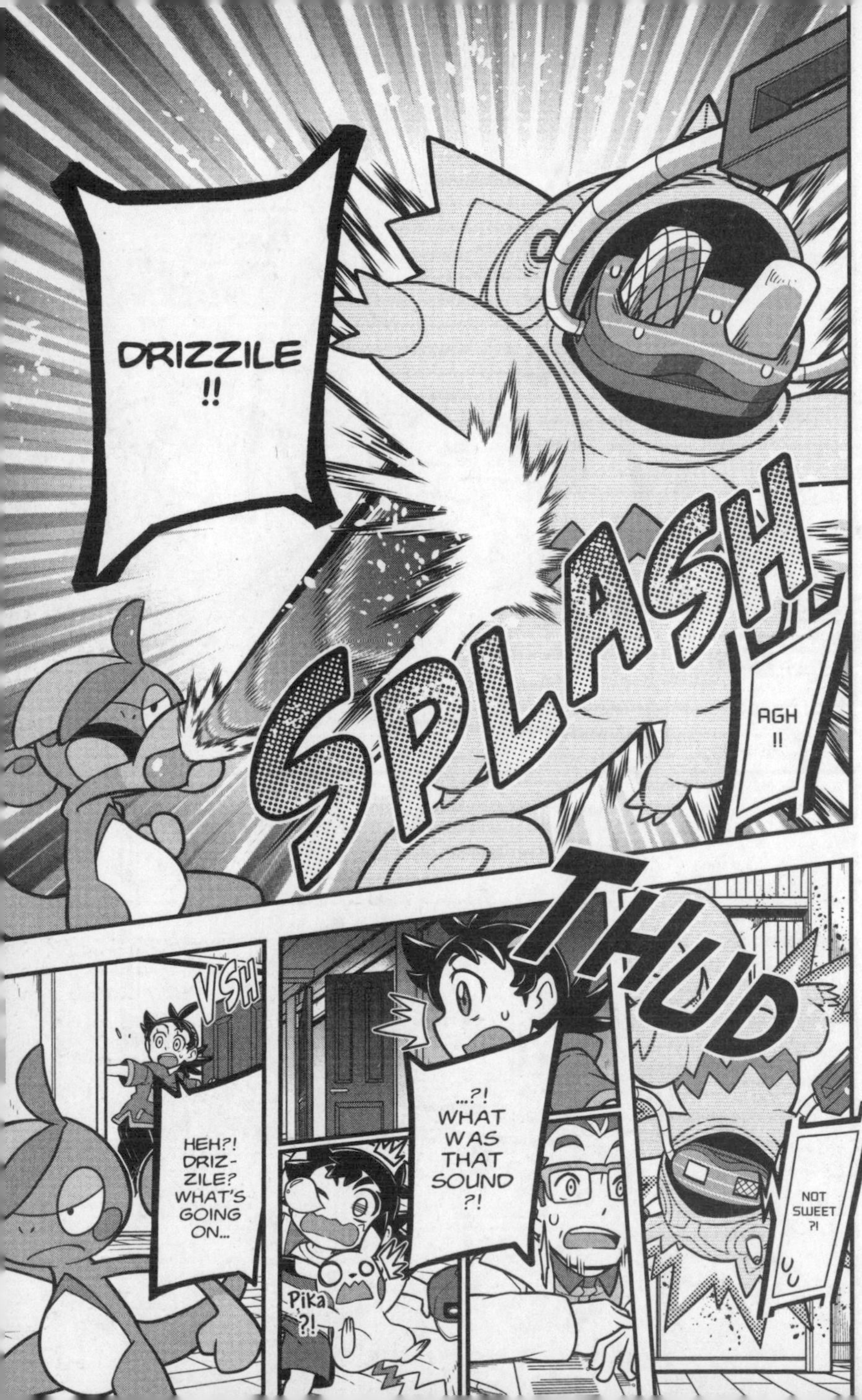
DRIZZILE !!
SPLASH
AGH !!
THUD
NOT SWEET ?!
...?! WHAT WAS THAT SOUND ?!
Pika ?!
VSH
HEH?! DRIZ-ZILE? WHAT'S GOING ON...

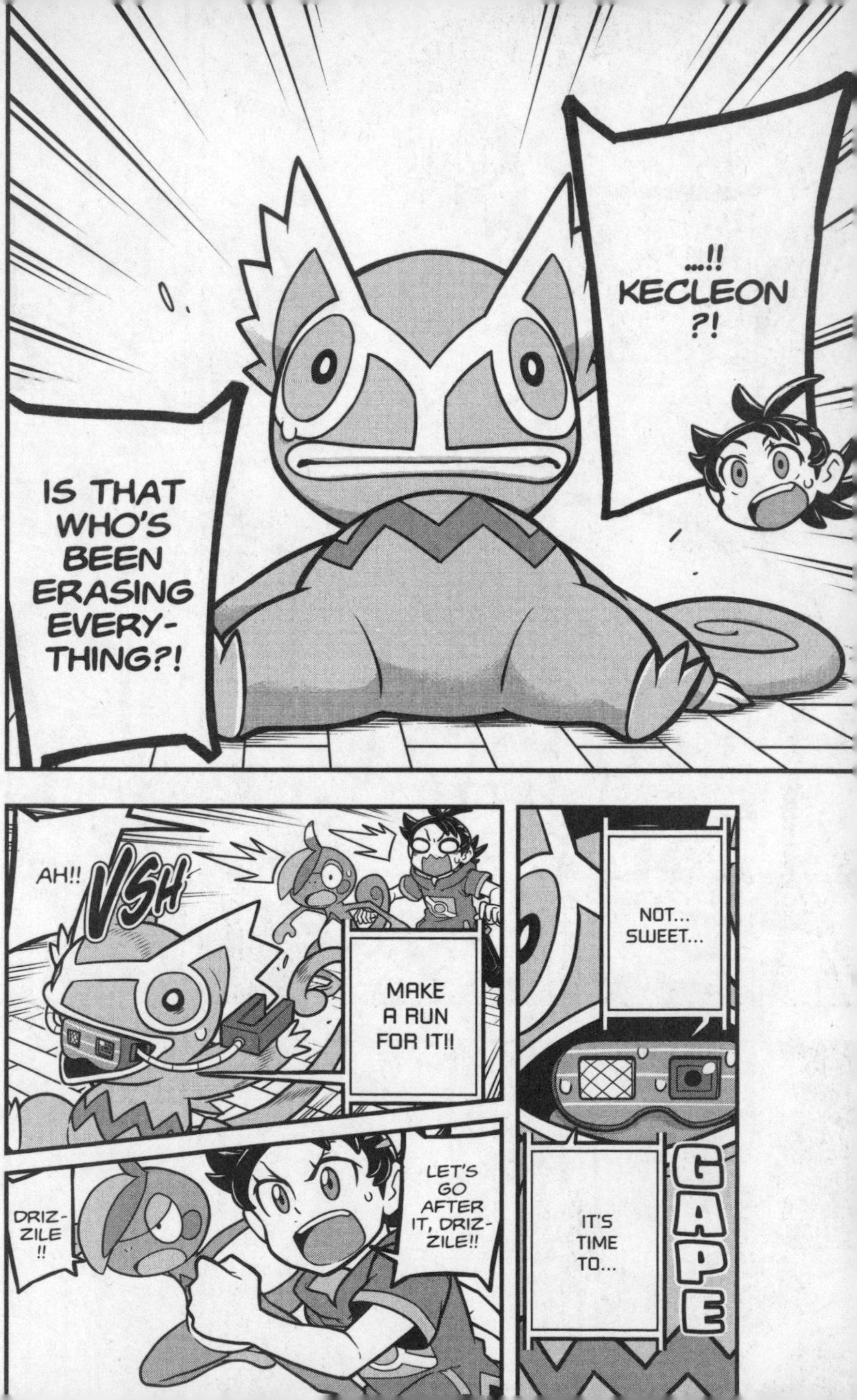
...!! KECLEON ?!
IS THAT WHO'S BEEN ERASING EVERY-THING?!
NOT... SWEET...
AH!!
VSH
MAKE A RUN FOR IT!!
IT'S TIME TO...
GAPE
LET'S GO AFTER IT, DRIZ-ZILE!!
DRIZ-ZILE !!

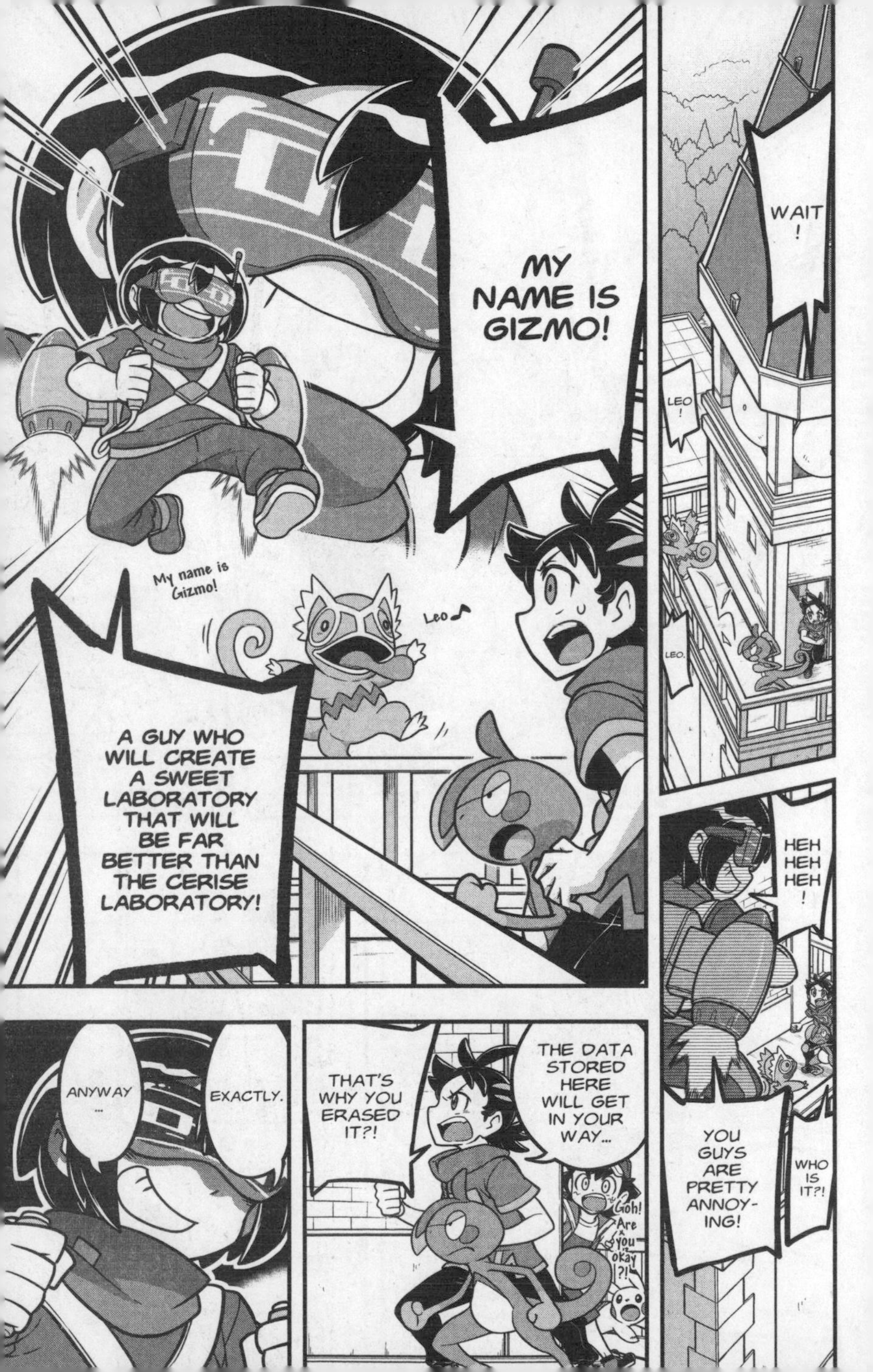
WAIT!
LEO!
LEO.
HEH HEH HEH!
WHO IS IT?!
YOU GUYS ARE PRETTY ANNOYING!
MY NAME IS GIZMO!
My name is Gizmo!
Leo♪
A GUY WHO WILL CREATE A SWEET LABORATORY THAT WILL BE FAR BETTER THAN THE CERISE LABORATORY!
THE DATA STORED HERE WILL GET IN YOUR WAY...
Goh! Are you okay?!
THAT'S WHY YOU ERASED IT?!
EXACTLY.
ANYWAY...

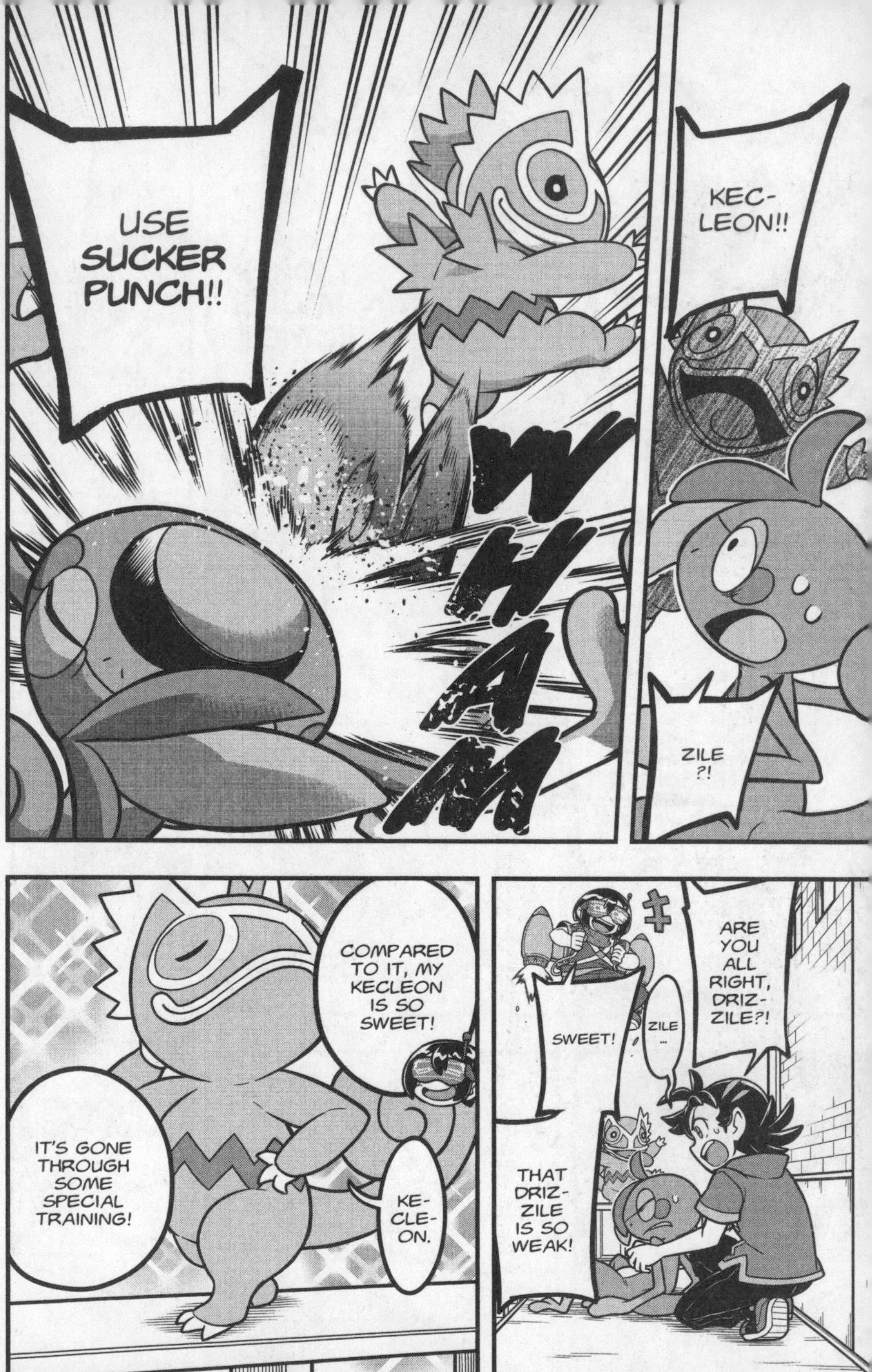
KEC-LEON!!
ZILE ?!
USE SUCKER PUNCH!!
WHAM
ARE YOU ALL RIGHT, DRIZ-ZILE?!
ZILE ...
SWEET!
THAT DRIZ-ZILE IS SO WEAK!
COMPARED TO IT, MY KECLEON IS SO SWEET!
KE-CLE-ON.
IT'S GONE THROUGH SOME SPECIAL TRAINING!

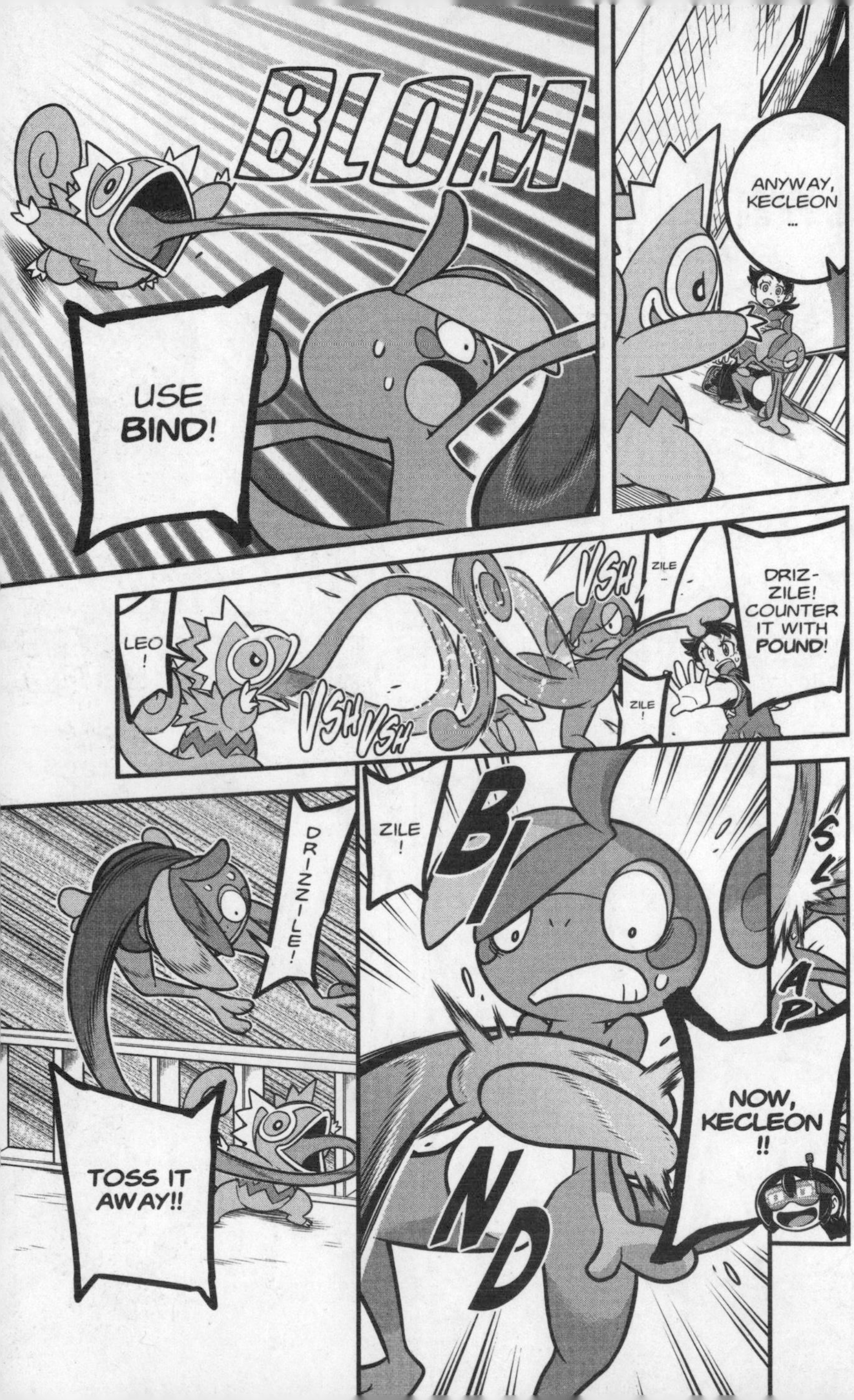
ANYWAY, KECLEON ...
BLOM
USE BIND!
DRIZ-ZILE! COUNTER IT WITH POUND!
ZILE ...
VSH
ZILE
LEO!
VSH VSH
SLAP
NOW, KECLEON!!
ZILE!
BIND
DRIZZILE!
TOSS IT AWAY!!

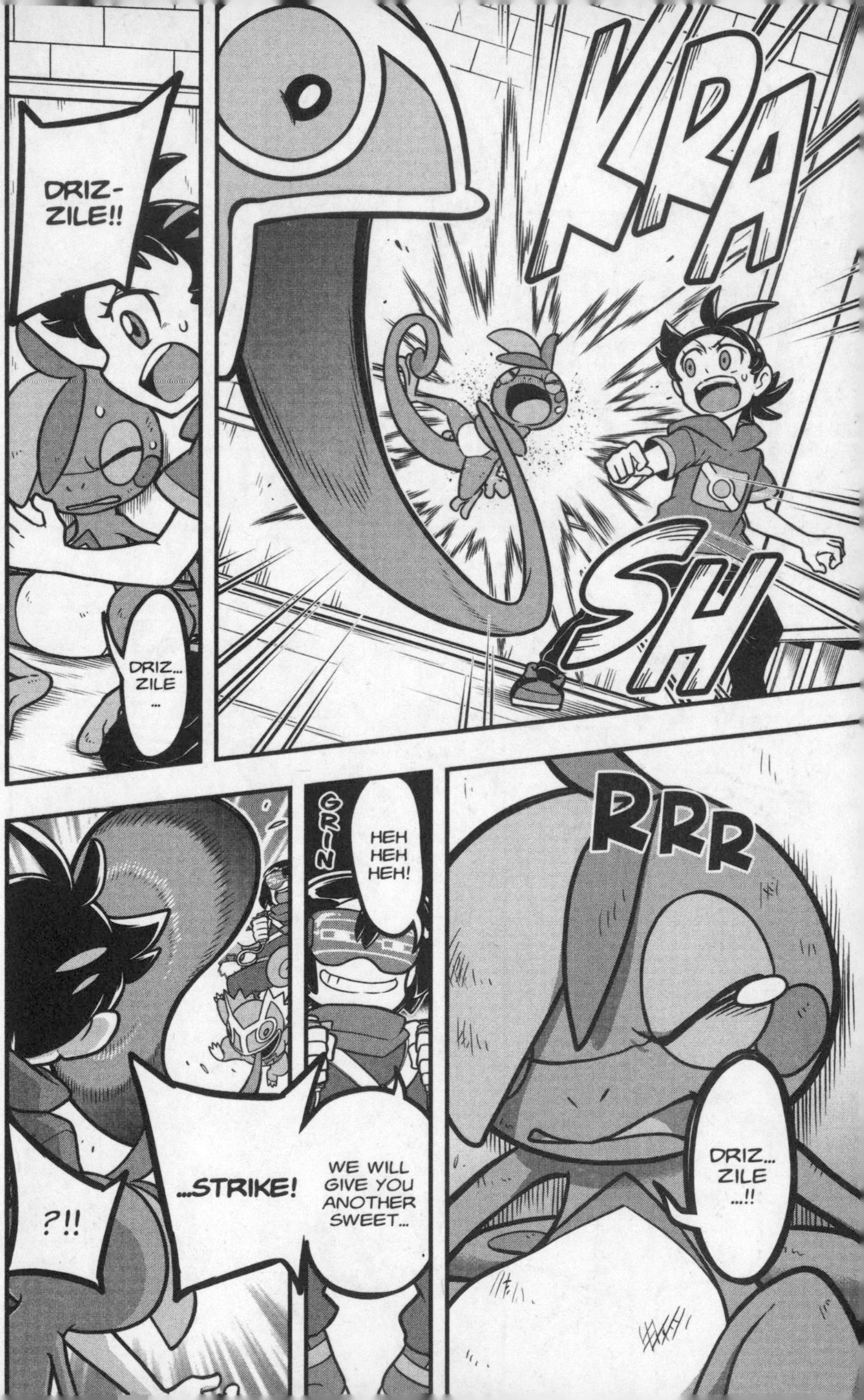
KRA
SH
DRIZ-ZILE!!
DRIZ... ZILE ...
RRR
DRIZ... ZILE ...!!
GRIN
HEH HEH HEH!
WE WILL GIVE YOU ANOTHER SWEET...
...STRIKE!
?!!

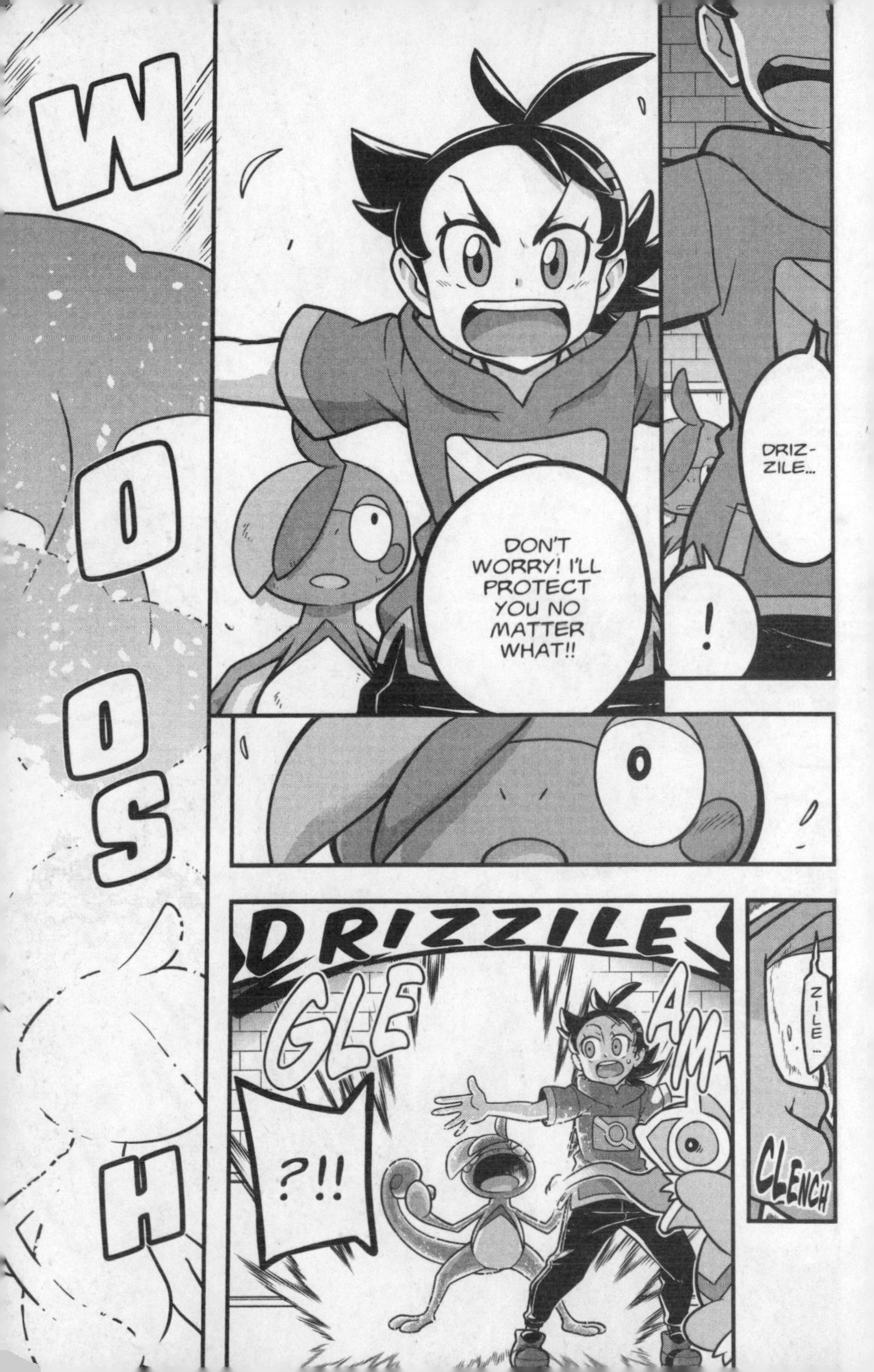
DRIZ-ZILE...
!
DON'T WORRY! I'LL PROTECT YOU NO MATTER WHAT!!
ZILE...
CLENCH
DRIZZILE
GLEAM
?!!
WOOSH

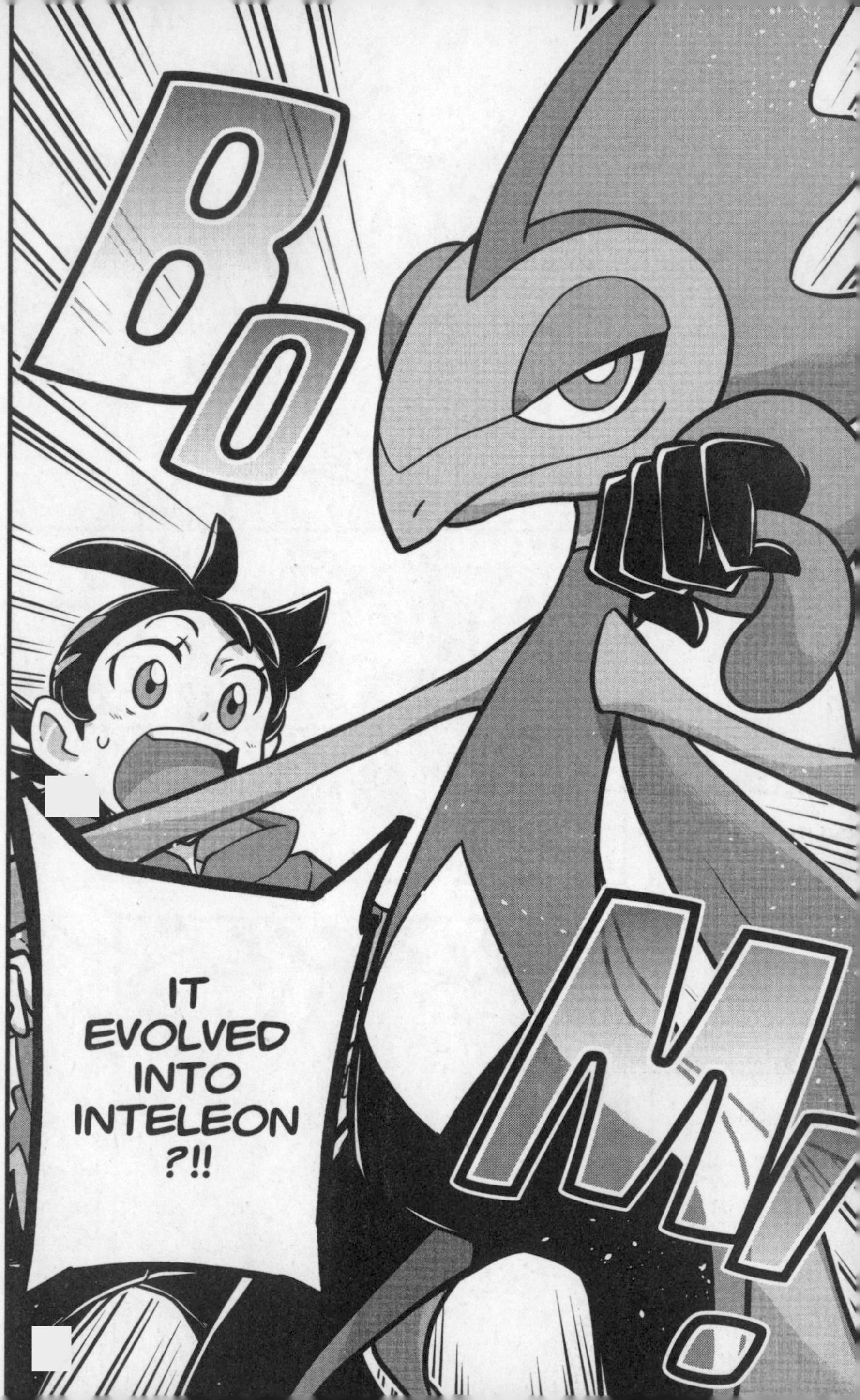
BOOM!
IT EVOLVED INTO INTELEON ?!!

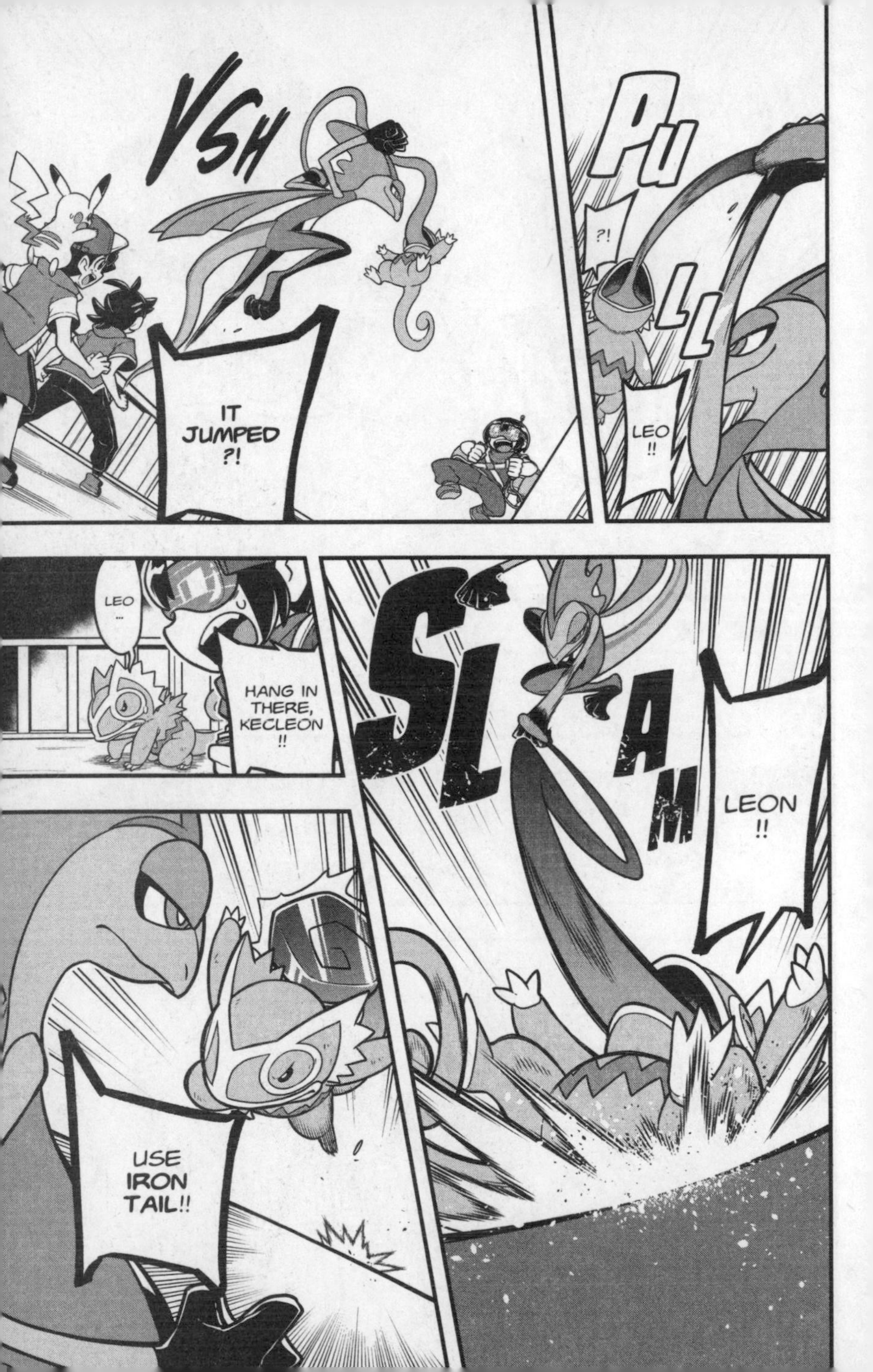
PULL
?!
LEO !!
VSH
IT JUMPED ?!
SLAM
LEON !!
LEO ...
HANG IN THERE, KECLEON !!
USE IRON TAIL!!

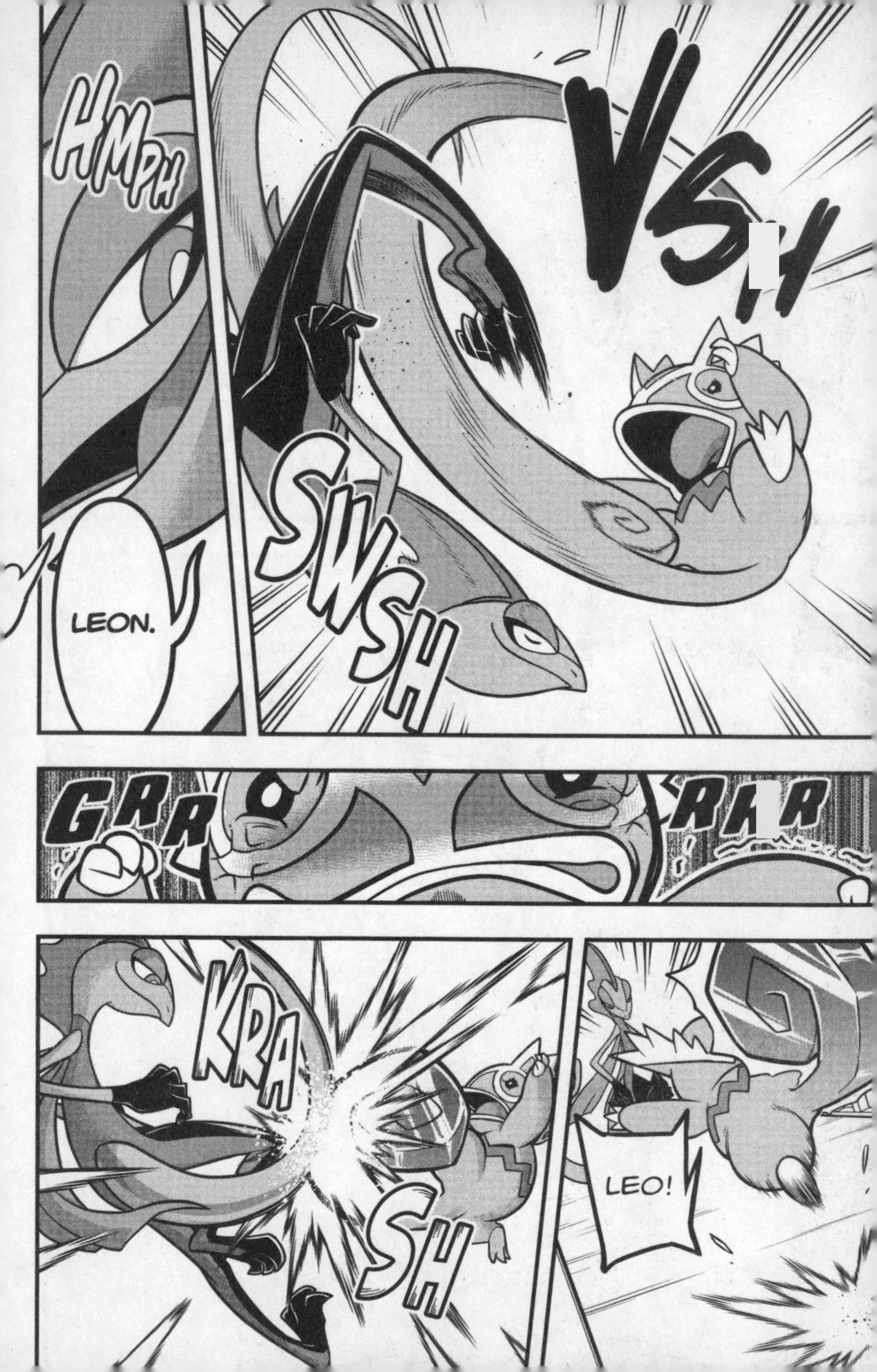
VSH
SWSH
HMPH
LEON.
GRR
RRR
LEO!
KRA
SH

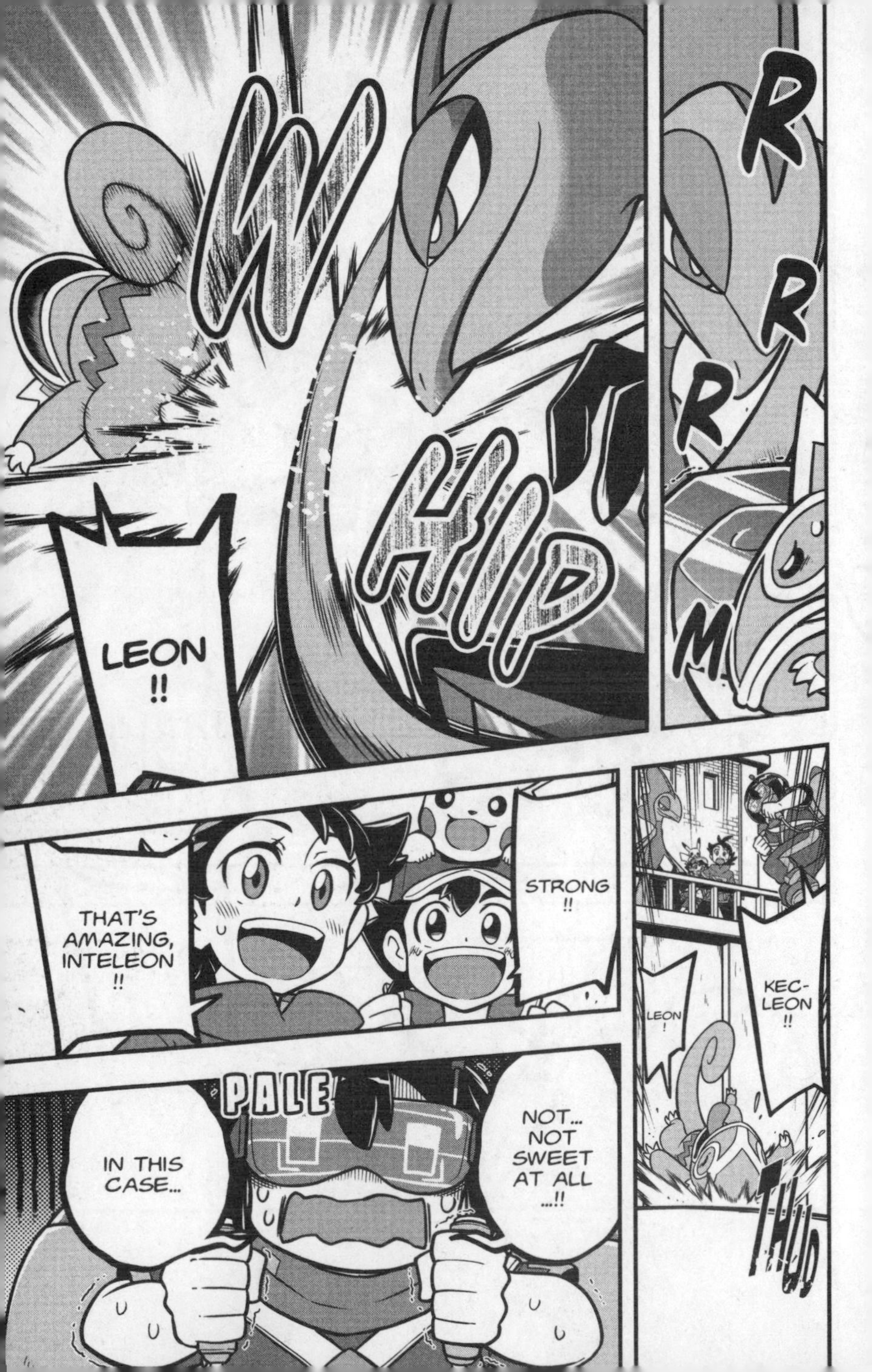
RRRM
WHIP
LEON !!
KEC-LEON !!
LEON !
THUD
STRONG !!
THAT'S AMAZING, INTELEON !!
PALE
NOT... NOT SWEET AT ALL ...!!
IN THIS CASE...

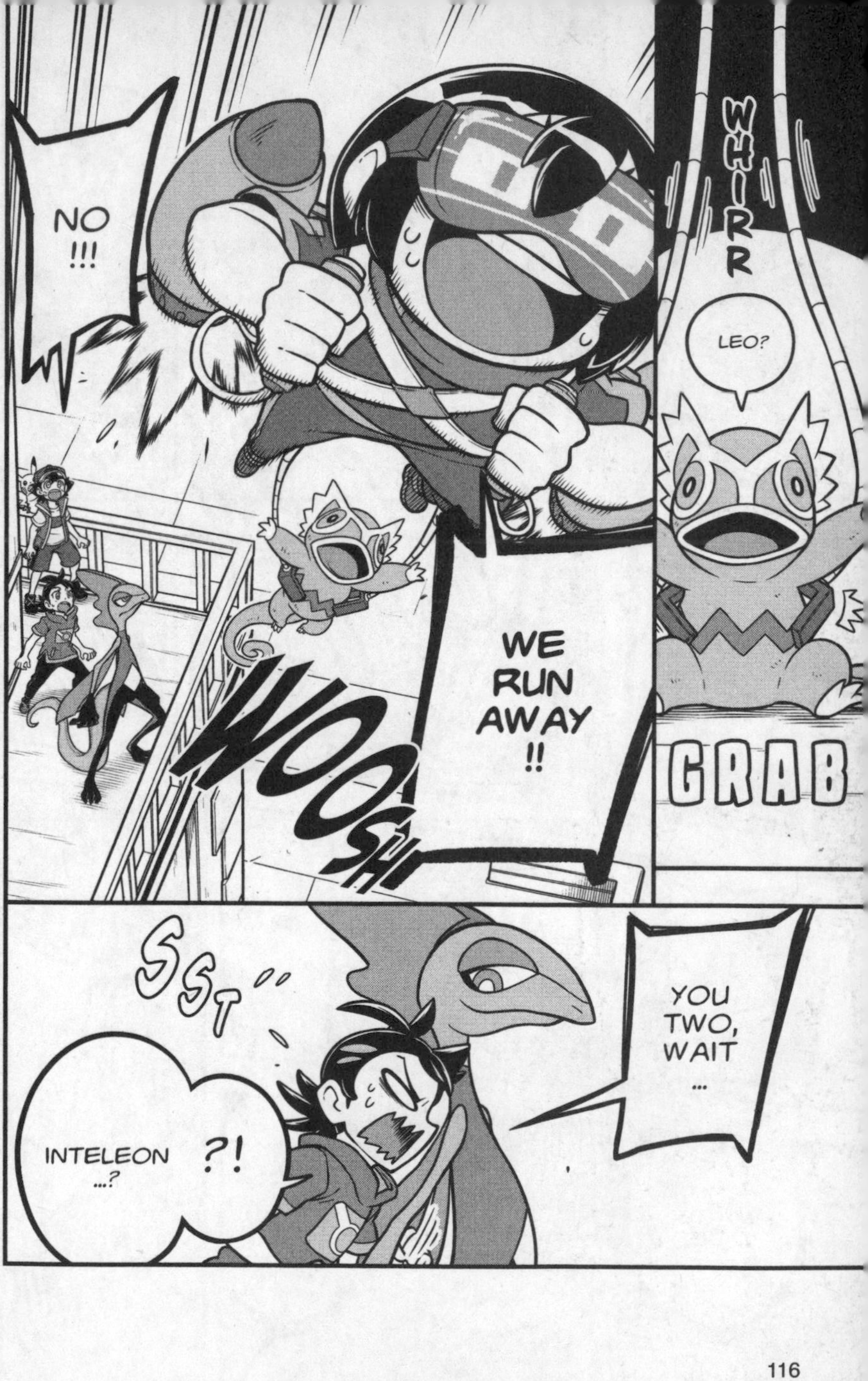
WHIRR
LEO?
GRAB
WE RUN AWAY !!
NO !!!
WOOSH
YOU TWO, WAIT ...
SST
INTELEON ...? ?!

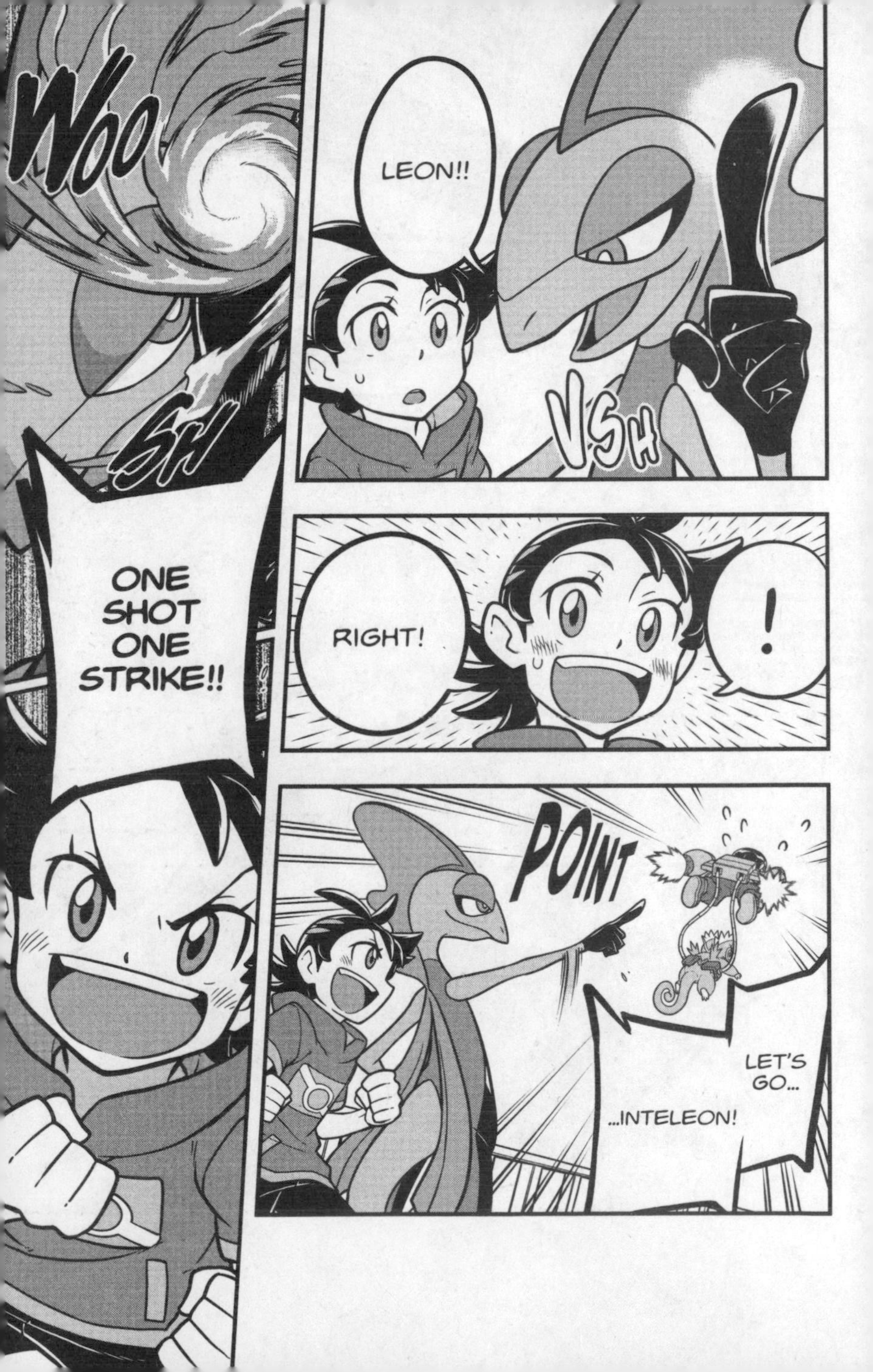
LEON!!
VSH
!
RIGHT!
POINT
LET'S GO...
...INTELEON!
WOO
SH
ONE SHOT ONE STRIKE!!

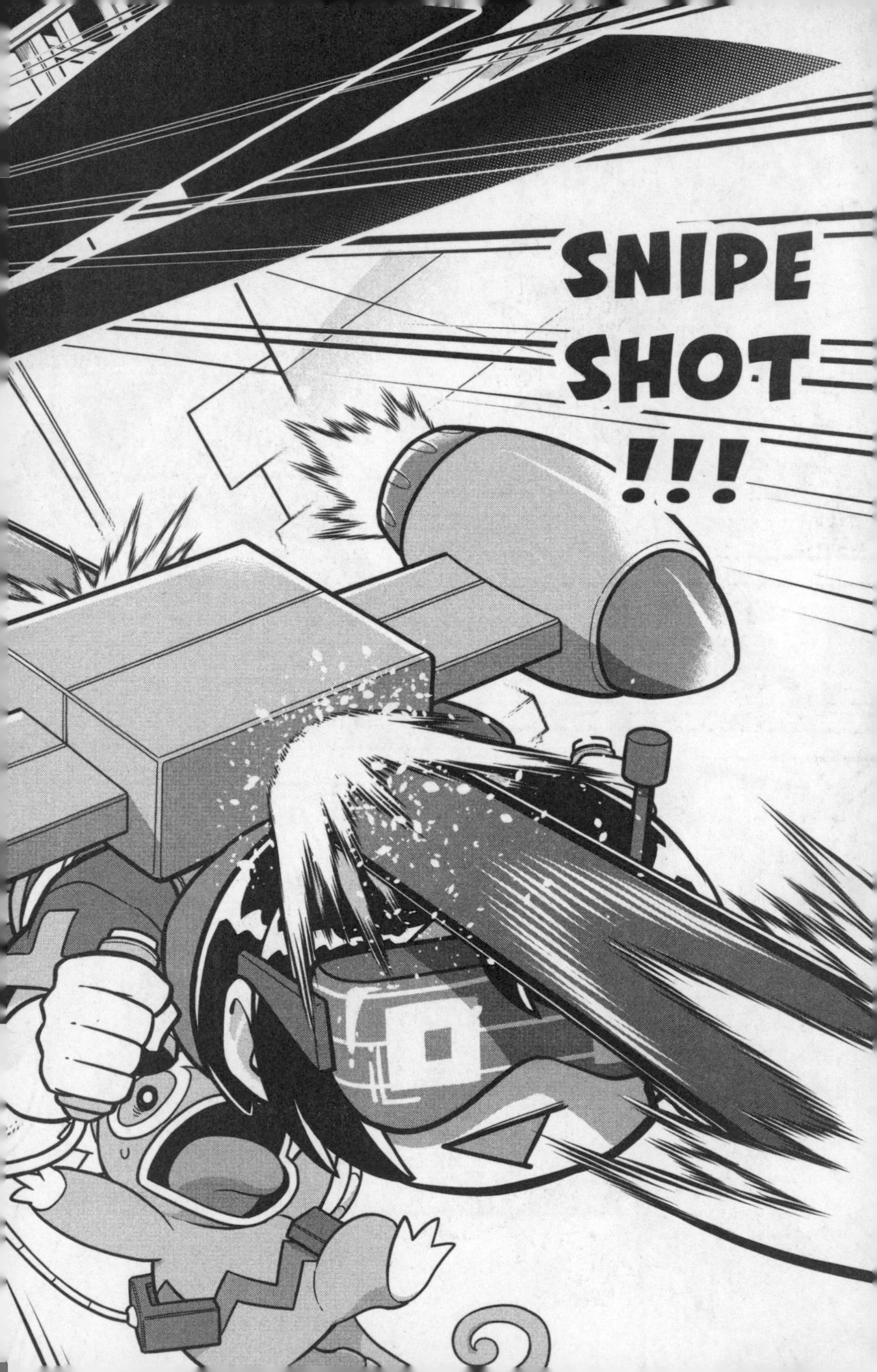
SNIPE SHOT!!!

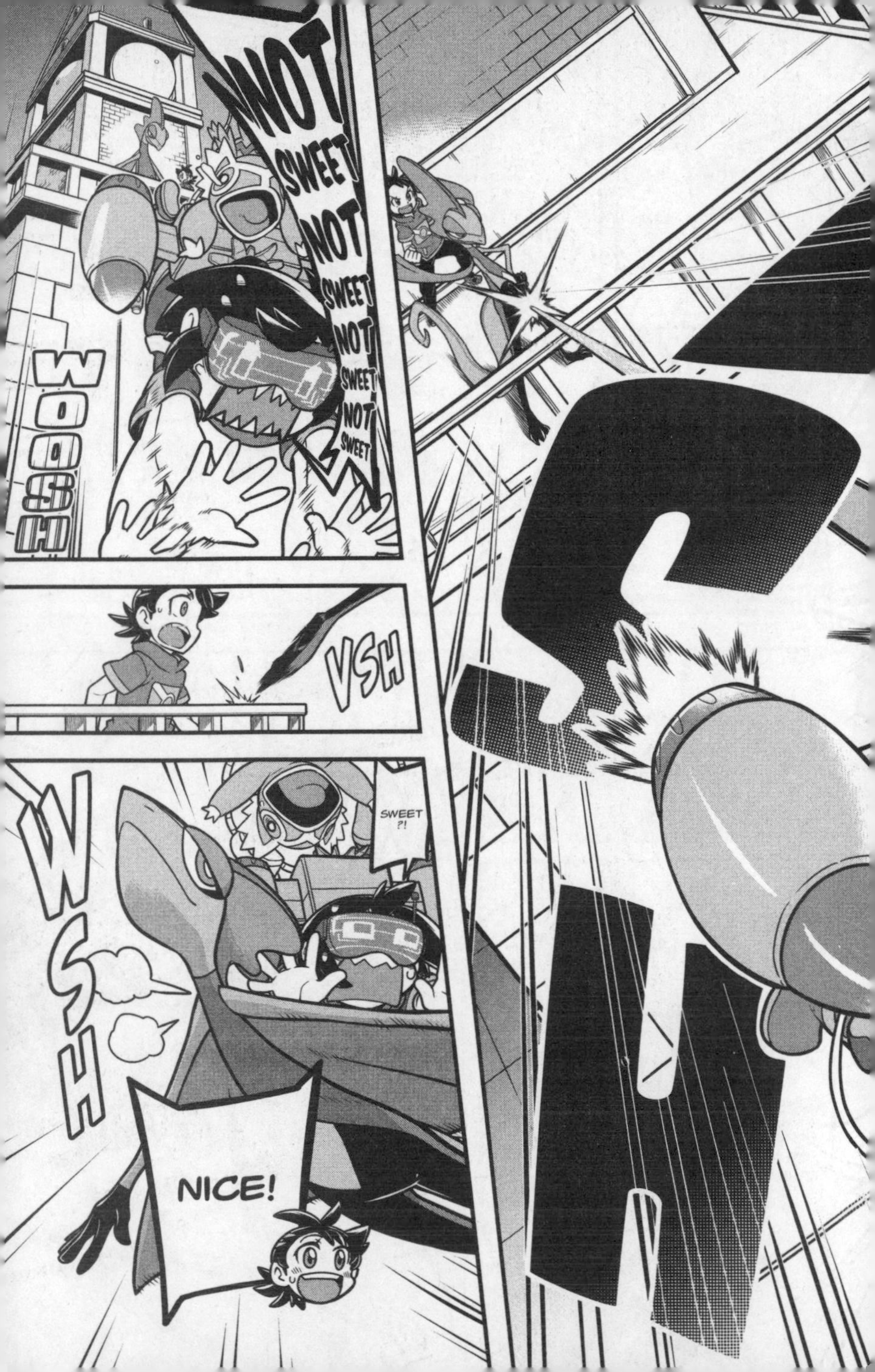
NOT SWEET NOT SWEET NOT SWEET NOT SWEET
WOOSH
VSH
SWEET?!
WSHH
NICE!

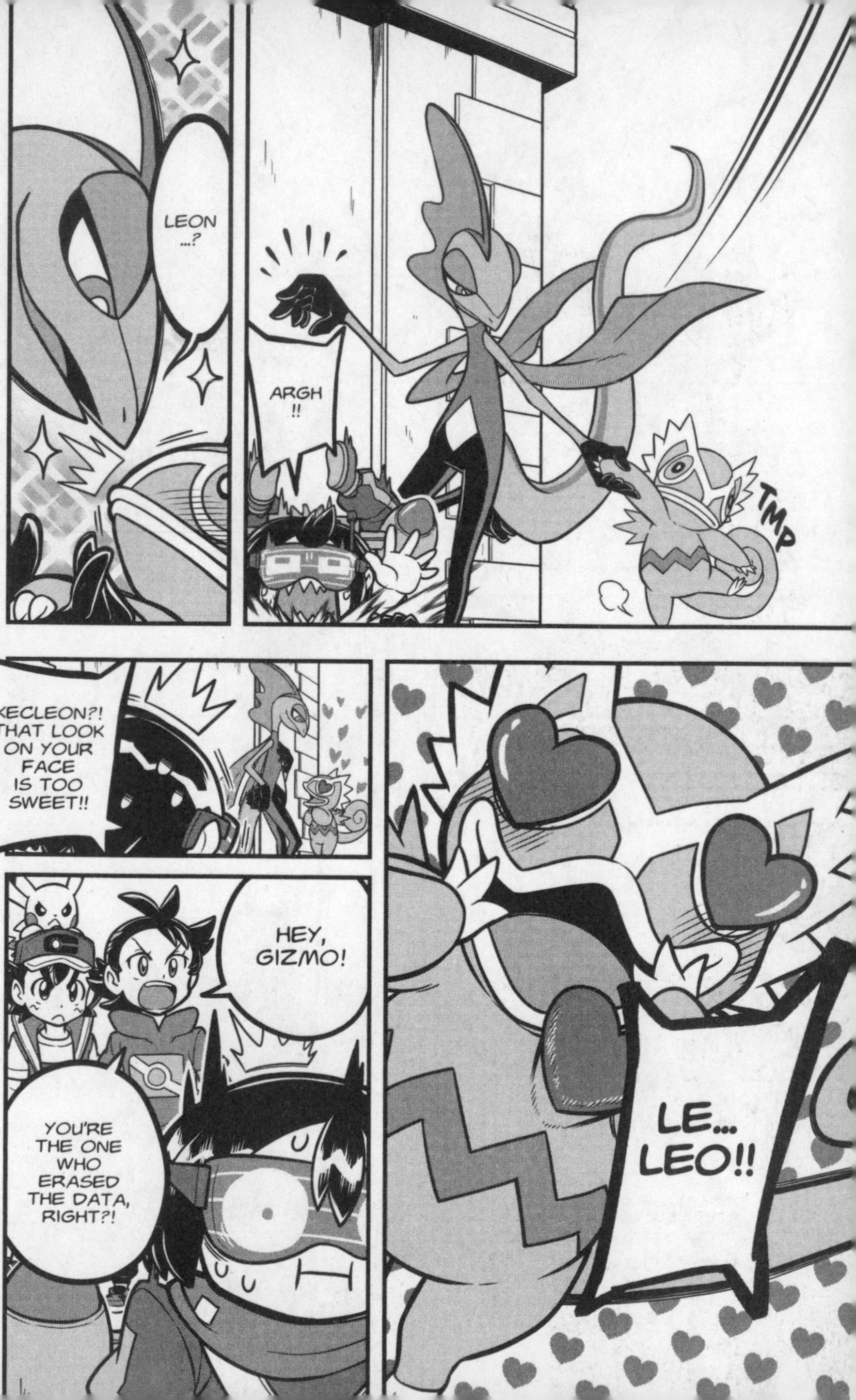
TMP
ARGH !!
LEON ...?
LE... LEO!!
KECLEON?! THAT LOOK ON YOUR FACE IS TOO SWEET!!
HEY, GIZMO!
YOU'RE THE ONE WHO ERASED THE DATA, RIGHT?!

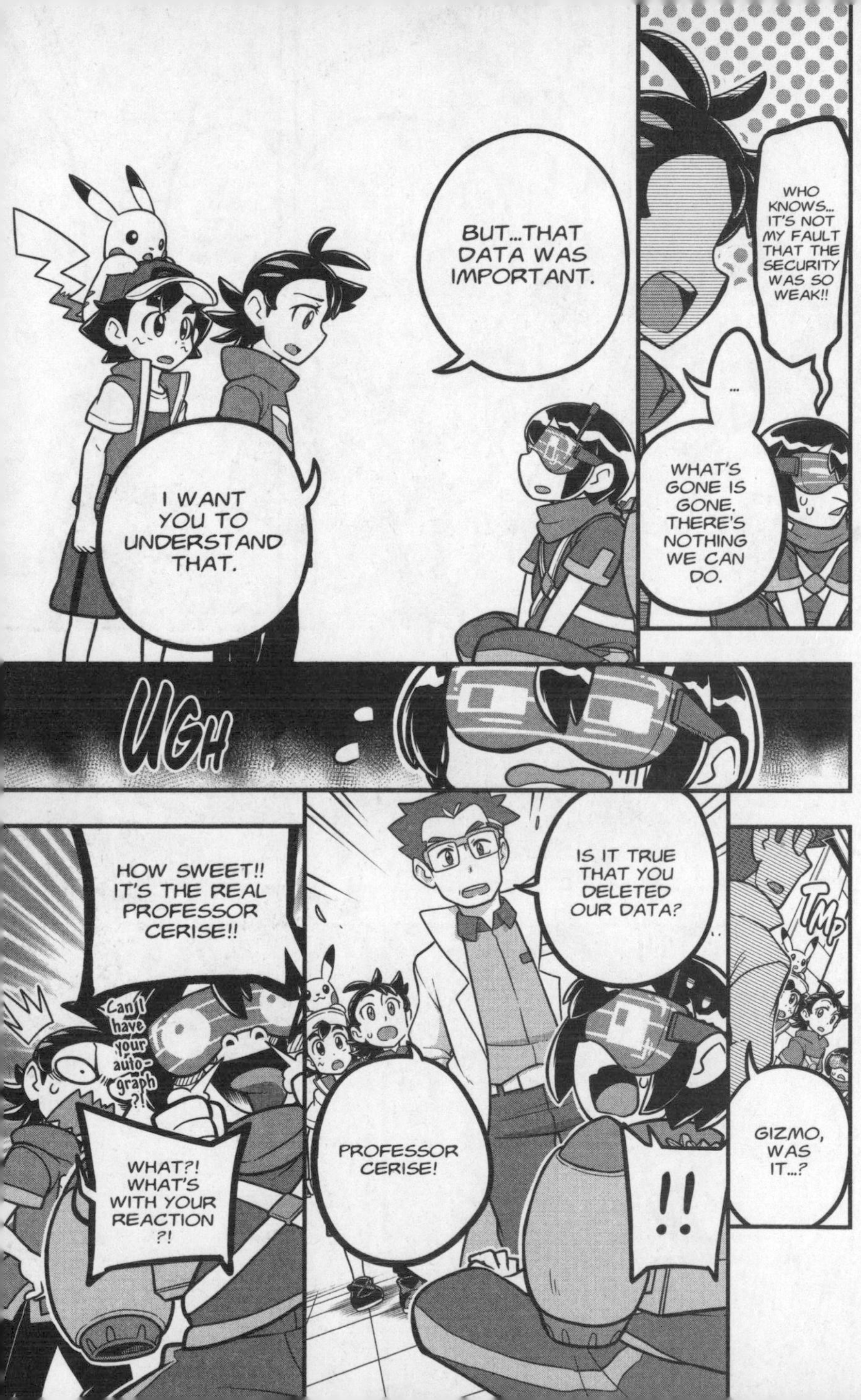
WHO KNOWS... IT'S NOT MY FAULT THAT THE SECURITY WAS SO WEAK!!
...
WHAT'S GONE IS GONE. THERE'S NOTHING WE CAN DO.
BUT...THAT DATA WAS IMPORTANT.
I WANT YOU TO UNDERSTAND THAT.
UGH
TMP
GIZMO, WAS IT...?
IS IT TRUE THAT YOU DELETED OUR DATA?
!!
PROFESSOR CERISE!
HOW SWEET!! IT'S THE REAL PROFESSOR CERISE!!
Can I have your autograph?!
WHAT?! WHAT'S WITH YOUR REACTION?!

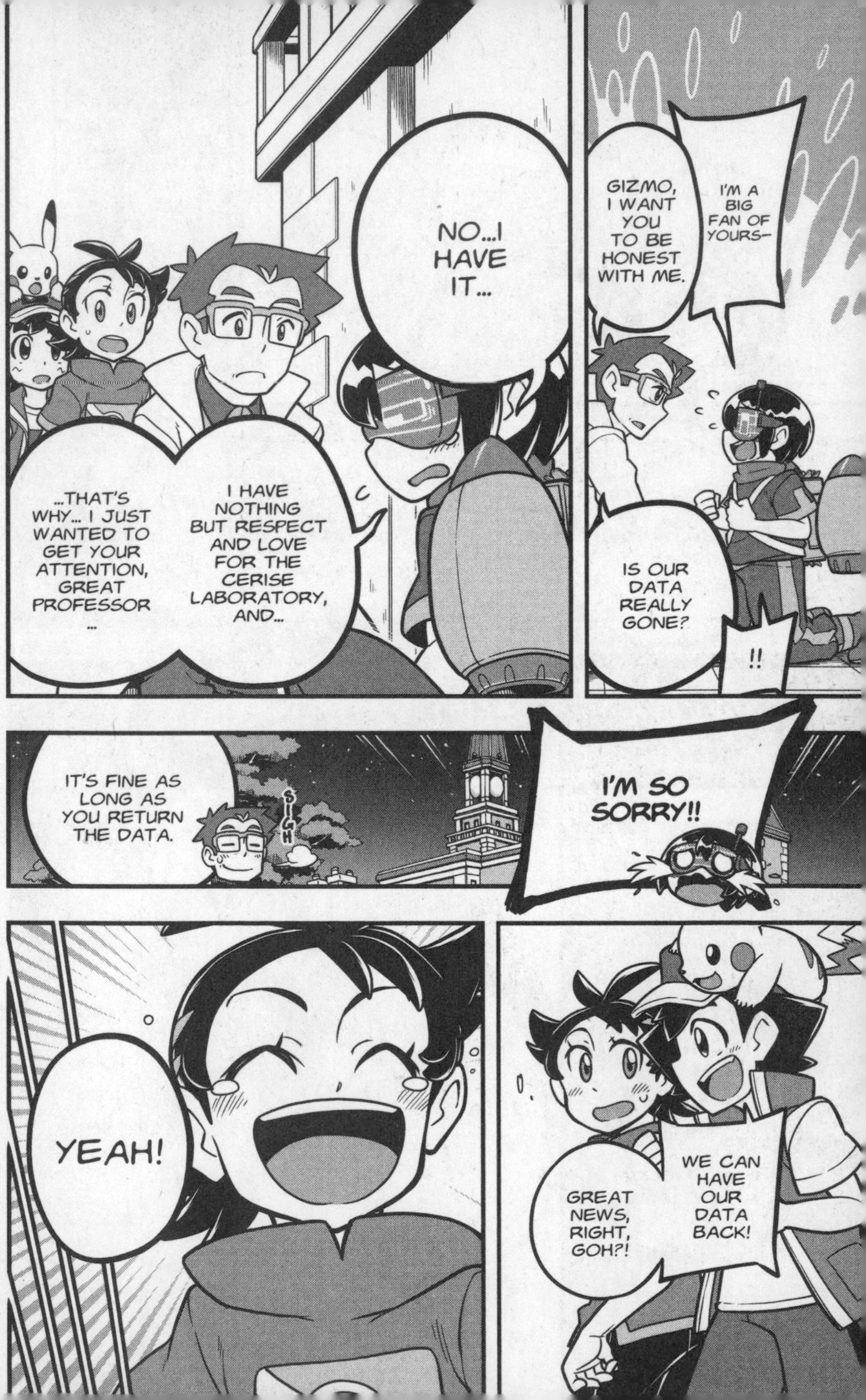
I'M A BIG FAN OF YOURS–
GIZMO, I WANT YOU TO BE HONEST WITH ME.
IS OUR DATA REALLY GONE?
!!
NO...I HAVE IT...
I HAVE NOTHING BUT RESPECT AND LOVE FOR THE CERISE LABORATORY, AND...
...THAT'S WHY... I JUST WANTED TO GET YOUR ATTENTION, GREAT PROFESSOR ...
I'M SO SORRY!!
SIGH
IT'S FINE AS LONG AS YOU RETURN THE DATA.
WE CAN HAVE OUR DATA BACK!
GREAT NEWS, RIGHT, GOH?!
YEAH!

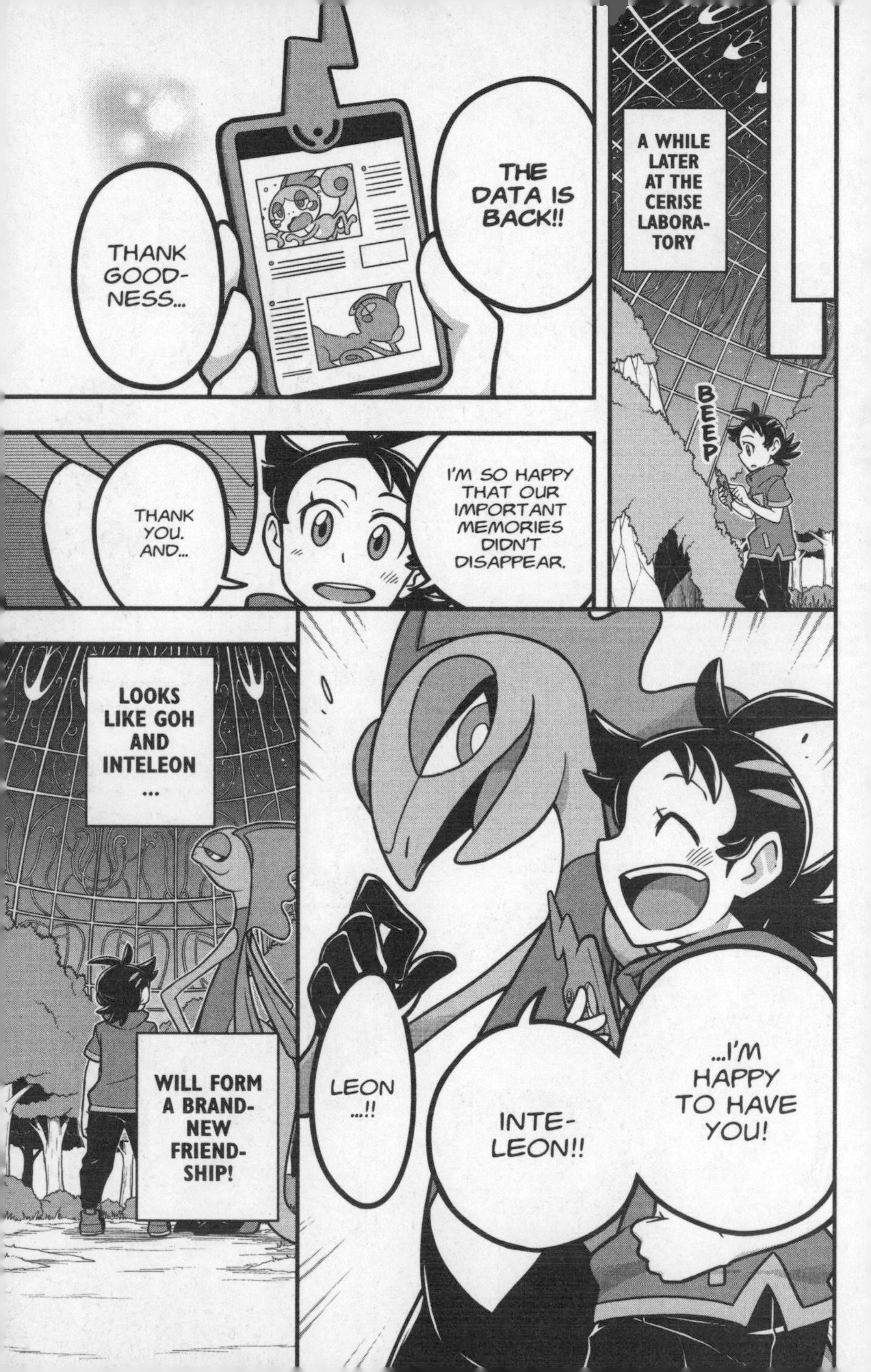
A WHILE LATER AT THE CERISE LABORA-TORY
BEEP
THE DATA IS BACK!!
THANK GOOD-NESS...
I'M SO HAPPY THAT OUR IMPORTANT MEMORIES DIDN'T DISAPPEAR.
THANK YOU. AND...
...I'M HAPPY TO HAVE YOU!
INTE-LEON!!
LEON ...!!
LOOKS LIKE GOH AND INTELEON ...
WILL FORM A BRAND-NEW FRIEND-SHIP!

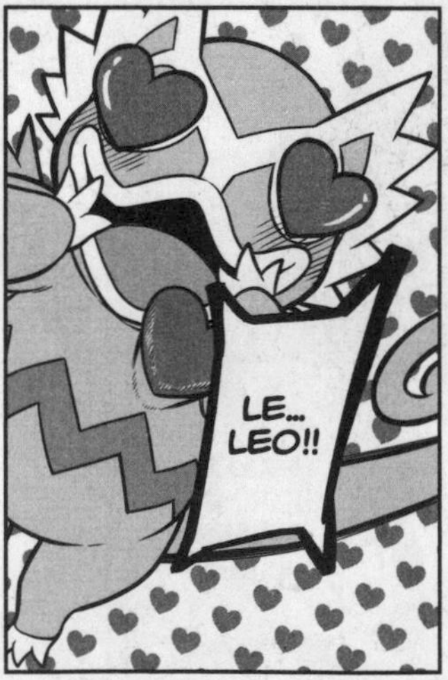
LE...
LEO!!

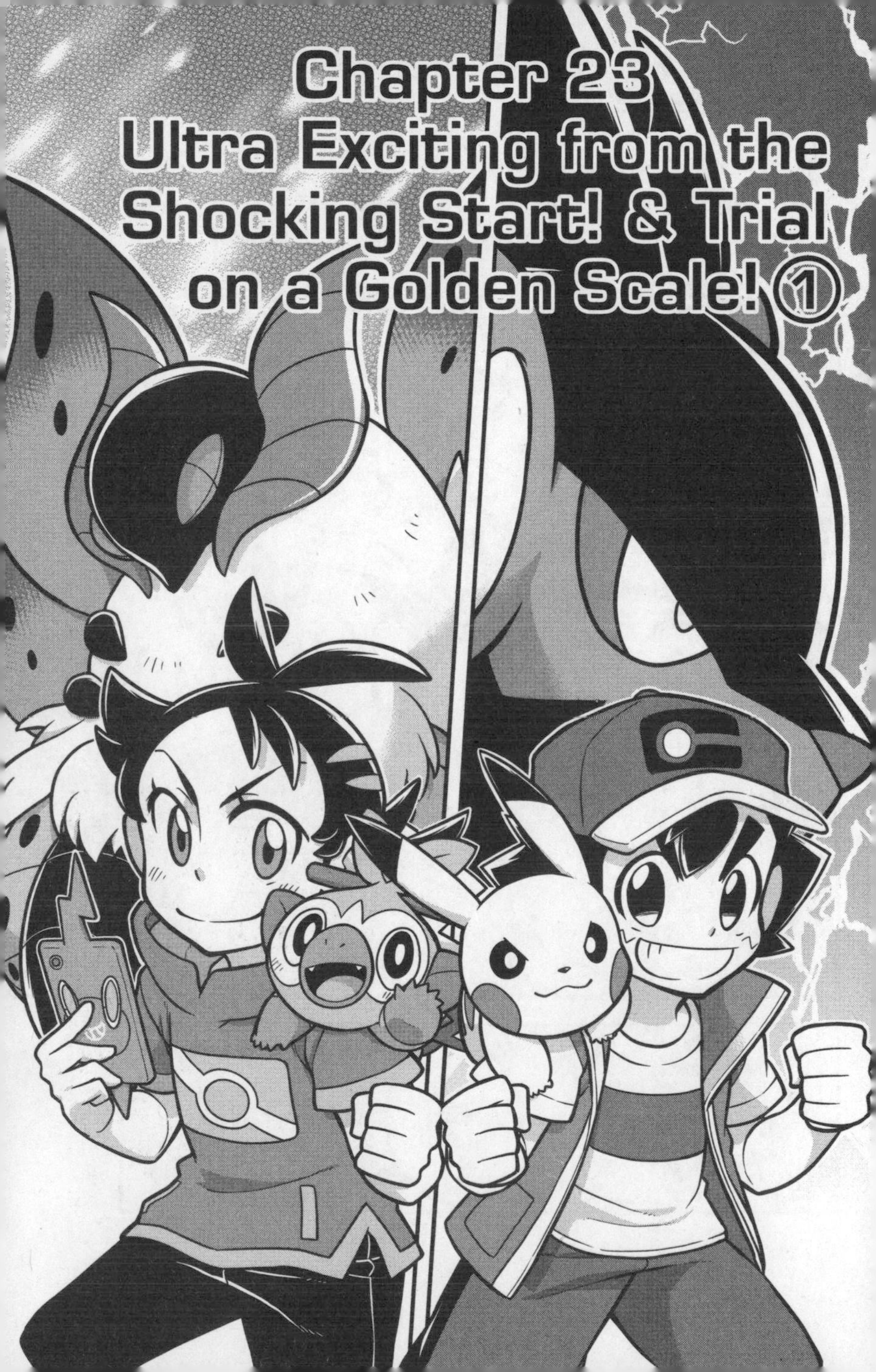
Chapter 23
Ultra Exciting from the Shocking Start! & Trial on a Golden Scale! ①

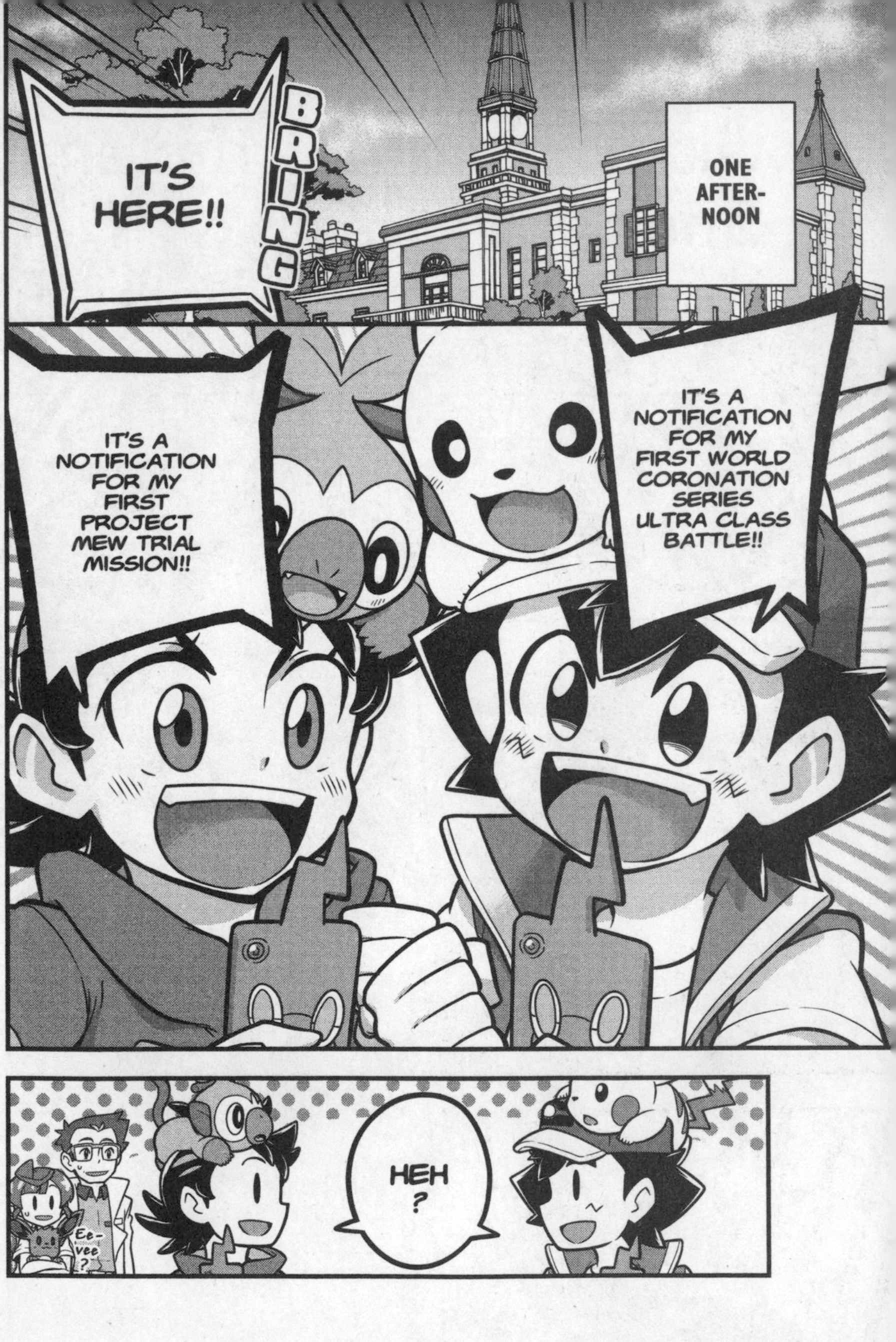
ONE AFTER-NOON
BRING
IT'S HERE!!
IT'S A NOTIFICATION FOR MY FIRST WORLD CORONATION SERIES ULTRA CLASS BATTLE!!
IT'S A NOTIFICATION FOR MY FIRST PROJECT MEW TRIAL MISSION!!
HEH?
Ee-vee?

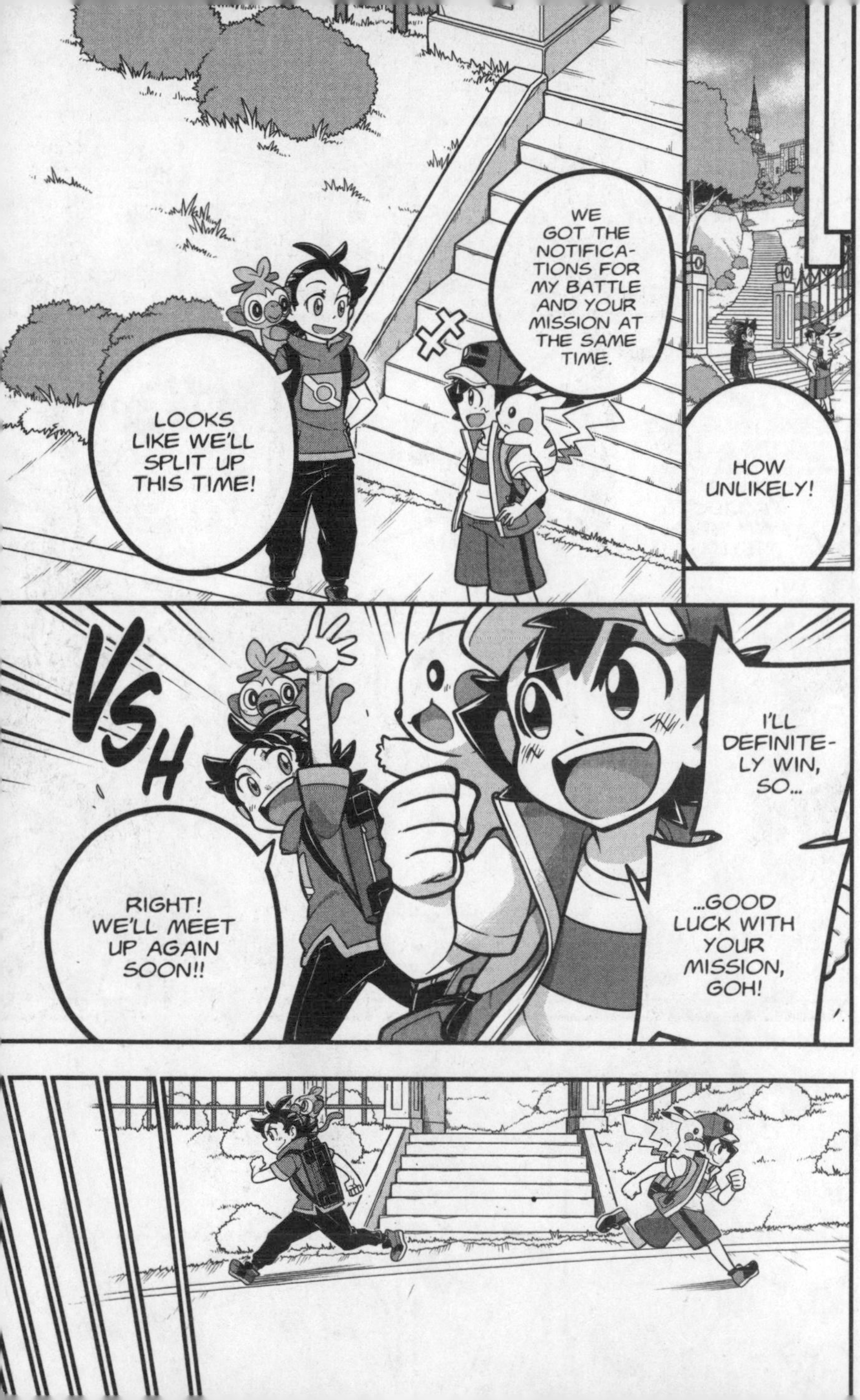
HOW UNLIKELY!
WE GOT THE NOTIFICATIONS FOR MY BATTLE AND YOUR MISSION AT THE SAME TIME.
LOOKS LIKE WE'LL SPLIT UP THIS TIME!
I'LL DEFINITELY WIN, SO...
VSH
...GOOD LUCK WITH YOUR MISSION, GOH!
RIGHT! WE'LL MEET UP AGAIN SOON!!

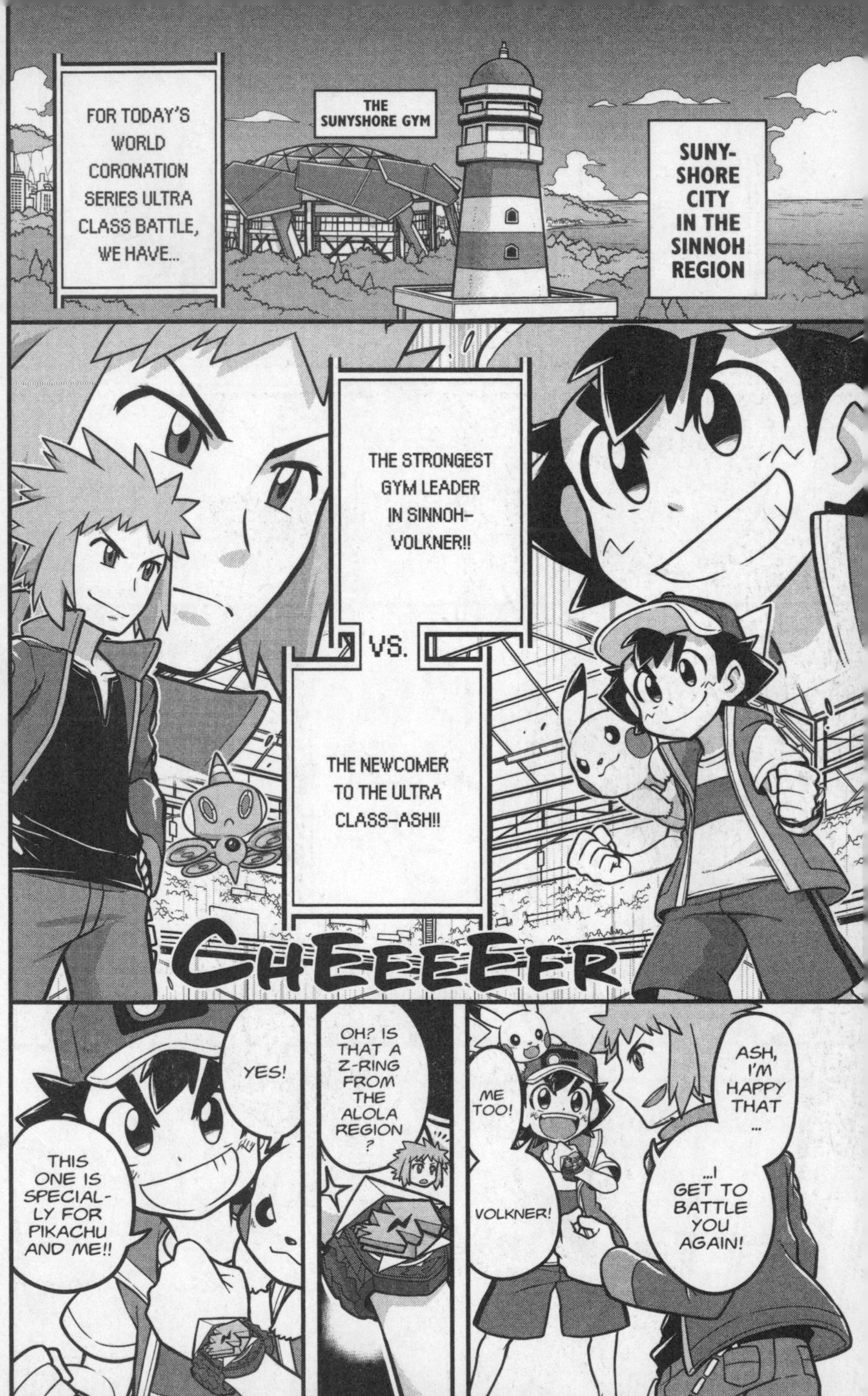
SUNY-SHORE CITY IN THE SINNOH REGION
THE SUNYSHORE GYM
FOR TODAY'S WORLD CORONATION SERIES ULTRA CLASS BATTLE, WE HAVE...
THE STRONGEST GYM LEADER IN SINNOH-VOLKNER!!
VS.
THE NEWCOMER TO THE ULTRA CLASS-ASH!!
CHEEEEER
ASH, I'M HAPPY THAT ...
...I GET TO BATTLE YOU AGAIN!
ME TOO!
VOLKNER!
OH? IS THAT A Z-RING FROM THE ALOLA REGION?
YES!
THIS ONE IS SPECIAL-LY FOR PIKACHU AND ME!!

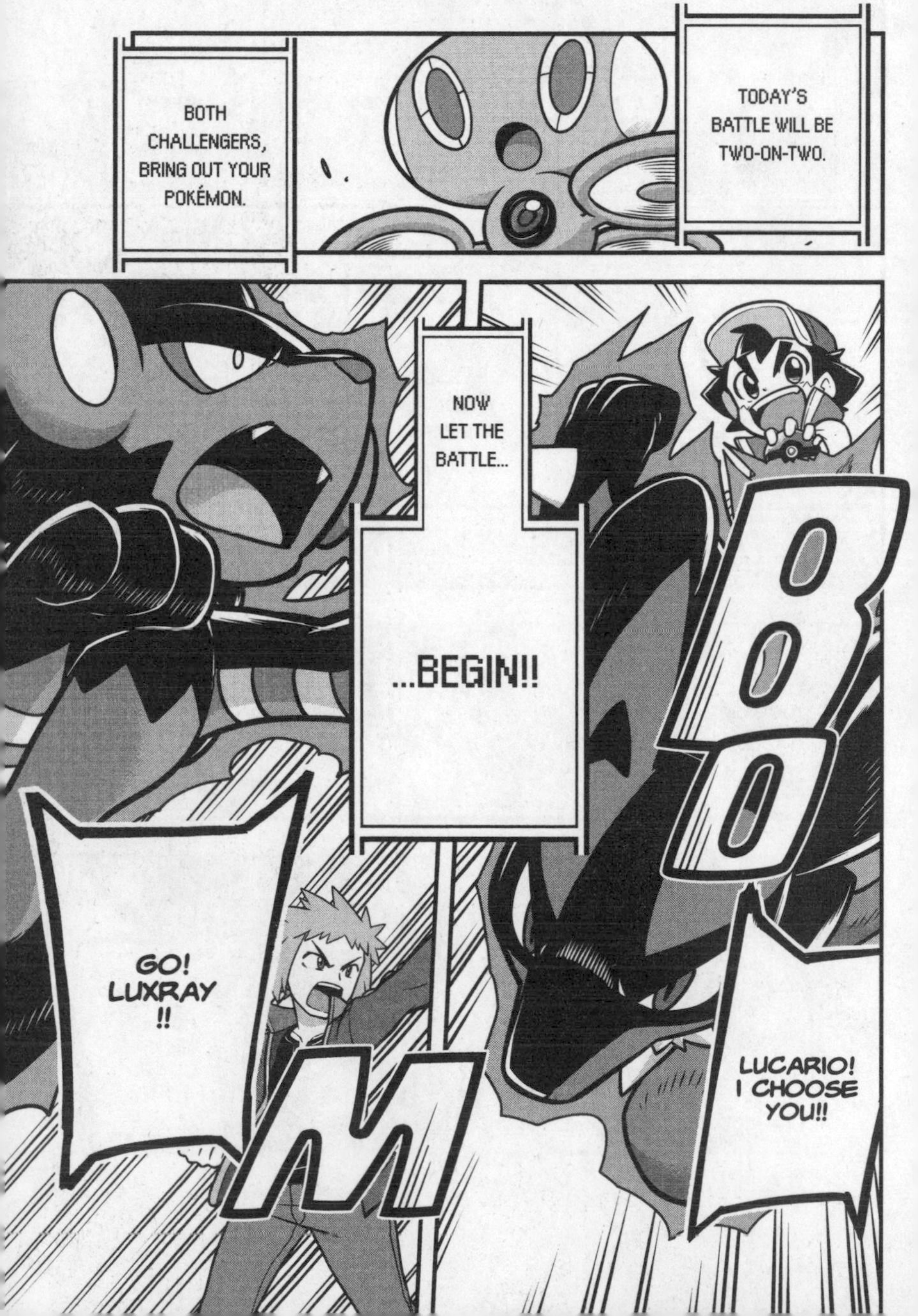
TODAY'S BATTLE WILL BE TWO-ON-TWO.
BOTH CHALLENGERS, BRING OUT YOUR POKÉMON.
NOW LET THE BATTLE...
...BEGIN!!
BOOM
LUCARIO! I CHOOSE YOU!!
GO! LUXRAY!!

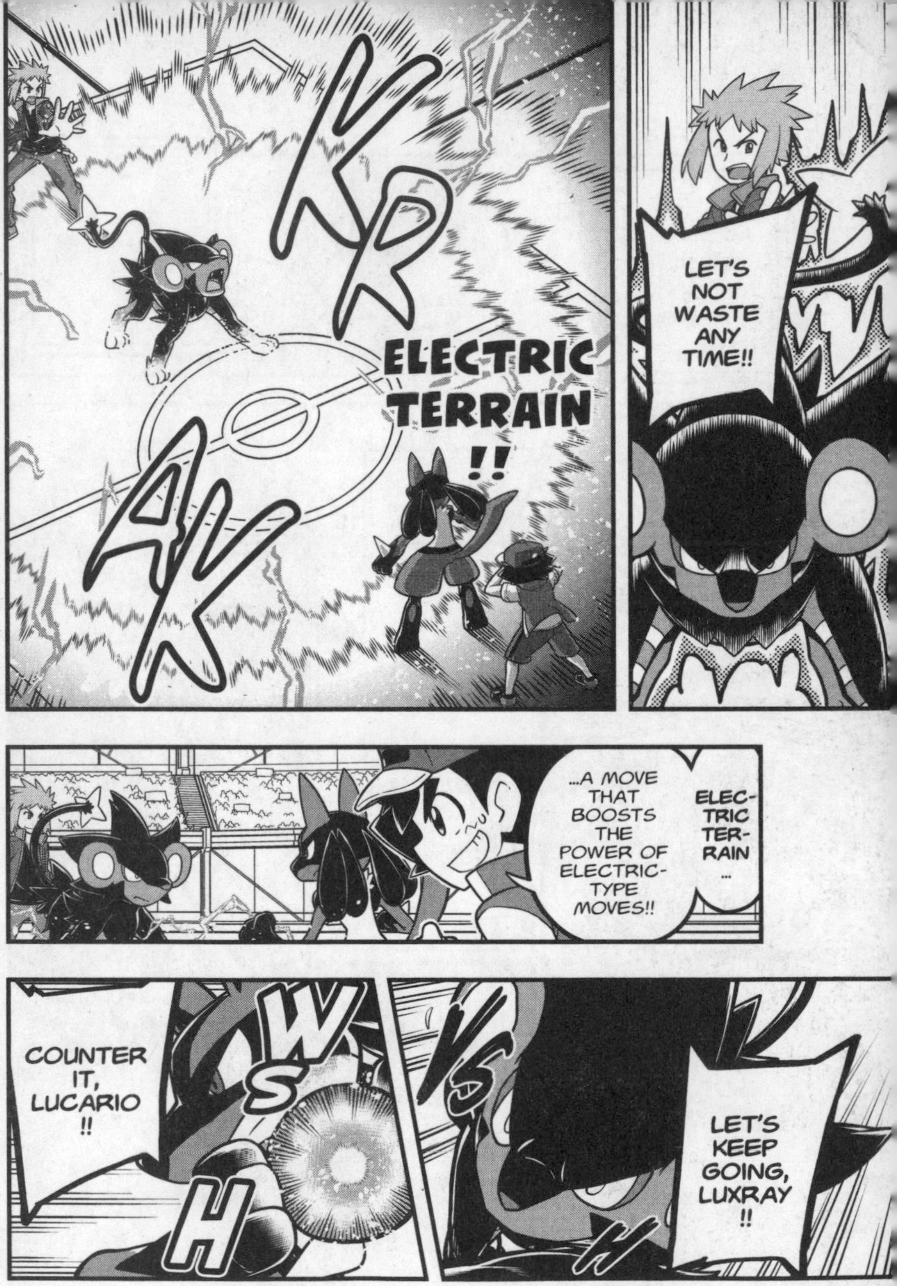
LET'S NOT WASTE ANY TIME!!
KRAK
ELECTRIC TERRAIN!!
ELECTRIC TERRAIN...
...A MOVE THAT BOOSTS THE POWER OF ELECTRIC-TYPE MOVES!!
LET'S KEEP GOING, LUXRAY!!
WSH
COUNTER IT, LUCARIO!!

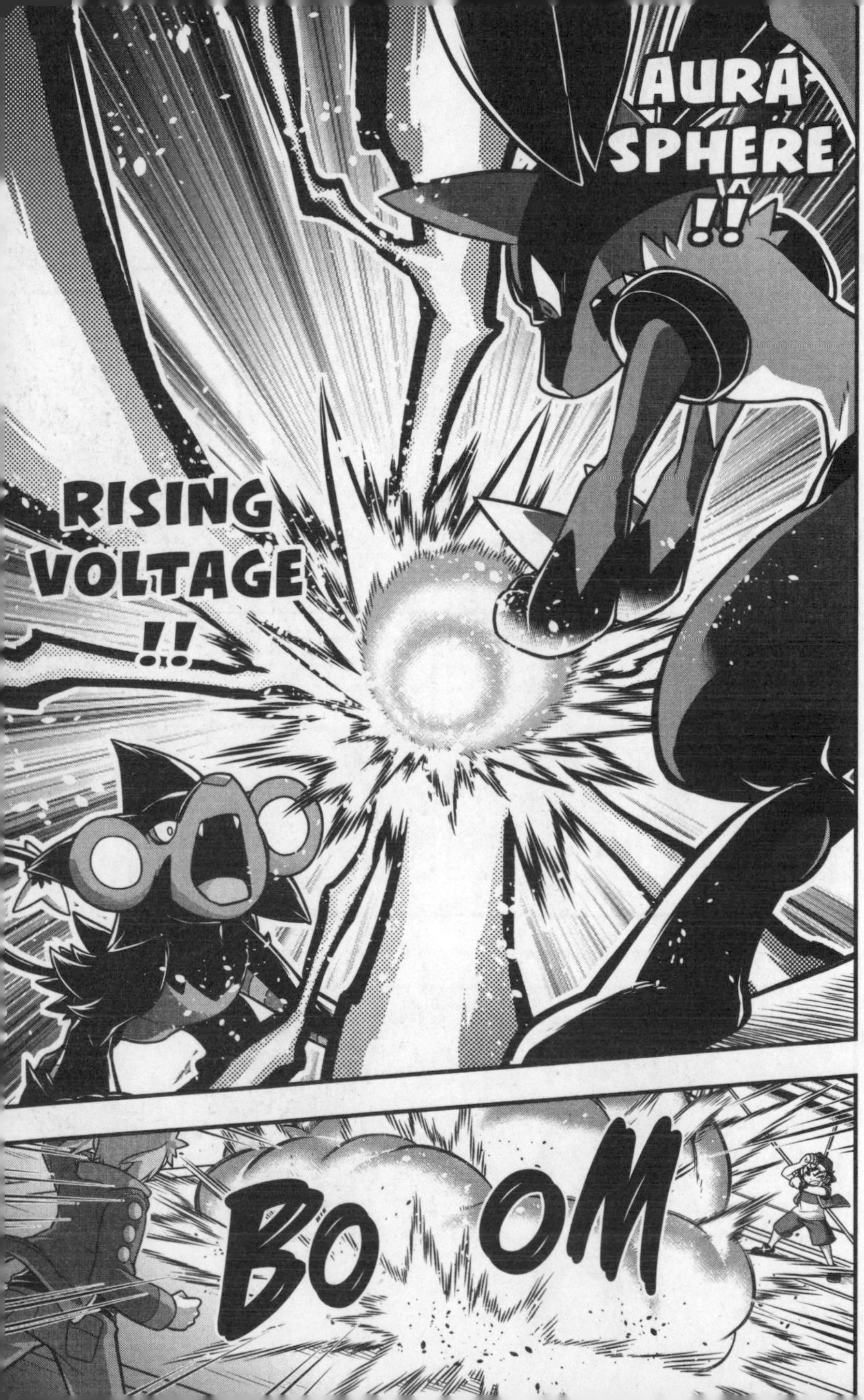
AURA SPHERE !!
RISING VOLTAGE !!
BO OM

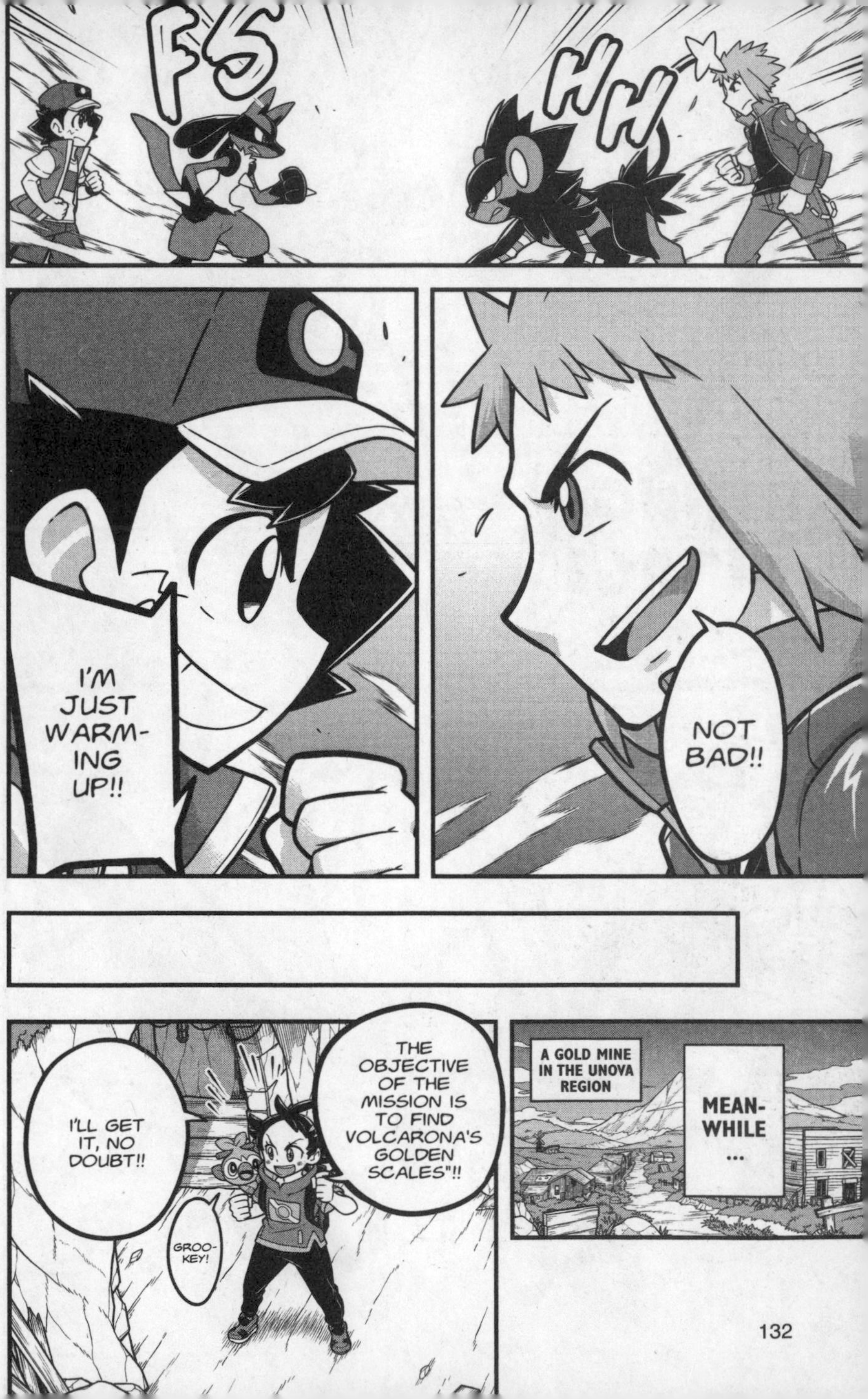
HH
FS
NOT BAD!!
I'M JUST WARMING-ING UP!!
MEAN-WHILE...
A GOLD MINE IN THE UNOVA REGION
THE OBJECTIVE OF THE MISSION IS TO FIND VOLCARONA'S GOLDEN SCALES"!!
I'LL GET IT, NO DOUBT!!
GROO-KEY!

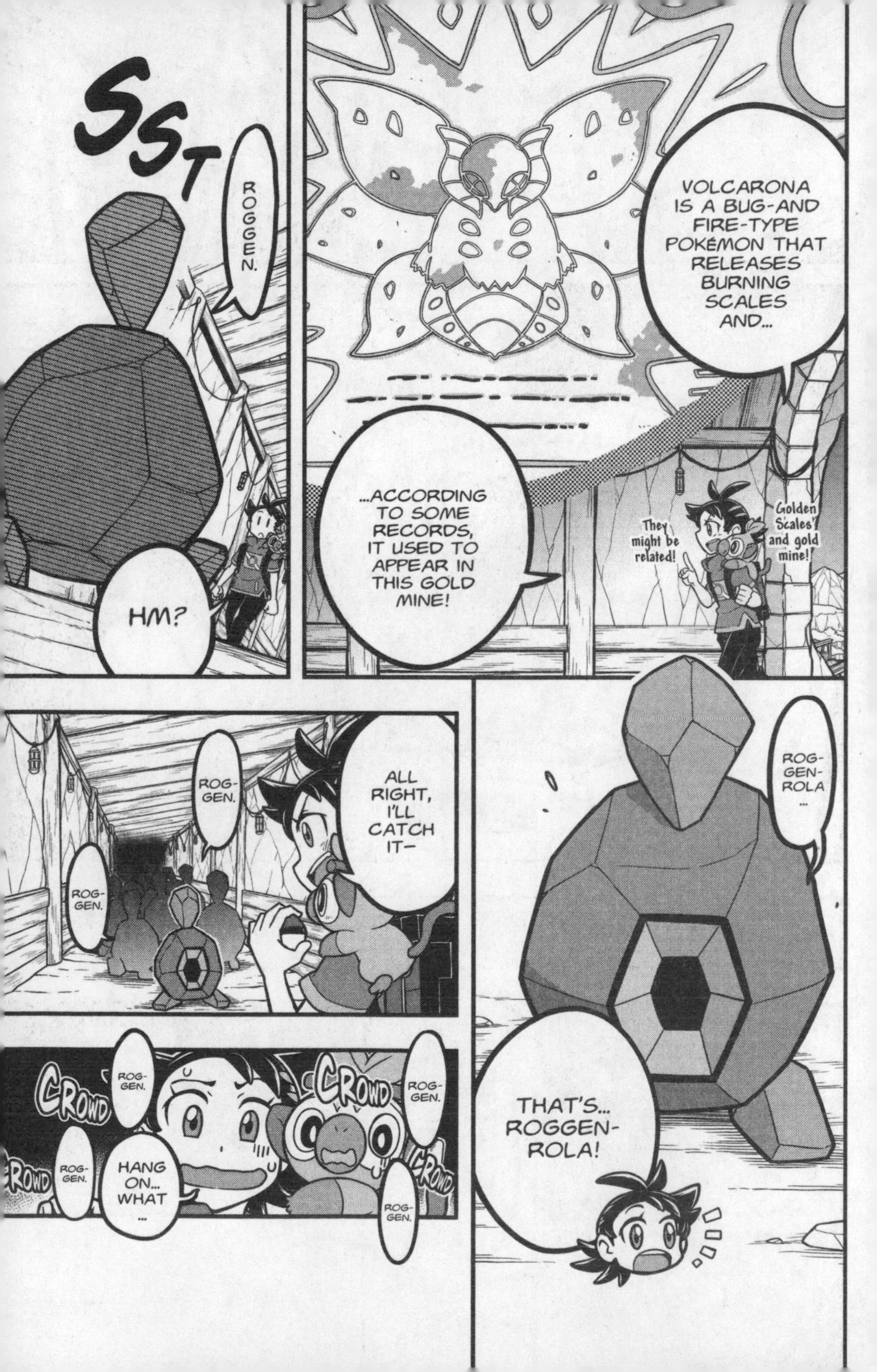
VOLCARONA IS A BUG-AND FIRE-TYPE POKÉMON THAT RELEASES BURNING SCALES AND...
...ACCORDING TO SOME RECORDS, IT USED TO APPEAR IN THIS GOLD MINE!
Golden Scales and gold mine!
They might be related!
SST
ROGGEN.
HM?
ROG-GEN-ROLA...
THAT'S... ROGGEN-ROLA!
ALL RIGHT, I'LL CATCH IT—
ROGGEN.
ROGGEN.
ROG-GEN.
CROWD
ROG-GEN.
CROWD
HANG ON... WHAT...
ROG-GEN.
CROWD
ROG-GEN.
CROWD

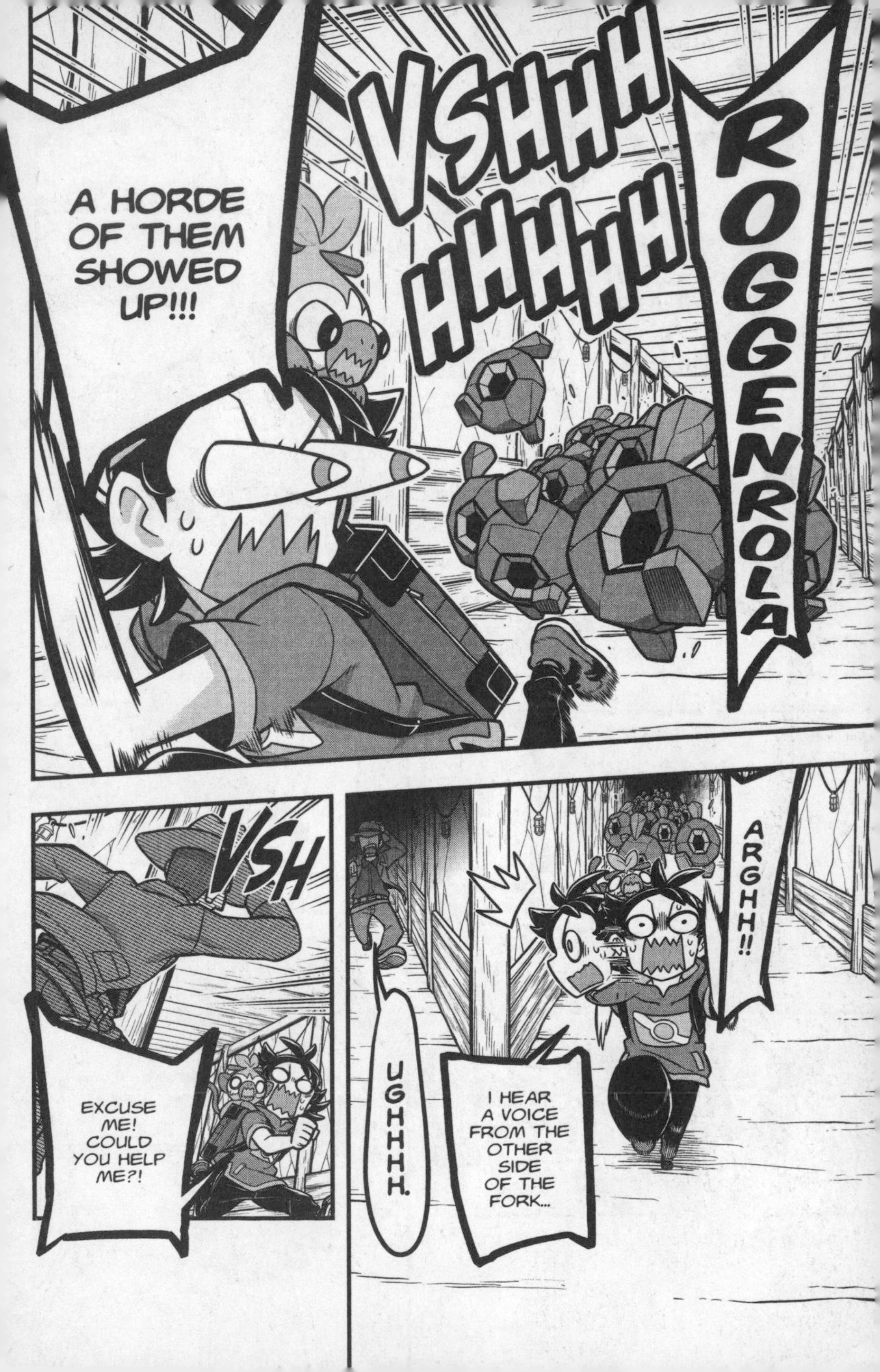
ROGGENROLA
VSHHH HHHHHH
A HORDE OF THEM SHOWED UP!!!
ARGHH!!
I HEAR A VOICE FROM THE OTHER SIDE OF THE FORK...
UGHHHH.
VSH
EXCUSE ME! COULD YOU HELP ME?!

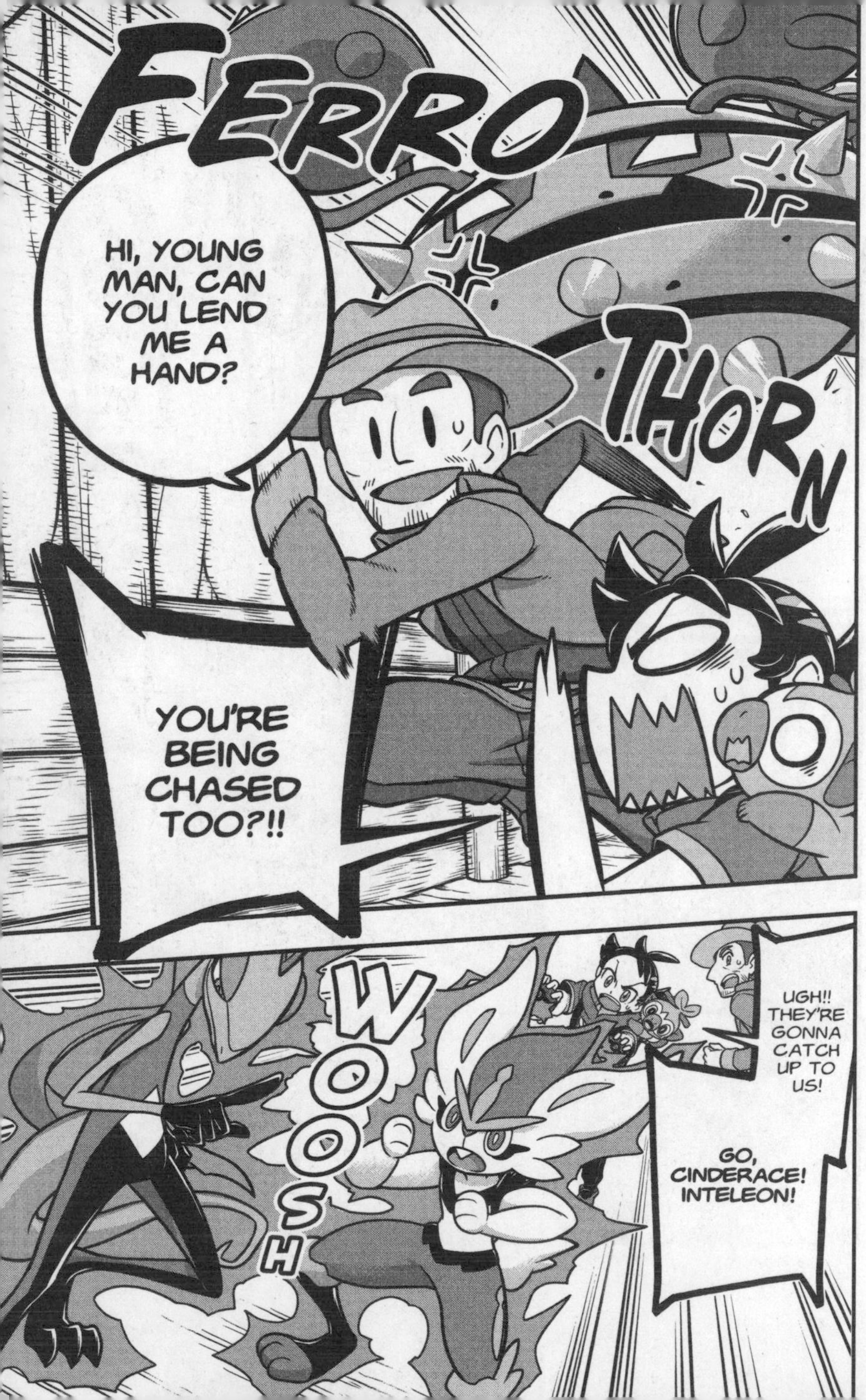
FERRO
THORN
HI, YOUNG MAN, CAN YOU LEND ME A HAND?
YOU'RE BEING CHASED TOO?!!
UGH!! THEY'RE GONNA CATCH UP TO US!
GO, CINDERACE! INTELEON!
WOOOSH

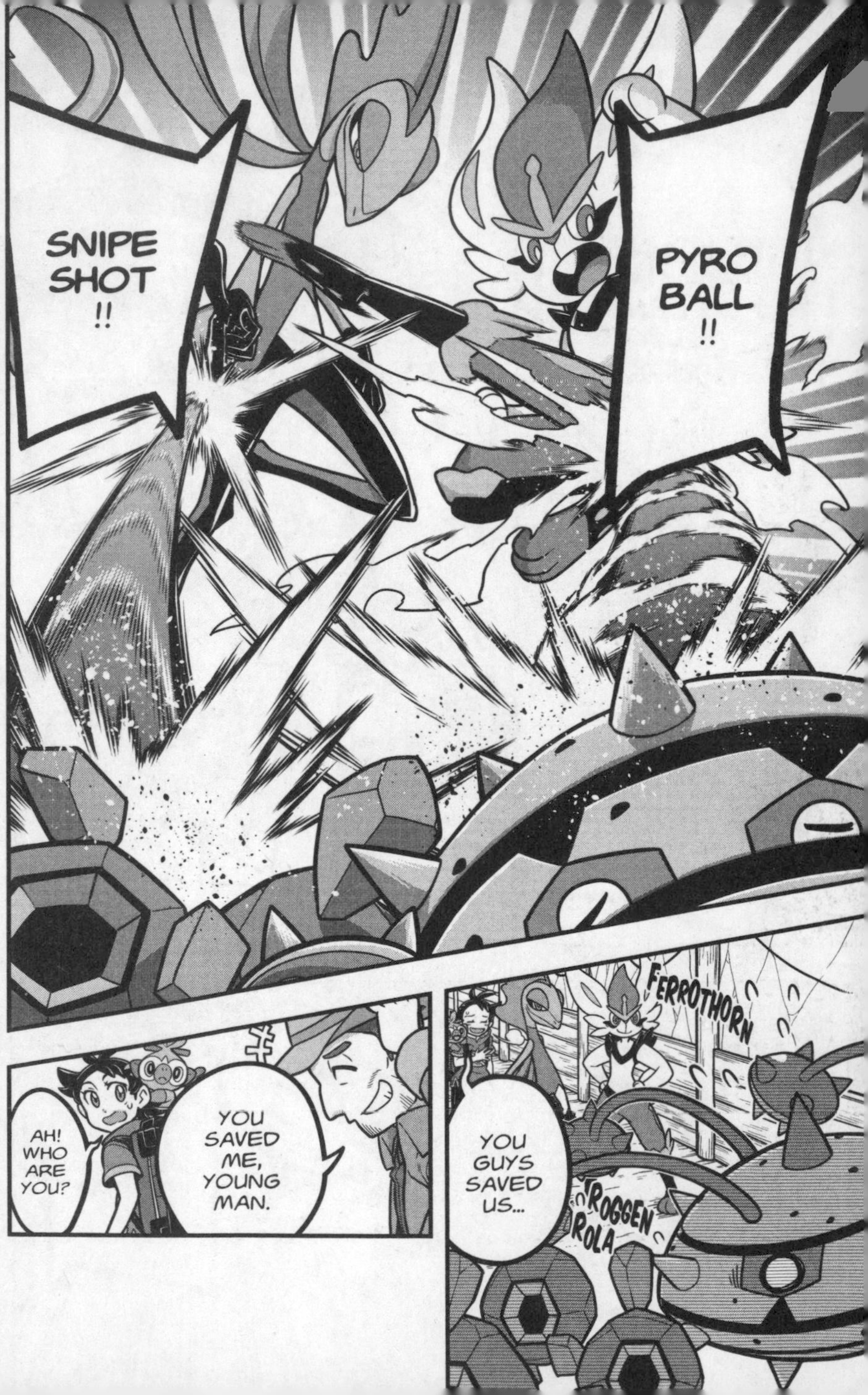
PYRO BALL !!
SNIPE SHOT !!
FERROTHORN
YOU GUYS SAVED US...
ROGGENROLA
YOU SAVED ME, YOUNG MAN.
AH! WHO ARE YOU?

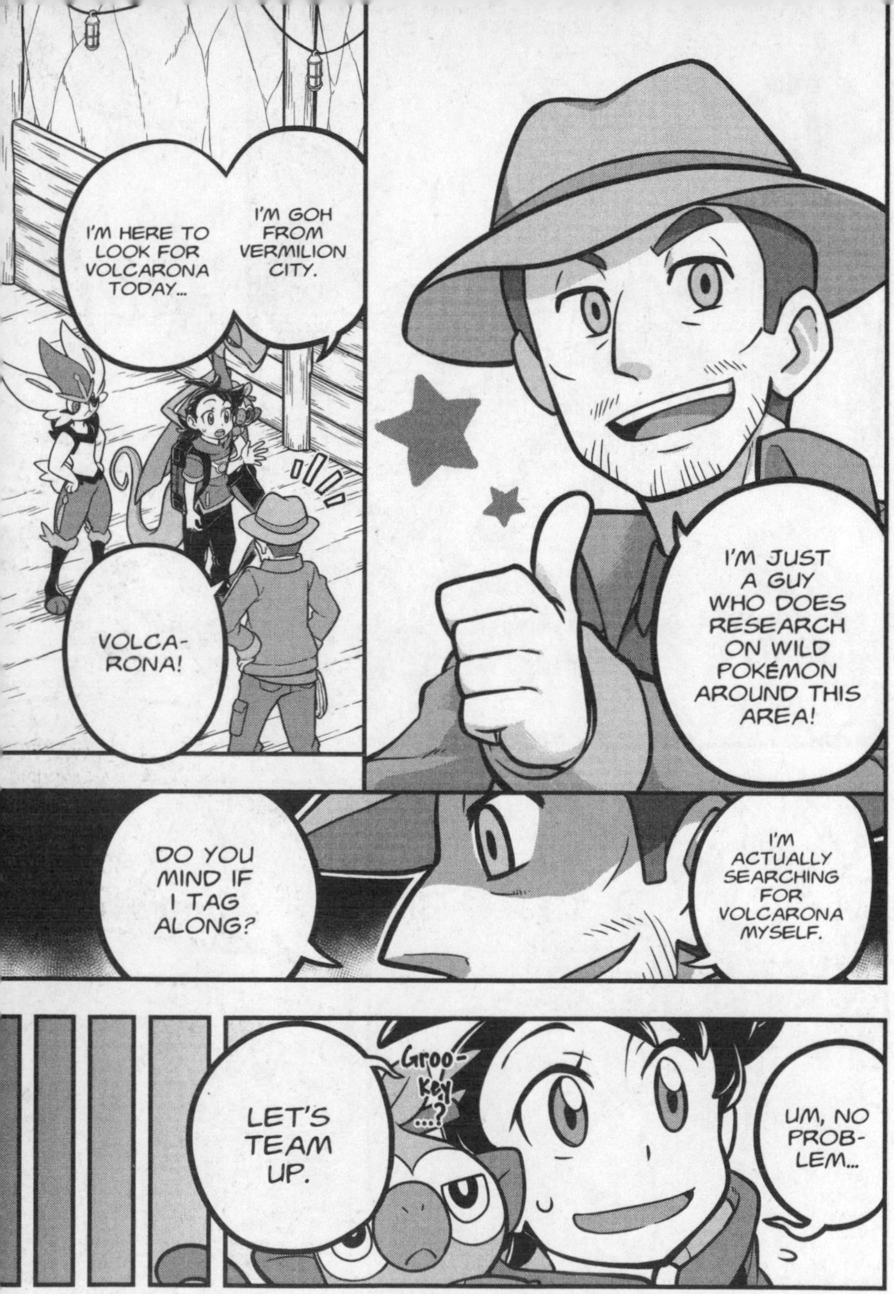
I'M JUST A GUY WHO DOES RESEARCH ON WILD POKÉMON AROUND THIS AREA!
I'M GOH FROM VERMILION CITY.
I'M HERE TO LOOK FOR VOLCARONA TODAY...
VOLCA-RONA!
I'M ACTUALLY SEARCHING FOR VOLCARONA MYSELF.
DO YOU MIND IF I TAG ALONG?
UM, NO PROB-LEM...
Groo-key...?
LET'S TEAM UP.

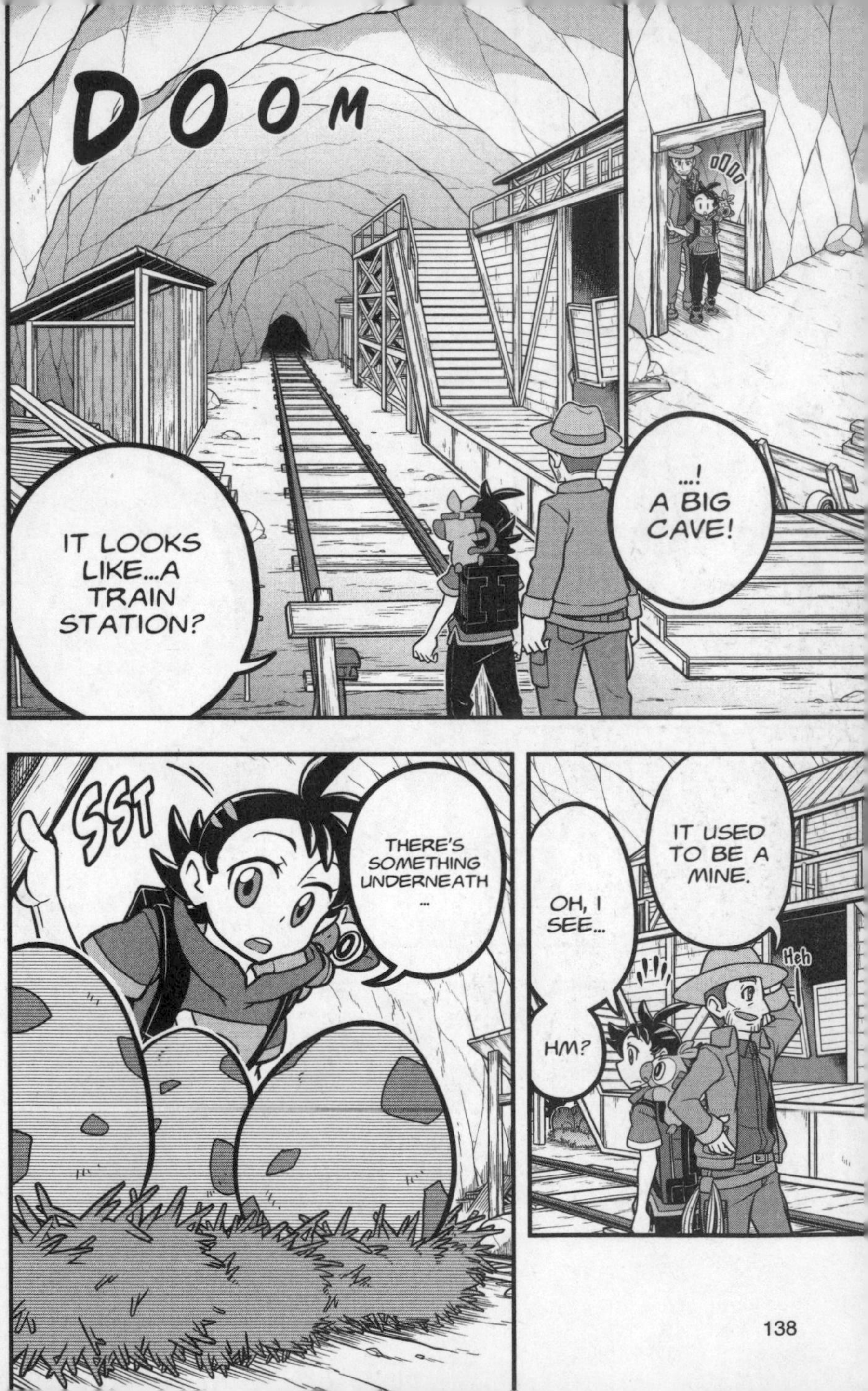
DOOM
...! A BIG CAVE!
IT LOOKS LIKE...A TRAIN STATION?
IT USED TO BE A MINE.
OH, I SEE...
Heh
HM?
SST
THERE'S SOMETHING UNDERNEATH ...

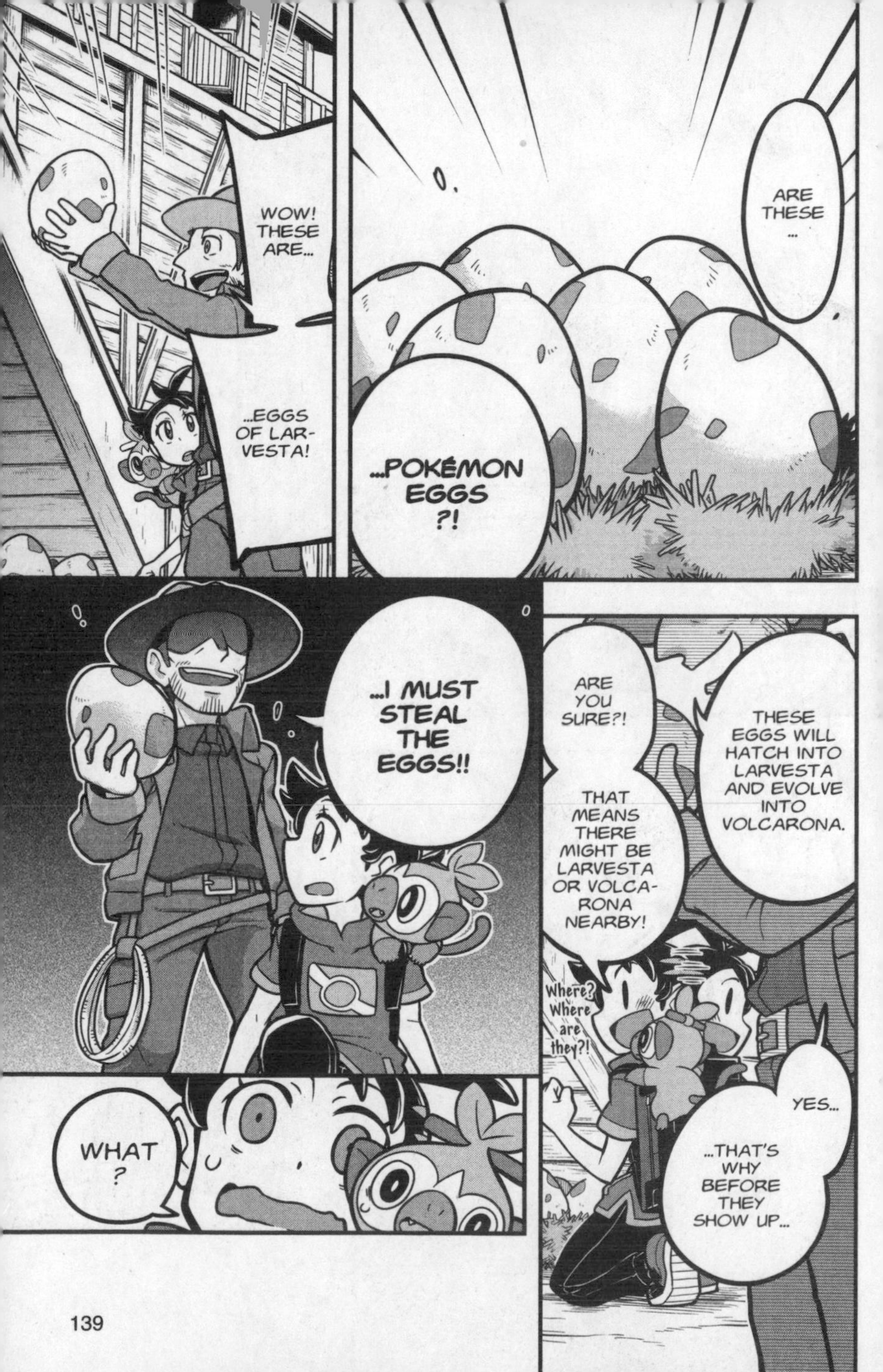
ARE THESE ...
...POKÉMON EGGS ?!
WOW! THESE ARE...
...EGGS OF LARVESTA!
THESE EGGS WILL HATCH INTO LARVESTA AND EVOLVE INTO VOLCARONA.
ARE YOU SURE?!
THAT MEANS THERE MIGHT BE LARVESTA OR VOLCARONA NEARBY!
Where? Where are they?!
YES...
...THAT'S WHY BEFORE THEY SHOW UP...
...I MUST STEAL THE EGGS!!
WHAT ?

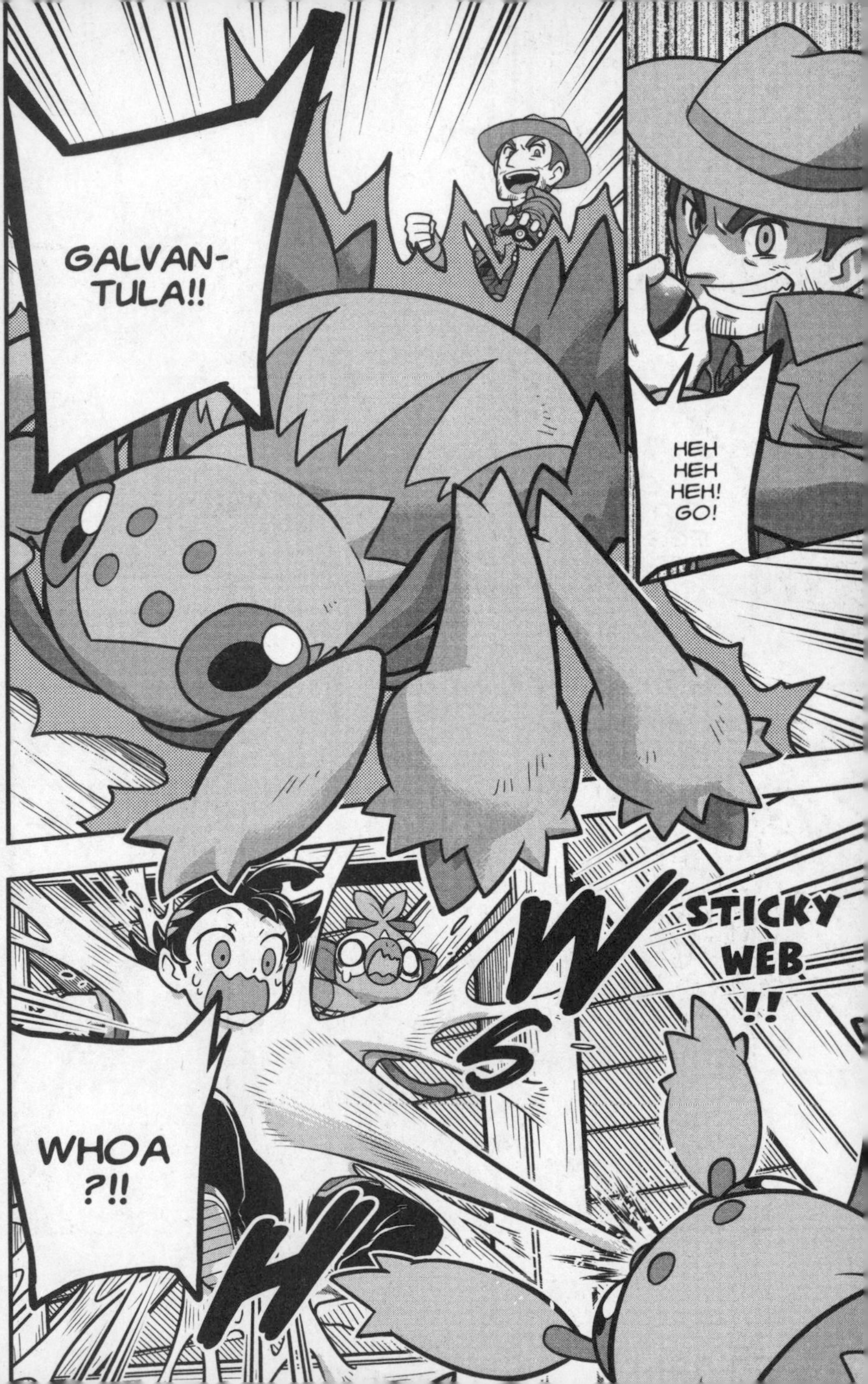
HEH HEH HEH! GO!
GALVAN-TULA!!
STICKY WEB!!
WHOA ?!!

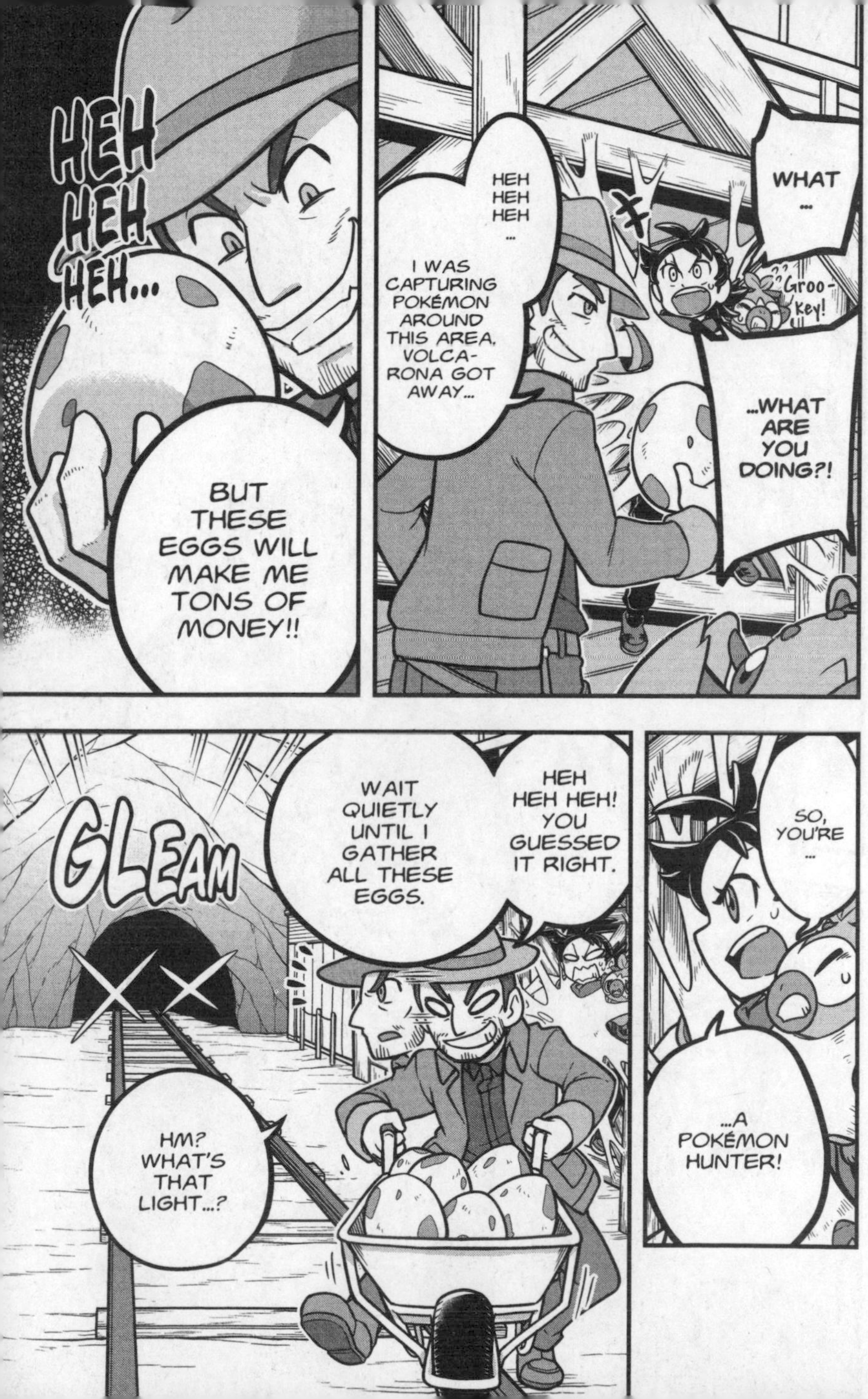
WHAT ...
Groo-key!
...WHAT ARE YOU DOING?!
HEH HEH HEH ... I WAS CAPTURING POKÉMON AROUND THIS AREA. VOLCARONA GOT AWAY...
HEH HEH HEH...
BUT THESE EGGS WILL MAKE ME TONS OF MONEY!!
SO, YOU'RE ...
...A POKÉMON HUNTER!
HEH HEH HEH! YOU GUESSED IT RIGHT.
WAIT QUIETLY UNTIL I GATHER ALL THESE EGGS.
GLEAM
HM? WHAT'S THAT LIGHT...?

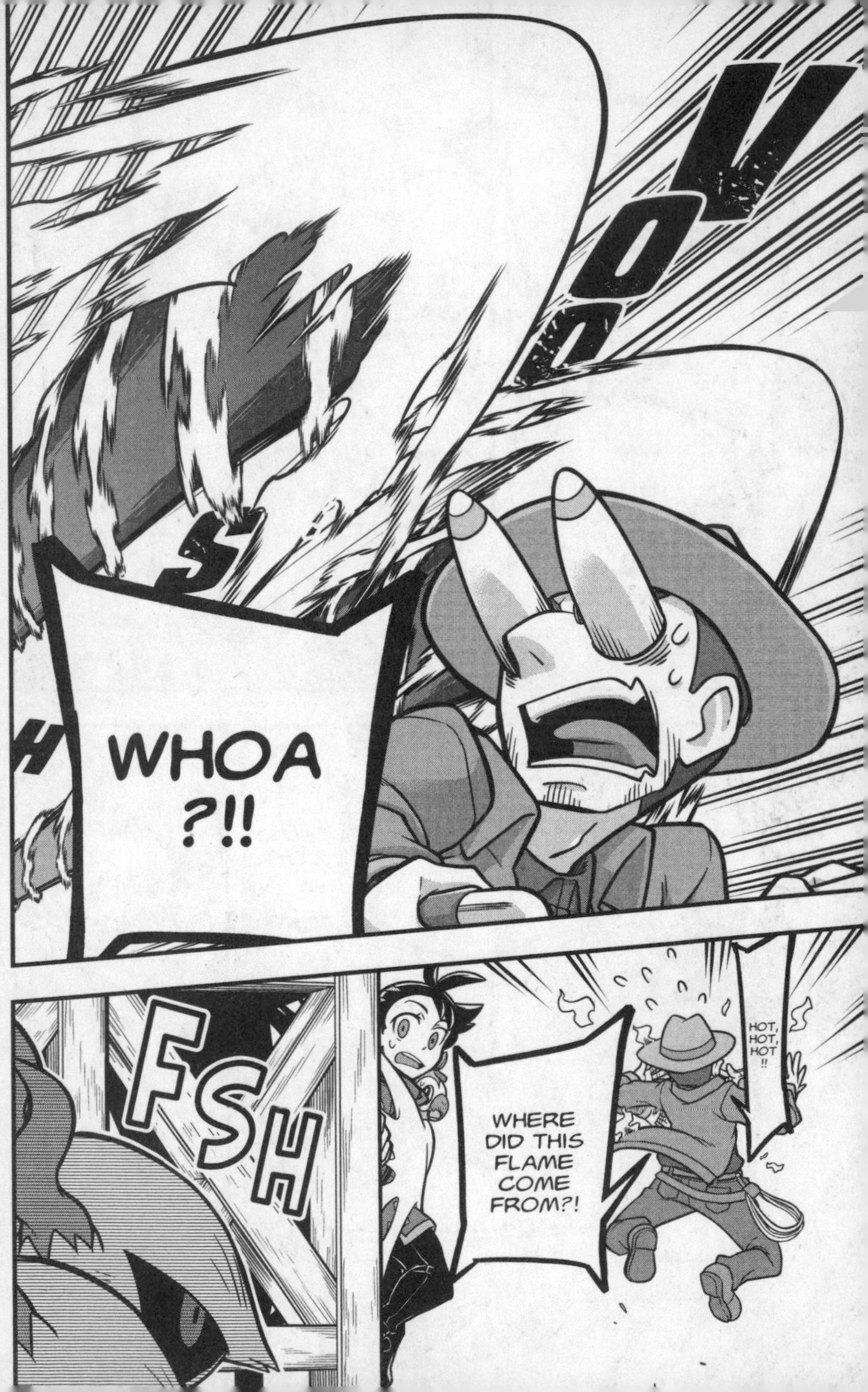
WHOA ?!!
HOT, HOT, HOT !!
WHERE DID THIS FLAME COME FROM?!
FSH

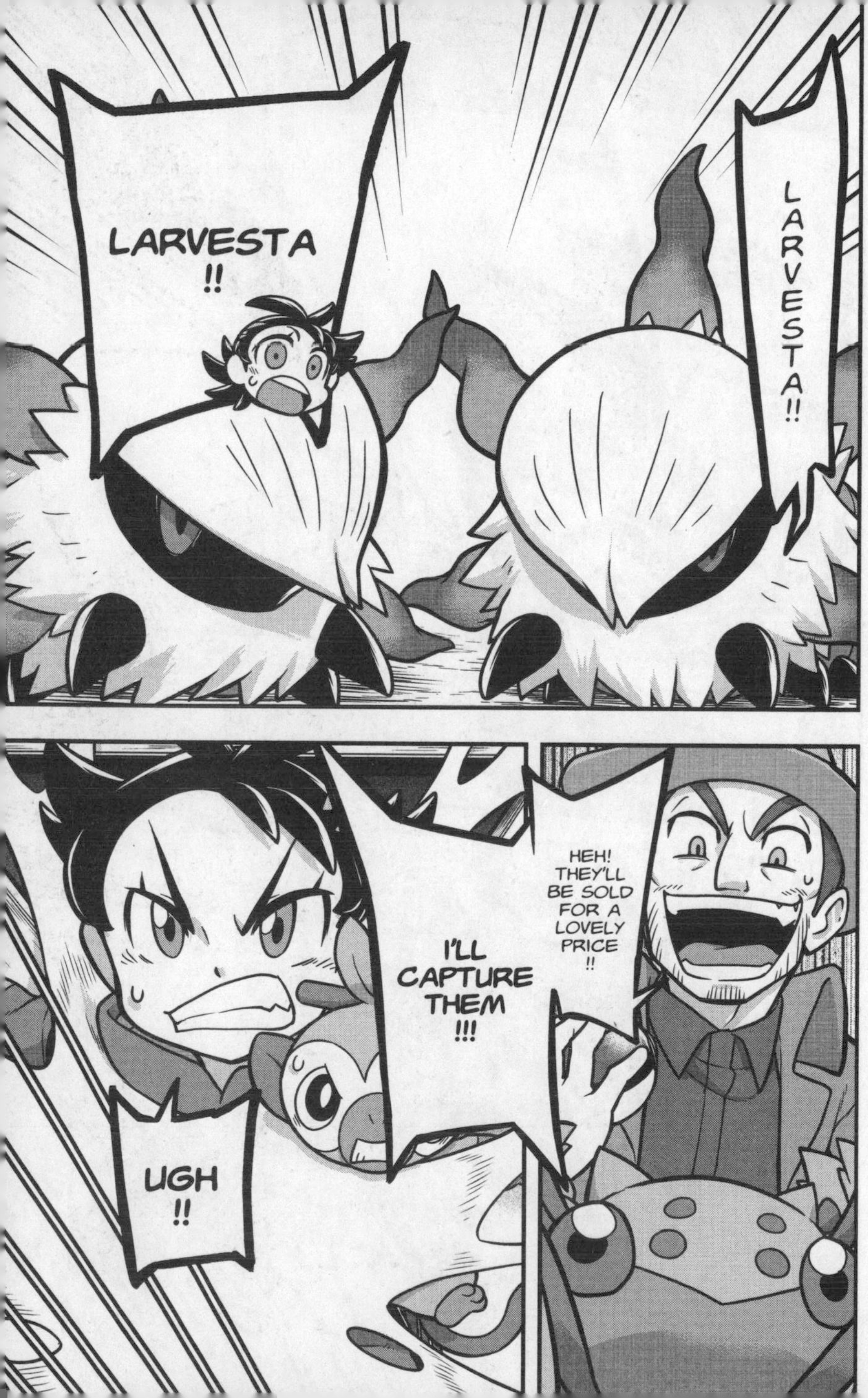
LARVESTA!!
LARVESTA!!
HEH! THEY'LL BE SOLD FOR A LOVELY PRICE!!
I'LL CAPTURE THEM!!!
UGH!!

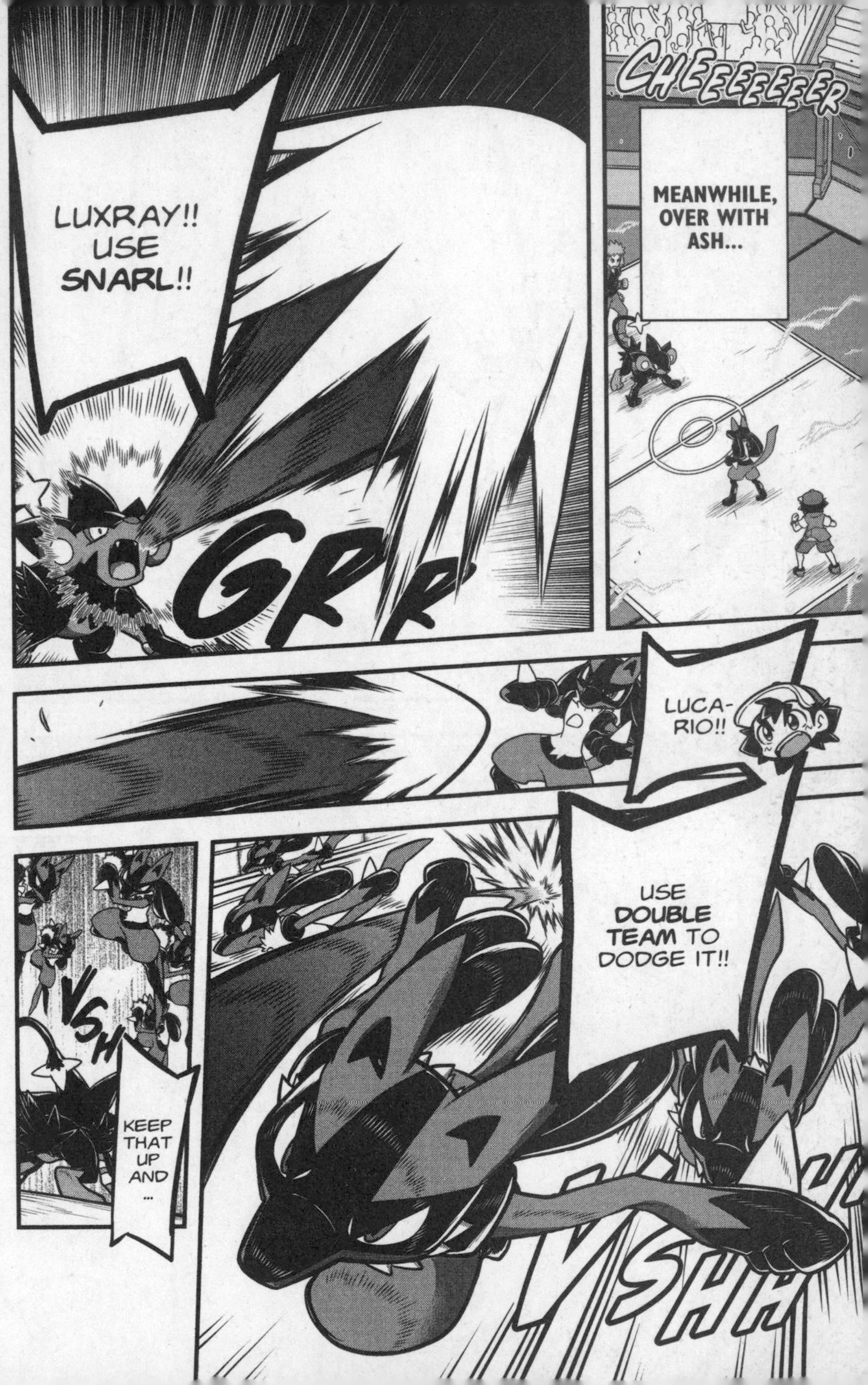
CHEEEEEEER
MEANWHILE, OVER WITH ASH...
LUXRAY!! USE SNARL!!
GRR
LUCA-RIO!!
USE DOUBLE TEAM TO DODGE IT!!
VSHH
VSH
KEEP THAT UP AND...

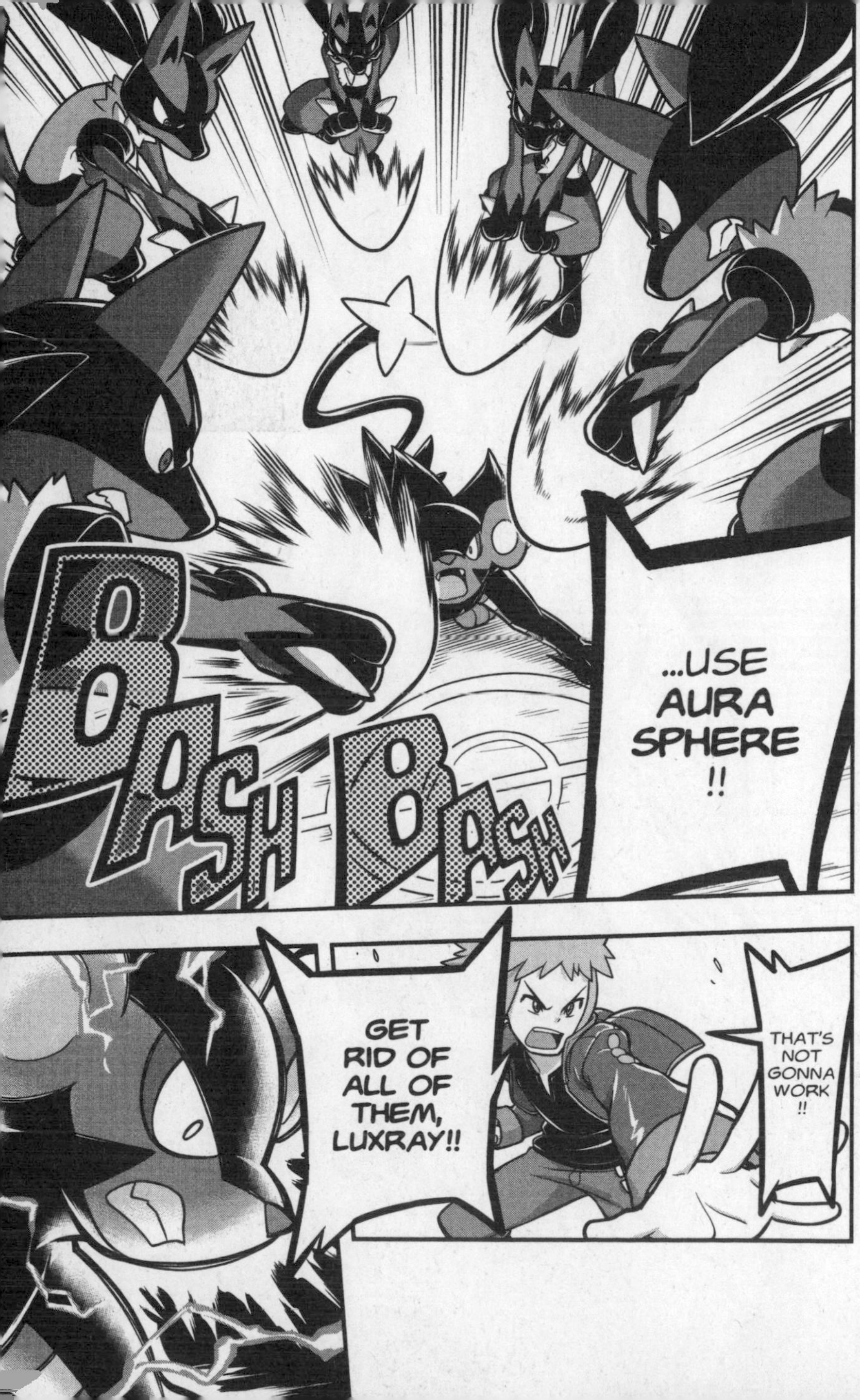
...USE AURA SPHERE !!
BASH
BASH
THAT'S NOT GONNA WORK !!
GET RID OF ALL OF THEM, LUXRAY!!

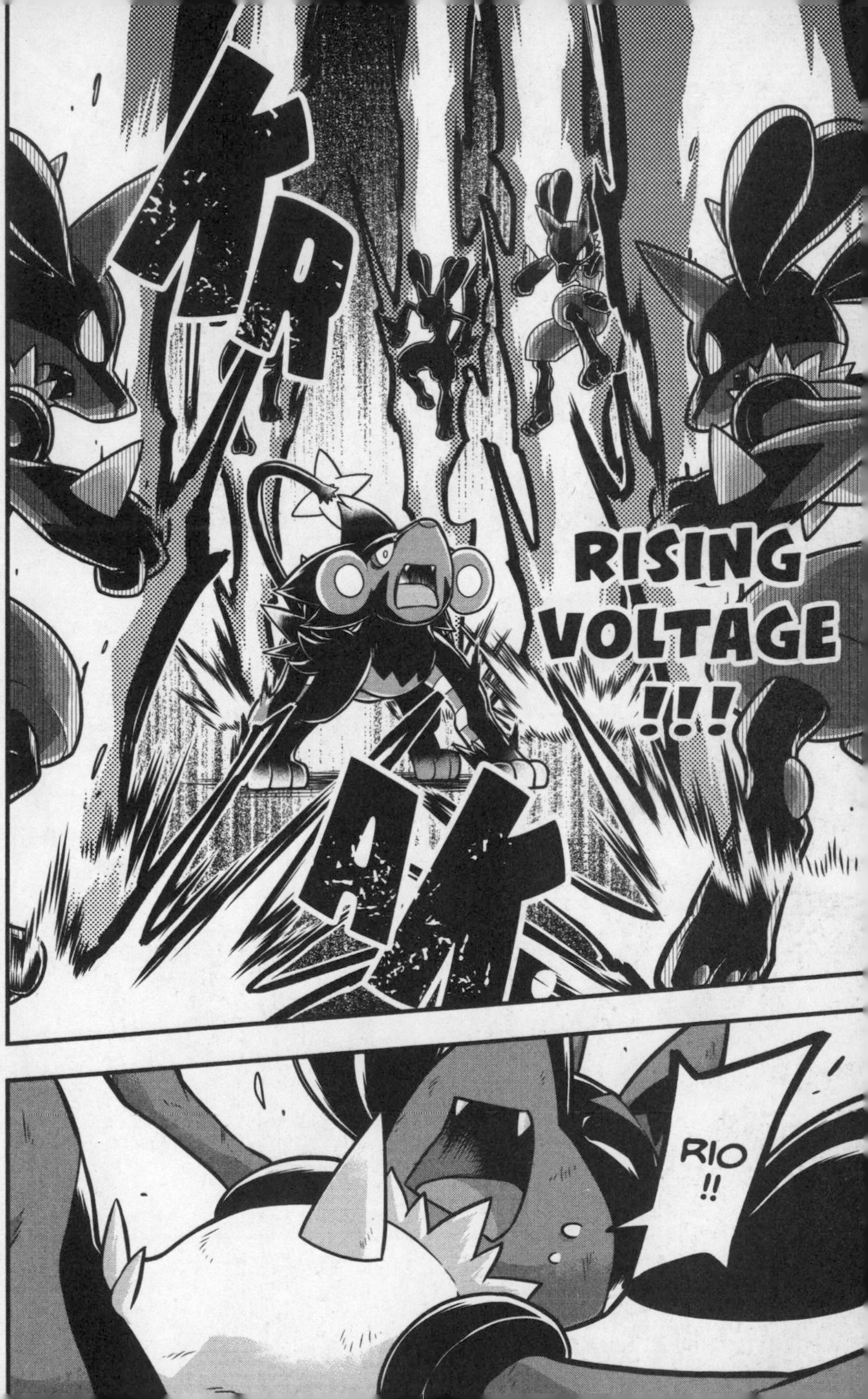
RISING VOLTAGE !!!
RIO !!

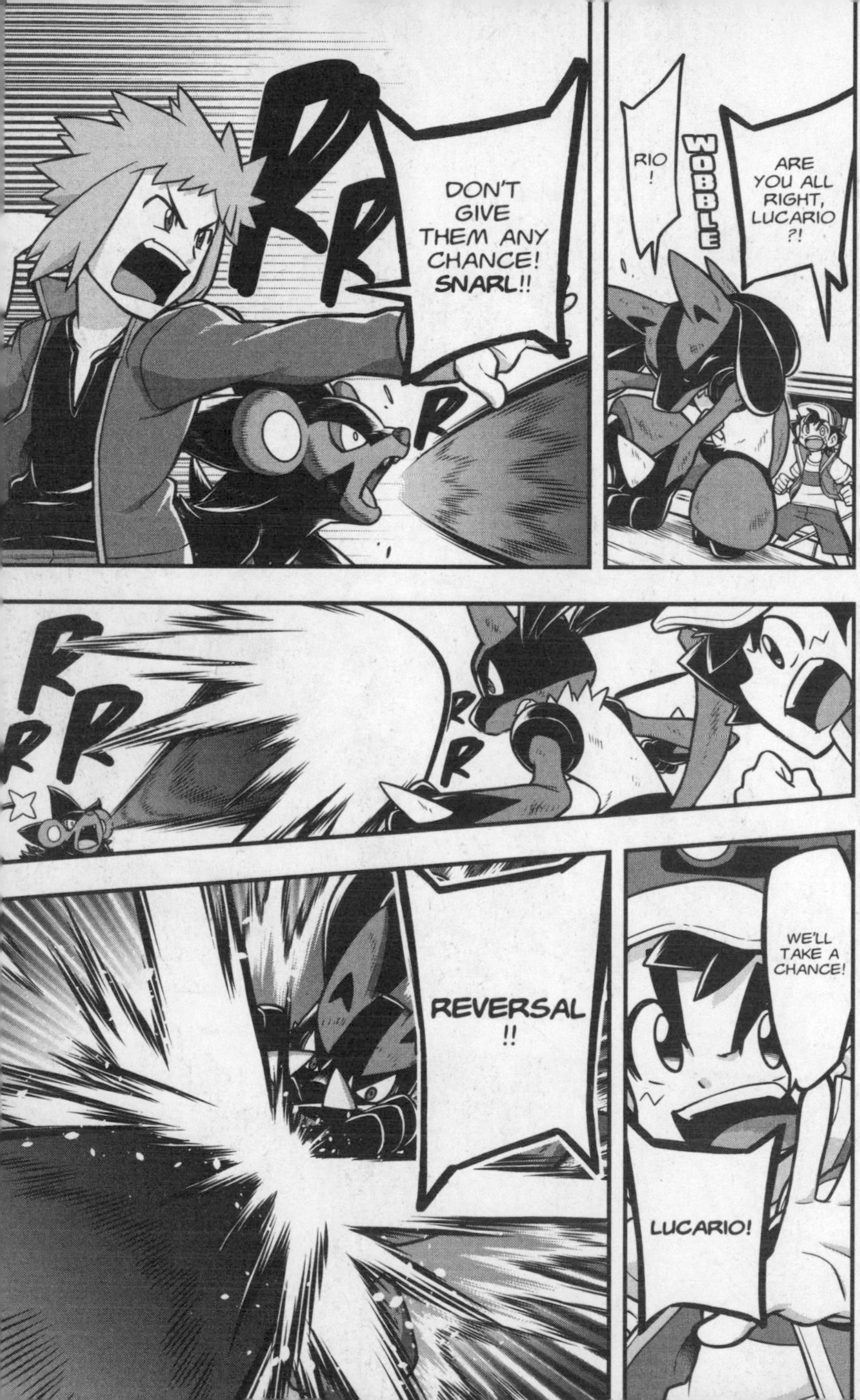
ARE YOU ALL RIGHT, LUCARIO?!
WOBBLE
RIO!
DON'T GIVE THEM ANY CHANCE! SNARL!!
WE'LL TAKE A CHANCE!
LUCARIO!
REVERSAL!!

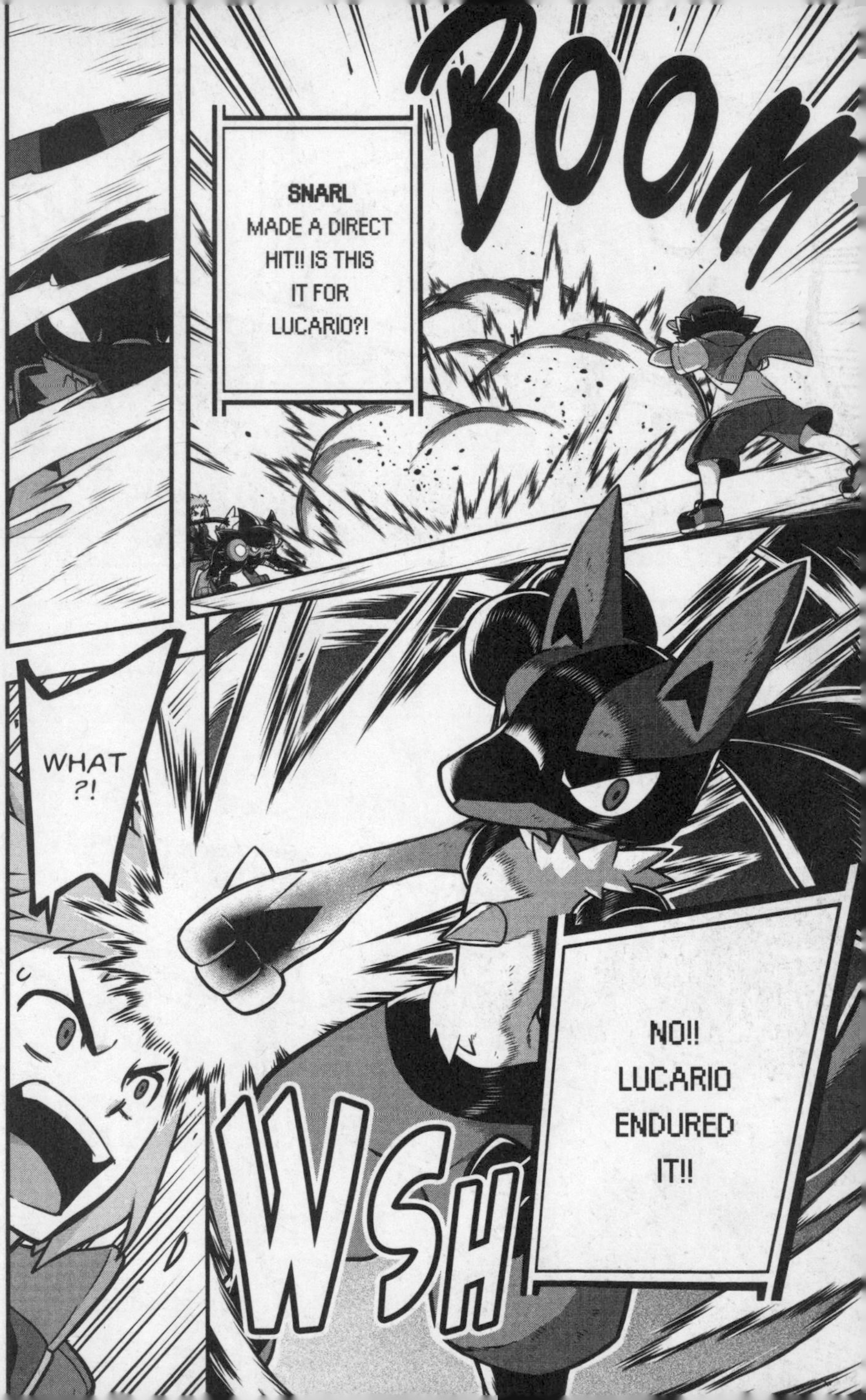
BOOM
SNARL MADE A DIRECT HIT!! IS THIS IT FOR LUCARIO?!
NO!! LUCARIO ENDURED IT!!
WSH
WHAT?!

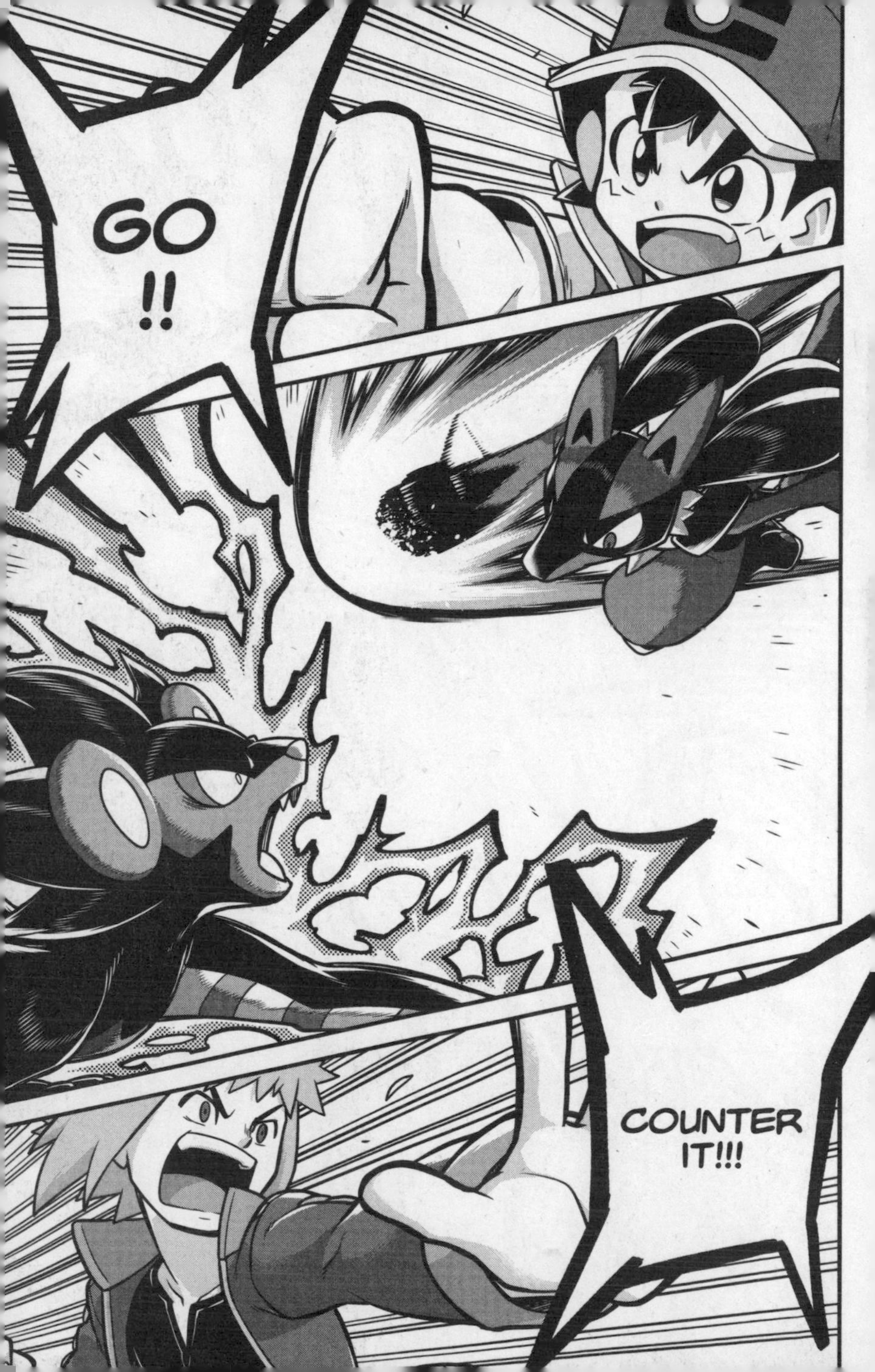
GO
!!
COUNTER
IT!!!

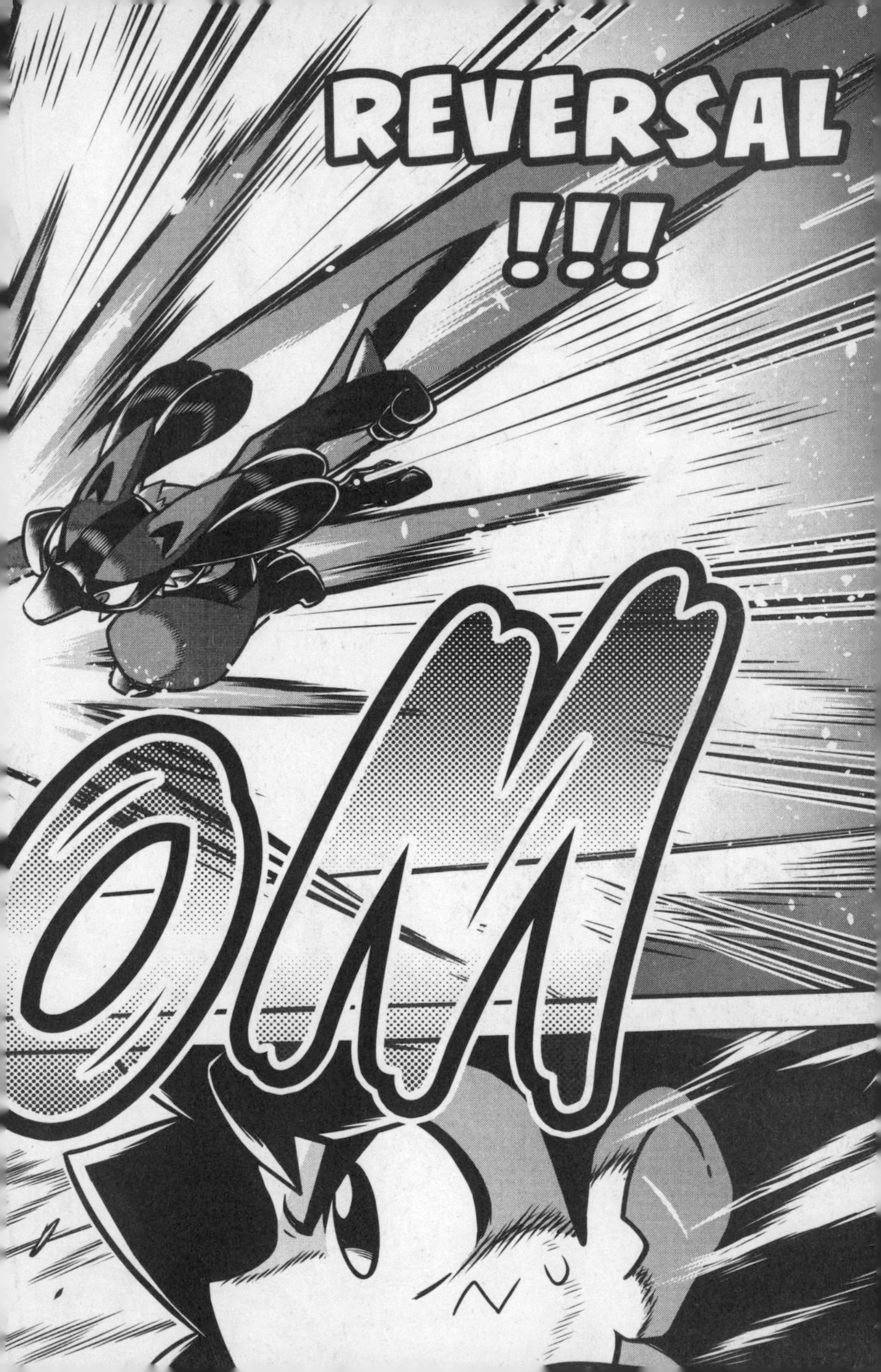
REVERSAL !!!
OM

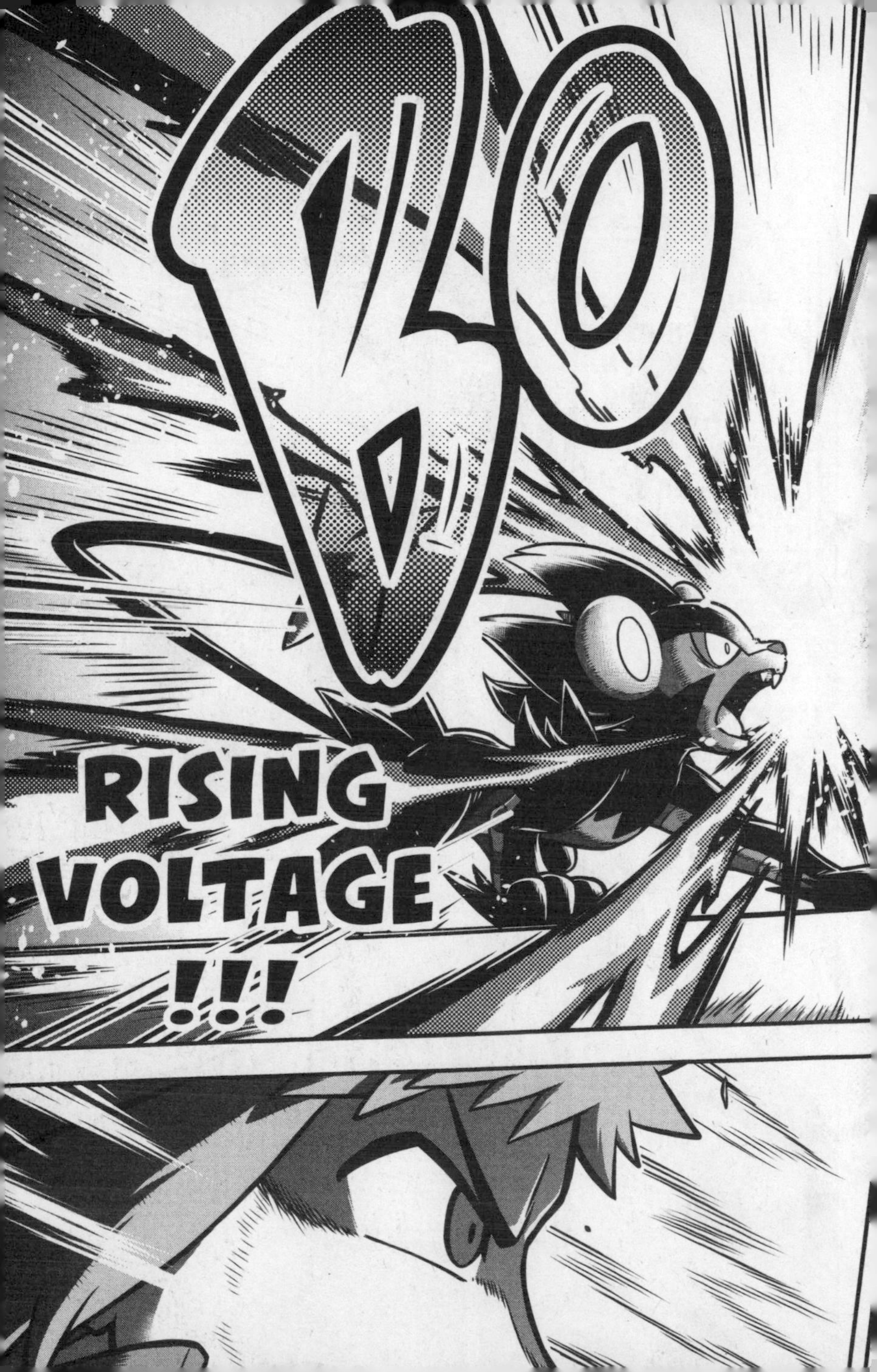
RISING VOLTAGE !!!

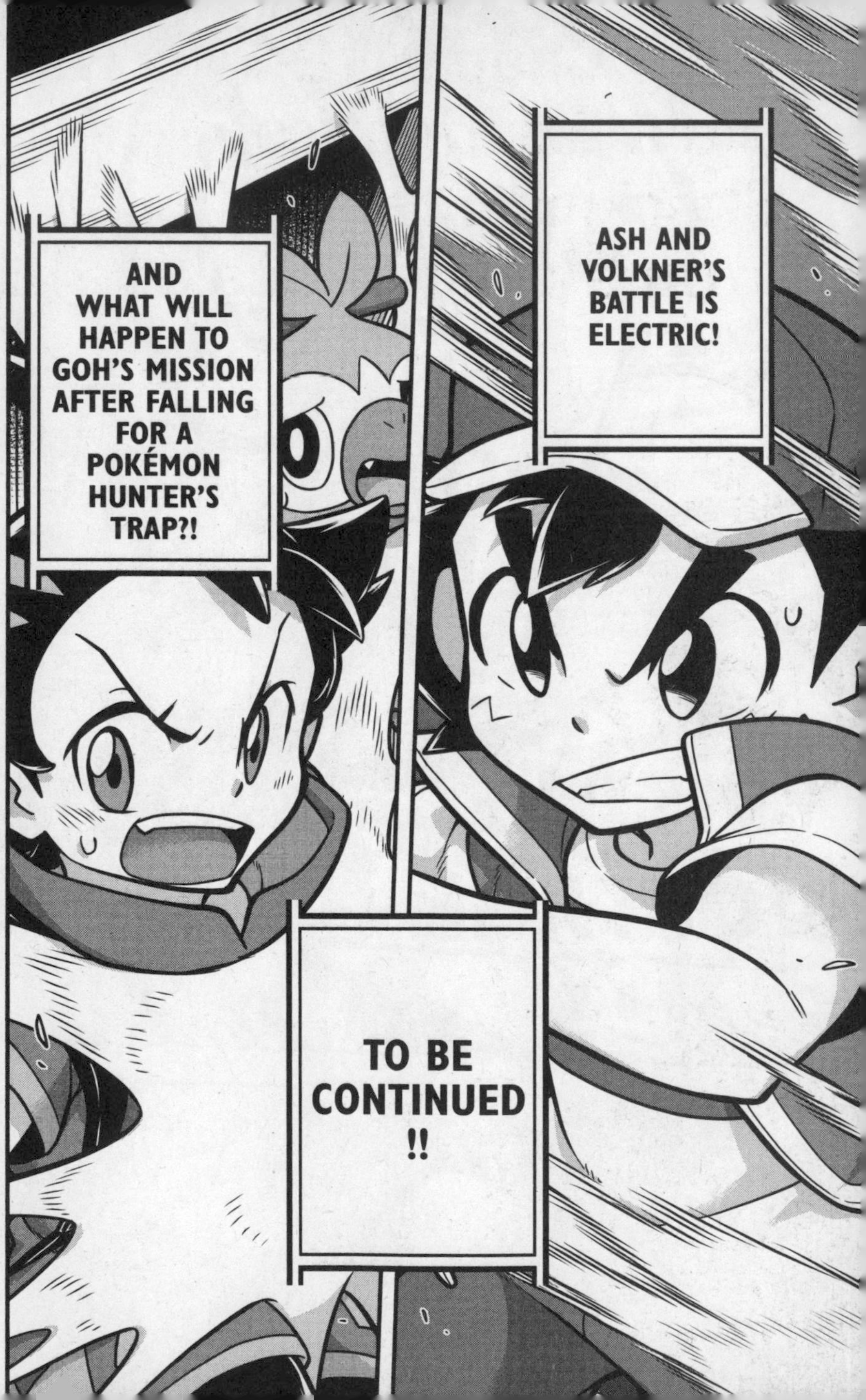
ASH AND VOLKNER'S BATTLE IS ELECTRIC!
AND WHAT WILL HAPPEN TO GOH'S MISSION AFTER FALLING FOR A POKÉMON HUNTER'S TRAP?!
TO BE CONTINUED !!

Chapter 24
Ultra Exciting from the Shocking Start! & Trial on a Golden Scale! ②

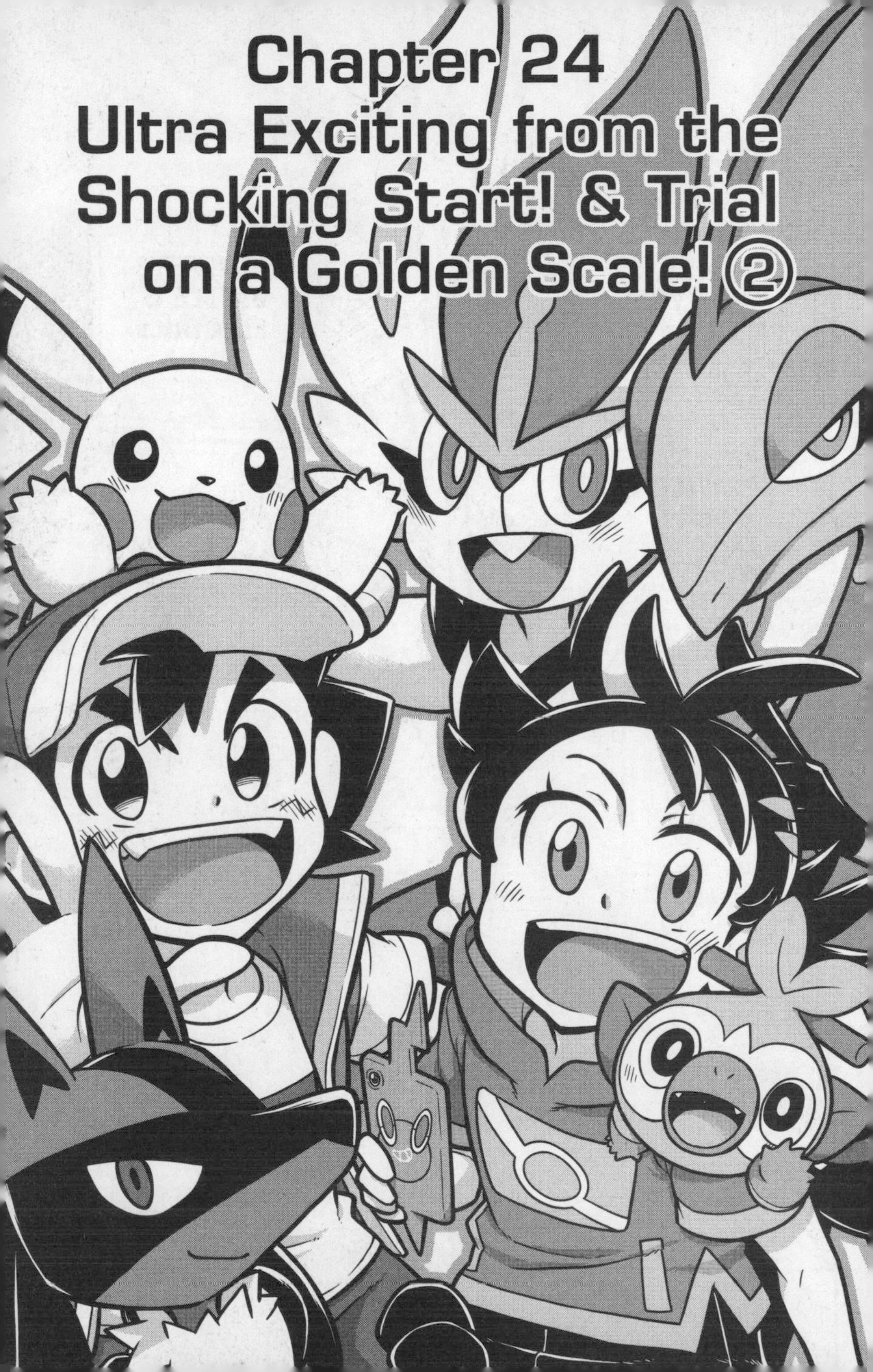

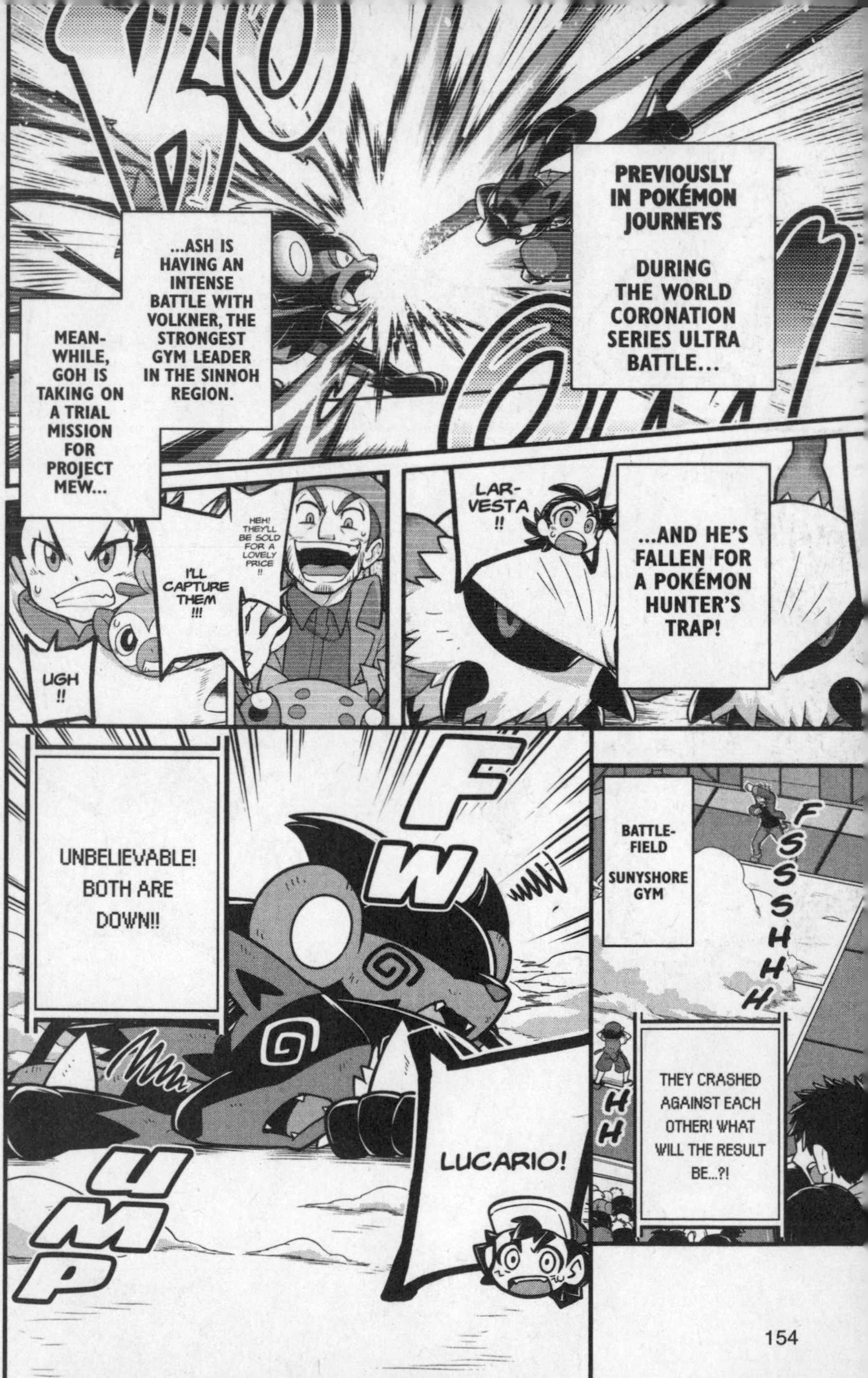
PREVIOUSLY IN POKÉMON JOURNEYS
DURING THE WORLD CORONATION SERIES ULTRA BATTLE...
...ASH IS HAVING AN INTENSE BATTLE WITH VOLKNER, THE STRONGEST GYM LEADER IN THE SINNOH REGION.
MEAN-WHILE, GOH IS TAKING ON A TRIAL MISSION FOR PROJECT MEW...
...AND HE'S FALLEN FOR A POKÉMON HUNTER'S TRAP!
LAR-VESTA !!
HEH! THEY'LL BE SOLD FOR A LOVELY PRICE !!
I'LL CAPTURE THEM !!!
UGH !!
BATTLE-FIELD
SUNYSHORE GYM
FSSSHHHHH
THEY CRASHED AGAINST EACH OTHER! WHAT WILL THE RESULT BE...?!
UNBELIEVABLE! BOTH ARE DOWN!!
FWUMP
LUCARIO!

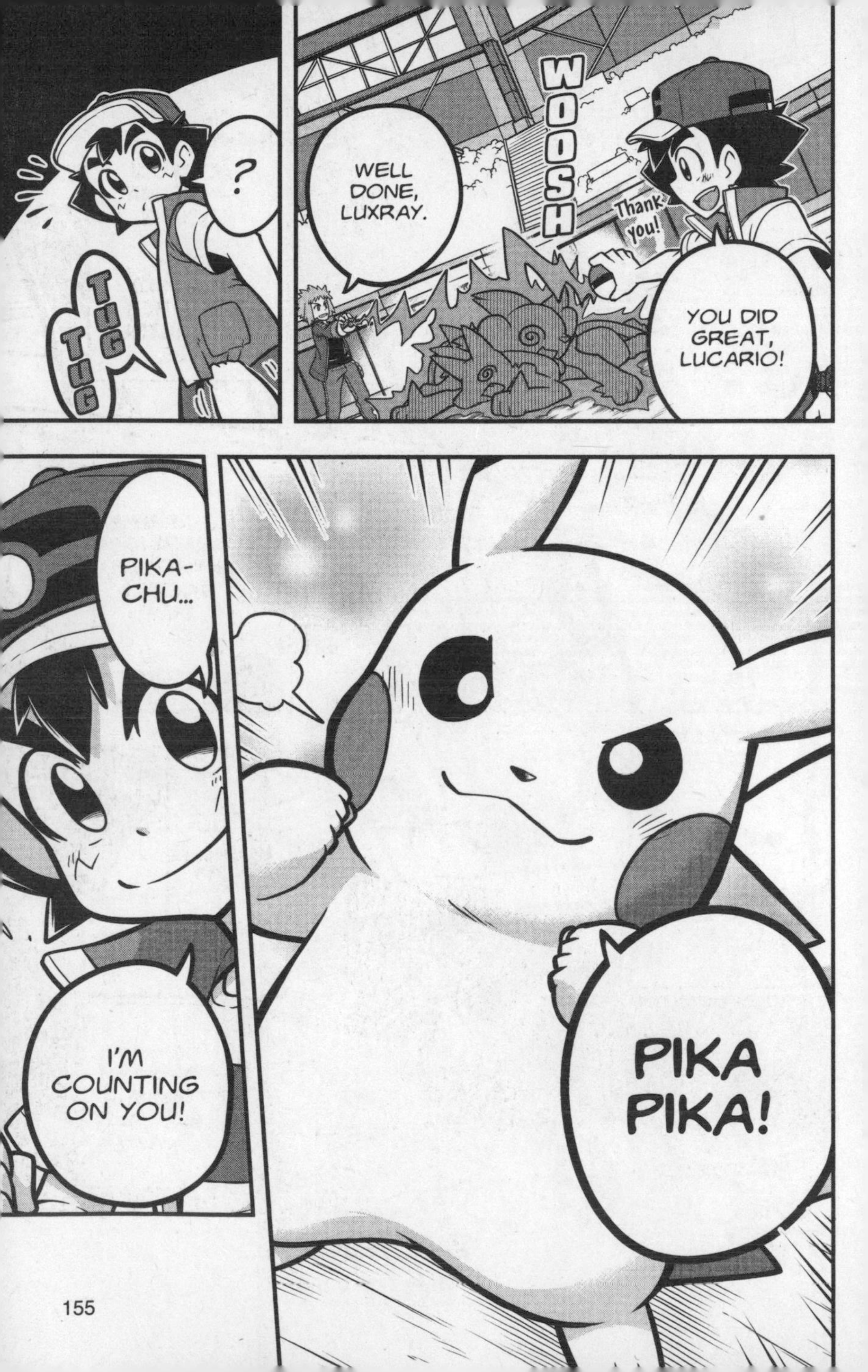
Thank you!
YOU DID GREAT, LUCARIO!
WOOSH
WELL DONE, LUXRAY.
?
TUG TUG
PIKA PIKA!
PIKA-CHU...
I'M COUNTING ON YOU!

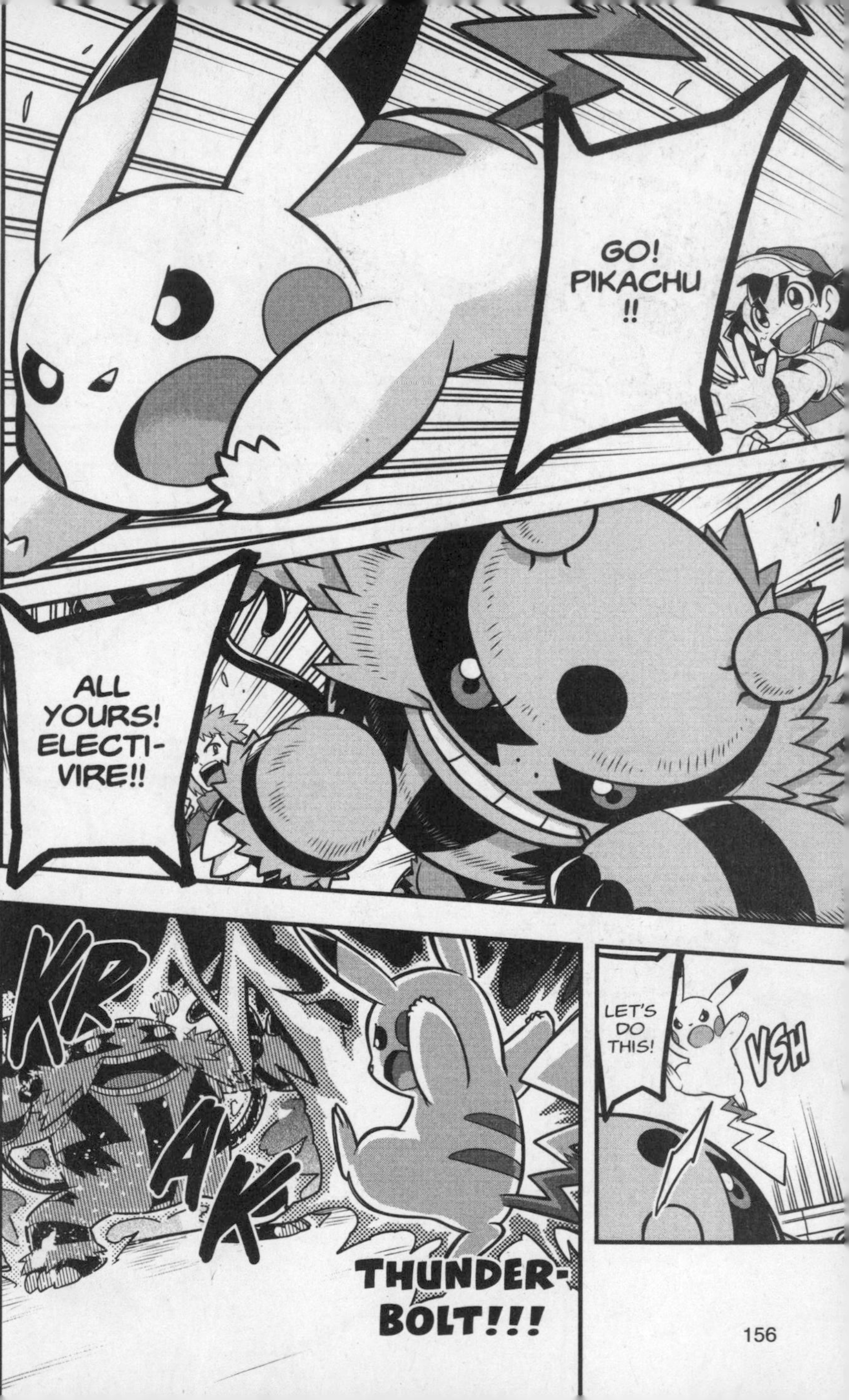
GO! PIKACHU!!
ALL YOURS! ELECTIVIRE!!
LET'S DO THIS!
VSH
KRAKK
THUNDERBOLT!!!

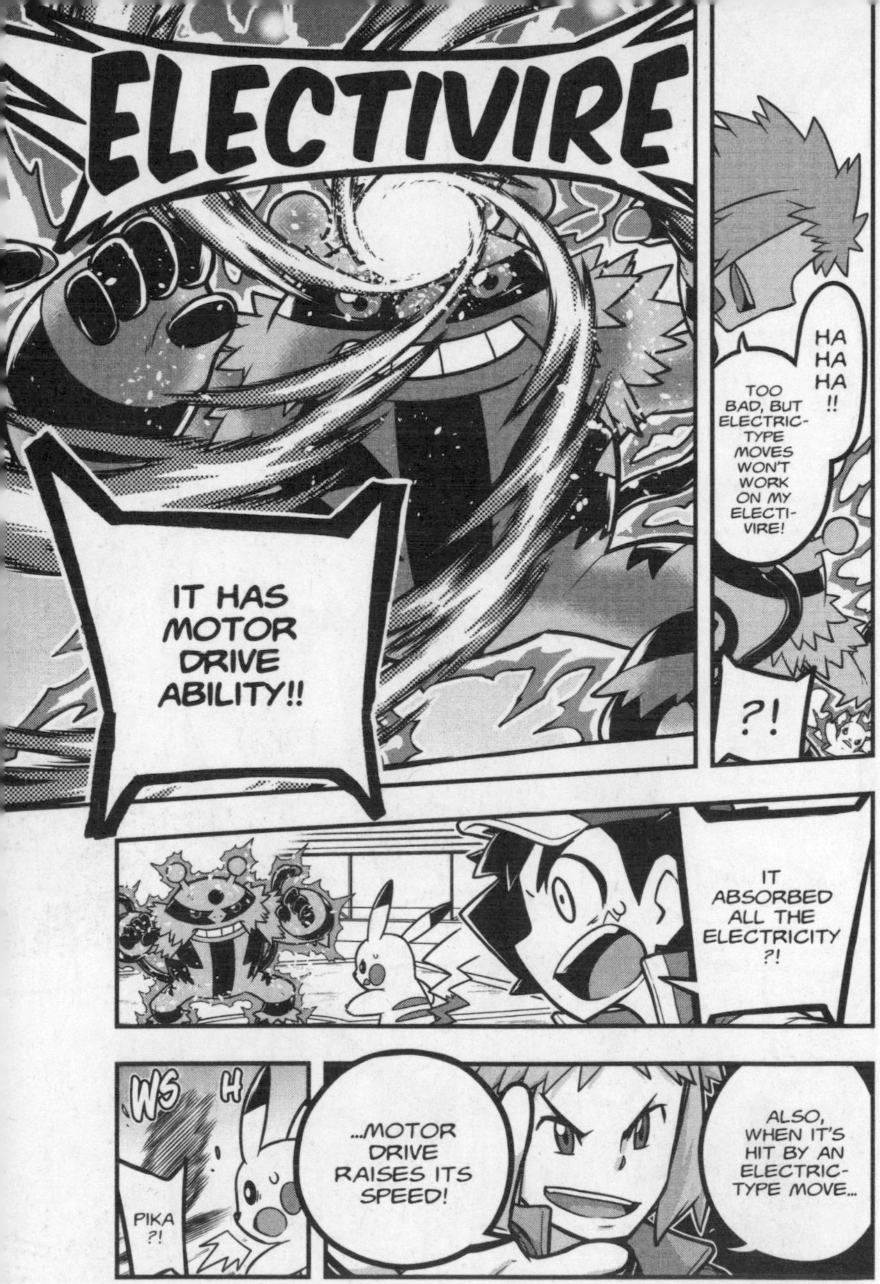
HA HA HA !!
TOO BAD, BUT ELECTRIC-TYPE MOVES WON'T WORK ON MY ELECTIVIRE!
?!
ELECTIVIRE
IT HAS MOTOR DRIVE ABILITY!!
IT ABSORBED ALL THE ELECTRICITY?!
ALSO, WHEN IT'S HIT BY AN ELECTRIC-TYPE MOVE...
...MOTOR DRIVE RAISES ITS SPEED!
WSH
PIKA?!

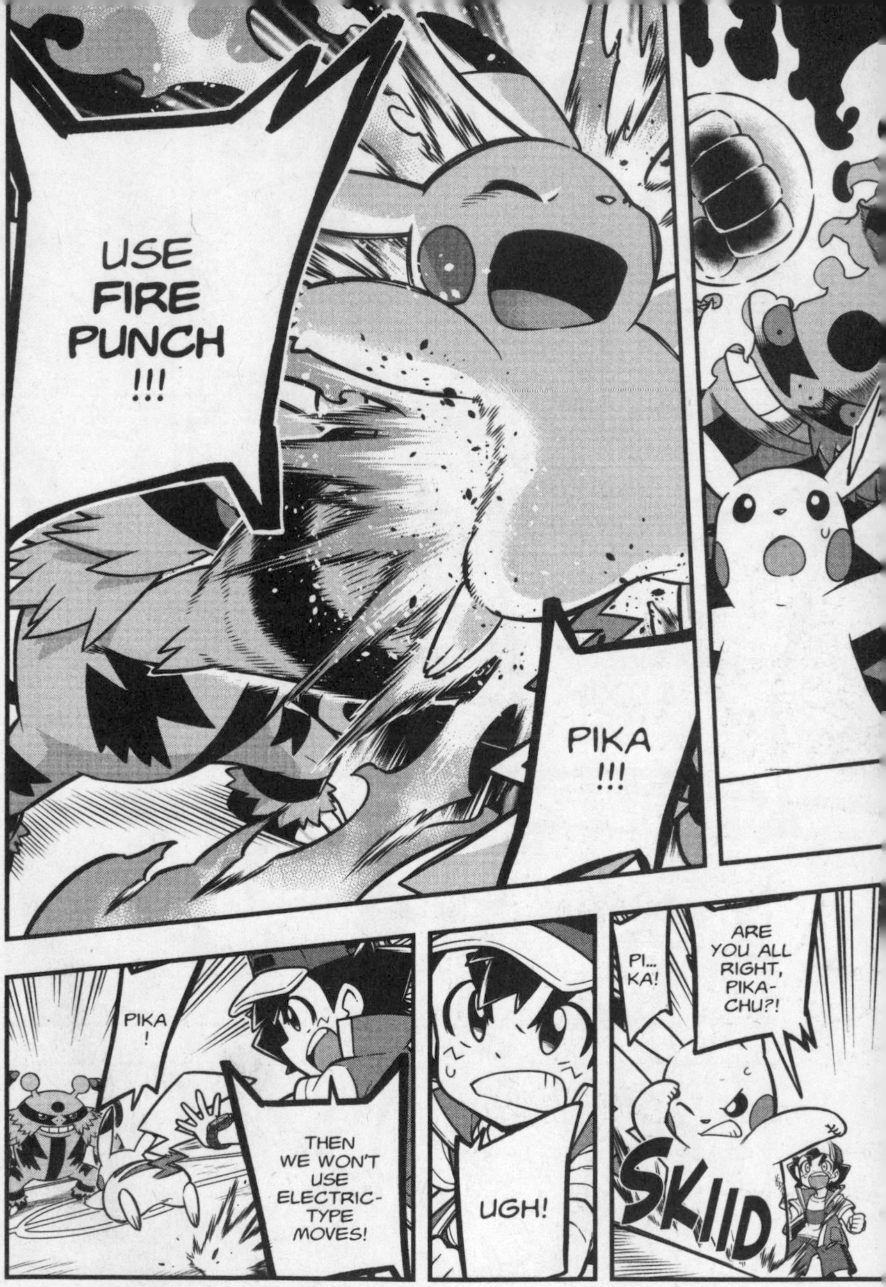
USE FIRE PUNCH !!!
PIKA !!!
ARE YOU ALL RIGHT, PIKA-CHU?!
PI... KA!
SKIID
UGH!
PIKA !
THEN WE WON'T USE ELECTRIC-TYPE MOVES!

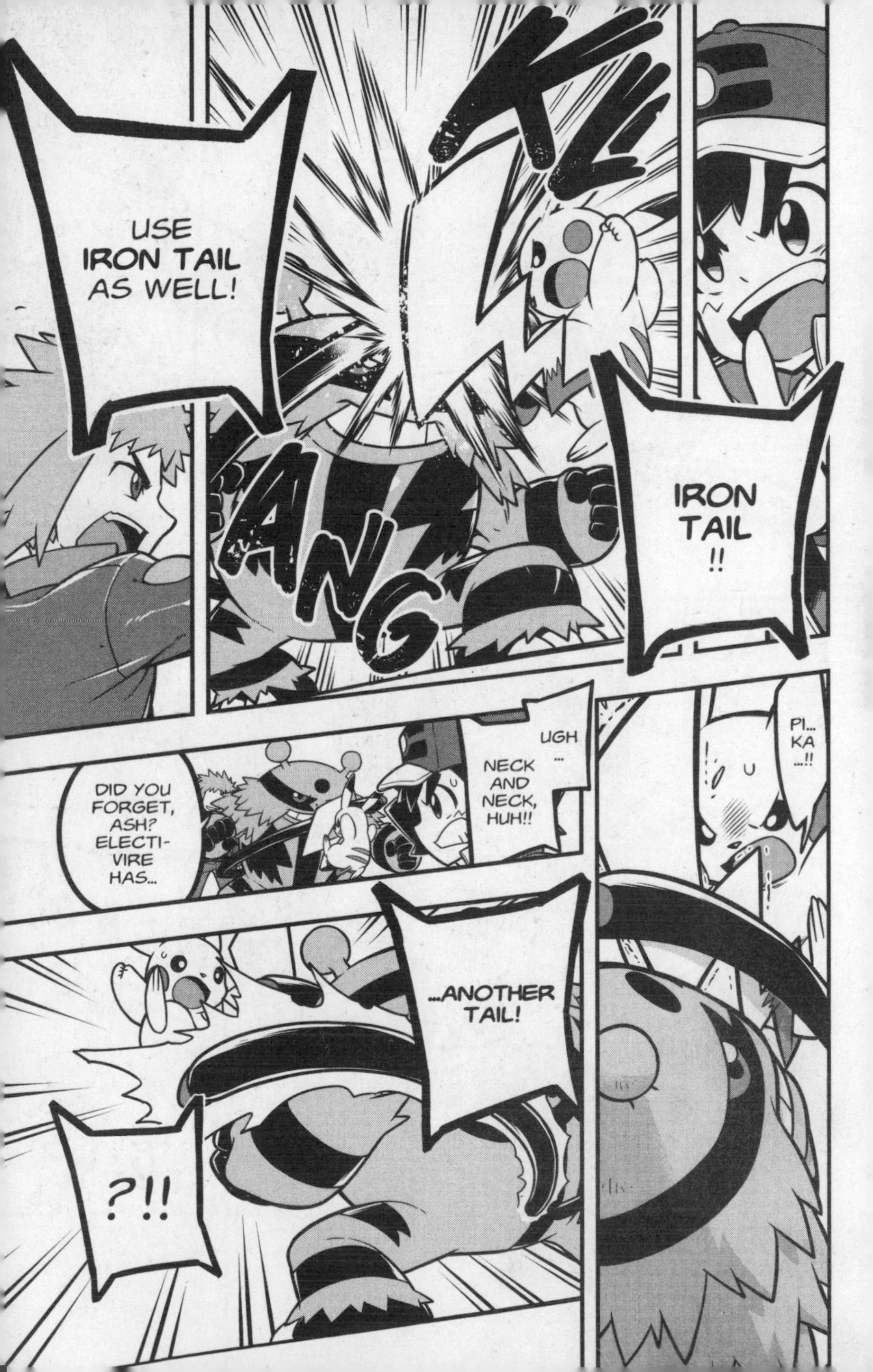
IRON TAIL !!
CLANG
USE IRON TAIL AS WELL!
PI... KA ...!!
UGH ...
NECK AND NECK, HUH!!
DID YOU FORGET, ASH? ELECTIVIRE HAS...
...ANOTHER TAIL!
?!!

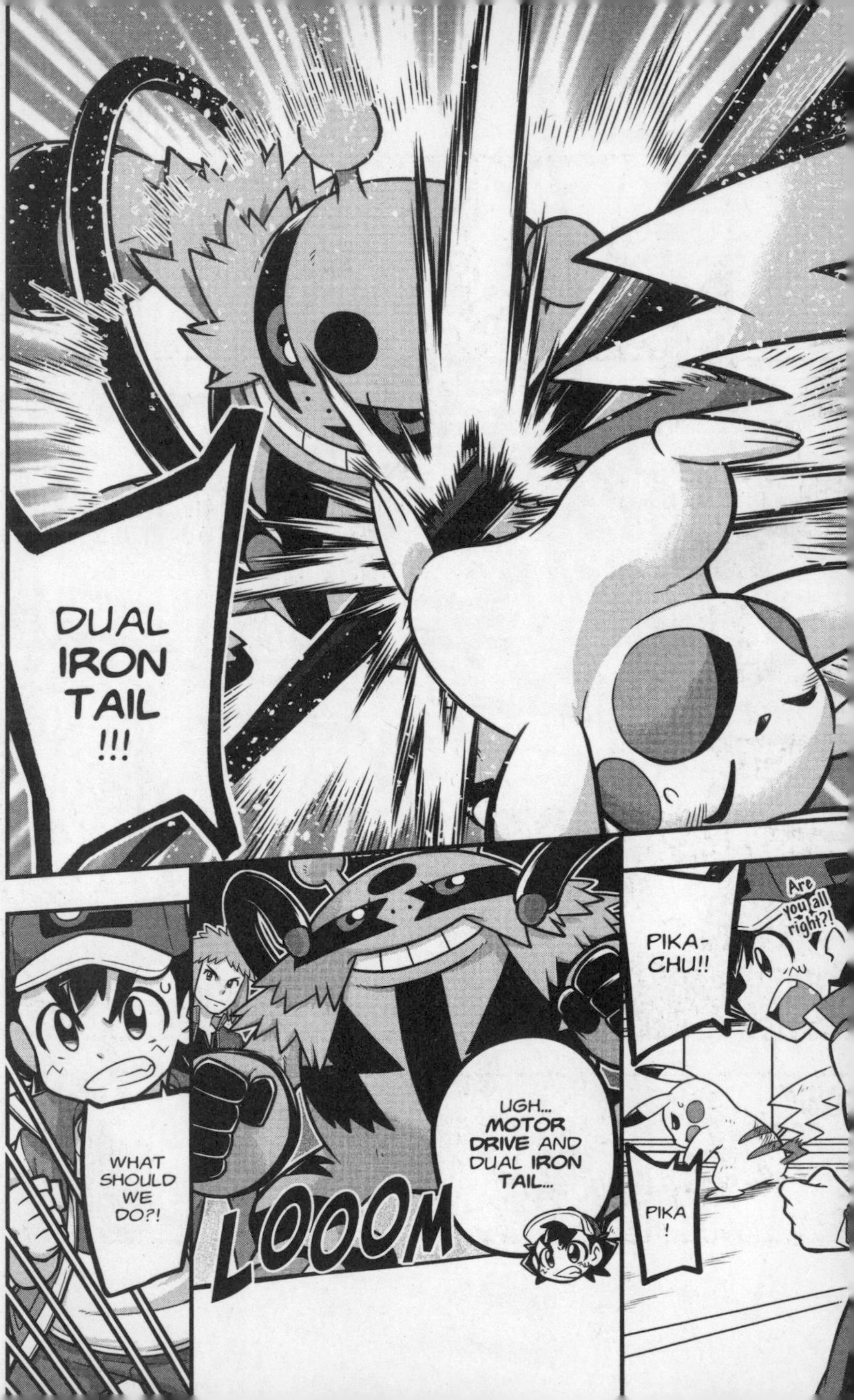
DUAL IRON TAIL!!!
Are you all right?!
PIKA-CHU!!
PIKA!
UGH... MOTOR DRIVE AND DUAL IRON TAIL...
LOOOM
WHAT SHOULD WE DO?!

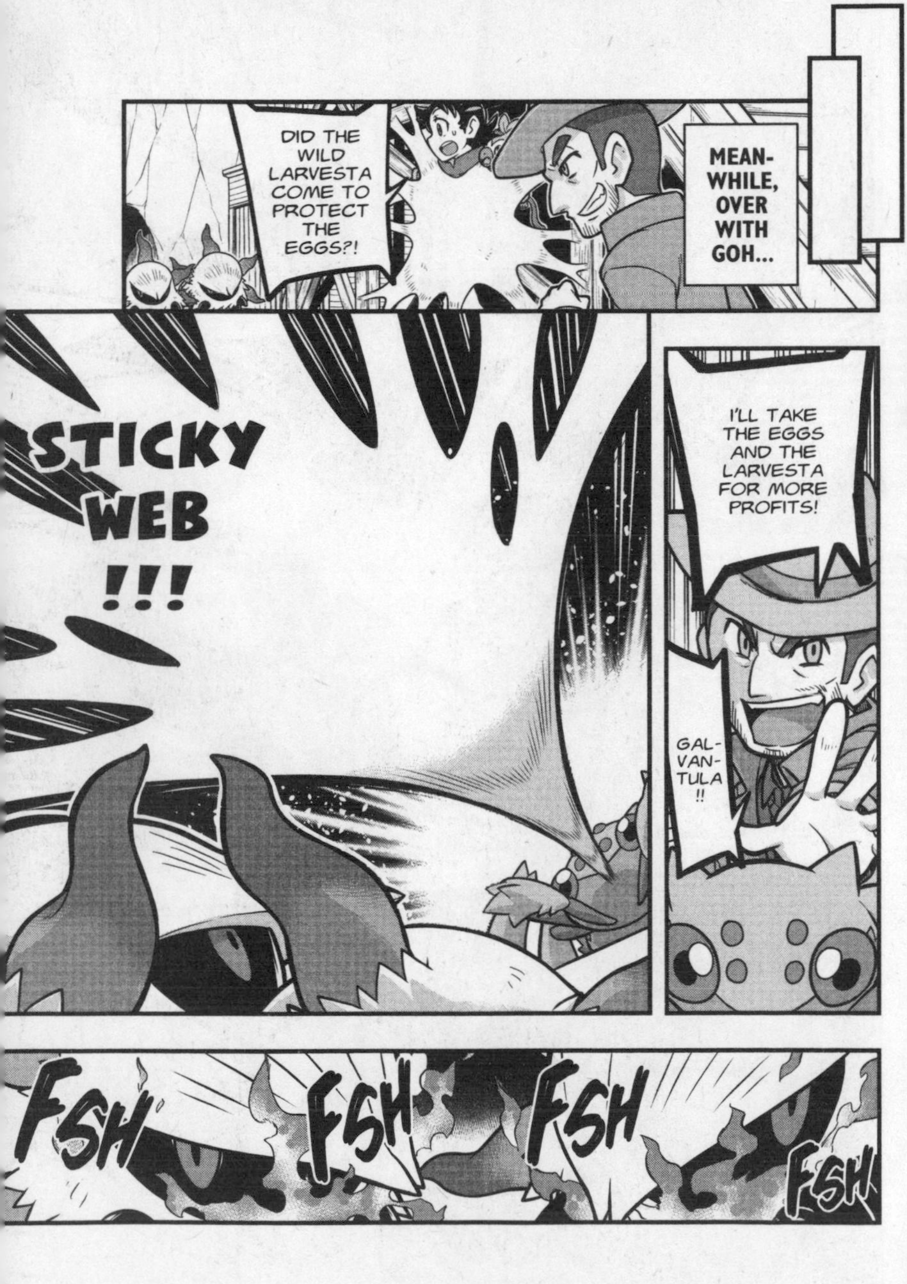
MEAN-WHILE, OVER WITH GOH...
DID THE WILD LARVESTA COME TO PROTECT THE EGGS?!
I'LL TAKE THE EGGS AND THE LARVESTA FOR MORE PROFITS!
GAL-VAN-TULA!!
STICKY WEB!!!
FSH
FSH
FSH
FSH

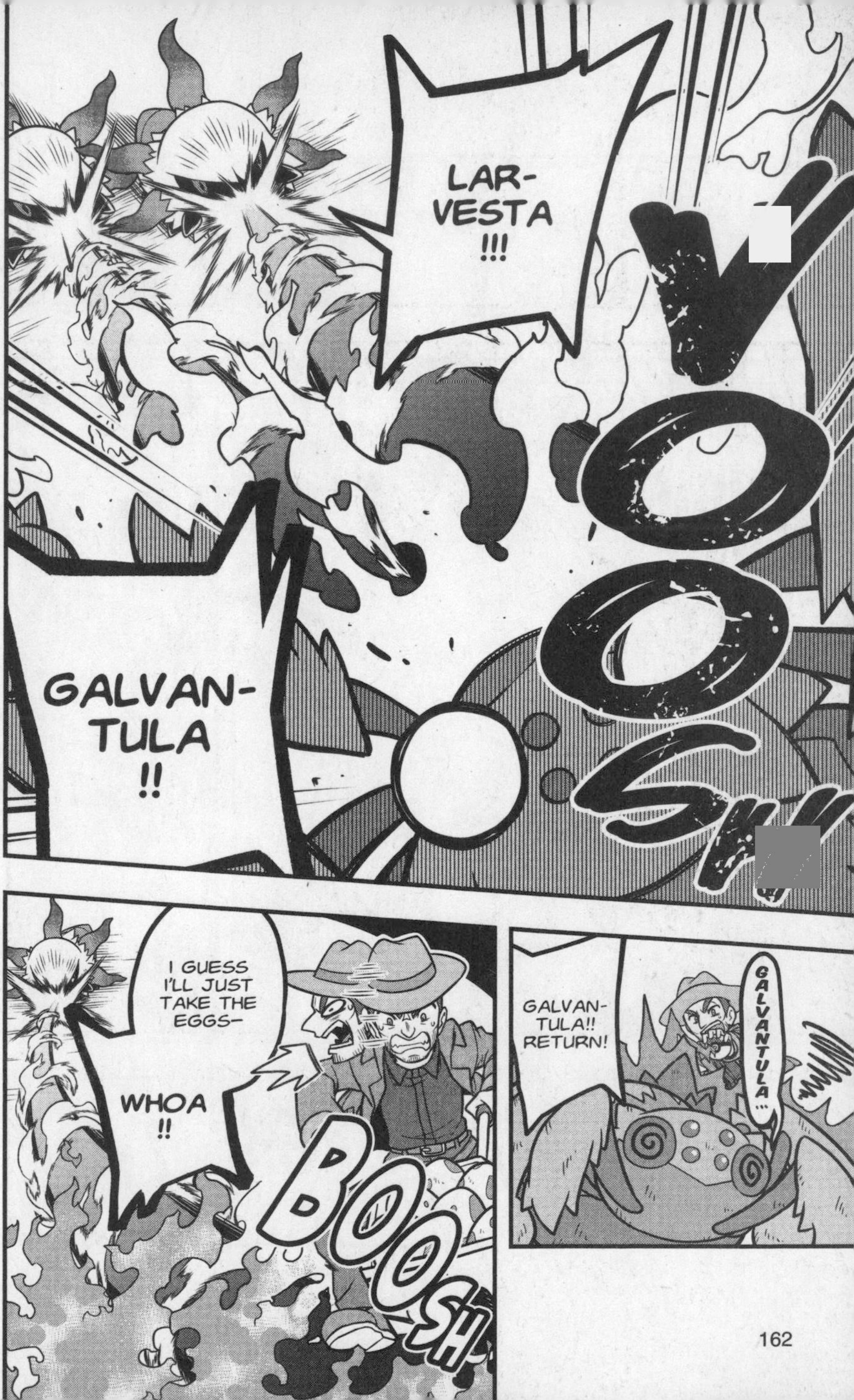
LAR-VESTA !!!
VOOSH
GALVAN-TULA !!
GALVAN-TULA!! RETURN!
GALVANTULA...
I GUESS I'LL JUST TAKE THE EGGS—
WHOA !!
BOOSH

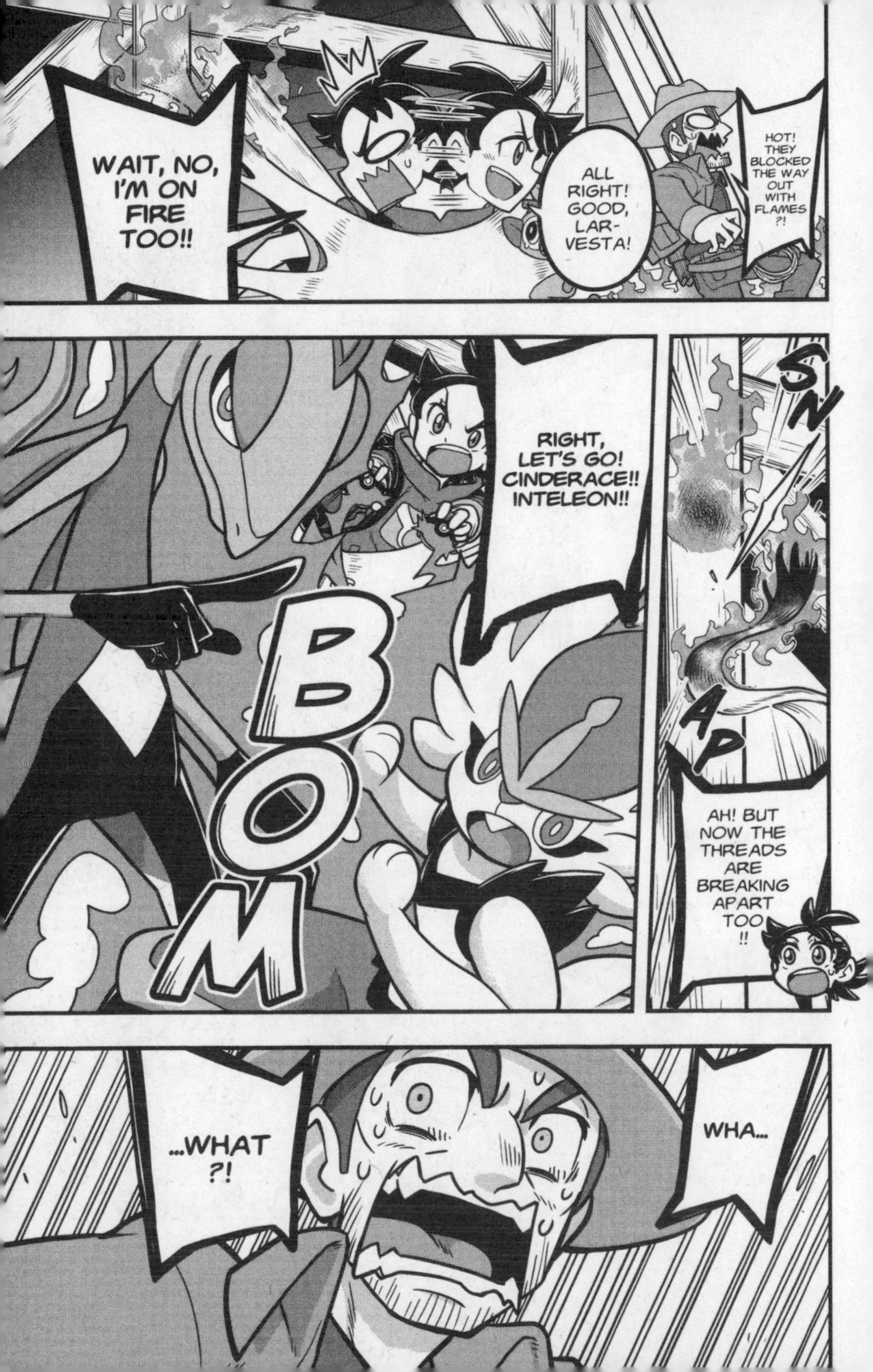
HOT! THEY BLOCKED THE WAY OUT WITH FLAMES ?!
ALL RIGHT! GOOD, LAR-VESTA!
WAIT, NO, I'M ON FIRE TOO!!
SNAP
AH! BUT NOW THE THREADS ARE BREAKING APART TOO !!
RIGHT, LET'S GO! CINDERACE!! INTELEON!!
BOOM
WHA...
...WHAT ?!

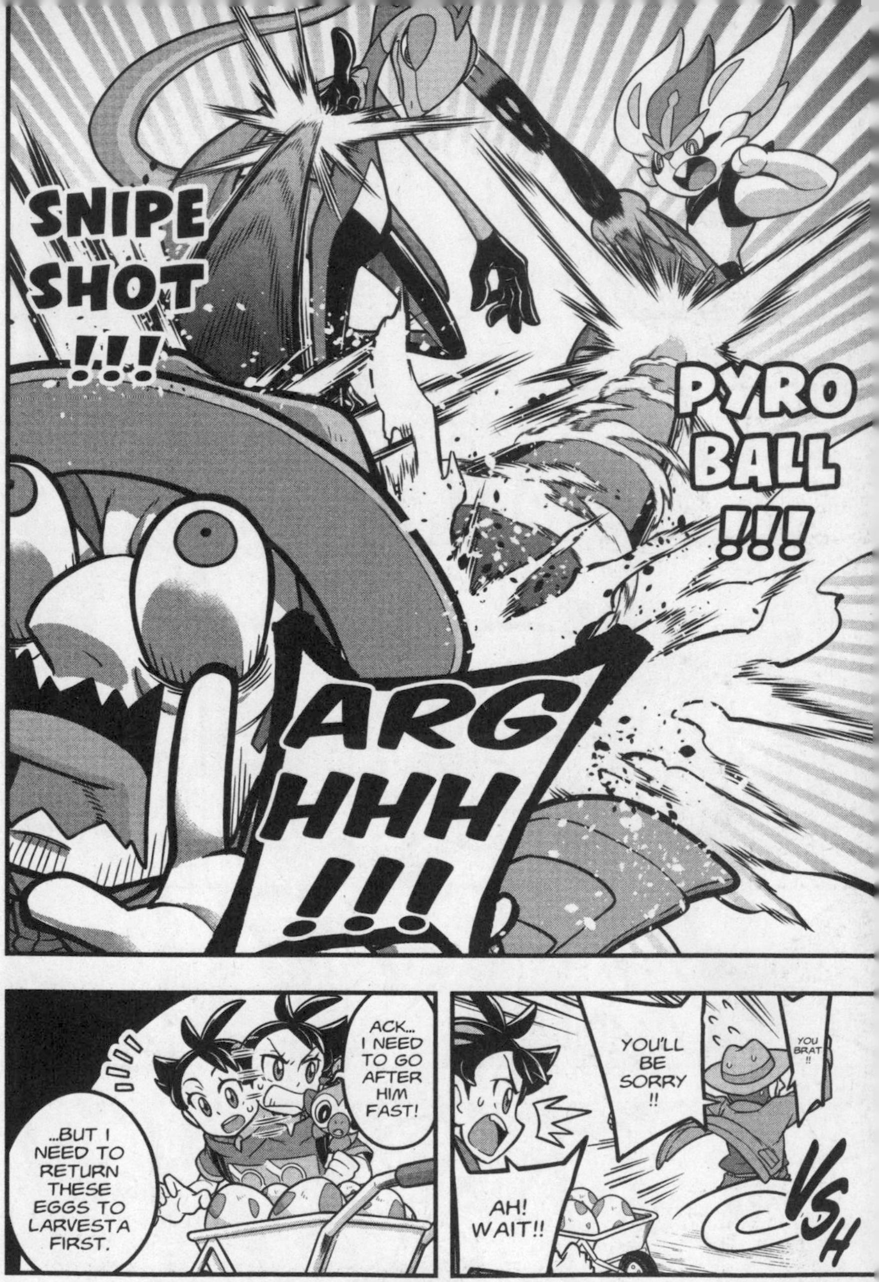
PYRO BALL !!!
SNIPE SHOT !!!
ARGHHH !!!
YOU BRAT !!
YOU'LL BE SORRY !!
VSH
AH! WAIT!!
ACK... I NEED TO GO AFTER HIM FAST!
!!!!
...BUT I NEED TO RETURN THESE EGGS TO LARVESTA FIRST.

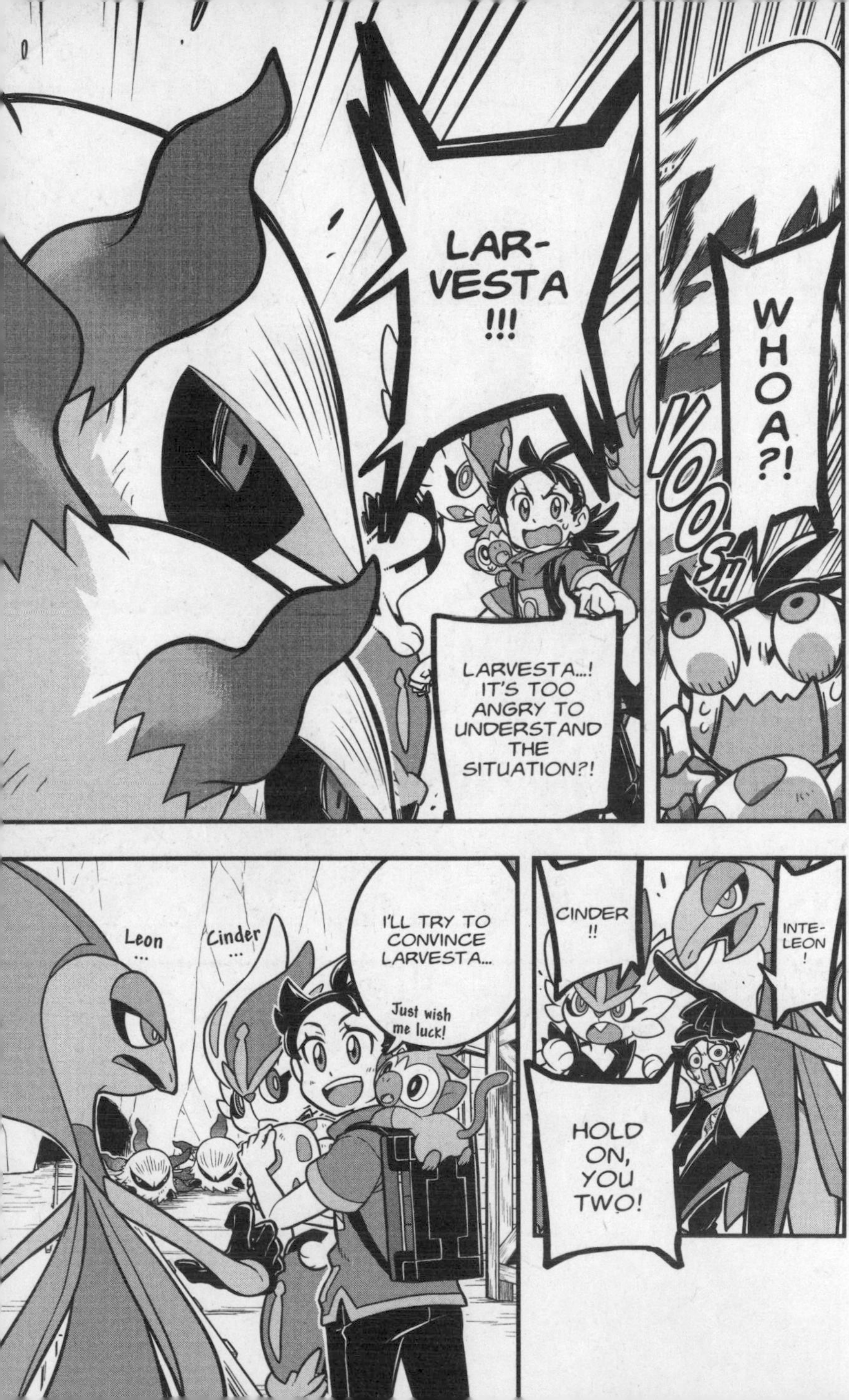
WHOA?!
VOOOSH
LAR-VESTA!!!
LARVESTA...! IT'S TOO ANGRY TO UNDERSTAND THE SITUATION?!
INTE-LEON!
CINDER!!
HOLD ON, YOU TWO!
I'LL TRY TO CONVINCE LARVESTA...
Just wish me luck!
Cinder...
Leon...

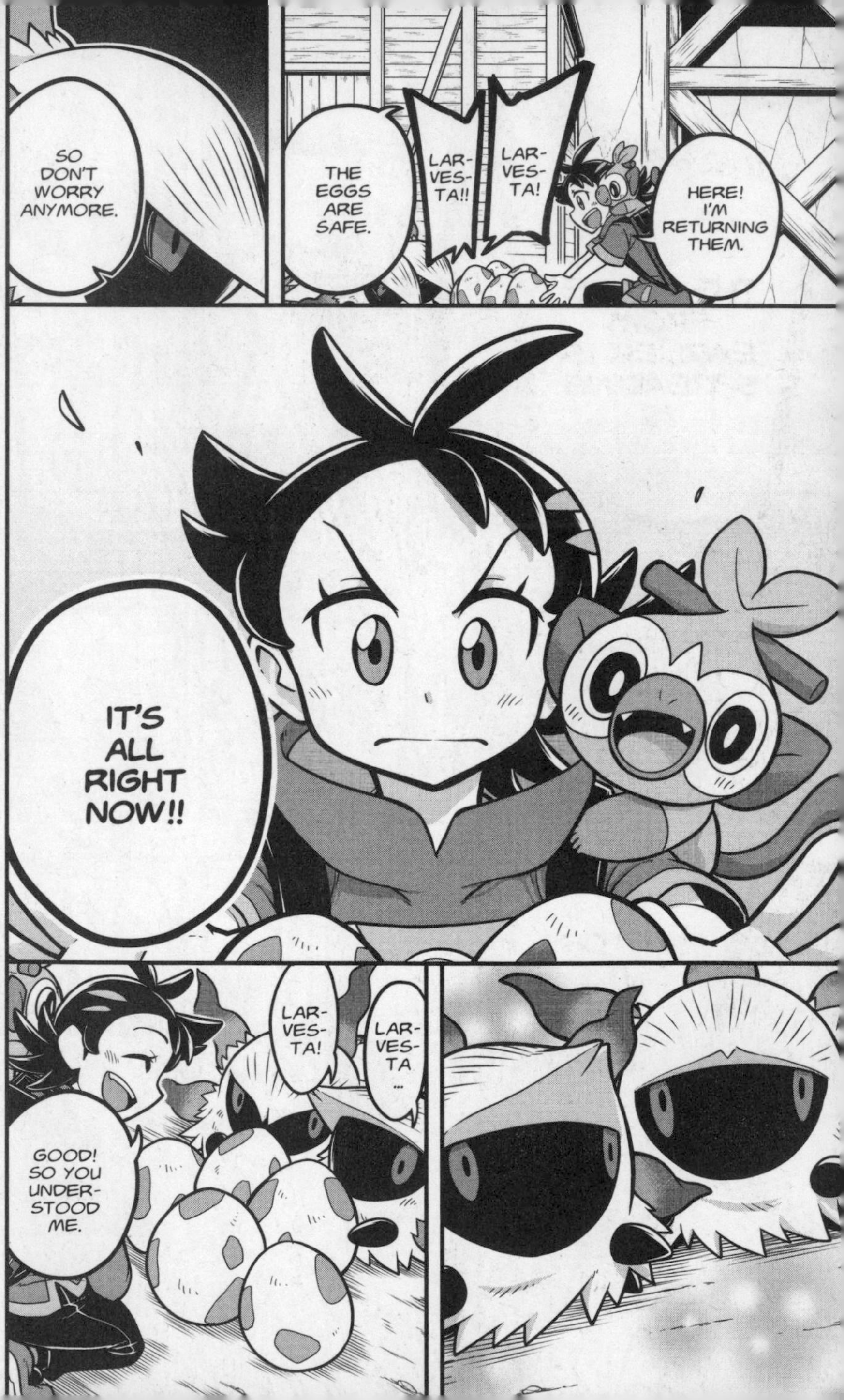
HERE! I'M RETURNING THEM.
LAR-VES-TA!
LAR-VES-TA!!
THE EGGS ARE SAFE.
SO DON'T WORRY ANYMORE.
IT'S ALL RIGHT NOW!!
LAR-VES-TA …
LAR-VES-TA!
GOOD! SO YOU UNDER-STOOD ME.

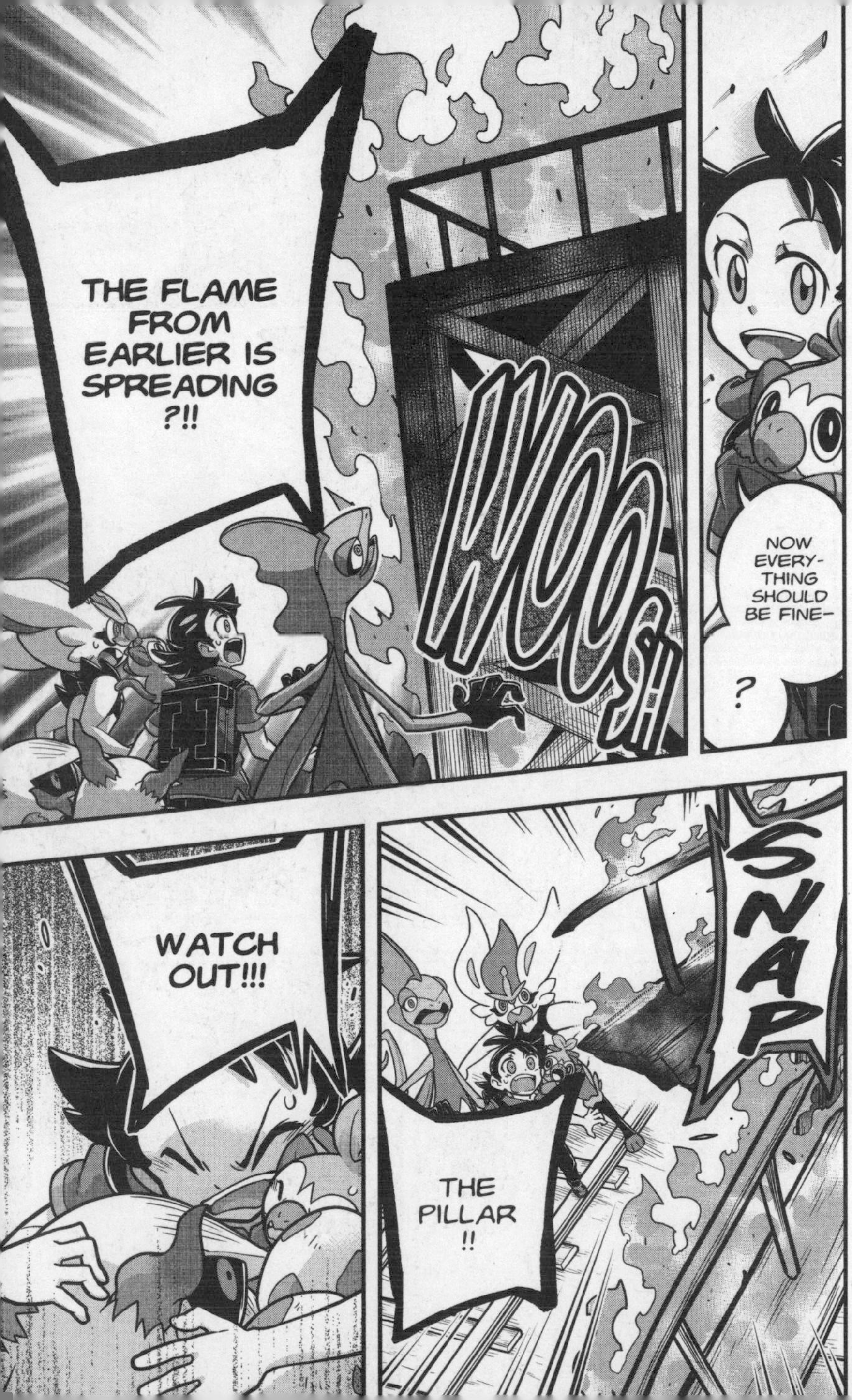
NOW EVERYTHING SHOULD BE FINE-
?
THE FLAME FROM EARLIER IS SPREADING ?!!
WHOOSH!!
SNAP
THE PILLAR !!
WATCH OUT!!!

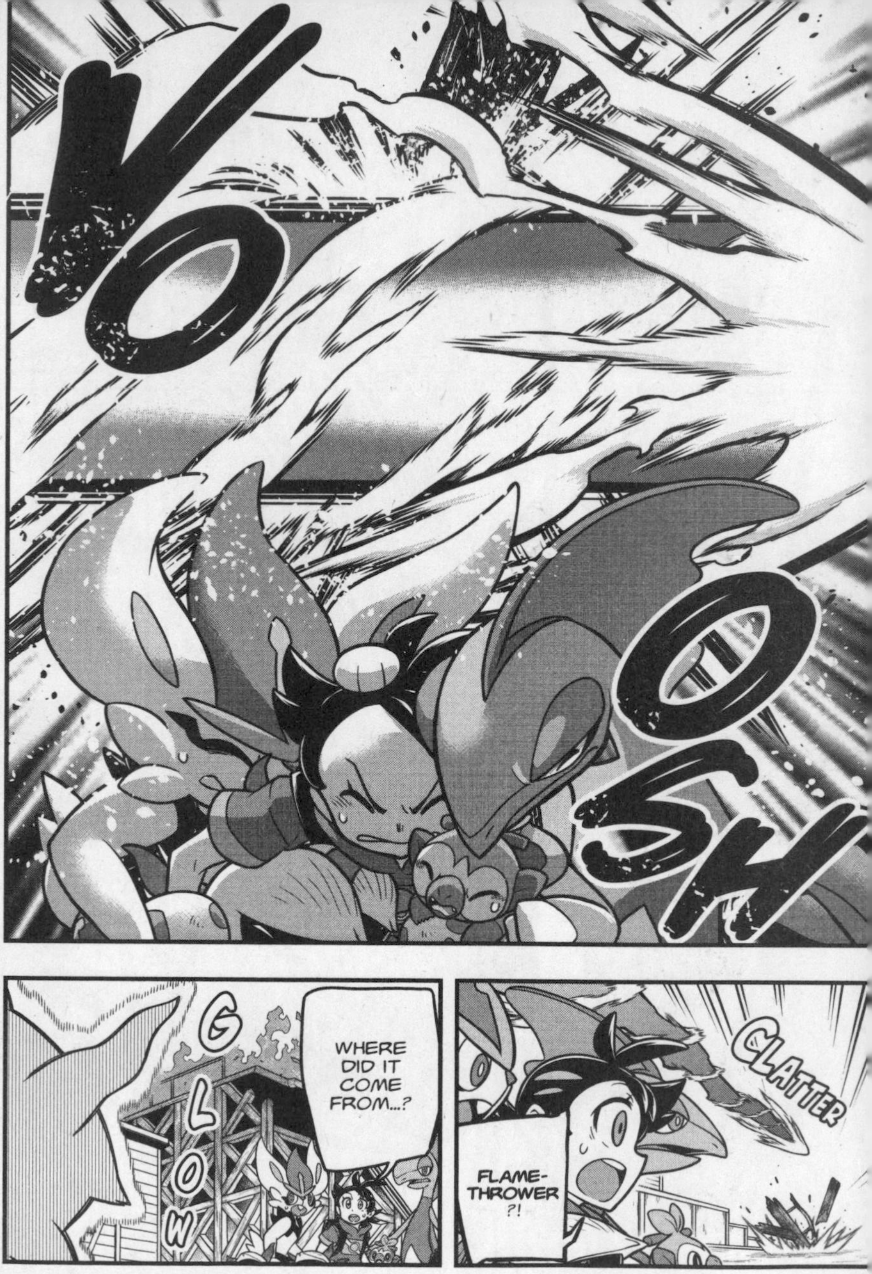
VOOSH
CLATTER
FLAME-THROWER?!
WHERE DID IT COME FROM...?
GLOW

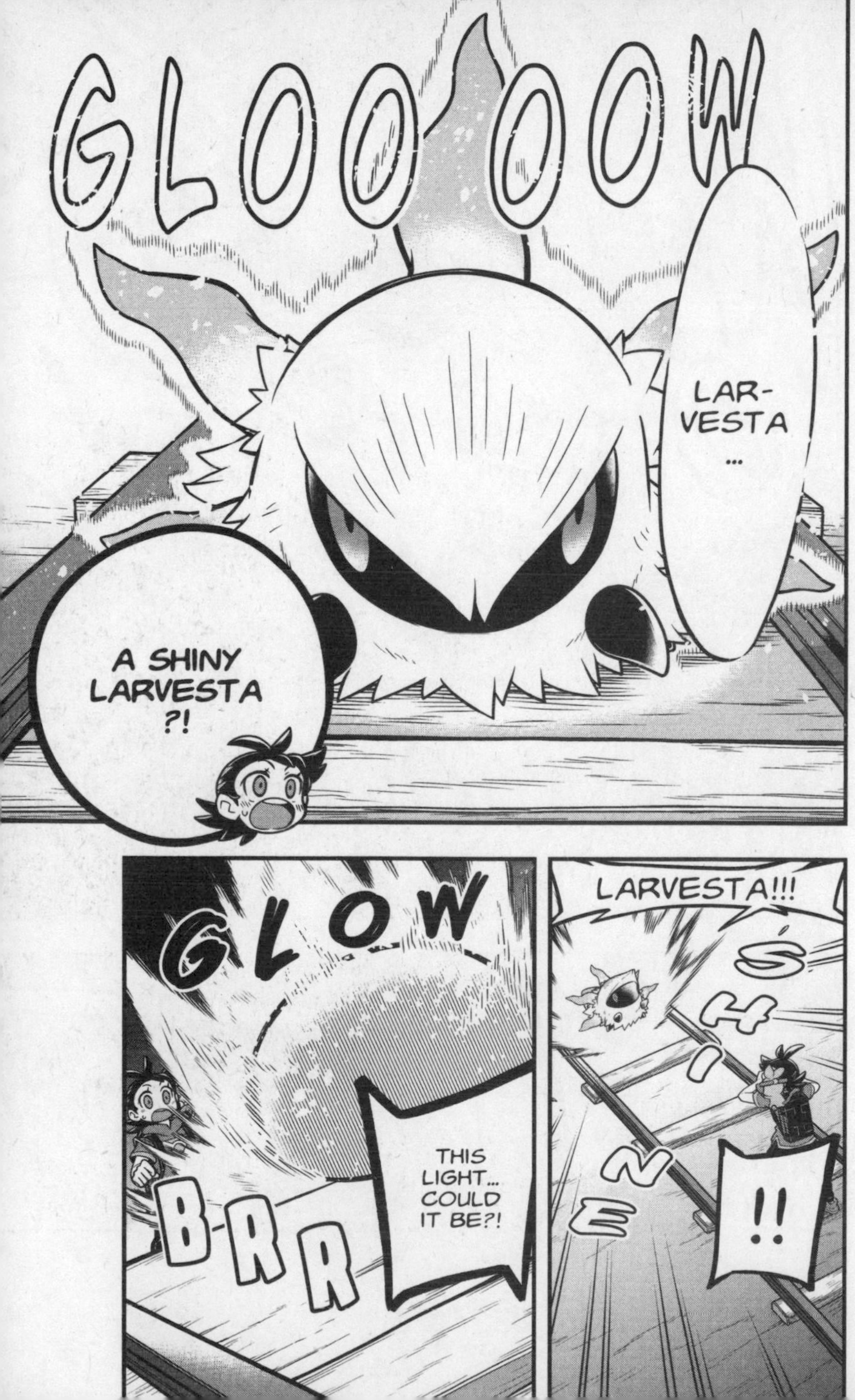
GLOOOOW
LAR-VESTA ...
A SHINY LARVESTA ?!
LARVESTA!!!
SHINE
!!
GLOW
THIS LIGHT... COULD IT BE?!
BRRR

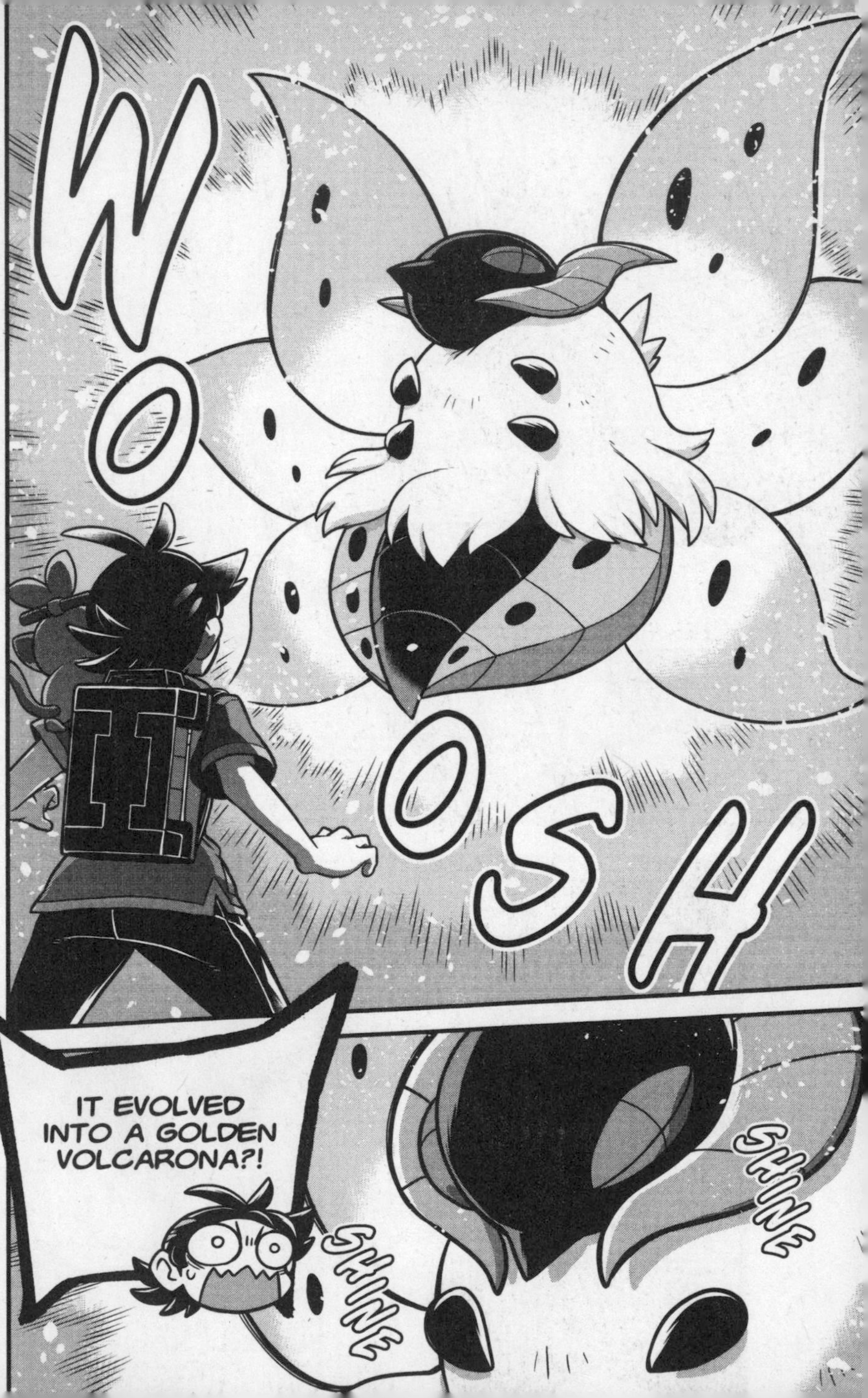
WHOOSH
SHINE
IT EVOLVED INTO A GOLDEN VOLCARONA?!
SHINE

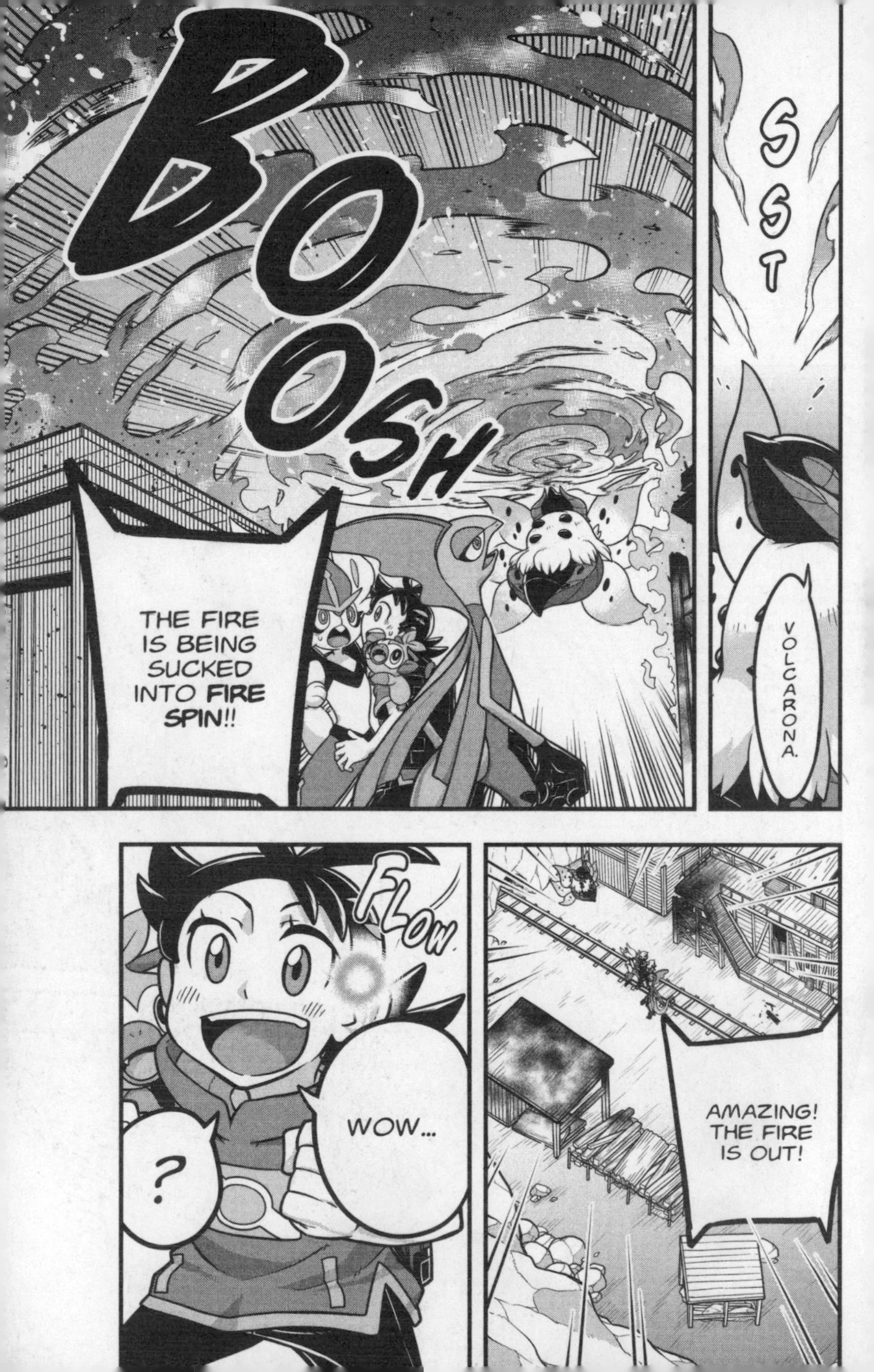
SSST
VOLCARONA.
BOOSH
THE FIRE IS BEING SUCKED INTO FIRE SPIN!!
AMAZING! THE FIRE IS OUT!
FLOW
WOW...
?

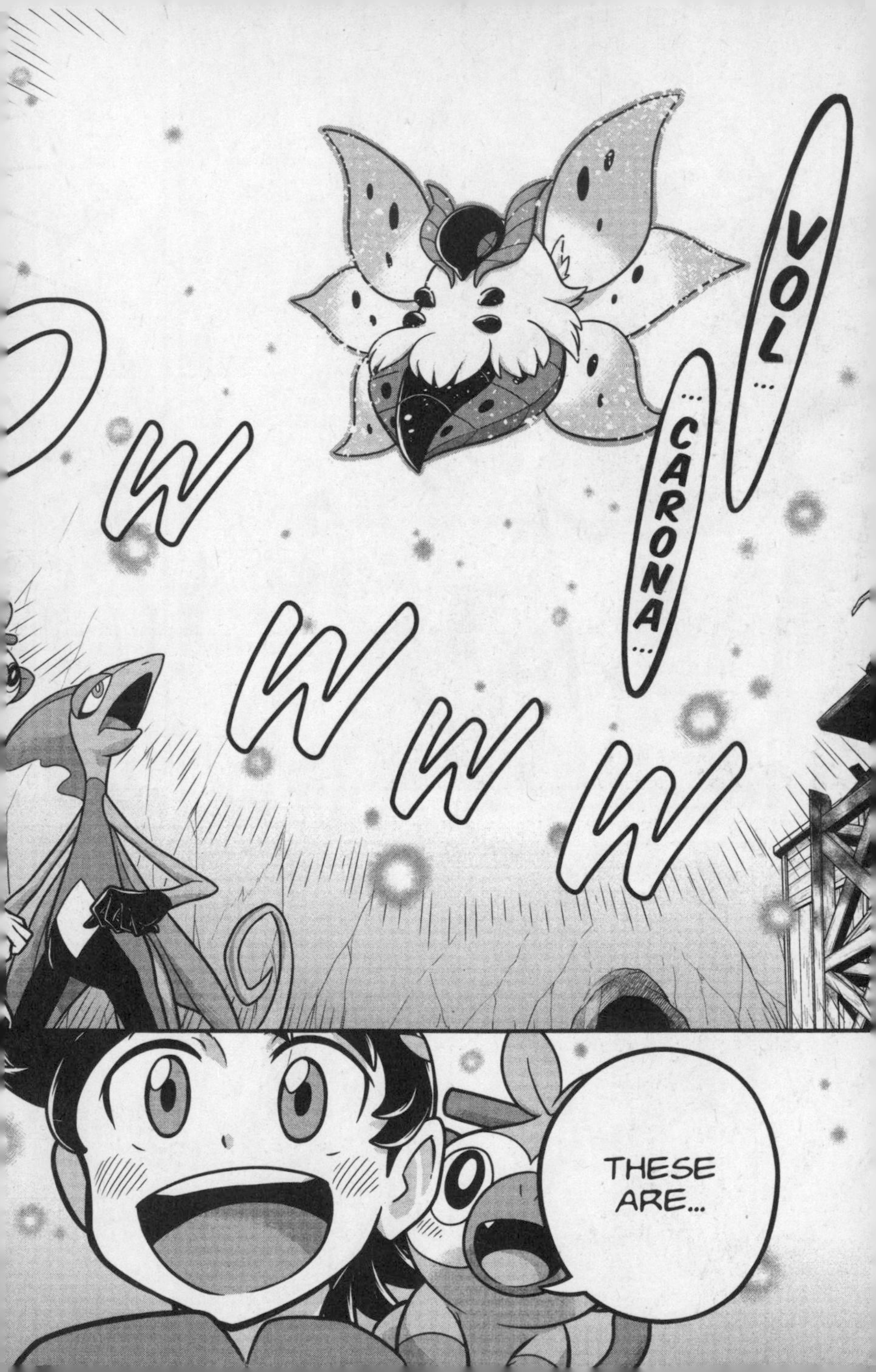
VOL...
...CARONA...
WWWW
THESE ARE...

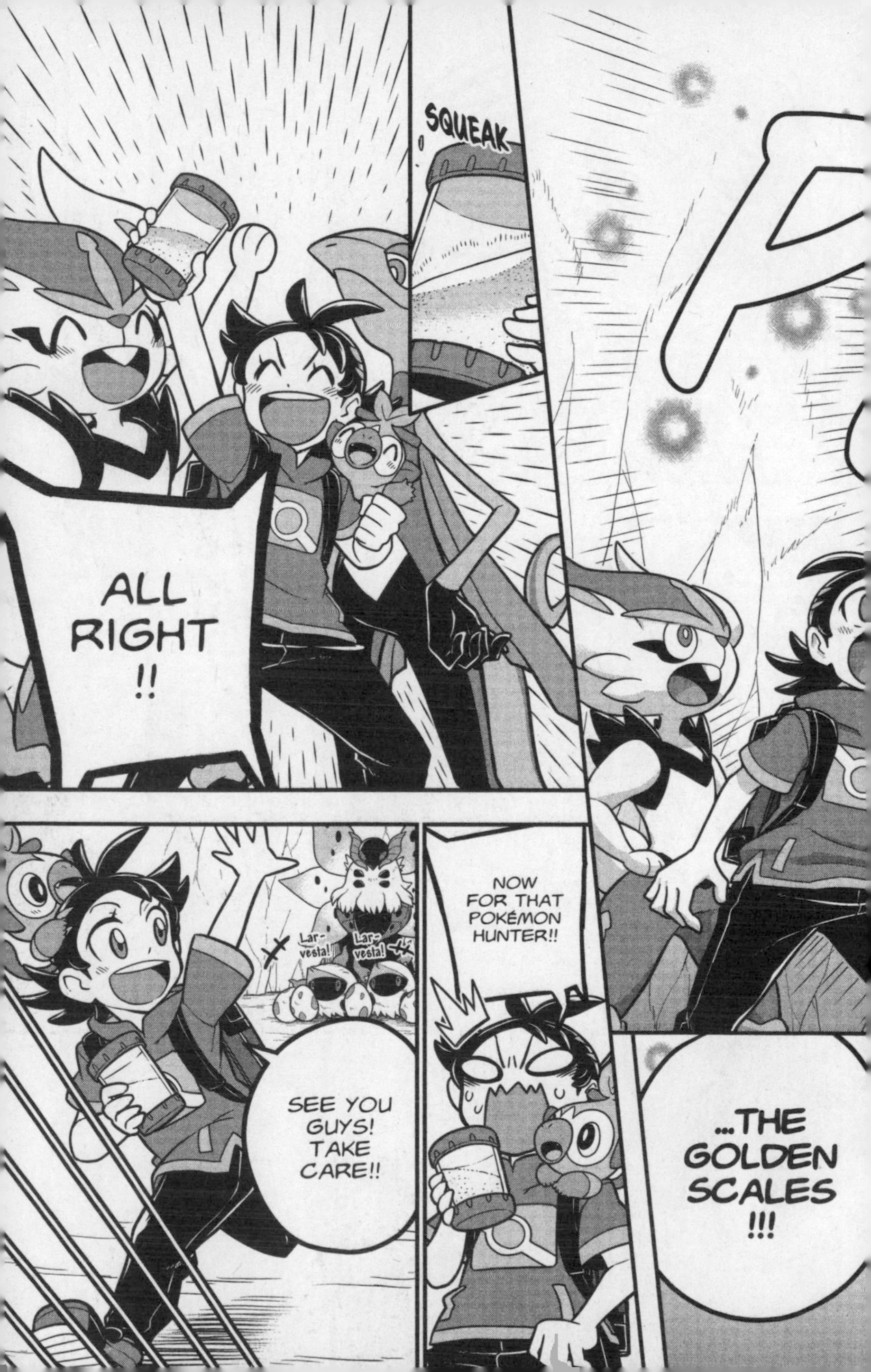
SQUEAK
ALL RIGHT!!
...THE GOLDEN SCALES!!!
NOW FOR THAT POKÉMON HUNTER!!
Lar-vesta!
Lar-vesta!
SEE YOU GUYS! TAKE CARE!!

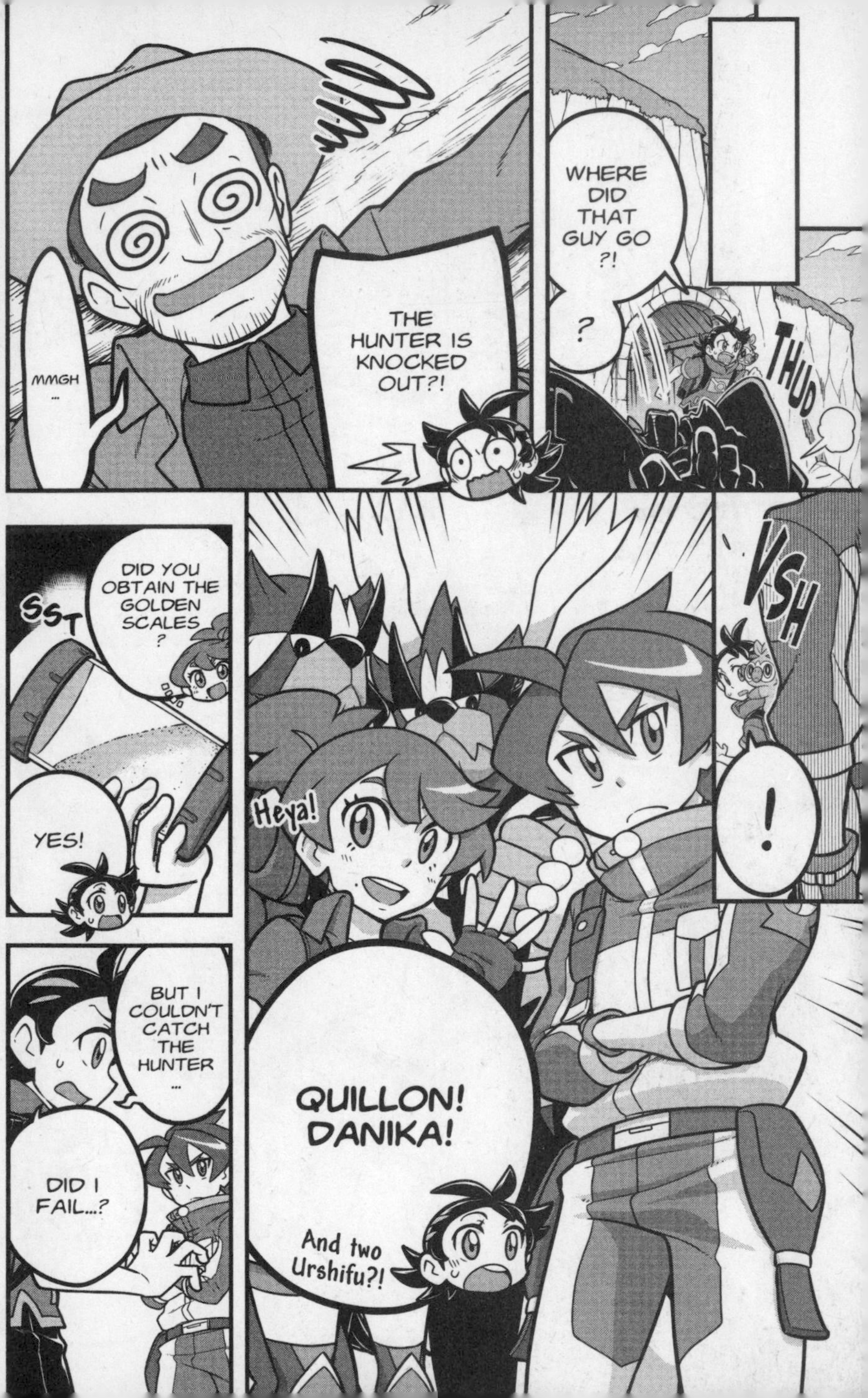
WHERE DID THAT GUY GO?!
?
THUD
THE HUNTER IS KNOCKED OUT?!
MMGH ...
VSH
!
Heya!
QUILLON! DANIKA!
And two Urshifu?!
DID YOU OBTAIN THE GOLDEN SCALES?
SST
YES!
BUT I COULDN'T CATCH THE HUNTER ...
DID I FAIL...?

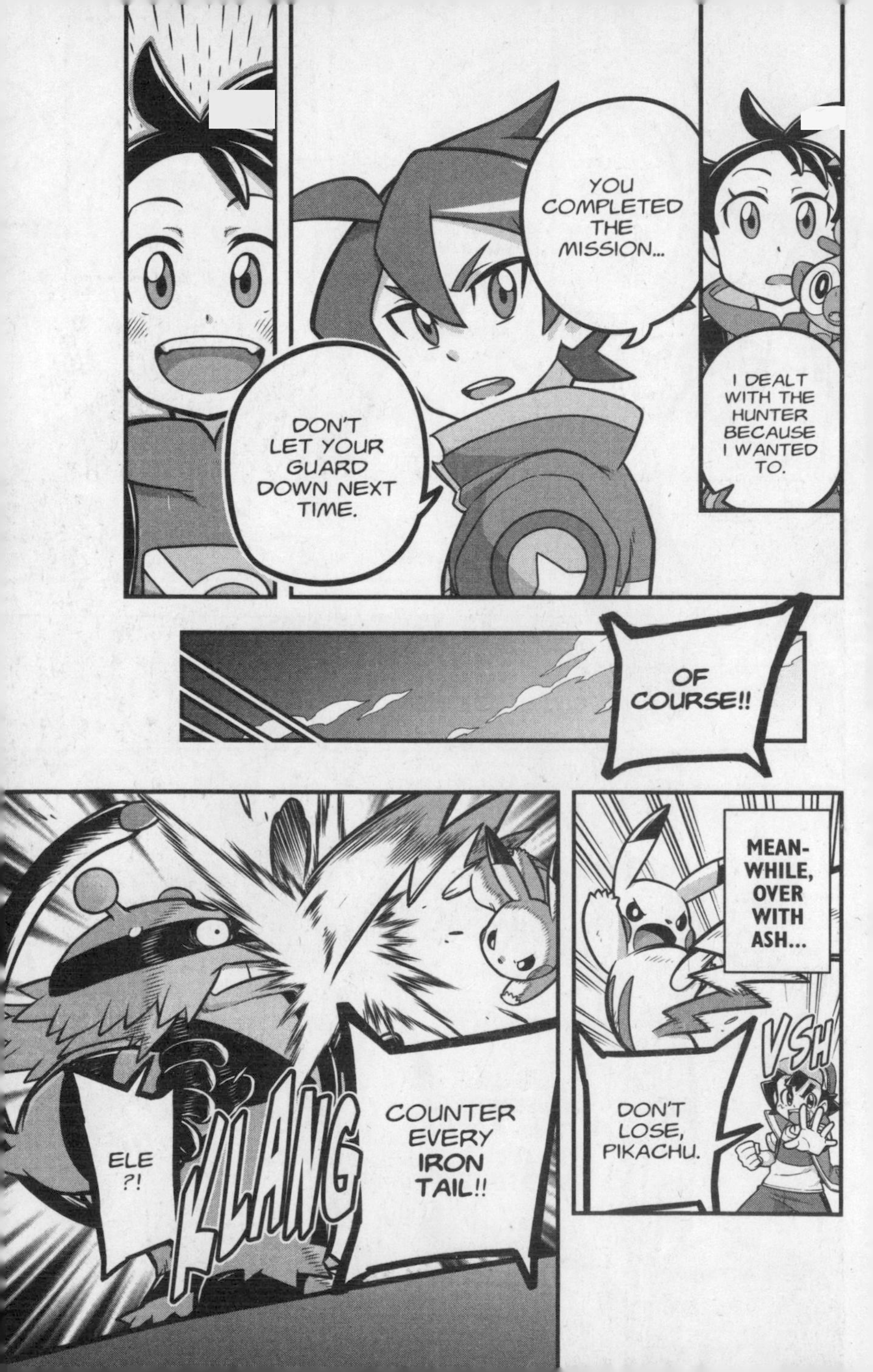
I DEALT WITH THE HUNTER BECAUSE I WANTED TO.
YOU COMPLETED THE MISSION...
DON'T LET YOUR GUARD DOWN NEXT TIME.
OF COURSE!!
MEAN-WHILE, OVER WITH ASH...
VSH
DON'T LOSE, PIKACHU.
COUNTER EVERY IRON TAIL!!
KLANG
ELE ?!

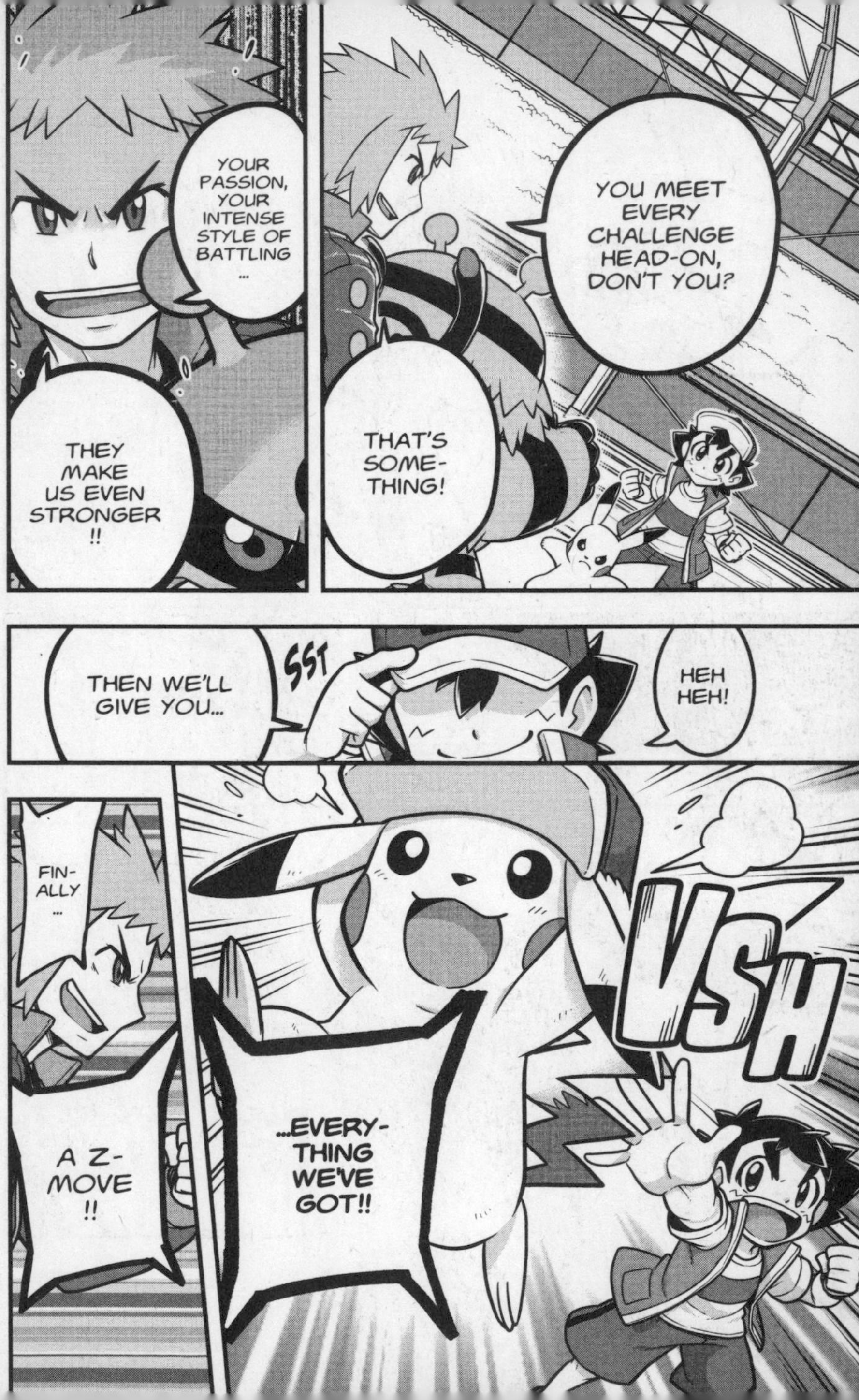
YOU MEET EVERY CHALLENGE HEAD-ON, DON'T YOU?
THAT'S SOME-THING!
YOUR PASSION, YOUR INTENSE STYLE OF BATTLING ...
THEY MAKE US EVEN STRONGER !!
HEH HEH!
SST
THEN WE'LL GIVE YOU...
VSH
...EVERY-THING WE'VE GOT!!
FIN-ALLY ...
A Z-MOVE !!

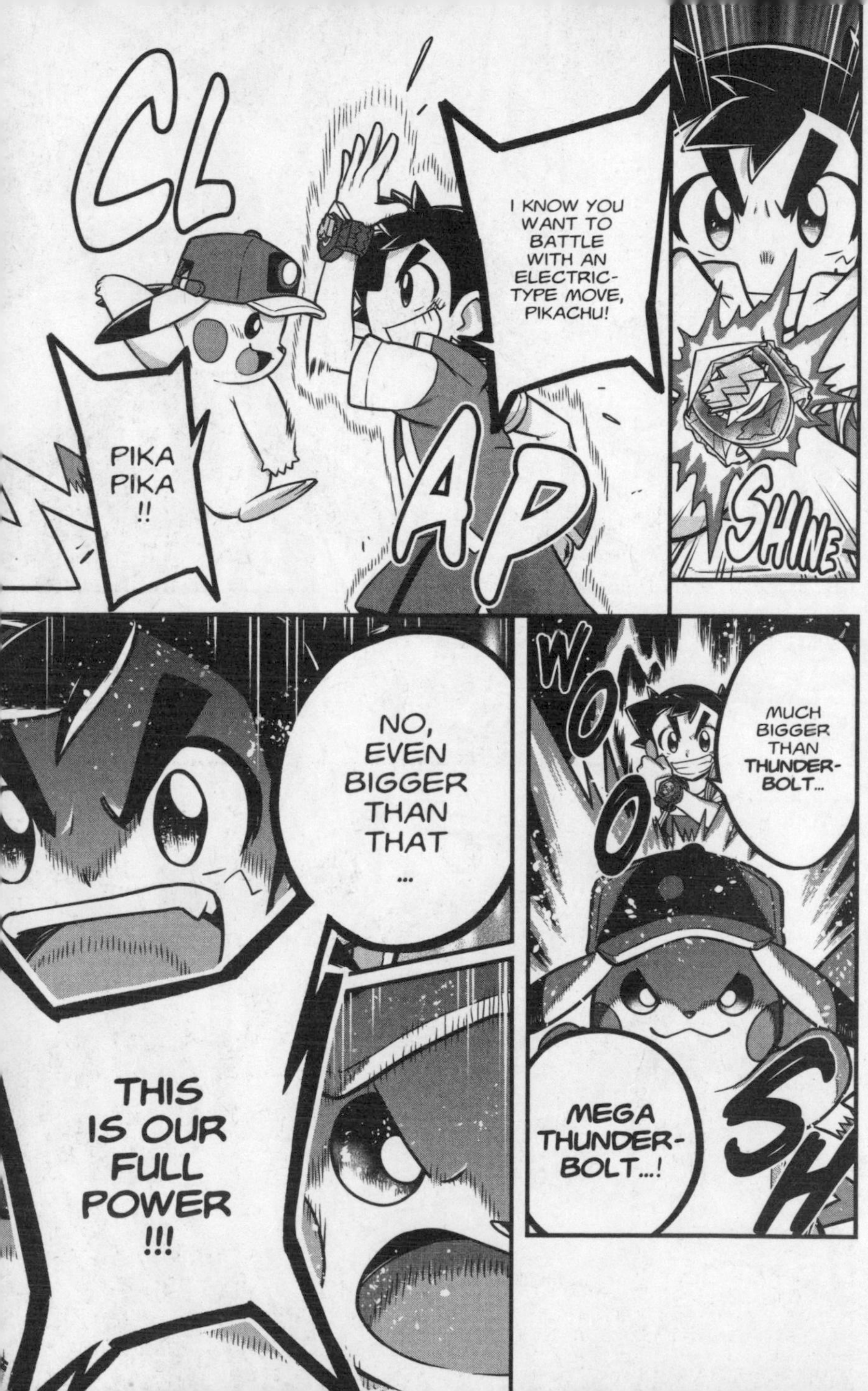
SHINE
I KNOW YOU WANT TO BATTLE WITH AN ELECTRIC-TYPE MOVE, PIKACHU!
CLAP
PIKA PIKA !!
WOO
MUCH BIGGER THAN THUNDER-BOLT...
MEGA THUNDER-BOLT...!
SH
NO, EVEN BIGGER THAN THAT ...
THIS IS OUR FULL POWER !!!

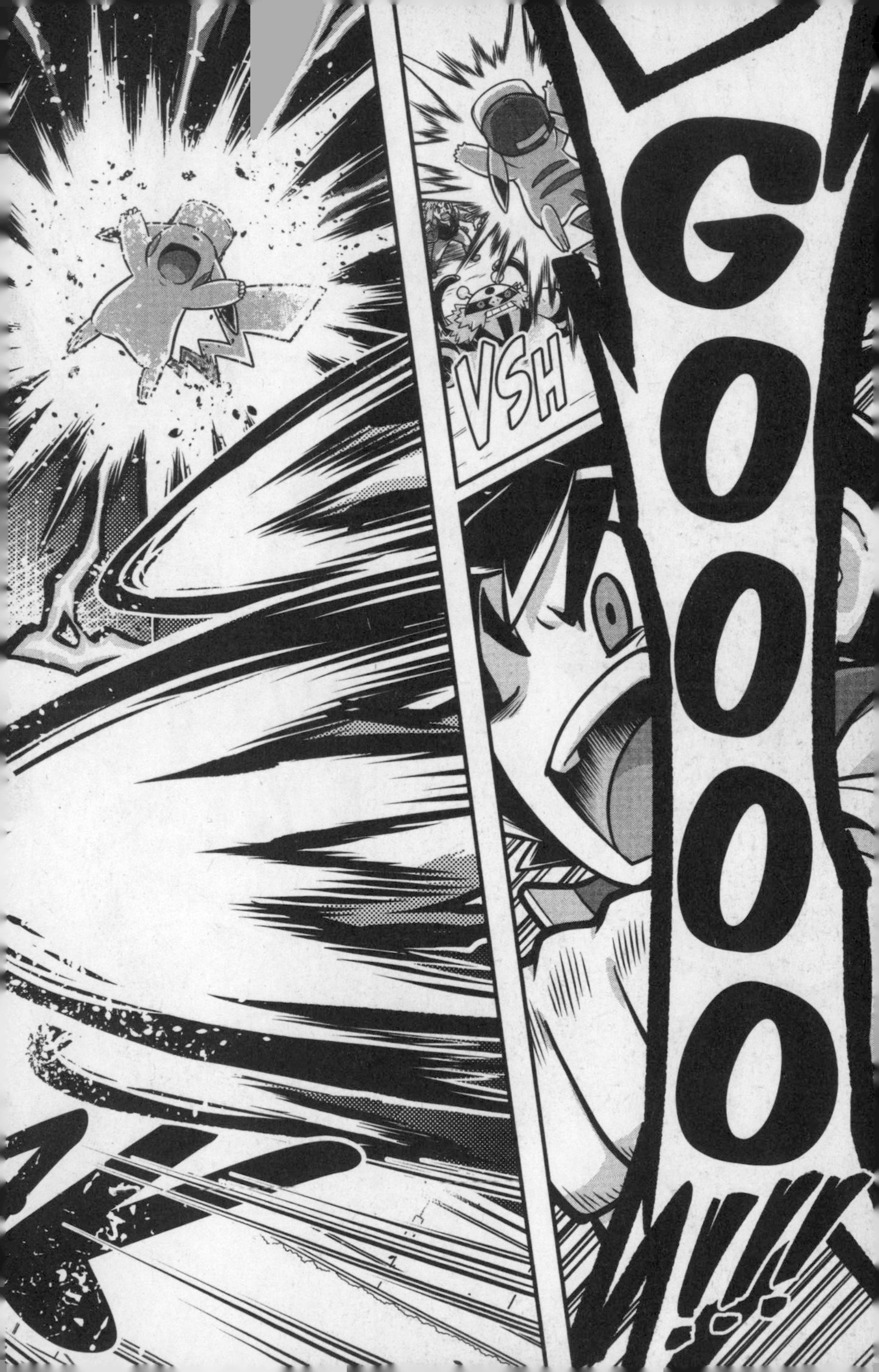
GOOOO!!
VSH

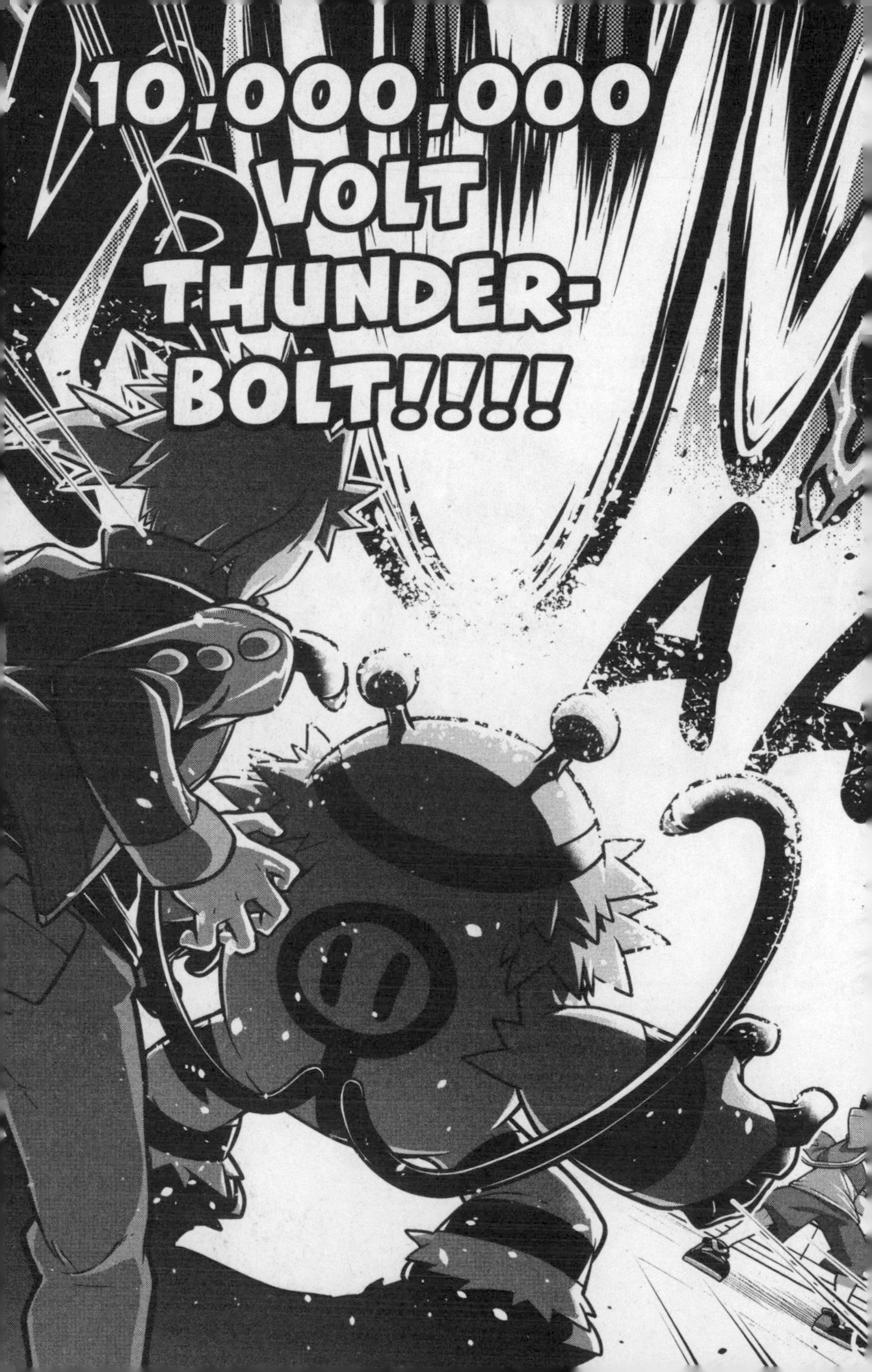
10,000,000 VOLT THUNDER-BOLT!!!!

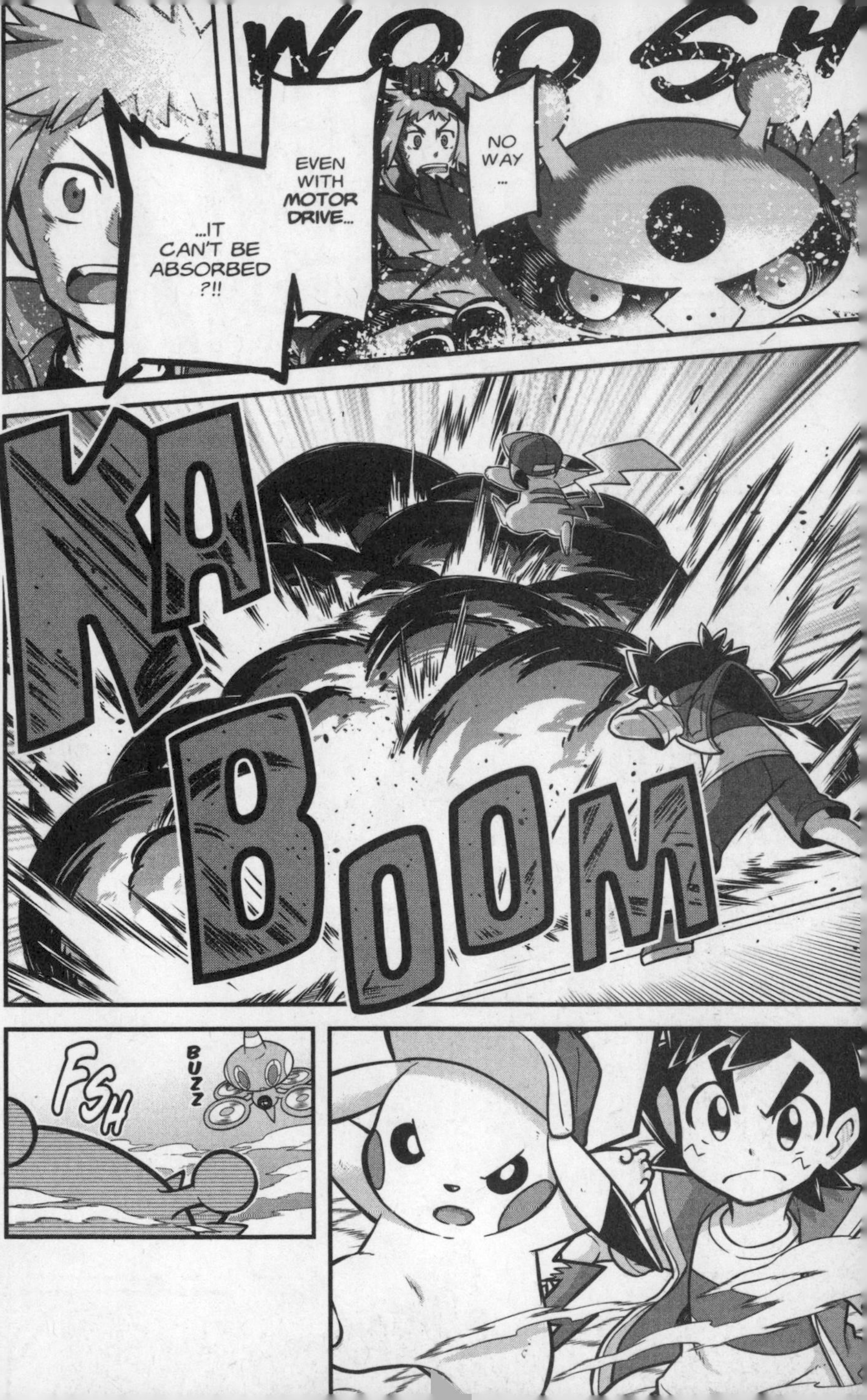
WOOSH
NO WAY ...
EVEN WITH MOTOR DRIVE...
...IT CAN'T BE ABSORBED?!!
KA-BOOM
FSH
BUZZ

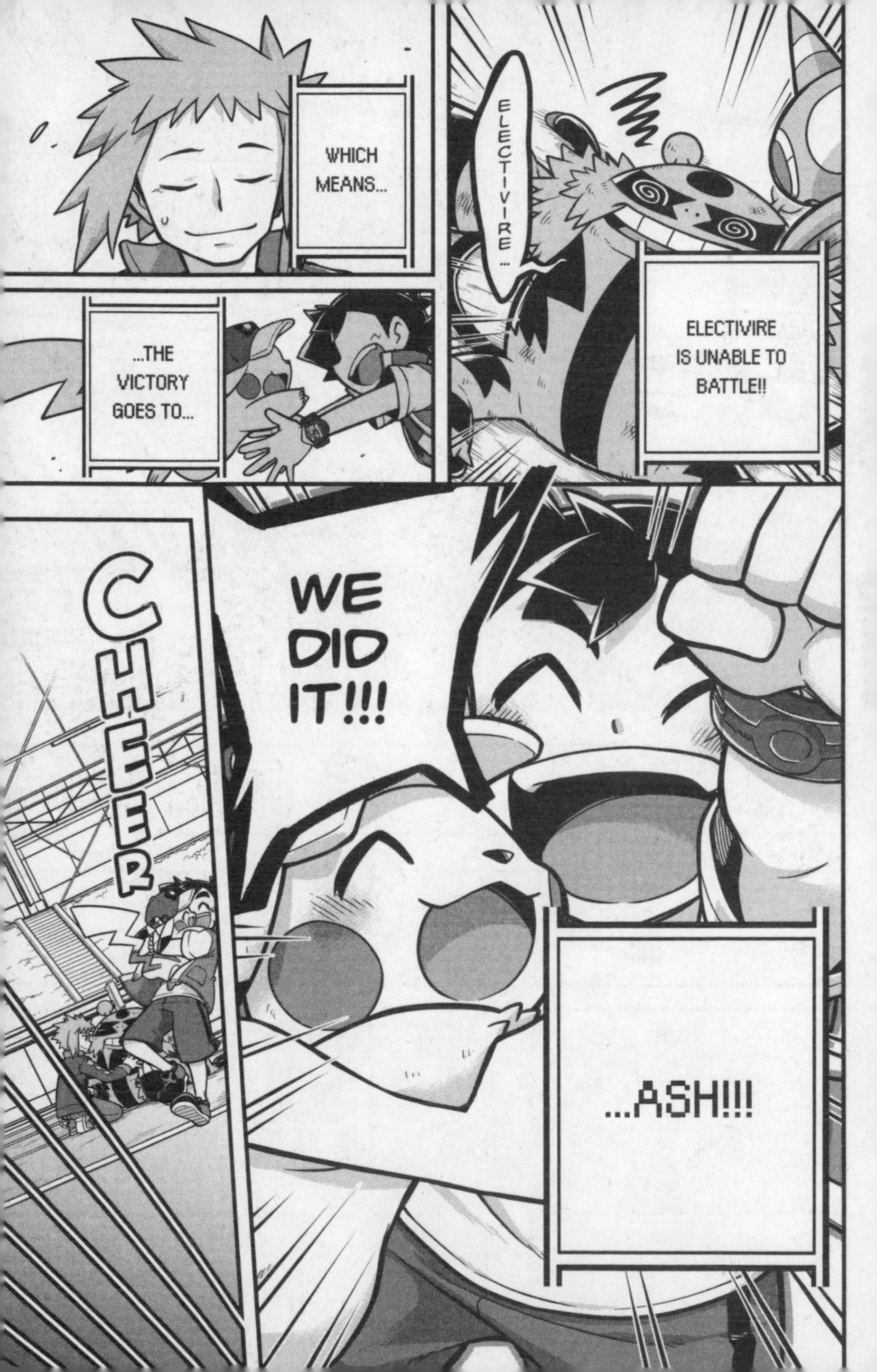
ELECTIVIRE...
ELECTIVIRE IS UNABLE TO BATTLE!!
WHICH MEANS...
...THE VICTORY GOES TO...
...ASH!!!
WE DID IT!!!
CHEER

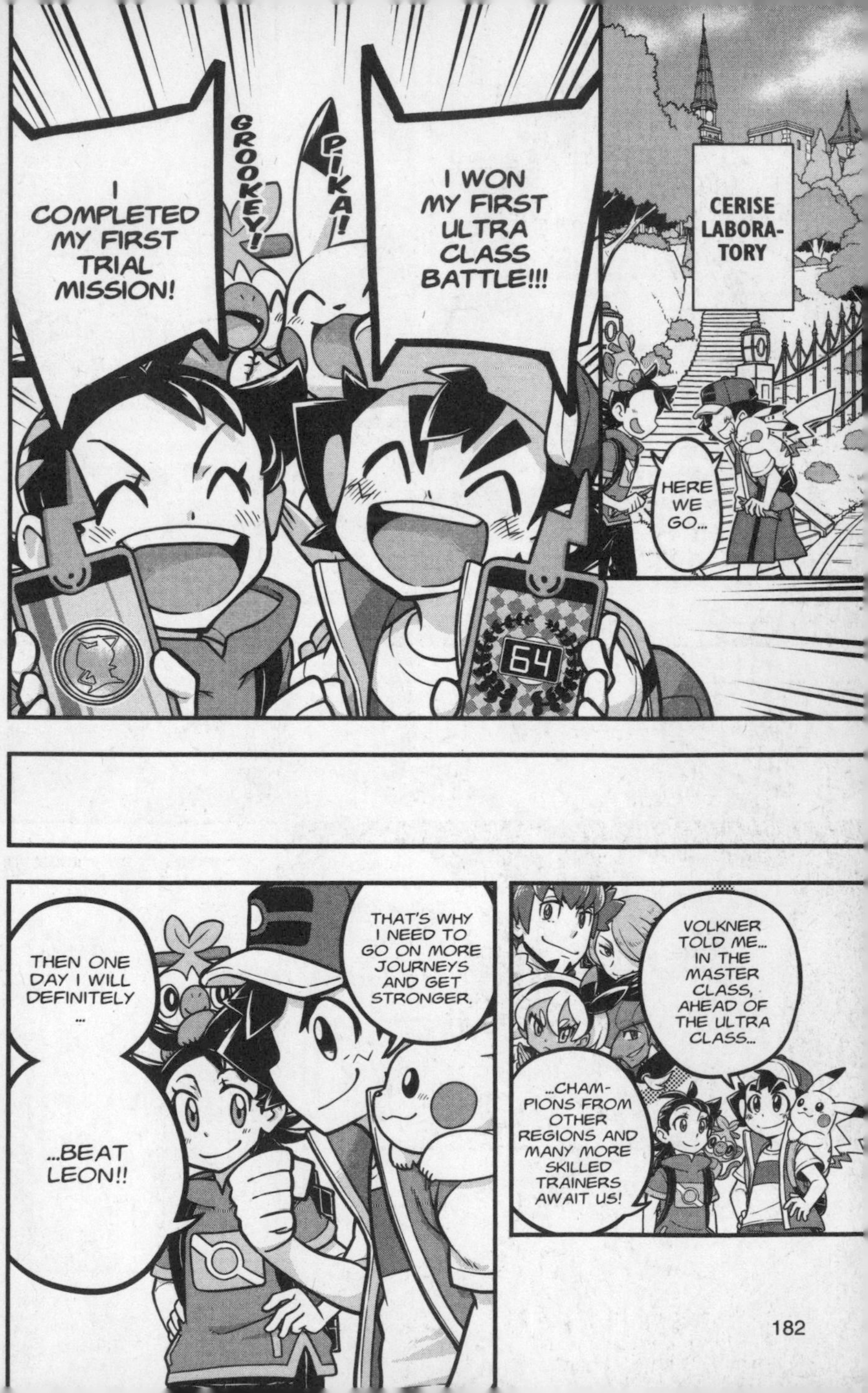
CERISE LABORATORY
HERE WE GO...
I WON MY FIRST ULTRA CLASS BATTLE!!!
PIKA!
GROOKEY!
I COMPLETED MY FIRST TRIAL MISSION!
VOLKNER TOLD ME... IN THE MASTER CLASS, AHEAD OF THE ULTRA CLASS...
...CHAMPIONS FROM OTHER REGIONS AND MANY MORE SKILLED TRAINERS AWAIT US!
THAT'S WHY I NEED TO GO ON MORE JOURNEYS AND GET STRONGER.
THEN ONE DAY I WILL DEFINITELY ...
...BEAT LEON!!

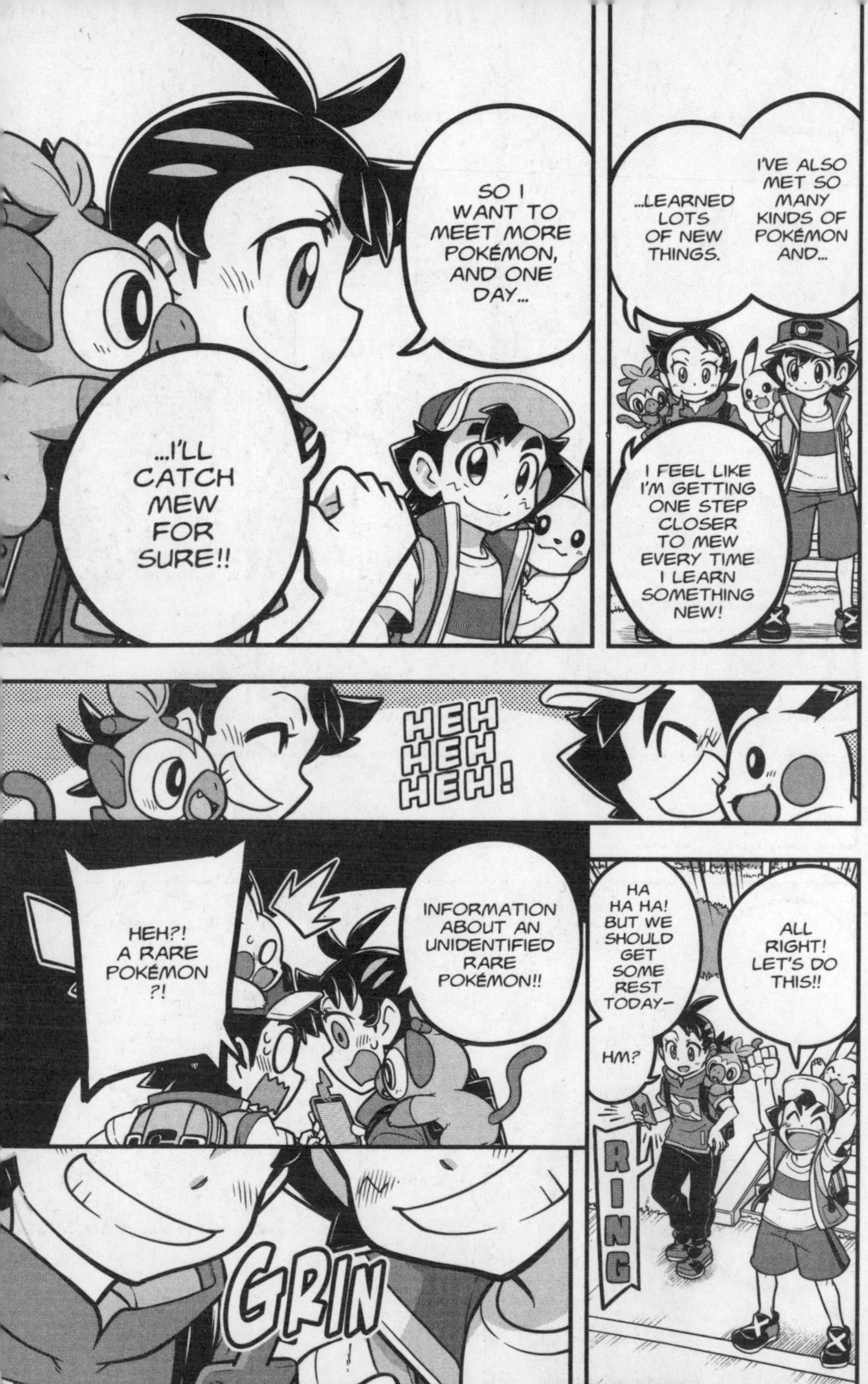
I'VE ALSO MET SO MANY KINDS OF POKÉMON AND...
...LEARNED LOTS OF NEW THINGS.
I FEEL LIKE I'M GETTING ONE STEP CLOSER TO MEW EVERY TIME I LEARN SOMETHING NEW!
SO I WANT TO MEET MORE POKÉMON, AND ONE DAY...
...I'LL CATCH MEW FOR SURE!!
HEH HEH HEH!
ALL RIGHT! LET'S DO THIS!!
HA HA HA! BUT WE SHOULD GET SOME REST TODAY—
HM?
RING
INFORMATION ABOUT AN UNIDENTIFIED RARE POKÉMON!!
HEH?! A RARE POKÉMON ?!
GRIN

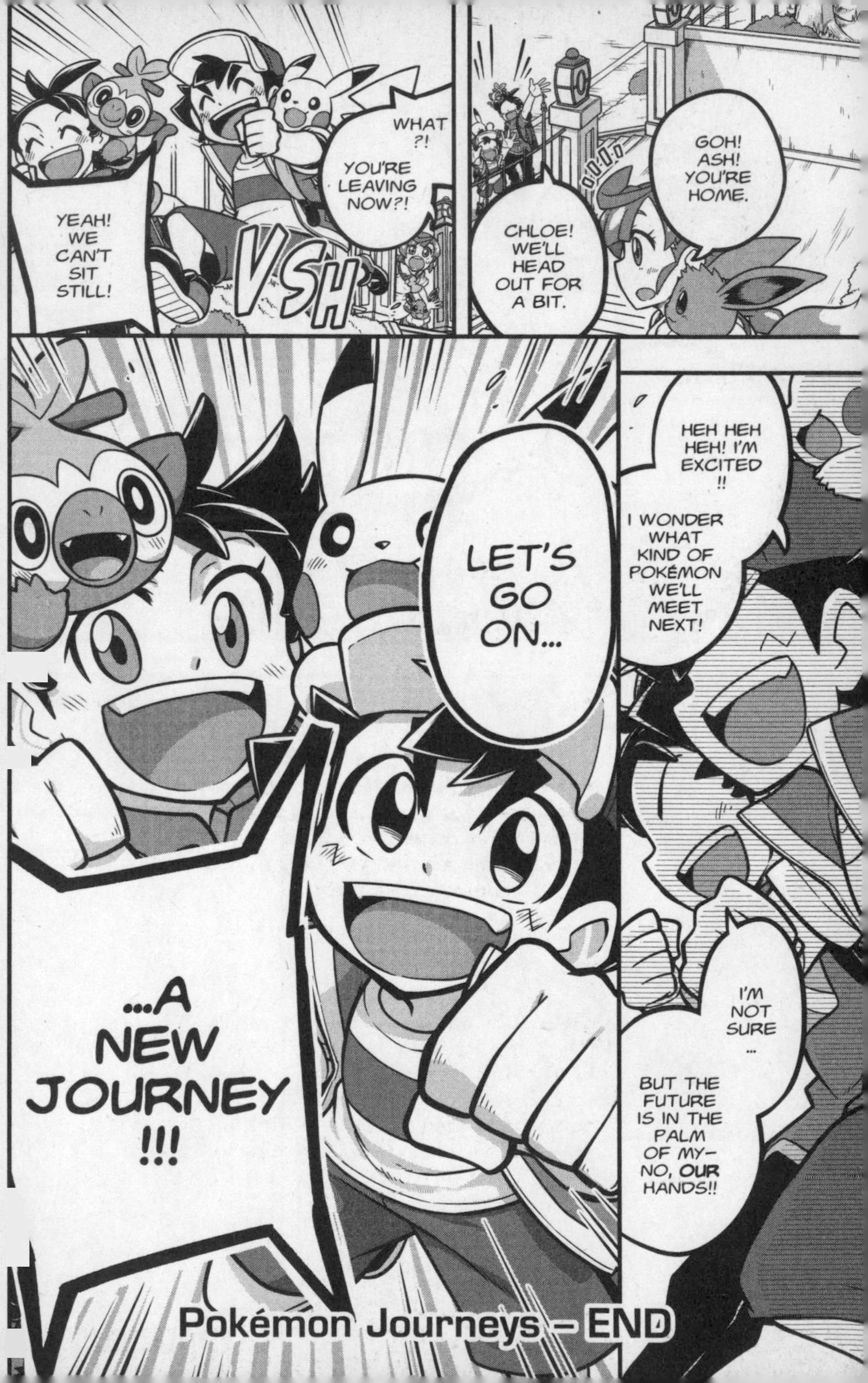
GOH! ASH! YOU'RE HOME.
CHLOE! WE'LL HEAD OUT FOR A BIT.
WHAT ?! YOU'RE LEAVING NOW?!
VSH
YEAH! WE CAN'T SIT STILL!
HEH HEH HEH! I'M EXCITED !!
I WONDER WHAT KIND OF POKÉMON WE'LL MEET NEXT!
I'M NOT SURE ...
BUT THE FUTURE IS IN THE PALM OF MY— NO, **OUR** HANDS!!
LET'S GO ON...
...A NEW JOURNEY !!!
Pokémon Journeys – END

Message From
MACHITO GOMI

Thank you for coming along with me! Ash's and Goh's journeys end here for now...but I'm sure their adventures will continue! Why? Because the future is in the palm of their hands!!

Machito Gomi was born in Tokyo on March 12, 1992. He won the Effort Award in the February 2013 Manga College competition. He is also the creator of *Bakejo! Youkai Jogakuen e Youkoso* (Bakejo! Welcome to Yokai Girls' School) and *Pokémon: Mewtwo Strikes Back—Evolution*.

Volume 4
VIZ Media Edition

STORY AND ART BY
MACHITO GOMI
SCRIPT BY
ATSUHIRO TOMIOKA, SHOJI YONEMURA & DEKO AKAO

Translation **Misa 'Japanese Ammo'**
English Adaptation **Molly Tanzer**
Touch-Up & Lettering **Joanna Estep**
Design **Kam Li**
Editor **Joel Enos**

©2022 Pokémon.
©1995–2021 Nintendo / Creatures Inc. / GAME FREAK inc.
TM, ®, and character names are trademarks of Nintendo.
POCKET MONSTERS - SATOSHI TO GOH NO MONOGATARI! - Vol. 4
by Machito GOMI
Script by Atsuhiro TOMIOKA, Shoji YONEMURA & Deko AKAO
© 2020 Machito GOMI
All rights reserved.
Original Japanese edition published by SHOGAKUKAN.
English translation rights in the United States of America, Canada, the United Kingdom, Ireland,
Australia and New Zealand arranged with SHOGAKUKAN.

Original Cover Design/Plus One

Printed in Canada

Published by VIZ Media, LLC
P.O. Box 77010
San Francisco, CA 94107

10 9 8 7 6 5 4 3 2 1
First printing, November 2022

ALL YOUR FAVORITE POKÉMON GAME CHARACTERS JUMP OUT OF THE SCREEN INTO THE PAGES OF THIS ACTION-PACKED MANGA!

POKÉMON™ ADVENTURES

COLLECTOR'S EDITION

Story by HIDENORI KUSAKA **Art by MATO**

A stylish new omnibus edition of the best-selling *Pokémon Adventures* manga, collecting all the original volumes of the series you know and love!

VIZ

The Pokémon COOKBOOK
Easy & Fun Recipes

by **Maki Kudo**

Create delicious dishes that look like your favorite Pokémon characters with more than 35 fun, easy recipes. Make a Poké Ball sushi roll, Pikachu ramen or mashed Meowth potatoes for your next party, weekend activity or powered-up lunch box.

VIZ
viz.com

Pokémon

HORIZON
SUN & MOON

Akira's summer vacation in the Alola region heats up when he befriends a Rockruff with a mysterious gemstone. Together, Akira hopes they can achieve his newfound dream of becoming a Pokémon Trainer and master the amazing Z-Move. But first, Akira needs to pass a test to earn a Trainer Passport. This becomes more difficult when Rockruff gets kidnapped! And then Team Kings shows up with—you guessed it—evil plans for world domination!

Story & Art
TENYA YABUNO

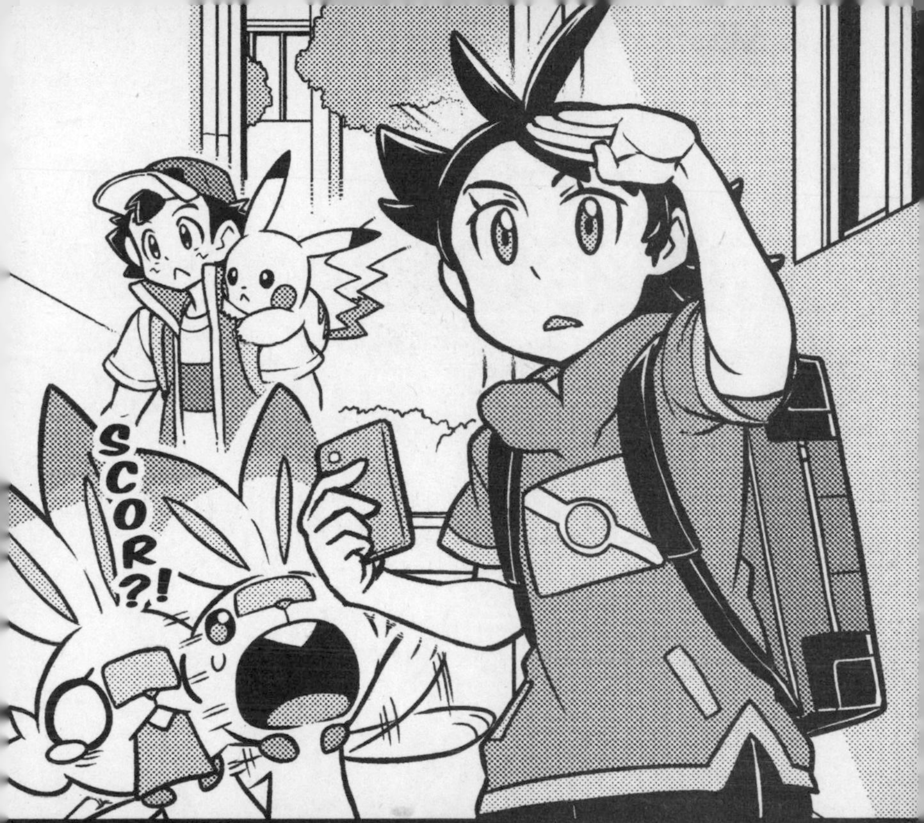
SCOR?!

THIS IS THE END OF THIS GRAPHIC NOVEL!

To properly enjoy this VIZ Media graphic novel, please turn it around and begin reading from right to left.

This book has been printed in the original Japanese format in order to preserve the orientation of the original artwork.

Have fun with it!

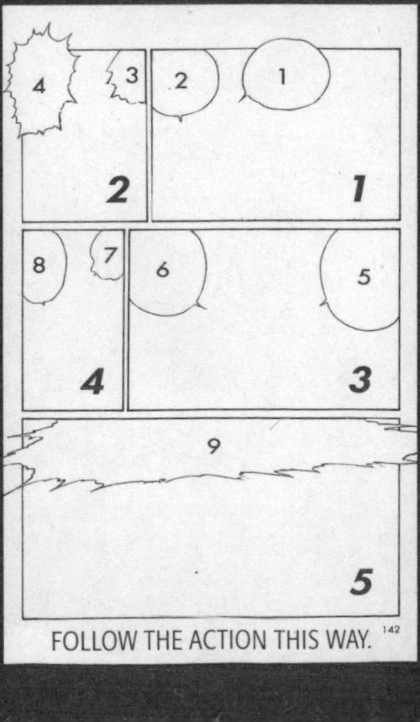
FOLLOW THE ACTION THIS WAY.

POKÉMON™

MEWTWO STRIKES BACK

EVOLUTION

Story and Art by *Machito Gomi*

Original Concept by Satoshi Tajiri
Supervised by Tsunekazu Ishihara
Script by Takeshi Shudo

A manga adventure inspired by the hit Pokémon movie!